STRANGE TH

STRANGE THINGS IN CLOSE-UP

The Nearly Complete Howard Waldrop

A Legend book
Published by Arrow Books Limited
62–65 Chandos Place, London WC2N 4NW

An imprint of Century Hutchinson Limited

London Melbourne Sydney Auckland
Johannesburg and agencies throughout
the world

First published in two separate volumes:

Howard Who? published 1986 by Doubleday & Company Inc., USA
All About Strange Monsters of the Recent Past published 1987 by
Ursus Imprints, USA

This Legend edition published as *Strange Things In Close-Up: The
Nearly Complete Howard Waldrop* © Howard Waldrop 1989

Introduction © 1986 George R. R. Martin

Howard Who? © Howard Waldrop 1986

"The Ugly Chickens" copyright © 1980 by Terry
Carr. From *Universe 10*, Doubleday & Company,
Inc., 1980.
"*Der Untergang des Abendlandesmenschen*"
copyright © 1976 by the Nemedian Chronicles. From
Chacal (later, *Shayol*) #1, Winter 1976.
"Ike at the Mike" copyright © 1982 by Omni
Publications International, Ltd. From *Omni*, June
1982.
"Dr. Hudson's Secret Gorilla" copyright © 1977 by
Flight Unlimited, Inc. From *Shayol* #1, November
1977.
". . . The World, as We Know't." copyright © 1982
by Flight Unlimited, Inc. From *Shayol* #6, Winter
1982.
"Green Brother" copyright © 1982 by Flight
Unlimited, Inc. From *Shayol* #5, Winter 1982.
"Mary Margaret Road-Grader" copyright © 1976 by
Damon Knight. From *Orbit 18*, Harper & Row,
1976.
"Save a Place in the Lifeboat for Me" copyright
© 1976 by Nickelodeon Graphic Arts Service. From
Nickelodeon #2, 1976.
"Horror, We Got" copyright © 1976 by Flight
Unlimited, Inc. From *Shayol* #3, Summer 1979.

"Man-Mountain Gentian" copyright © 1983 by Omni Publications International, Ltd. From *Omni*, September 1983.

"God's Hooks!" copyright © 1982 by Terry Carr. From *Universe 12*, Doubleday & Company, Inc., 1982.

"Heirs of the Perisphere" copyright © 1985 by Playboy Inc. From *Playboy*, July 1985.

All About Strange Monsters of the Recent Past
© Howard Waldrop 1987

"All About Strange Monsters of the Recent Past" copyright © 1980 by Flight Unlimited, Inc. From *Shayol* #4 (volume 1, number 4), 1980.

"Helpless, Helpless" copyright © 1984 by Howard Waldrop. From *Light Years and Dark*, edited by Michael Bishop, Berkley Books, 1984.

"Fair Game" copyright © 1986 by Howard Waldrop. From *Afterlives*, edited by Pamela Sargent and Ian Watson, Vintage Books (Random House), 1986.

"What Makes Heironymous Run?" copyright © 1985 by Flight Unlimited, Inc. From *Shayol* #7 (volume 3, number 1), 1985.

"The Lions Are Asleep This Night" copyright © 1986 by Omni Publications International Ltd. From *Omni*, August 1986.

"Flying Saucer Rock and Roll" copyright © 1984 by Omni Publications International Ltd. From *Omni*, January 1985.

"He-We-Await" appears here for the first time. Copyright © 1987 by Howard Waldrop.

"The Left-Handed Muse" © Lewis Shiner 1987.

This book is sold subject to the condition that it shall not, by way of trade or otherwise, be lent, resold, hired out, or otherwise circulated without the publisher's prior consent in any form of binding or cover other than that in which it is published and without a similar condition including this condition being imposed on the subsequent purchaser

Printed and bound in Great Britain by
Courier International, Tiptree, Essex

ISBN 0 09964440 1

Contents

Howard Who?

The Ugly Chickens	9
Der Untergang des Abendlandesmenschen	35
Ike at the Mike	49
Dr. Hudson's Secret Gorilla	65
". . . The World, as We Know't."	79
Green Brother	98
Mary Margaret Road-Grader	116
Save a Place in the Lifeboat for me	135
Horror, We Got	158
Man-Mountain Gentian	174
God's Hooks!	193
Heirs of the Perisphere	215

All About Strange Monsters of the Recent Past

All About Strange Monsters of The Recent Past	237
Helpless, Helpless	247
Fair Game	259
What Makes Heironymous Run?	276
The Lions Are Asleep This Night	292
Flying Saucer Rock and Roll	315
He-We-Await	338
The Left-Handed Muse by Lewis Shiner	360

Introduction

By George R. R. Martin

Let's begin with some riddles. What do Dwight David Eisenhower and the dodo have in common? How are Japanese sumo wrestlers like Disney cartoon characters? What's the common link between Izaak Walton, Abbott & Costello, and George Armstrong Custer? If you ran into a gorilla in a powdered wig at a tractor pull, what would that remind you of? And while you're pondering all that, just who was that masked man anyway?

The last one is easy. The masked man is Howard Waldrop, a short squinty-eyed fellow with an atrocious accent and a wardrobe like Mork from Ork. He was born in Mississippi, grew up in Texas, and has bounced around the Lone Star State most of his adult life, from Arlington to Grand Prairie to Bryan to Austin, where he now resides. He knows everything there is to know about B movies, he can sing fifties rock and TV theme songs all night long (and often does), he likes to fish, and he just happens to be the most startling, original, and entertaining short story writer in science fiction today.

The word *unique* is much abused these days, but in Howard's case it applies. We live in a derivative age, and nowhere is that more apparent than in the books we read. Every new horror writer is compared to Stephen King. Our fantasists all seem to write in the tradition of J. R. R. Tolkien, Robert E. Howard, or Stephen R. Donaldson. The hot young talents in SF are routinely proclaimed as the next Robert A. Heinlein, the new Isaac Asimov, the angriest young man since Harlan Ellison, unless they happen to be female, in which case they are dutifully likened to Andre Norton, Ursula K. LeGuin, and Marion Zimmer Bradley. If you listen to the blurb-writers, these days it seems that everybody writes like somebody else.

Howard Waldrop's short fiction is squarely in the tradition

Strange Things in Close-Up

of Howard Waldrop. There's never been anyone like him, in or out of science fiction. His voice is his own; singular, distinctive, quirky, and—once you've encountered it—more than a little addictive. I'm tempted to say that the only thing that's like a Howard Waldrop story is another Howard Waldrop story, except that it wouldn't be true. Howard's stories differ as much from each other as from your run-of-the-mill SF and fantasy. The only thing they have in common is that they're all a little bit different.

Howard doesn't like to write the same thing twice. Well-meaning friends keep telling him that the best way to get rich and famous is to write the same thing over and over and over and over again, to keep frying up those robot duneburgers of gore and serving them to a hungry public, but Howard keeps wandering off and getting interested in Groucho Marx, Chinese proletarian novels, and the mound-builder Indians. Suddenly books start piling up in his office, a maniacal gleam lights his tiny little eyes, and he begins to talk incessantly about a strange new story he's going to write. Meanwhile, he consumes those piles of books during breaks in his daily regimen of building bookcases and watching old movies on television. Then, when all of his friends are just about ready to skin him alive, out it comes all in a rush: the latest Waldrop wonderment.

It's an odd way to work, but it's Howard's way, as uniquely his own as the stories it produces. He's been doing it for a long time. People have been paying him for it ever since 1970, but he started long before that, writing stories just for the love of writing. I couldn't tell you just when Howard began to scrawl words on paper, but I suspect that it was about nine seconds after he first learned to hold a Crayola in his stubby little fingers.

I do know that he was born in Mississippi on September 15, 1946 (a date he's immortalized in one of his recent short stories), that later on his family moved to Texas, and that he's been a thorough-going Texan ever since. He was already writing up a storm by the time he first came to my attention.

That was in 1963; we were both in high school, him in Arlington, Texas and me in Bayonne, New Jersey, and both of us were publishing our juvenilia in the comic book fan magazines of the day, tiny publications printed in purple with fast-fading ditto masters and circulated to literally *dozens* of eager

Introduction

readers, most of them high school kids, like Howard himself. Even then, Howard was unique. Everyone else who wrote for those tiny little fanzines (including, I blush to admit, myself) imitated the professional funny-books and wrote about superheroes. Howard wrote detective stories set in France at the time of the Musketeers. The readers loved him, but didn't quite know what to make of him, and they'd write in puzzlement to the fanzine letter columns to say, "Boy, Howard Waldrop's story was really great, but it was all about Cardinal Richelieu. What powers did *he* have, anyway?" He's been pleasing and puzzling readers ever since.

Everyone who read him back then knew right off that Howard was too good to stay an amateur for long, and sure enough we were all right. He made his first professional sale in 1970, just before he got drafted. The Army sent him to Georgia, gave him a typewriter, and taught him all the words to "I Want to Be an Airborne Ranger," but otherwise did him little good. The story had more lasting effects on his life and career. It was a little thing called "Lunchbox," and the editor who bought it was the legendary John W. Campbell, Jr. During the decades that he had edited *Astounding* (later *Analog*), Campbell had discovered and introduced an astonishing number of SF greats, and in fishing Howard Waldrop out of the slush pile, he demonstrated that his eye for talent hadn't deserted him. Campbell's untimely death came before he could actually print Howard's debut story, but in a very real sense it can still be said that Howard Waldrop was Campbell's last great gift to science fiction.

Two years as an army journalist slowed him down a little, but there was no stopping Howard permanently, and once he was discharged he returned to Texas to begin to write and sell all sorts of things. He even wrote a novel, a collaboration with his landlord. It was called *The Texas-Israeli War*, by Jake Saunders and Howard Waldrop, and it's still in print today.

Those were heady days in Texas, for reasons entirely unconnected with the Dallas Cowboy Cheerleaders. Hot young writers were popping up all over the Lone Star State, and selling stories to every contemporary market, large and small. The brilliant Tom Reamy was just beginning to publish, Lisa Tuttle was turning heads with her early stories, Bruce Sterling was in the process of becoming a Harlan Ellison Discovery, and all of

Strange Things in Close-Up

them—along with Howard and a half-dozen others—were part of a loosely organized floating workshop they called the Turkey City Neopro Rodeo. Collaboration was endemic among the Turkey City writers, and Howard shared bylines with a number of them, producing some forgettable journeyman stories and others that are still being talked about, most notably "Custer's Last Jump," about the way Crazy Horse and the Plains Indian Air Force destroyed Custer's paratroops at the Battle of the Little Big Horn. It was berserk, brilliant, and an omen of the things soon to come from Howard's clanking manual typewriter.

It was around then that people finally started noticing Howard Waldrop. He was nominated for *two* Nebulas in 1977: for "Custer" and again for "Mary Margaret Road-Grader," Howard's solo tour de force about post-holocaust tractor pulls, which you'll find in this collection. He didn't take home any trophies that year, but it was only a matter of time. Other nominations for other awards followed, and in 1981 his classic story "The Ugly Chickens" (that's also included here) won both the Nebula and the prestigious World Fantasy Award, and came within a dodo feather of copping the Hugo as well, for a rare triple crown.

Nowadays, Howard seems to be just about everywhere. Once, to find the latest Waldrop stories, you had to buy Terry Carr's distinguished hardcover anthology series *Universe*, or seek out small circulation semi-professional magazines like *Shayol*, *Chacal* and *Nickelodeon*. These days Howard is publishing in *Omni* and *Playboy* . . . but you'll still find him in *Universe* and *Shayol* as well. He's not the kind who forgets where he came from. His name turns up monotonously on the shortlists for every major award in the field and most of the minor ones, and no wonder. The stories keep getting stranger and stranger, but they're getting better and better too.

He even had another go at a novel recently, this time without any help from his landlord. The end result was called *Them Bones*, time travel as only Waldrop would write it, and it was published to loud huzzas as part of Terry Carr's revived Ace Specials line.

As good as it was, however, *Them Bones* still wasn't a patch on Howard's short stories. Short fiction remains Waldrop's forte, and believe me, nobody does it better. You've got a

Introduction

damned fine sampler of Waldrop in the pages that follow, the famous stories and the obscure ones, plucked from magazines with hundreds or hundreds of thousands of readers. The only thing they all have in common is their quality. If this is your first taste of Howard, I envy you. Bet you can't read just one.

Oh, yes, you'll be wanting the answers to the riddles. Howard Waldrop. Howard Waldrop. Howard Waldrop. And finally, Howard Waldrop. There's only one of him, but—lucky for us—he spreads himself around.

HOWARD WHO?

To the editors who first bought them—Terry (Bob and Marta sorta for a few minutes). Pat & Arnie, Ellen, Damon, Tom, Alice; Pat (who bought the whole thing); Joe (who sold the whole thing); but mostly for Ruthie, who could have been a contender, instead of a bum, which is what I am.

Introduction to
The Ugly Chickens

Howard Who?, indeed. If people know my work at all, it's probably this story. It was up for four awards and won two of them, and was reprinted ten times in the first year after publication.

Well, I had no idea when I wrote it. I really didn't. Terry Carr had been wanting a story from me for Universe 10 *for a year. It took me the first six months of 1979 to write this. I did most of the work on a friend's kitchen table, with notes and books scattered all around, like a collage that could be called Writer At Work.*

When I finished, I didn't know if I had a story or a monster on my hands. Anyway I sent it to Terry. Let me tell you what happened then.

Terry had strained his back and was Taking a Lot of Medicine. (Also I'd taken too long to do the story). Anyway, when the story got there, the book was already filled up. But Terry, even in his haze, loved the story, called Marta Randall, who lived up the hill (and who, with Robert Silverberg, was editing New Dimensions, *another original anthology series). She ran down the hill, read the story, and fired off a letter to me. I sent the story to Terry; I got back a letter from Marta, offering a contract at twice the money Terry was paying. Sounded real good to me.*

So I went off to an sf convention, read "The Ugly Chickens" (just after they showed the old Warner Bros. cartoon Porky in Wackyland*) and in general had a good time.*

I walked back in the door at home and the phone rang.

"Hello, Howard. This is Terry."

Like Scrooge McDuck, I could see silver dollars with wings on them flying out the window.

What happened was that Terry's Medicine Had Worn Off,

and an agent called to tell him that — hah hah . . . one of the stories he'd bought for Universe *as an original had already been sold in Ireland or something. Now Terry needed "The Ugly Chickens" real bad. At half the money.*

"What does Marta think about all this?" I asked.

"She says if you'll write another *story for New Dimensions, she'll let me have 'Ugly Chickens' back. Okay? Huh? Huh?"*

"Okay," I said. Thereby starting the rumor that I sell my stories to the lowest bidder. (Which is why editors are always offering me a penny a word on publication, thinking this gives them an inside edge on seeing my works first.)

(For Marta, I wrote "Flying Saucer Rock and Roll," which, along with a story by Ed Bryant and one by Connie Willis, guaranteed that Pocket Books ended publication of the New Dimensions *series with # 12, and pulled copies of # 13 from publication after review copies had already been sent out. Go figure that. They knew the job was dangerous when they took it.)*

Terry Carr and I go back a long way, to Universe 4, *where I sold him my second story, ever. Lest you think it's all friendship, we were once at a party with a hundred or so other writers at a worldcon (they all run together after a while). I was wearing a tee-shirt printed with long green arms clawing their way up from below the belt-line, like the Creature from the Black Lagoon was there.*

There was one of those lulls, and somebody asked, "What's down there, Howard?"

And before I could think, Terry Carr's voice boomed throughout the whole room: "It's a good writer, trying to get out," he said.

The Ugly Chickens

My car was broken, and I had a class to teach at eleven. So I took the city bus, something I rarely do.

I spent last summer crawling through The Big Thicket with cameras and tape recorder, photographing and taping two of the last ivory-billed woodpeckers on the earth. You can see the films at your local Audubon Society showroom.

This year I wanted something just as flashy but a little less taxing. Perhaps a population study on the Bermuda cahow, or the New Zealand *takahe*. A month or so in the warm (not hot) sun would do me the world of good. To say nothing of the advance of science.

I was idly leafing through Greenway's *Extinct and Vanishing Birds of the World*. The city bus was winding its way through the ritzy neighborhoods of Austin, stopping to let off the chicanas, black women and Vietnamese who tended the kitchens and gardens of the rich.

"I haven't seen any of those ugly chickens in a long time," said a voice close by.

A grey-haired lady was leaning across the aisle toward me.

I looked at her, then around. Maybe she was a shopping-bag lady. Maybe she was just talking. I looked straight at her. No doubt about it, she was talking to me. She was waiting for an answer.

"I used to live near some folks who raised them when I was a girl," she said. She pointed.

I looked down at the page my book was open to.

What I should have said was: "That is quite impossible, madam. This is a drawing of an extinct bird of the island of Mauritius. It is perhaps the most famous dead bird in the world. Maybe you are mistaking this drawing for that of some rare

Strange Things in Close-Up

Asiatic turkey, peafowl or pheasant. I am sorry, but you *are* mistaken."

I should have said all that.

What she said was, "Oops, this is my stop," and got up to go.

My name is Paul Linberl. I am twenty-six years old, a graduate student in ornithology at the University of Texas, a teaching assistant. My name is not unknown in the field. I have several vices and follies, but I don't think foolishness is one of them.

The stupid thing for me to do would have been to follow her.

She stepped off the bus.

I followed her.

I came into the departmental office, trailing scattered papers in the whirlwind behind me. "Martha! Martha!" I yelled.

She was doing something in the supply cabinet.

"Jesus, Paul! What do you want?"

"Where's Courtney?"

"At the conference in Houston. You know that. You missed your class. What's the matter?"

"Petty cash. Let me at it!"

"Payday was only a week ago. If you can't . . ."

"It's business! It's fame and adventure and the chance of a lifetime! It's a long sea voyage that leaves . . . a plane ticket. To either Jackson, Mississippi or Memphis. Make it Jackson, it's closer. I'll get receipts! I'll be famous. Courtney will be famous. *You'll* even be famous! This university will make even *more* money! I'll pay you back. Give me some paper. I gotta write Courtney a note. When's the next plane out? Could you get Marie and Chuck to take over my classes Tuesday and Wednesday? I'll try to be back Thursday unless something happens. Courtney'll be back tomorrow, right? I'll call him from, well, wherever. Do you have some coffee? . . ."

And so on and so forth. Martha looked at me like I was crazy. But she filled out the requisition anyway.

"What do I tell Kemejian when I ask him to sign these?"

"Martha, babe, sweetheart. Tell him I'll get his picture in *Scientific American*."

"He doesn't read it."

The Ugly Chickens

"*Nature*, then!"

"I'll see what I can do," she said.

The lady I had followed off the bus was named Jolyn (Smith) Jimson. The story she told me was so weird that it had to be true. She knew things only an expert, or someone with firsthand experience, could know. I got names from her, and addresses, and directions, and tidbits of information. Plus a year: 1927.

And a place. Northern Mississippi.

I gave her my copy of the Greenway book. I told her I'd call her as soon as I got back into town. I left her standing on the corner near the house of the lady she cleaned for twice a week. Jolyn Jimson was in her sixties.

Think of the dodo as a baby harp seal with feathers. I know that's not even close, but it saves time.

In 1507, the Portuguese, on their way to India, found the (then unnamed) Mascarene Islands in the Indian Ocean—three of them a few hundred miles apart, all east and north of Madagascar.

It wasn't until 1598, when that old Dutch sea captain Cornelius van Neck bumped into them, that the islands received their names—names which changed several times through the centuries as the Dutch, French and English changed them every war or so. They are now known as Rodriguez, Réunion and Mauritius.

The major feature of these islands were large flightless birds, stupid, ugly, bad-tasting birds. Van Neck and his men named them *dod-aarsen*, stupid ass, or dodars, silly birds, or solitaires.

There were three species—the dodo of Mauritius, the real grey-brown, hooked-beak clumsy thing that weighed twenty kilos or more; the white, somewhat slimmer, dodo of Réunion; and the solitaires of Rodriguez and Réunion, which looked like very fat, very dumb light-colored geese.

The dodos all had thick legs, big squat bodies twice as large as a turkey's, naked faces, and big long downcurved beaks ending in a hook like a hollow linoleum knife. They were flightless. Long ago they had lost the ability to fly, and their wings had degenerated to flaps the size of a human hand with only three or four feathers in them. Their tails were curly and fluffy, like a child's afterthought at decoration. They had absolutely no natural enemies. They nested on open ground. They probably hatched their eggs wherever they happened to lay them.

No natural enemies until van Neck and his kind showed up. The Dutch, French and Portuguese sailors who stopped at the Mascarenes to replenish stores found that besides looking stupid, dodos *were* stupid. They walked right up to them and hit them on the head with clubs. Better yet, dodos could be herded around like sheep. Ship's logs are full of things like: "Party of ten men ashore. Drove half-a-hundred of the big turkey-like birds into the boat. Brought to ship where they are given the run of the decks. Three will feed a crew of 150."

Even so, most of the dodo, except for the breast, tasted bad. One of the Dutch words for them was *walghvogel*, disgusting bird. But on a ship three months out on a return from Goa to Lisbon, well, food was where you found it. It was said, even so, that prolonged boiling did not improve the flavor.

Even so, the dodos might have lasted, except that the Dutch, and later the French, colonized the Mascarenes. These islands became plantations and dumping-places for religious refugees. Sugar cane and other exotic crops were raised there.

With the colonists came cats, dogs, hogs and the cunning *Rattus norwegicus* and the Rhesus monkey from Ceylon. What dodos the hungry sailors left were chased down (they were dumb and stupid, but they could run when they felt like it) by dogs in the open. They were killed by cats as they sat on their nests. Their eggs were stolen and eaten by monkeys, rats and hogs. And they competed with the pigs for all the low-growing goodies of the islands.

The last Mauritius dodo was seen in 1681, less than a hundred years after man first saw them. The last white dodo walked off the history books around 1720. The solitaires of Rodriguez and Réunion, last of the genus as well as the species, may have lasted until 1790. Nobody knows.

Scientists suddenly looked around and found no more of the Didine birds alive, anywhere.

This part of the country was degenerate before the first Snopes ever saw it. This road hadn't been paved until the late fifties, and it was a main road between two country seats. That didn't mean it went through civilized country. I'd travelled for miles

The Ugly Chickens

and seen nothing but dirt banks red as Billy Carter's neck and an occasional church. I expected to see Burma Shave signs, but realized this road had probably never had them.

I almost missed the turn-off onto the dirt and gravel road the man back at the service station had marked. It led onto the highway from nowhere, a lane out of a field. I turned down it and a rock the size of a golf ball flew up over the hood and put a crack three inches long in the windshield of the rent-a-car I'd gotten in Grenada.

It was a hot muggy day for this early. The view was obscured in a cloud of dust every time the gravel thinned. About a mile down the road, the gravel gave out completely. The roadway turned into a rutted dirt pathway, just wider than the car, hemmed in on both sides by a sagging three-strand barbed wire fence.

In some places the fenceposts were missing for a few meters. The wire lay on the ground and in some places disappeared under it for long stretches.

The only life I saw was a mockingbird raising hell with something under a thorn bush the barbed wire had been nailed to in place of a post. To one side now was a grassy field which had gone wild, the way everywhere will look after we blow ourselves off the face of the planet. The other was fast becoming woods—pine, oak, some black gum and wild plum, fruit not out this time of the year.

I began to ask myself what I was doing here. What if Ms. Jimson were some imaginative old crank who—but no. Wrong, maybe, but even the wrong was worth checking. But I knew she hadn't lied to me. She had seemed incapable of lies—a good ol' girl, backbone of the South, of the earth. Not a mendacious gland in her being.

I couldn't doubt her, or my judgement, either. Here I was, creeping and bouncing down a dirt path in Mississippi, after no sleep for a day, out on the thin ragged edge of a dream. I *had* to take it on faith.

The back of the car sometimes slid where the dirt had loosened and gave way to sand. The back tire stuck once, but I rocked out of it. Getting back out again would be another matter. Didn't anyone ever use this road?

The woods closed in on both sides like the forest primaeval, and the fence had long since disappeared. My odometer said ten kilometers and it had been twenty minutes since I'd turned off the highway. In the rearview mirror, I saw beads of sweat and dirt in the wrinkles of my neck. A fine patina of dust covered everything inside the car. Clots of it came through the windows.

The woods reached out and swallowed the road. Branches scraped against the windows and the top. It was like falling down a long dark leafy tunnel. It was dark and green in there. I fought back an atavistic urge to turn on the headlights. The roadbed must be made of a few centuries of leaf mulch. I kept constant pressure on the accelerator and bulled my way through.

Half a log caught and banged and clanged against the car bottom. I saw light ahead. Fearing for the oil pan, I punched the pedal and sped out.

I almost ran through a house.

It was maybe ten meters from the trees. The road ended under one of the windows. I saw somebody waving from the corner of my eye.

I slammed on the brakes.

A whole family was on the porch, looking like a Walker Evans Depression photograph, or a fever dream from the mind of a "Hee Haw" producer. The house was old. Strips of peeling paint a meter long tapped against the eaves.

"Damned good thing you stopped," said a voice. I looked up. The biggest man I had ever seen in my life leaned down into the driver-side window.

"If we'd have heard you sooner, I'd've sent one of the kids down to the end of the driveway to warn you," he said.

Driveway?

His mouth was stained brown at the corners. I figured he chewed tobacco until I saw the sweet-gum snuff brush sticking from the pencil pocket in the bib of his overalls. His hands were the size of a catcher's mitts. They looked like they'd never held anything smaller than an axe handle.

"How y'all?" he said, by way of introduction.

"Just fine," I said. I got out of the car.

"My name's Lindberl," I said, extending my hand. He took it. For an instant, I thought of bear traps, shark's mouths, closing elevator doors. The thought went back to wherever it is they stay.

The Ugly Chickens

"This the Gudger place?" I asked.

He looked at me blankly with his grey eyes. He wore a diesel truck cap, and had on a checked lumberjack shirt beneath his overalls. His rubber boots were the size of the ones Karloff wore in *Frankenstein*.

"Naw. I'm Jim Bob Krait. That's my wife Jenny, and there's Luke and Skeeno and Shirl." He pointed to the porch.

The people on the porch nodded.

"Lessee? Gudger? No Gudgers round here I know of. I'm sorta new here," I took that to mean he hadn't lived here for more than twenty years or so.

"Jennifer!" he yelled. "You know of anybody named Gudger?" To me he said, "My wife's lived around here all her life."

His wife came down onto the second step of the porch landing. "I think they used to be the ones what lived on the Spradlin place before the Spradlins. But the Spradlins left around the Korean War. I didn't know any of the Gudgers myself. That's while we was living over to Water Valley."

"You an insurance man?" asked Mr. Krait.

"Uh . . . no," I said. I imagined the people on the porch leaning toward me, all ears. "I'm a . . . I teach college."

"Oxford?" asked Krait.

"Uh, no. University of Texas."

"Well, that's a damn long way off. You say you're looking for the Gudgers?"

"Just their house. The area. As your wife said, I understand they left during the Depression, I believe."

"Well, they musta had money," said the gigantic Mr. Krait. "Nobody around here was rich enough to *leave* during the Depression."

"Luke!" he yelled. The oldest boy on the porch sauntered down. He looked anemic and wore a shirt in vogue with the Twist. He stood with his hands in his pockets.

"Luke, show Mr. Lindbergh—"

"Lindberl."

"Mr Lindberl here the way up to the old Spradlin place. Take him as far as the old log bridge, he might get lost before then."

"Log bridge broke down, daddy."

"When?"

Strange Things in Close-Up

"October, daddy."

"Well, hell, somethin' else to fix! Anyway, to the creek."

He turned to me. "You want him to go along on up there, see you don't get snakebit?"

"No, I'm sure I'll be fine."

"Mind if I ask what you're going up there for?" he asked. He was looking away from me. I could see having to come right out and ask was bothering him. Such things usually came up in the course of conversation.

"I'm a—uh, bird scientist. I study birds. We had a sighting—someone told us the old Gudger place—the area around here—I'm looking for a rare bird. It's hard to explain."

I noticed I was sweating. It was hot.

"You mean like a goodgod? I saw a goodgod about twenty-five years ago, over next to Bruce," he said.

"Well, no." (A goodgod was one of the names for an ivory-billed woodpecker, one of the rarest in the world. Any other time I would have dropped my jaw. Because they were thought to have died out in Mississippi by the teens, and by the fact that Krait knew they *were* rare.)

I went to lock my car up, then thought of the protocol of the situation. "My car be in your way?" I asked.

"Naw. It'll be just fine," said Jim Bob Krait. "We'll look for you back by sundown, that be all right?"

For a minute, I didn't know whether that was a command or an expression of concern.

"Just in case I get snakebit," I said. "I'll try to be careful up there."

"Good luck on findin' them rare birds," he said. He walked up to the porch with his family.

"Les go," said Luke.

Behind the Krait house was a henhouse and pigsty where hogs lay after their morning slop like islands in a muddy bay, or some Zen pork sculpture. Next we passed broken farm machinery gone to rust, though there was nothing but uncultivated land as far as the eye could see. How the family made a living I don't know. I'm told you can find places just like this throughout the South.

We walked through woods and across fields, following a sort

The Ugly Chickens

of path. I tried to memorize the turns I would have to take on the way back. Luke didn't say a word the whole twenty minutes he accompanied me, except to curse once when he stepped into a bull nettle with his tennis shoes.

We came to a creek which skirted the edge of a woodsy hill. There was a rotted log forming a small dam. Above it the water was nearly a meter deep, below it, half that much.

"See that path?" he asked.

"Yes."

"Follow it up around the hill, then across the next field. Then you cross the creek again on the rocks, and over the hill. Take the left-hand path. What's left of the house is about three quarters the way up the next hill. If you come to a big bare rock cliff, you've gone too far. You got that?"

I nodded.

He turned and left.

The house had once been a dog-run cabin, like Ms. Jimson had said. Now it was fallen in on one side, what they call sigoglin (or was it antisigoglin?). I once heard a hymn on the radio called "The Land Where No Cabins Fall." This was the country songs like that were written in.

Weeds grew everywhere. There were signs of fences, a flattened pile of wood that had once been a barn. Further behind the house were the outhouse remains. Half a rusted pump stood in the backyard. A flatter spot showed where the vegetable garden had been; in it a single wild tomato, pecked by birds, lay rotting. I passed it. There was lumber from three outbuildings, mostly rotten and green with algae and moss. One had been a smokehouse and woodshed combination. Two had been chicken roosts. One was larger than the other. It was there I started to poke around and dig.

Where? Where? I wish I'd been on more archaeological digs, knew the places to look. Refuse piles, midden heaps, kitchen scrap piles, compost boxes. Why hadn't I been born on a farm so I'd know instinctively where to search.

I prodded around the grounds. I moved back and forth like a setter casting for the scent of quail. I wanted more, more. I still wasn't satisfied.

Dusk. Dark, in fact. I trudged into the Kraits' front yard. The toe sack I carried was full to bulging. I was hot, tired, streaked with fifty years of chicken shit. The Kraits were on their porch. Jim Bob lumbered down like a friendly mountain.

I asked him a few questions, gave them a Xerox of one of the dodo pictures, left them addresses and phone numbers where they could reach me.

Then into the rent-a-car. Off to Water Valley, acting on information Jennifer Krait gave me. I went to the postmaster's house at Water Valley. She was getting ready for bed. I asked questions. She got on the phone. I bothered people until one in the morning. Then back into the trusty rent-a-car.

On to Memphis as the moon came up on my right. Interstate 55 was a glass ribbon before me. WLS from Chicago was on the radio.

I hummed along with it, I sang at the top of my voice.

The sack full of dodo bones, beaks, feet and eggshell fragments kept me company on the front seat.

Did you know a museum once traded an entire blue whale skeleton for one of a dodo?

Driving, driving.

THE DANCE OF THE DODOS

I used to have a vision sometimes—I had it long before this madness came up. I can close my eyes and see it by thinking hard. But it comes to me most often, most vividly when I am reading and listening to classical music, especially Pachelbel's *Canon in D*.

It is near dusk in The Hague and the light is that of Frans Hals, of Rembrandt. The Dutch royal family and their guests eat and talk quietly in the great dining hall. Guards with halberds and pikes stand in the corners of the room. The family is arranged around the table; the King, Queen, some princesses, a prince, a couple of other children, an invited noble or two. Servants come out with plates and cups but they do not intrude.

On a raised platform at one end of the room an orchestra plays dinner music—a harpsichordist, viola, cello, three violins and woodwinds. One of the royal dwarfs sits on the edge of the platform, his foot slowly rubbing the back of one of the dogs sleeping near him.

As the music of Pachelbel's *Canon in D* swells and rolls through the hall, one of the dodos walks in clumsily, stops, tilts its head, its eyes bright as a pool of tar. It sways a little, lifts its foot tentatively, one then another, rocks back and forth in time to the cello.

The violins swirl. The dodo begins to dance, its great ungainly body now graceful. It is joined by the other two dodos who come into the hall, all three in sort of a circle.

The harpsichord begins its counterpoint. The fourth dodo, the white one from Réunion, comes from its place under the table and joins the circle with the others.

It is most graceful of all, making complete turns where the others only sway and dip on the edge of the circle they have formed.

The music rises in volume; the first violinist sees the dodos and nods to the King. But he and the others at the table have already seen. They are silent, transfixed—even the servants stand still, bowls, pots and kettles in their hands forgotten.

Around the dodos dance with bobs and weaves of their ugly heads. The white dodo dips, takes half a step, pirouettes on one foot, circles again.

Without a word the King of Holland takes the hand of the Queen, and they come around the table, children before the spectacle. They join in the dance, waltzing (anachronism) among the dodos while the family, the guests, the soldiers watch and nod in time with the music.

Then the vision fades, and the afterimage of a flickering fireplace and a dodo remains.

The dodo and its kindred came by ships to the ports of civilized men. The first we have record of is that of Captain van Neck who brought back two in 1599—one for the King of Holland, and one which found its way through Cologne to the menagerie of Emperor Rudolf II.

This royal aviary was at Schloss Neugebau, near Vienna. It was here the first paintings of the dumb old birds were done by Georg and his son Jacob Hoefnagel, between 1602 and 1610. They painted it among more than ninety species of birds which kept the Emperor amused.

Another Dutch artist named Roelandt Savery, as someone

said, "made a career out of the dodo." He drew and painted them many times, and was no doubt personally fascinated by them. Obsessed, even. Early on, the paintings are consistent; the later ones have inaccuracies. This implies he worked from life first, then from memory as his model went to that place soon to be reserved for all its species. One of his drawings has two of the Raphidae scrambling for some goodie on the ground. His works are not without charm.

Another Dutch artist (they seemed to sprout up like mushrooms after a spring rain) named Peter Withoos also stuck dodos in his paintings, sometimes in odd and exciting places—wandering around during their owner's music lessons, or stuck with Adam and Eve in some Edenic idyll.

The most accurate representation, we are assured, comes from half a world away from the religious and political turmoil of the seafaring Europeans. There is an Indian miniature painting of the dodo which now rests in a museum in Russia. The dodo could have been brought by the Dutch or Portuguese in their travels to Goa and the coasts of the Indian subcontinent. Or they could have been brought centuries before by the Arabs who plied the Indian Ocean in their triangular-sailed craft, and who may have discovered the Mascarenes before the Europeans cranked themselves up for the First Crusade.

At one time early in my bird-fascination days (after I stopped killing them with BB guns but before I began to work for a scholarship), I once sat down and figured out where all the dodos had been.

Two with van Neck in 1599, one to Holland, one to Austria. Another was in Count Solm's park in 1600. An account speaks of "one in Italy, one in Germany, several to England, eight or nine to Holland." William Boentekoe van Hoorn knew of "one shipped to Europe in 1640, another in 1685" which he said was "also painted by Dutch artists." Two were mentioned as "being kept in Surrat House in India as pets," perhaps one of which is the one in the painting. Being charitable, and considering "several" to mean at least three, that means twenty dodos in all.

There had to be more, when boatloads had been gathered at the time.

What do we know of the Didine birds? A few ships' logs,

The Ugly Chickens

some accounts left by travellers and colonists. The English were fascinated by them. Sir Hamon L'Estrange, a contemporary of Pepys, saw exhibited "a Dodar from the Island of Mauritius . . . it is not able to flie, being so bigge." One was stuffed when it died, and was put in the Museum Tradescantum in South Lambeth. It eventually found its way into the Ashmolean Museum. It grew ratty and was burned, all but a leg and the head, in 1750. By then there were no more dodos, but nobody had realized that yet.

Francis Willughby got to describe it before its incineration. Earlier, old Carolus Clusius in Holland studied the one in Count Solm's park. He collected everything known about the Raphidae, describing a dodo leg Pieter Pauw kept in his natural history cabinet, in *Exoticarium libri decem* in 1605, eight years after their discovery.

François Leguat, a Huguenot who lived on Réunion for some years, published an account of his travels in which he mentioned the dodos. It was published in 1690 (after the Mauritius dodo was extinct) and included the information that "some of the males weigh forty-five pound. One egg, much bigger than that of a goos is laid by the female, and takes seven weeks hatching time."

The Abbe Pingre visited the Mascarenes in 1761. He saw the last of the Rodriguez solitaires, and collected what information he could about the dead Mauritius and Réunion members of the genus.

After that, only memories of the colonists, and some scientific debate as to *where* the Raphidae belonged in the great taxonomic scheme of things—some said pigeons, some said rails—were left. Even this nitpicking ended. The dodo was forgotten.

When Lewis Carroll wrote *Alice in Wonderland* in 1865, most people thought he invented the dodo.

The service station I called from in Memphis was busier than a one-legged man in an ass-kicking contest. Between bings and dings of the bell, I finally realized the call had gone through.

The guy who answered was named Selvedge. I got nowhere with him. He mistook me for a real estate agent, then a lawyer. Now he was beginning to think I was some sort of a con man. I wasn't doing too well, either. I hadn't slept in two days. I must have sounded like a speed freak. My only progress was that I found that Ms. Annie Mae Gudger (childhood playmate of Jolyn Jimson) was now, and had been, the respected Ms. Annie Mae Radwin. This guy Selvedge must have been a secretary or toady or something.

We were having a conversation comparable to that between a shrieking macaw and a pile of mammoth bones. Then there was another click on the line.

"Young man?" said the other voice, an old woman's voice, Southern, very refined but with a hint of the hills in it.

"Yes? Hello! Hello!"

"Young man, you say you talked to a Jolyn somebody? Do you mean Jolyn Smith?"

"Hello! Yes! Ms. Radwin, Ms. Annie Mae Radwin who used to be Gudger? She lives in Austin now. Texas. She used to live near Water Valley, Mississippi. Austin's where I'm from. I . . ."

"Young man," asked the voice again, "are you sure you haven't been put up to this by my hateful sister Alma?"

"Who? No, ma'am. I met a woman named Jolyn . . ."

"I'd like to talk to you, young man," said the voice. Then offhandedly, "Give him directions to get here, Selvedge."

Click.

I cleaned out my mouth as best I could in the service station restroom, tried to shave with an old clogged Gillette disposable in my knapsack and succeeded in gapping up my jawline. I changed into a clean pair of jeans, the only other shirt I had with me and combed my hair. I stood in front of the mirror.

I still looked like the dog's lunch.

The house reminded me of Presley's mansion, which was somewhere in the neighborhood. From a shack on the side of a Mississippi hill to this, in forty years. There are all sorts of ways of making it. I wondered what Annie Mae Gudger's had been. Luck? Predation? Divine intervention? Hard work? Trover and replevin?

Selvedge led me toward the sun room. I felt like Philip Marlowe going to meet a rich client. The house was filled with that furniture built sometime between the turn of the century and

The Ugly Chickens

the 1950s—the ageless kind. It never looks great, it never looks ratty, and every chair is comfortable.

I think I was expecting some formidable woman with sleeve blotters and a green eyeshade hunched over a roll-top desk with piles of paper whose acceptance or rejection meant life or death for thousands.

Who I met was a charming lady in a green pantsuit. She was in her sixties, her hair still a straw wheat color. It didn't look dyed. Her eyes were blue as my first-grade teacher's had been. She was wiry and looked as if the word fat was not in her vocabulary.

"Good morning, Mr. Lindberl." She shook my hand. "Would you like some coffee? You look as if you could use it."

"Yes, thank you."

"Please sit down." She indicated a white wicker chair at a glass table. A serving tray with coffeepot, cups, tea bags, croissants, napkins and plates lay on the tabletop.

After I swallowed half a cup of coffee at a gulp, she said, "What you wanted to see me about must be important?"

"Sorry about my manners," I said. "I know I don't look it, but I'm a biology assistant at the University of Texas. An ornithologist. Working on my master's. I met Ms. Jolyn Jimson two days ago . . ."

"How is Jolyn? I haven't seen her in, oh, Lord, it must be on to fifty years. The time gets away."

"She seemed to be fine. I only talked to her half an hour or so. That was . . ."

"And you've come to see me about? . . ."

"Uh. The . . . about some of the poultry your family used to raise, when they lived near Water Valley."

She looked at me a moment. Then she began to smile.

"Oh, you mean the ugly chickens?" she said.

I smiled. I almost laughed. I knew what Oedipus must have gone through.

It is now 4:30 in the afternoon. I am sitting at the downtown Motel 6 in Memphis. I have to make a phone call and get some sleep and catch a plane.

Annie Mae Gudger Radwin talked for four hours, answering

my questions, setting me straight on family history, having Selvedge hold all her calls.

The main problem was that Annie Mae ran off in 1928, the year *before* her father got his big break. She went to Yazoo City, and by degrees and stages worked her way northward to Memphis and her destiny as the widow of a rich mercantile broker.

But I get ahead of myself.

Grandfather Gudger used to be the overseer for Colonel Crisby on the main plantation near McComb, Mississippi. There was a long story behind that. Bear with me.

Colonel Crisby himself was the scion of a seafaring family with interests in both the cedars of Lebanon (almost all cut down for masts for His Majesty's and others' navies) and Egyptian cotton. Also teas, spices and any other salable commodity which came their way.

When Colonel Crisby's grandfather reached his majority in 1802, he waved good-bye to the Atlantic Ocean at Charleston S.C. and stepped westward into the forest. When he stopped, he was in the middle of the Chickasaw Nation, where he opened a trading post and introduced slaves to the Indians.

And he prospered, and begat Colonel Crisby's father, who sent back to South Carolina for everything his father owned. Everything—slaves, wagons, horses, cattle, guinea fowl, peacocks and dodos, which everybody thought of as atrociously ugly poultry of some kind, one of the seafaring uncles having bought them off a French merchant in 1721. (I surmised these were white dodos from Réunion, unless they had been from even earlier stock. The dodo of Mauritius was already extinct by then.)

All this stuff was herded out west to the trading post in the midst of the Chickasaw Nation. (The tribes around there were of the confederation of the Dancing Rabbits.)

And Colonel Crisby's father prospered, and so did the guinea fowl and the dodos. Then Andrew Jackson came along and marched the Dancing Rabbits off up the Trail of Tears to the heaven of Oklahoma. And Colonel Crisby's father begat Colonel Crisby, and put the trading post in the hands of others, and moved his plantation westward still to McComb.

Everything prospered but Colonel Crisby's father, who died.

The Ugly Chickens

And the dodos, with occasional losses to the avengin' weasel and the egg-sucking dog, reproduced themselves also.

Then along came Granddaddy Gudger, a Simon Legree role model, who took care of the plantation while Colonel Crisby raised ten companies of men and marched off to fight the War of the Southern Independence.

Colonel Crisby came back to the McComb plantation earlier than most, he having stopped much of the same volley of Minié balls that caught his commander, General Beauregard Hanlon, on a promontory bluff during the Siege of Vicksburg.

He wasn't dead, but death hung around the place like a gentlemanly bill collector for a month. The colonel languished, went slap-dab crazy and freed all his slaves the week before he died (the war lasted another two years after that). Not having any slaves, he didn't need an overseer.

Then comes the Faulkner part of the tale, straight out of *As I Lay Dying*, with the Gudger family returning to the area of Water Valley (before there was a Water Valley), moving through the demoralized and tattered displaced persons of the South, driving their dodos before them. For Colonel Crisby had given them to his former overseer for his faithful service. Also followed the story of the bloody murder of Granddaddy Gudger at the hands of the Freedman's militia during the rising of the first Klan, and of the trials and tribulations of Daddy Gudger in the years between 1880 and 1910, when he was between the ages of four and thirty-four.

Alma and Annie Mae were the second and fifth of Daddy Gudger's brood, born three years apart. They seemed to have hated each other from the very first time Alma looked into little Annie Mae's crib. They were kids by Daddy Gudger's second wife (his desperation had killed the first) and their father was already on his sixth career. He had been a lumberman, a stump preacher, a plowman-for-hire (until his mules broke out in farcy buds and died of the glanders), a freight hauler (until his horses died of overwork and the hardware store repossessed the wagon), a politician's roadie (until the politician lost the election). When Alma and Annie Mae were born, he was failing as a sharecropper. Somehow Gudger had made it through the Depression of 1898 as a boy, and was too poor after that to notice more about economics than the price of Beech-Nut tobacco at the store.

Alma and Annie Mae fought, and it helped none at all that Alma, being the oldest daughter, was both her mother and father's darling. Annie Mae's life was the usual unwanted poor-white-trash-child's hell. She vowed early to run away, and recognized her ambition at thirteen.

All this I learned this morning. Jolyn (Smith) Jimson was Annie Mae's only friend in those days—from a family even poorer than the Gudgers. But somehow there was food, and an occasional odd job. And the dodos.

"My family hated those old birds," said the cultured Annie Mae Radwin, nee Gudger, in the solarium. "He always swore he was going to get rid of them someday, but just never seemed to get around to it. I think there was more to it than that. But they were so much *trouble*. We always had to keep them penned up at night, and go check for their eggs. They wandered off to lay them, and forgot where they were. Sometimes no new ones were born at all in a year.

"And they got so *ugly*. Once a year. I mean, terrible-looking, like they were going to die. All their feathers fell off, and they looked like they had mange or something. Then the whole front of their beaks fell off, or worse, hung halfway on for a week or two. They looked like big old naked pigeons. After that they'd lose weight, down to twenty or thirty pounds, before their new feathers grew back.

"We were always having to kill foxes that got after them in the turkey house. That's what we called their roost, the turkey house. And we found their eggs all sucked out by cats and dogs. They were so stupid we had to drive them into their roost at night. I don't think they could have found it standing ten feet from it."

She looked at me.

"I think much as my father hated them, they meant something to him. As long as he hung on to them, he knew he was as good as Granddaddy Gudger. You may not know it, but there was a certain amount of family pride about Granddaddy Gudger. At least in my father's eyes. His rapid fall in the world had a sort of grandeur to it. He'd gone from a relatively high position in the old order, and maintained some grace and stature after the

The Ugly Chickens

Emancipation. and though he lost everything, he managed to keep those ugly old chickens the colonel had given him as sort of a symbol.

"And as long as he had them, too, my daddy thought himself as good as his father. He kept his dignity, even when he didn't have anything else."

I asked what happened to them. She didn't know, but told me who did and where I could find her.

That's why I'm going to make a phone call.

"Hello. Dr. Courtney. Dr. Courtney? This is Paul. Memphis. Tennessee. It's too long to go into. No, of course not, not yet. But I've got evidence. What? Okay, how do trochanters, coracoids, tarsometatarsi and beak sheaths sound? From their henhouse, where else? Where would you keep *your* dodos, then?

"Sorry. I haven't slept in a couple of days. I need some help. Yes, yes. Money. Lots of money.

"Cash. Three hundred dollars, maybe. Western Union, Memphis, Tennessee. Whichever one's closest to the airport. Airport. I need the department to set up reservations to Mauritius for me...

"No. No. Not wild goose chase, wild *dodo* chase. Tame dodo chase. I *know* there aren't any dodos on Mauritius! I know that. I could explain. I know it'll mean a couple of grand ... if ... but ...

"Look, Dr. Courtney. Do you want *your* picture in *Scientific American*, or don't you?"

I am sitting in the airport cafe in Port Louis, Mauritius. It is now three days later, five days since that fateful morning my car wouldn't start. God bless the Sears Diehard people. I have slept sitting up in a plane seat, on and off, different planes, different seats, for twenty-four hours, Kennedy to Paris, Paris to Cairo, Cairo to Madagascar. I felt like a brand-new man when I got here.

Now I feel like an infinitely sadder and wiser brand-new man. I have just returned from the hateful sister Alma's house in the exclusive section of Port Louis, where all the French and British officials used to live.

Courtney will get his picture in *Scientific American*, me too,

Strange Things in Close-Up

all right. There'll be newspaper stories and talk shows for a few weeks for me, and I'm sure Annie Mae Gudger Radwin on one side of the world and Alma Chandler Gudger Moliere on the other will come in for their share of glory.

I am putting away cup after cup of coffee. The plane back to Tananarive leaves in an hour. I plan to sleep all the way back to Cairo, to Paris, to New York, pick up my bag of bones, sleep back to Austin.

Before me on the table is a packet of documents, clippings and photographs. I have come half the world for this. I gaze from the package, out the window across Port Louis to the bulk of Mt. Pieter Boothe, which overshadows the city and its famous racecourse.

Perhaps I should do something symbolic. Cancel my flight. Climb the mountain and look down on man and all his handiworks. Take a pitcher of martinis with me. Sit in the bright semitropical sunlight (it's early dry winter here). Drink the martinis slowly, toasting Snuffo, God of Extinction. Here's one for the Great Auk. This is for the Carolina Parakeet. Mud in your eye, Passenger Pigeon. This one's for the Heath Hen. Most importantly, here's one each for the Mauritius dodo, the white dodo of Réunion, the Réunion solitaire, the Rodriguez solitaire. Here's to the Raphidae, great Didine birds that you were.

Maybe I'll do something just as productive, like climbing Mt. Pieter Boothe and pissing into the wind.

How symbolic. The story of the dodo ends where it began, on this very island. Life imitates cheap art. Like the Xerox of the Xerox of a bad novel. I never expected to find dodos still alive here (this is the one place they would have been noticed). I still can't believe Alma Chandler Gudger Moliere could have lived here twenty-five years and not *know* about the dodo, never set foot inside the Port Louis Museum, where they have skeletons and a stuffed replica the size of your little brother.

After Annie Mae ran off, the Gudger family found itself prospering in a time the rest of the country was going to hell. It was 1929. Gudger delved into politics again, and backed a man who knew a man who worked for Theodore "Sure Two-Handed Sword of God" Bilbo, who had connections everywhere. Who introduced him to Huey "Kingfish" Long just after that gentleman lost the Louisiana governor's election one of the times.

The Ugly Chickens

Gudger stumped around Mississippi, getting up steam for Long's Share the Wealth plan, even before it had a name.

The upshot was that the Long machine in Louisiana knew a rabble-rouser when it saw one, and invited Gudger to move to the Sportsman's Paradise, with his family, all expenses paid, and start working for the Kingfish at the unbelievable salary of $62.50 a week. Which prospect was like turning a hog loose under a persimmon tree, and before you could say Backwoods Messiah, the Gudger clan was on its way to the land of pelicans, graft and Mardi Gras.

Almost. But I'll get to that.

Daddy Gudger prospered all out of proportion with his abilities, but many men did that during the Depression. First a little, thence to more, he rose in bureaucratic (and political) circles of the state, dying rich and well-hated with his fingers in *all* the pies.

Alma Chandler Gudger became a debutante (she says Robert Penn Warren put her in his book) and met and married Jean Carl Moliere, only heir to rice, indigo and sugar cane growers. They had a happy wedded life, moving first to the West Indies, later to Mauritius, where the family sugar cane holdings were one of the largest on the island. Jean Carl died in 1959. Alma was his only survivor.

So local family makes good. Poor sharecropping Mississippi people turn out to have a father dying with a smile on his face, and two daughters who between them own a large portion of the planet.

I open the envelope before me. Ms. Alma Moliere had listened politely to my story (the university had called ahead and arranged an introduction through the director of the Port Louis Museum, who knew Ms. Moliere socially) and told me what she could remember. Then she sent a servant out to one of the storehouses (large as a duplex) and he and two others came back with boxes of clippings, scrapbooks and family photos.

"I haven't looked at any of this since we left St. Thomas," she said. "Let's go through it together."

Most of it was about the rise of Citizen Gudger.

"There's not many pictures of us before we came to Louisiana. We were so frightfully poor then, hardly anyone we knew had a camera. Oh, look. Here's one of Annie Mae. I thought I threw all those out after Mamma died."

This is the photograph. It must have been taken about 1927. Annie Mae is wearing some unrecognizable piece of clothing that approximates a dress. She leans on a hoe, smiling a snaggle-toothed smile. She looks to be ten or eleven. Her eyes are half hidden by the shadow of the brim of a gapped straw hat she wears. The earth she is standing in barefoot has been newly turned. Behind her is one corner of the house, and the barn beyond has its upper hay-windows open. Out-of-focus people are at work there.

A few feet behind her, a huge male dodo is pecking at something on the ground. The front two thirds of it shows, back to the stupid wings and the edge of the upcurved tail feathers. One foot is in the photo, having just scratched at something, possibly an earthworm, in the new-plowed clods. Judging by its darkness, it is the grey, or Mauritius, dodo.

The photograph is not very good, one of those 3½ x 5 jobs box camera used to take. Already I can see this one, and the blowup of the dodo, taking up a double-page spread in *S.A.* Alma told me around then they were down to six or seven of the ugly chickens, two whites, the rest grey-brown.

Besides this photo, two clippings are in the package, one from the Bruce *Banner-Times*, the other from the Oxford newspaper; both are columns by the same woman dealing with "Doings in Water Valley." Both mention the Gudger family moving from the area to seek its fortune in the swampy state to the west, and telling how they will be missed. Then there's a yellowed clipping from the front page of the Oxford newspaper with a small story about the Gudger Farewell Party in Water Valley the Sunday before (dated October 19, 1929).

There's a handbill in the package, advertising the Gudger Family Farewell Party, Sunday Oct. 15, 1929 Come One Come All. (The people in Louisiana who sent expense money to move Daddy Gudger must have overestimated the costs by an exponential factor. I said as much.)

"No," Alma Moliere said. "There was a lot, but it wouldn't have made any difference. Daddy Gudger was like Thomas Wolfe and knew a shining golden opportunity when he saw one. Win, lose or draw, he was never coming back *there* again. He

The Ugly Chickens

would have thrown some kind of soiree whether there had been money for it or not. Besides, people were much more sociable then, you mustn't forget."

I asked her how many people came.

"Four or five hundred," she said. "There's some pictures here somewhere." We searched awhile, then we found them.

Another thirty minutes to my flight. I'm not worried sitting here. I'm the only passenger, and the pilot is sitting at the table next to mine talking to an RAF man. Life is much slower and nicer on these colonial islands. You mustn't forget.

I look at the other two photos in the package. One is of some men playing horseshoes and washer-toss, while kids, dogs and women look on. It was evidently taken from the east end of the house looking west. Everyone must have had to walk the last mile to the old Gudger place. Other groups of people stand talking. Some men in shirtsleeves and suspenders, stand with their heads thrown back, a snappy story, no doubt, just told. One girl looks directly at the camera from close up, shyly, her finger in her mouth. She's about five. It looks like any snapshot of a family reunion which could have been taken anywhere, anytime. Only the clothing marks it as backwoods 1920s.

Courtney will get his money's worth. I'll write the article, make phone calls, plan the talk show tour to coincide with publication. Then I'll get some rest. I'll be a normal person again; get a degree, spend my time wading through jungles after animals which will be dead in another twenty years, anyway.

Who cares? The whole thing will be just another media event, just this year's Big Deal. It'll be nice getting normal again. I can read books, see movies, wash my clothes at the laundromat, listen to Jonathan Richman on the stereo. I can study and become an authority on some minor matter or other.

I can go to museums and see all the wonderful dead things there.

"That's the memory picture," said Alma. "They always took them at big things like this, back in those days. Everybody who was there would line up and pose for the camera. Only we couldn't fit everybody in. So we had two made. This is the one with us in it."

The house is dwarfed by people. All sizes, shapes, dress and age. Kids and dogs in front, women next, then men at the back. The only exceptions are the bearded patriarchs seated towards the front with the children—mens whose eyes face the camera but whose heads are still ringing with something Nathan Bedford Forrest said to them one time on a smoke-filled field. This photograph is from another age. You can recognize Daddy and Mrs. Gudger if you've seen their photograph before. Alma pointed herself out to me.

But the reason I took the photograph is in the foreground. Tables have been built out of sawhorses, with doors and boards nailed across them. They extend the entire width of the photograph. They are covered with food, more food than you can imagine.

"We started cooking three days before. So did the neighbors. Everybody brought something," said Alma.

It's like an entire Safeway had been cooked and set out to cool. Hams, quarters of beef, chickens by the tubful, quail in mounds, rabbit, butterbeans by the bushel, yams, Irish potatoes, an acre of corn, eggplant, peas, turnip greens, butter in five-pound molds, cornbread and biscuits, gallon cans of molasses, redeye gravy by the pot.

And five huge birds—twice as big as turkeys, legs capped like for Thanksgiving, drumsticks the size of Schwarzenegger's biceps, whole-roasted, lying on their backs on platters large as cocktail tables.

The people in the crowd sure look hungry.

"We ate for days," said Alma.

I already have the title for the *Scientific American* article. It's going to be called "The Dodo Is *Still* Dead."

Introduction to
Der Untergang Des Abendlandesmenschen

Adding to my reputation to selling to low bidders is the fact that half the stories in this book first appeared in Shayol, *or magazines associated with it. Why, when you're such a hotshot big-time writer, people ask, did you send stories first to the lowest-paying market?*

Here's how. Let's say I finished typing up a story on Thursday and mailed it off. On Tuesday, Pat Cadigan and Arnie Fenner (the editor and publisher of what is now, alas, an ex-magazine) would send me a check. A few months later would appear a beautifully printed magazine with covers by Don Punchatz or Roger Stine, and my story would be illustrated by Hank Jankus or Robert Haas, and not one word would be changed. (Unless, of course, something in the original manuscript hadn't made much sense, in which case they would have called me in the course of production and asked me to explain, in my own words, exactly what it was I was trying to say.)

It wasn't just me. The table of contents of all the Shayol's *reads like a Who's Who of everyone who was trying to do something with the SF or fantasy short story. The magazine will be missed.*

This story was written early in 1975 (it says here in my story log). I remember the exact genesis; a photo of William S. Hart in a stage production of Ben-Hur *from 1908. I'd been reading a lot of Conan Doyle, and I looked at the picture and said, "The man was born to play Sherlock Holmes." One thing led to another—silent German Expressionistic films, books about the Weimar Republic, the idea of a sky that flickers. All the things that fall together when a story idea gets ahold of you.*

The title is a take-off on Oswald Spengler's guaranteed sleep-inducer Der Untergang des Abendlandes, *a book of pseudo-*

historical philosophy that somehow became a 1920s bestseller when translated over here as The Decline of the West. *My title comes out, I'm told, as* The Down-Going of the Men of the Sun-Setting Lands. *Or,* End of the Cowboys, *if you will.*

Der Untergang des Abendlandesmenschen

They rode through the flickering landscape to the tune of organ music.

Bronco Billy, short like an old sailor, and William S., tall and rangy as a windblown pine. Their faces, their horses, the landscape all darkened and became light; were at first indistinct, then sharp and clear as they rode across one ridge and down into the valley beyond.

Ahead of them, in much darker shades, was the city of Bremen, Germany.

Except for the organ and piano music, it was quiet in most of Europe.

In the vaults below the Opera, in the City of Lights, Erik the phantom played the *Toccata and Fugue* while the sewers ran blackly by.

In Berlin, Cesare the somnambulist slept. His mentor Caligari lectured at the University, and waited for his chance to send the monster through the streets.

Also in Berlin, Dr. Mabuse was dead and could no longer control the underworld.

But in Bremen...

In Bremen, something walked the night.

To the cities of china eggs and dolls, in the time of sawdust bread and the price of six million marks for a postage stamp, came Bronco Billy and William S. They had ridden hard for two days and nights, and the horses were heavily lathered.

They reined in, and tied their mounts to a streetlamp on the Wilhelmstrasse.

Strange Things in Close-Up

"What say we get a drink, William S.?" asked the shorter cowboy. "All this damn flickering gives me a headache."

William S. struck a pose three feet away from him, turned his head left and right, and stepped up to the doors of the *Gasthaus* before them.

With his high-pointed hat and checked shirt, William S. looked like a weatherbeaten scarecrow, or a child's version of Abraham Lincoln before the beard. His eyes were like shiny glass, through which some inner hellfires shone.

Bronco Billy hitched up his pants. He wore Levis, which on him looked too large, a dark vest, lighter shirt, big leather chaps with three tassels at hip, knee and calf. His hat seemed three sizes too big.

Inside the tavern, things were murky grey, black and stark white. And always, the flickering.

They sat down at a table and watched the clientele. Ex-soldiers, in the remnants of uniforms, seven years after the Great War had ended. The unemployed, spending their last few coins on beer. The air was thick with grey smoke from pipes and cheap cigarettes.

Not too many people had noticed the entrance of William S. and Bronco Billy.

Two had.

"Quirt!" said an American captain, his hand on his drinking buddy, a sergeant.

"What?" asked the sergeant, his hand on the barmaid.

"Look who's here!"

The sergeant peered toward the haze of flickering grey smoke where the cowboys sat.

"Damn!" he said.

"Want to go over and chat with 'em?" asked the captain.

"&%#*$ no!" cursed the sergeant. "This ain't our #%& *!*ing picture."

"I suppose you're right," said the captain, and returned to his wine.

"You must remember, my friend," said William S. after the waiter brought them beer, "that there can be no rest in the pursuit of evil."

Der Untergang Des Abendlandesmenschen

"Yeah, but hell, William S., this is along way from home."

William S. lit a match, put it to a briar pipe containing his favorite shag tobacco. He puffed on it a few moments, then regarded his companion across his tankard.

"My dear Bronco Billy," he said. "No place is too far to go in order to thwart the forces of darkness. This is something Dr. Helioglabulus could not handle by himself, else he should not have summoned us."

"Yeah, but William S., my butt's sore as a rizen after two days in the saddle. I think we should bunk down before we see this doctor fellow."

"Ah, that's where you're wrong, my friend," said the tall, hawknosed cowboy. "Evil never sleeps. Men must."

"Well, I'm a man," said Bronco Billy. "I say let's sleep."

Just then, Dr. Helioglabulus entered the tavern.

He was dressed as a Tyrolean mountain guide, in *Lederhosen* and feathered cap, climbing boots and suspenders. He carried with him an alpenstock, which made a large *clunk* each time it touched the floor.

He walked through the flickering darkness and smoke and stood in front of the table with the two cowboys.

William S. had risen.

"Dr.–"he began.

"Eulenspiegel," said the other, an admonitory finger to his lips.

Bronco Billy rolled his eyes heavenward.

"Dr. Eulenspiegel, I'd like you to meet my associate and chronicler, Mr. Bronco Billy."

The doctor clicked his heels together.

"Have a chair," said Bronco Billy, pushing one out from under the table with his boot. He tipped his hat up off his eyes.

The doctor, in his comic opera outfit, sat.

"Helioglabulus," whispered William S., "whatever are you up to?"

"I had to come incognito. There are . . . others who should not learn of my presence here."

Bronco Billy looked from one to the other and rolled his eyes again.

"Then the game is afoot?" asked William S., his eyes more alight than ever.

"Game such as man has never before seen," said the doctor.

"I see," said William S., his eyes narrowing as he drew on his pipe. "Moriarty?"

"Much more evil."

"More evil?" asked the cowboy, his fingertips pressed together. "I cannot imagine such."

"Neither could I, up until a week ago," said Helioglabulus. "Since then, the city has experienced wholesale terrors. Rats run the streets at night, invade houses. This tavern will be deserted by nightfall. The people lock their doors and say prayers, even in this age. They are reverting to the old superstitions."

"They have just cause?" asked William S.

"A week ago, a ship pulled into the pier. On board was—one man!" He paused for dramatic effect. Bronco Billy was unimpressed. The doctor continued. "The crew, the passengers were gone. Only the captain was aboard, lashed to the wheel. And he was—drained of blood!"

Bronco Billy became interested.

"You mean," asked William S., bending over his beer, "that we are dealing with—the undead?"

"I am afraid so," said Dr. Helioglabulus, twisting his mustaches.

"Then we shall need the proper armaments," said the taller cowboy.

"I have them," said the doctor, taking cartridge boxes from his backpack.

"Good!" said William S. "Bronco Billy, you have your revolver?"

"What!? Whatta ya mean, 'Do you have your revolver?' Just what do you mean? Have you ever seen me without my guns, William S.? Are you losing your mind?"

"Sorry, Billy," said William S., looking properly abashed.

"Take these," said Helioglabulus.

Bronco Billy broke open his two Peacemakers, dumped the .45 shells on the table. William S. unlimbered his two Navy .36s and pushed the recoil rod down in the cylinders. He punched each cartridge out onto the tabletop.

Der Untergang Des Abendlandesmenschen

Billy started to load up his pistols, then took a closer look at the shells, held one up and examined it.

"Goddam, William S.," he yelled. "Wooden bullets! Wooden bullets?"

Helioglabulus was trying to wave him to silence. The tall cowboy tried to put his hand on the other.

Everyone in the beer hall had heard him. There was a deafening silence, all the patrons turned toward their table.

"Damn," said Bronco Billy. "You can't shoot a wooden bullet fifteen feet and expect it to hit the broad side of a corncrib. What the hell we gonna shoot wooden bullets at?"

The tavern began to empty, people rushing from the place, looking back in terror. All except five men at a far table.

"I am afraid, my dear Bronco Billy," said William S., "that you have frightened the patrons, and warned the evil ones of our presence."

Bronco Billy looked around.

"You mean those guys over there?" he nodded toward the other table. "Hell, William S., we both took on twelve men one time."

Dr. Helioglabulus sighed. "No, no, you don't understand. Those men over there are harmless; crackpot revolutionists. William and I are speaking of *nosferatu* . . ."

Bronco Billy continued to stare at him.

". . . the undead . . ."

No response.

". . . er, ah, vampires . . ."

"You mean," asked Billy, "like Theda Bara?"

"Not vamps, my dear friend," said the hawknosed wrangler. "Vampires. Those who rise from the dead and suck the blood of the living."

"Oh," said Bronco Billy. Then he looked at the cartridges. "These kill 'em?"

"Theoretically," said Helioglabulus.

"Meaning you don't know?"

The doctor nodded.

"In that case," said Bronco Billy, "we go halfies." He began to load his .45s with one regular bullet, then a wooden one, then another standard.

William S. had already filled his with wooden slugs.

41

Strange Things in Close-Up

"Excellent," said Helioglabulus. "Now, put these over your hatbands. I hope you never have to get close enough for them to be effective."

What he handed them were silver hatbands. Stamped on the shiny surface of the bands was a series of crosses. They slipped them on their heads, settling them on their hat brims.

"What next?" asked Bronco Billy.

"Why, we wait for nightfall, for the *nosferatu* to strike!" said the doctor.

"Did you hear them, Hermann?" asked Joseph.

"Sure. You think we ought to do the same?"

"Where would we find someone to make wooden bullets for pistols such as ours?" asked Joseph.

The five men sitting at the table looked toward the doctor and the two cowboys. All five were dressed in the remnants of uniforms belonging to the war. The one addressed as Hermann still wore the Knight's Cross on the faded splendor of his dress jacket.

"Martin," said Hermann. "Do you know where we can get wooden bullets?"

"I'm sure we could find someone to make them for the automatics," he answered. "Ernst, go to Wartman's; see about them."

Ernst stood, then slapped the table. "Every time I hear the word vampire, I reach for my Browning!" he said.

They all laughed. Martin, Hermann, Joseph, Ernst most of all. Even Adolf laughed a little.

Soon after dark, someone ran into the place, white of face. "The vampire!" he yelled, pointing vaguely toward the street, and fell out.

Bronco Billy and William S. jumped up. Helioglabulus stopped them. "I'm too old, and will only hold you up," he said. "I shall try to catch up later. Remember . . . the crosses. The bullets in the heart!"

As they rushed out past the other table, Ernst, who had left an hour earlier, returned with two boxes.

"Quick, Joseph!" he said as the two cowboys went through the door, "Follow them! We'll be right behind. Your pistol!"

Joseph turned, threw a Browning automatic pistol back to

Der Untergang Des Abendlandesmenschen

Hermann, then went out the doors as hoofbeats clattered in the street.

The other four began to load their pistols from the boxes of cartridges.

The two cowboys rode toward the commotion.

"Yee-haw!" yelled Bronco Billy. They galloped down the well-paved streets, their horses' hooves striking sparks from the cobbles.

They passed the police and others running toward the sounds of screams and dying. Members of the Free Corps, ex-soldiers and students, swarmed the streets in their uniforms. Torches burned against the flickering black night skies.

The city was trying to overcome the *nosferatu* by force.

Bronco Billy and William S. charged toward the fighting. In the center of a square stood a coach, all covered in black crepe. The driver, a plump, cadaverous man, held the reins to four black horses. The four were rearing high in their traces, their hooves menacing the crowd.

But it was not the horses which kept the mob back.

Crawling out of a second-story hotel window was a vision from nightmare. Bald, with pointed ears, teeth like a rat, beady eyes bright in the flickering night, the vampire climbed from a bedroom to the balcony. The front of his frock coat was covered with blood, his face and arms were smeared. A man's hand stuck halfway out the window, and the curtains were spattered black.

The *nosferatu* jumped to the ground, and the crowd parted as he leaped from the hotel steps to the waiting carriage. Then the driver cracked his whip over the horses—there was no sound—and the team charged, tumbling people like leaves before the night wind.

The carriage seemed to float to the two cowboys who rode after it. There was no sound of hoofbeats ahead, no noise from the harness, no creak of axles. It was as if they followed the wind itself through the nighttime streets of Bremen.

They sped down the flickering main roads. Once, when Bronco Billy glanced behind him, he thought he saw motorcycle headlights following. But he devoted most of his attention to the fleeing coach.

Strange Things in Close-Up

William S. rode beside him. They gained on the closed carriage.

Bronco Billy drew his left-hand pistol (he was ambidextrous) and fired at the broad back of the driver. He heard the splintery clatter of the wooden bullet as it ricocheted off the coach. Then the carriage turned ahead of them.

He was almost smashed against a garden wall by the headlong plunge of his mount, then he recovered, leaning far over in the saddle, as if his horse were a sailboat and he a sailor heeling against the wind.

Then he and William S. were closing with the hearse on a long broad stretch of the avenue. They pulled even with the driver.

And for the first time, the hackles rose on Bronco Billy's neck as he rode beside the black-crepe coach. There was no sound but him, his horse, their gallop. He saw the black-garbed driver crack the long whip, heard no *snap*, heard no horses, heard no wheels.

His heart in his throat, he watched William S. pull even on the other side. The driver turned that way, snapped his whip toward the taller cowboy. Bronco Billy saw his friend's hat fly away, cut in two,

Billy took careful aim and shot the lead horse in the head, twice. It dropped like a ton of cement, and the air was filled with a vicious, soundless image—four horses, the driver, the carriage, he, his mount and William S. all flying through the air in a tangle. Then the side of the coach caught him and the incessant flickering went out.

He must have awakened a few seconds later. His horse was atop him, but he didn't think anything was broken. He pushed himself out from under it.

The driver was staggering up from the flinders of the coach—strange, thought Bronco Billy, now I hear the sounds of the wheels turning, the screams of the dying horses. The driver pulled a knife. He started toward the cowboy.

Bronco Billy found his right-hand pistol, still in its holster. He pulled it, fired directly into the heart of the fat man. The driver folded from the recoil, then stood again.

Billy pulled the trigger.

Der Untergang Des Abendlandesmenschen

The driver dropped as the wooden bullet turned his heart to giblets.

Bronco Billy took all the regular ammo out of his pistol and began to cram the wooden ones in.

As he did, motorcycles came screaming to a stop beside him, and the five men from the tavern climbed from them or their sidecars.

He looked around for William S. but could not see him. Then he heard the shooting from the rooftop above the street—twelve shots, quick as summer thunder.

One of William S.'s revolvers dropped four stories and hit the ground beside him.

The Germans were already up the stairs ahead of Bronco Billy as he ran.

When the carriage had crashed into them, William S. had been thrown clear. He jumped up in time to see the vampire run into the doorway of the residential block across the way. He tore after while the driver pulled himself from the wreckage and Bronco Billy was crawling from under his horse.

Up the stairs he ran. He could now hear the pounding feet of the living dead man ahead, unlike the silence before the wreck. A flickering murky hallway was before him, and he saw the door at the far end close.

William S. smashed into it, rolled. He heard the scrape of teeth behind him, and saw the rat-like face snap shut inches away. He came up, his pistols leveled at the vampire.

The bald-headed thing grabbed the open door, pulled it before him.

William S. stood, feet braced, a foot from the door and began to fire into it. His colt .36 inches in front of his face, he fired again and again into the wooden door, watching chunks and splinters shear away. He heard the vampire squeal, like a rat trapped behind a trash can, but still he fired until both pistols clicked dry.

The door swung slowly awry, pieces of it hanging.

The *nosferatu* grinned, and carefully pushed the door closed. It hissed and crouched.

William S. reached up for his hat.

Strange Things in Close-Up

And remembered that the driver had knocked it off his head before the collision.

The thing leaped.

One of his pistols was knocked over the parapet.

Then he was fighting for his life.

The five Germans, yelling to each other, slammed into the doorway at the end of the hall. From beyond, they heard the sounds of scuffling, labored breathing, the rip and tear of cloth.

Bronco Billy charged up behind them.

"The door! It's jammed," said one.

"His hat!" yelled Bronco Billy. "He lost his hat!"

"Hat?" asked the one called Joseph, in English. "Why his hat?" The others shouldered against the gaped door. Through it, they saw flashes of movement and the flickering night sky.

"Crosses!" yelled Bronco Billy. "Like this!" he pointed to his hatband.

"Ah!" said Joseph. "Crosses."

He pulled something from the one called Adolf, who hung back a little, threw it through the hole in the door.

"*Cruzen!*" yelled Joseph.

"The cross!" screamed Bronco Billy. "William S. The cross!"

The sound of scuffling stopped.

Joseph tossed his pistol through the opening.

They continued to bang on the door.

The thing had its talons on his throat when the yelling began. The vampire was strangling him. Little circles were swimming in his sight. He was down beneath the monster. It smelled of old dirt, raw meat, of death. Its rat eyes were bright with hate.

Then he heard the yell, "A cross!" and something fluttered at the edge of his vision. He let go one hand from the vampire and grabbed it up.

It felt like cloth. He shoved it at the thing's face.

Hands let go.

William S. held the cloth before him as breath came back in a rush. He staggered up, and the *nosferatu* put its hands over its face. He pushed toward it.

Then the Browning Automatic pistol landed beside his foot, and he heard noises at the door behind him.

Der Untergang Des Abendlandesmenschen

Holding the cloth, he picked up the pistol.

The vampire hissed like a radiator.

William S. aimed and fired. The pistol was fully automatic.

The wooden bullets opened the vampire like a zipper coming off.

The door crashed outward, the five Germans and Bronco Billy rushed through.

William S. held to the doorframe and caught his breath. A crowd was gathering below, at the site of the wrecked hearse and the dead horses. Torchlights wobbled their reflection on the houses across the road. It looked like something from Dante.

Helioglabulus came onto the roof, took one look at the vampire and ran his alpenstock, handle first, into its ruined chest.

"Just to make sure," he said.

Bronco Billy was clapping William S. on the back. "Shore thought you'd gone to the last roundup," he said.

The five Germans were busy with the vampire's corpse.

William S. looked at the piece of cloth still clenched tightly in his own hand. He opened it. It was an armband.

On its red cloth was a white circle with a twisted black cross.

Like the decorations Indians used on their blankets, only in reverse.

He looked at the Germans. Four of them wore the armbands; the fifth, wearing an old corporal's uniform, had a torn sleeve.

They were slipping a yellow armband over the arm of the vampire's coat. When they finished, they picked the thing up and carried it to the roof edge. It looked like a spitted pig.

The yellow armband had two interlocking triangles, like the device on the chest of the costumes William S. had worn when he played *Ben-Hur* on Broadway. The Star of David.

The crowd below screamed as the corpse fell toward them.

There were shouts, then.

The unemployed, the war-wounded, the young, the bitter, the disillusioned. Then the shouting stopped . . . and they began to chant.

The five Germans stood on the parapet, looking down at the milling people. They talked among themselves.

Bronco Billy held William S. until he caught his breath.

They heard the crowds disperse, fill in again, break, drift off, reform, reassemble, grow larger.

47

Strange Things in Close-Up

"Well, pard," said Bronco Billy. "Let's mosey over to a hotel and get some shut-eye."

"That would be nice," said William S.

Helioglabulus joined them.

"We should go by the back way," he said.

"I don't like the way this crowd is actin'," said Bronco Billy.

William S. walked to the parapet, looked out over the city.

Under the dark flickering sky, there were other lights. Here and there, synagogues began to flicker.

And then to burn.

Introduction to
Ike at the Mike

Look. This shouldn't have been my story, it should have been someone else's.

Leigh Kennedy and I were watching a documentary on the birth of 1950s Rock and Roll, and there was this thirty-second montage of photos of two heroes of the time, Eisenhower and Presley.

Light bulbs went off in both our heads. We started talking.

"Lew and Chad need to do this story," I said. Lew Shiner was an Elvis Presley authority, in fact he'd collaborated on an unpublished book about the man. (It had one of the greatest opening paragraphs in history: "It was August. It was hot. The King was dead.") Chad Oliver had been at this writing business for thirty years and knew everything there was to know about jazz and swing music, and so on and so forth. I called them up and told them I had an idea for them, and that I would see them at a party in a couple of days.

There, I sat them down and said, "Look. Here's the idea . . ."
They both choked. "Me? Sacrilege?" said Lew.
"I just can't do that to music," said Chad.

"Well, damn your eyes, then, I'll do it myself," I said. So I went down and did all the research they had memorized, as much research as I could stand, anyway, and wrote this one snowy night, on a doily-decked dining room table while visiting people in Denver, Colorado.

It promptly sold to Omni for more money than I'd ever seen in my life, and was up for the Hugo after it was published.

Maybe next time I come around throwing off story sparks, Chad and Lew will listen.

Ike at the Mike

Ambassador Pratt leaned over toward Senator Presley.

"My mother's ancestors don't like to admit it," he said, "but they all came to the island from the Carpathians two centuries ago. Their name then was something like Karloff." He smiled, then laughed through his silver mustache.

"Hell," said Presley, with the tinge of the drawl which came to his speech when he was excited, as he was tonight. "My folks been dirt farmers all the way back to Adam. They don't even remember coming from anywhere. That don't mean they ain't wonderful folks, though."

"Of course not," said Pratt. "My father was a shopkeeper. He worked to send all my older brothers into the Foreign Service. But when my time came, I thought I had another choice. I wanted to run off to Canada or Australia, perhaps try my hand at acting. (I was in several local dramatic clubs, you know?) My father took me aside before my service exams. The day before, I remember quite distinctly. He said, 'William' (he was the only member of the family who used my full name), 'William,' he said, 'actors do not get paid the last workday of each and every month.' Well, I thought about it awhile, and next day passed my exams with absolute top grades."

Pratt smiled once more an ingratiating smile. There was something a little scary about it, thought Presley, sort of like Raymond Massey's smile in *Arsenic and Old Lace*. But the smile had gotten Pratt through sixty years of government service. It had been a smile which made the leaders of small countries grin back as Kings George, number after number, took yet more of their lands. It was a good smile; it made everyone remember his grandfather. Even Presley.

"Folks is funny," said Presley. "God knows I used to get up

Ike at the Mike

at barn dances and sing myself silly. I was just a kid, playing around."

"My childhood is so far behind me," said Ambassador Pratt. "I hardly remember it. I was small, then I had the talk with my father, and went to Service school, then found myself in Turkey. Which at that time owned a large portion of the globe. The Sick Man of Europe, it was called. You know I met Lawrence, of Arabia, don't you? Before the Great War. He was an archaeologist then. Came to us to get the Ottomans to give him permission to dig up Petra. They thought him to be a fool. Wanted the standard 90 percent share of everything, just the same."

"You've seen a lot of the world change," said Senator E. Aaron Presley. He took a sip of wine. "I've had trouble enough keeping up with it since I was elected congressman six years ago. I almost lost touch during my senatorial campaign, and I'll be damned if everything hadn't changed again by the time I got back here."

Pratt laughed. He was eighty years old, far past retirement age, still bouncing around like a man of sixty. He had alternately retired and had every British P. M. since Churchill call him out of seclusion to patch up relations with this or that nation.

Presley was thirty-three, the youngest senator in the country for a long time. The U.S. was in bad shape, and he was one of the symbols of the new hope. There was talk of revolution, several cities had been burned, there was a war on in South America (again). Social change, lifestyle readjustment, call it what they would. The people of Mississippi had elected Presley senator after five years as representative, as a sign of renewed hope. At the same time they had passed a tough new wiretap act, and had turned out for massive Christian revivalist meetings.

1968 looked to be the toughest year yet for America.

But there were still things that made it all worth living. Nights like tonight. A huge appreciation dinner, with the absolute top of Washington society turned out in its gaudiness. Most of Congress, President Kennedy, Vice President Shriver. Plus the usual hangers-on.

Presley watched them. Old Dick Nixon, once a senator from California. He came back to Washington to be near the action, though he'd lost his last election in '58.

The President was there, of course, looking as young as he

Strange Things in Close-Up

had when he was reelected in 1964, the first two-term president since Huey "Kingfish" Long, Jr., thought Presley. He was a hell of a good man in his Yankee way. His three young brothers were in the audience somewhere, representatives from two states.

Waiters hustled in and out of the huge banquet room. Presley watched the sequined gowns and the feathers on the women; the spectacular pumpkin-blaze of a neon orange suit of some hotshot Washington lawyer. The lady across the table had engaged Pratt in conversation about Wales. The ambassador was explaining that he had seen Wales once, back in 1923 on holiday, but that he didn't think it had changed much since then.

E. Aaron studied the table where the guests of honour sat— The President and First Lady, the veep and his wife, and Armstrong and Eisenhower, with their spouses.

Armstrong and Eisenhower. Two of the finest citizens of the land. Armstrong, the younger, in his sixty-eighth year, getting a little jowly. Born with the century, thought Presley. Symbol of his race and of his time. A man deserving of honor and respect.

But Eisenhower. Eisenhower was Presley's man. The senator had read all the biographies, reread all the old newspaper files, listened to him every chance he got.

If Presley had an ideal, it was Eisenhower. As both a leader and a person. A little too liberal, maybe, in his personal opinions, but that was the only possible drawback the man had. When it came time for action, Eisenhower, the "Ike" of the popular press, came through.

Senator Presley tried to catch his eye. He was only three tables away, and could see Ike through the hazy pall of smoke from after-dinner cigarettes and pipes. It was no use, though.

Eisenhower looked worried, distracted. He wasn't used to testimonials. He'd come out of semiretirement to attend, only because Armstrong had convinced him to do it. They were both getting presidential medals.

But it wasn't for the awards that all the other people were here, or the speeches that would follow, it . . .

Pratt turned to him

"I've noticed his preoccupation, too," he said.

Presley was a little taken aback. But Pratt is a sharp old

cookie, and he'd been around god knows how many people through wars, floods, conference tables. He'd probably drank enough tea in his life to float the Battleship *Kropotkin*.

"Quite a man," said Presley, afraid to let his true misty-eyed feelings show themselves. "Pretty much man of the century, far as I'm concerned."

"I've been with Churchill, and Lenin and Chiang," said Ambassador Pratt, "but they were just cagey, politicians, movers of men and material, as far as I'm concerned. I saw him once before, early on, must have been '38. Nineteen thirty-eight. I was very, very impressed then. Time has done nothing to change that."

"He's just not used to this kind of thing," said Presley.

"Perhaps it was that Patton fellow."

"Wild George? That who you mean?"

"Oh, didn't you hear?" asked Pratt, eyes all concern.

"I was in committee most of the week. If it wasn't about the new drug bill, I didn't hear about it."

"Oh. Of course. This Patton fellow died a few days ago, it seems. Circumstances rather sad, I think. Eisenhower and Mr Armstrong just returned from his funeral this afternoon."

"Gee, that's too bad. You know they worked together, Patton and Ike, for thirty years or so—"

The toastmaster, one of those boisterous, bald-headed, abrasive California types, rose. People began to applaud and stub out their cigarettes. Waiters disappeared as if a magic wand had been waved.

Well, thought Presley, an hour of pure boredom coming up, as he and Pratt applauded also. Some jokes, the President, the awarding of the medals, the obligatory standing ovation (though all of the senator's feelings were going to be in his part of it, anyway). Then the entertainment.

Ah, thought Presley. The thing everybody has come for.

Because, after the ceremony, they were going to bring out the band, Armstrong's band. Not just the one he toured with, but what was left of the old guys. *The* Armstrong Band, and they were going to rip the joint.

But also, also . . .

For the first time in twenty years, since Presley had been a boy, a kid in his teens . . .

Strange Things in Close-Up

Eisenhower was going to break his vow. Eisenhower was going to dust off that clarinet.

For two hours, Ike was going to play with Armstrong, just like in the old days.

"Cheer up," said gravelly-voiced Pops, while the President was making his way to the rostrum. Armstrong smiled at Eisenhower. "You're gonna blow 'em right outta the grooves."

"All reet," said Ike.

The thunderous applause was dying down. Backstage, Ike handed the box with the Presidential medal to his wife of twenty years, Helen Forrest, the singer. "Here goes, honey," he said. "Come out when you feel like it."

They were in the outer hall back of the platform set up behind the head tables. Some group of young folksingers, very nervous but very good, were out there killing time while Armstrong's band set up.

"Hey hey," said Pops. He'd pinned the Presidential medal, ribbon and all, to the front of his jacket through the boutonniere hole. "Wouldn't old Jelly Roll like to have seen me now?"

"Hey hey," yelled some of the band right back.

"Quiet, quiet!" yelled Pops. "Let them kids out there sing. They're good. Listen to 'em. Reminds me of me when I was young."

Ike had been licking his reed and doing tongue exercises. "You never were young, Pops," he said. "You were born older than me."

"That's a lie!" said Pops. "You could be my father."

"Maybe he is!" yelled Perkins, the guitar man.

Ike nearly swallowed his mouthpiece. The drummer did a paradiddle.

"Hush, hush, you clowns!" yelled Pops.

Ike smiled and looked up at the drummer, a young kid. But he'd been with Pops's new band for a couple of years, so he must be all right.

Eisenhower heaved a sigh when no one was looking. He had to get the tightness out of his chest. It had started at George S.'s funeral, a pain crying did not relieve. No one but he and Helen knew that he had had two mild heart attacks in the last six years. Hell, he thought. I'm almost eighty years old. I'm entitled to a few heart attacks. But not here, not tonight.

They dimmed the work lights. Pops had run into the back kitchen and blown a few screaming notes which they had heard through two concrete walls. He was ready.

"When you gonna quit playing, Pops?" asked Ike.

"Man, I ain't ever gonna quit. They're gonna have to dig me up three weeks after I die and break this horn to stop the noise comin' outta the ground." He looked at the lights. "Ease on off to the left there, Ike. Let us get them all ready for you. Come in on the chorus of the third song."

"Which one's that?" asked Ike, looking for his play sheet.

"You'll know it when you hear it," said Pops. He took out his handkerchief. "You taught it to me."

Ike went into the wings.

The crowd was tasteful, expectant.

The band hit the music hard, from the opening, and Armstrong led off with the "King Porter Stomp." His horn was flashing sparks, and the medal on his jacket front caught the spotlight like a big golden eye.

Then they launched into "Basin Street Blues," the horn sweet and slow and mellow, the band doing nothing but carrying a light line behind. Armstrong was totally in his music, staring not at the audience but down and at his horn.

He had come a long way since he used to hawk coal from the back of a wagon; since he was thrown in the Colored Waifs Home in New Orleans for firing off a pistol on New Year's Eve, 1913. One noise more or less shouldn't have mattered on that night, but it did, and the cops caught him. It was those music lessons at the Home that started him on the way, through New Orleans and Memphis and Chicago to the world beyond.

Armstrong might have been a criminal, he might have been a bum, he might have been killed unknown and unmourned in some war somewhere. But he wasn't: He was born to play that music. It wouldn't have mattered what world he would have been born into. As soon as his fingers closed around the cornet, music was changed forever.

The audience applauded wildly, but they weren't there just for Armstrong. They were waiting. And they got him.

Strange Things in Close-Up

The band hit up something that began nondescriptly—a slow blues beginning with the drummer heavy on his brushes.

The tune began to change, and as it changed, a pure sweet clarinet began to play above the other instruments, and Ike walked onstage playing his theme song, "Don't You Know What It Means to Miss New Orleans?"

His clarinet soared above the audience. Presley wasn't the only one who got chill bumps all the way down the backs of his ankles.

Ike and Armstrong traded off slow pure verses of the song; Ike's the sweet music of a craftsman, Armstrong's the heartfelt remembrance of things as they were. Ike never saw Storyville; Armstrong had to leave it when the Navy closed it down.

Together they built to a moving finale, and descended into a silence like the dimming of lights, with Ike's clarinet the last one to wink out.

The cream of Washington betrayed its origins with applause.

And before they knew what to do, the tune was the opening screech of "Mississippi Mud."

Ike and Armstrong traded licks, running on and off the melody. Pops wiped his face with his handkerchief; his face seemed all teeth and sweat. Ike's bald head shone, the freckles standing out above the wisps of white hair on his temples.

They played and played.

Ike's boyhood had been on the flat pan of Kansas, small-town church America at the turn of the century. A town full of laborers and businessmen, barbershops, milliners and ice-cream parlors.

He had done all the usual things—swum naked in the creek, run through town finding things to build up or tear down. He had hunted and fished and gone to services on Sunday; he had camped out overnight or for days at a time with his brothers, made fun of his girl cousins, stolen watermelons.

He first heard recorded music on an old Edison cylinder machine at the age of eight, long-hair music and opera his aunt collected.

There was a firehouse band which played each Wednesday night in the park across the street from the station. There were real band concerts on Sunday, mostly military music, marches and the instrumental parts of ballads, on the courthouse lawn.

Eisenhower heard it all. Music was part of his background, and he didn't think much of it. His brother had taken piano lessons for a while, but gave it up as, in his words, "sissy."

So Ike grew up in Kansas, where the music was as flat as the land.

Daniel Louis Armstrong was rared back, tooting out some wild lines of "Night and Day." In the old days it didn't matter how well you played; it was the angle of your back and the tilt of your horn. The band was really tight; they were playing for their lives.

The trombone player came out of his seat, jumped down onto the stage on his knees and matched Armstrong for a few bars.

The audience yelled.

Eisenhower tapped his foot and smiled, watching Armstrong and the trombone man.

The drummer was giving a lot of rim shots. The whole ballroom sounded like the overtaxed heart of a bird ready to fly away to meet Jesus.

Ike took off his coat and unknotted his tie down to the first button.

The crowd went wild.

Late August 1908.

The train was late. Young Dwight David Eisenhower hurried across the endless steel grid of the Kansas City rail yards. He was catching the train to New York City. There he would board another bound for West Point.

He carried his admission papers, a congratulatory letter from his congressman (gotten after some complicated negotiations—it looked for a while like he would be Midshipman Eisenhower), his train ticket and twenty-one dollars emergency money in his jacket.

He'd asked the porter for the track number. It was next to the station proper. A spur track confused him. He looked down the tracks, couldn't see a number (trains waited all around, ready to hurl themselves toward distant cities . . .) and went to the station entrance.

Strange Things in Close-Up

Four black men, ragged of dress, were smiling and playing near the door. What they played young David had never heard before—it was syncopated music, but not like a rag, not a march, something in between, something like nothing else. He had never heard polyrhythms like them before—they stopped him dead.

The four had a banjo, a cornet, a violin, and a clarinet. They played, smiled, danced a little for the two or three people watching them. A hat lay on the ground before them. In it were a few dimes, pennies, and a single new half-dime.

They finished the song. A couple of people said, "Very nice, very nice" and added a few cents to the hat. They walked away.

The four men started to talk among themselves.

"What was that song?" asked young David.

The man with the cornet looked at him through large horn-rimmed spectacles. "That song was called 'Struttin' with Some Barbecue,' young sir," he said.

Dwight David reached into his pocket and took out a shiny one-dollar gold piece,

"Play it again," he said.

They nearly killed themselves this time, running through it. It was great art, it was on the street, and they were getting a whole dollar for it. David watched them, especially the clarinet player, who made his instrument soar above the others. They finished the number and all tipped their hats to him.

"Is that hard to learn to play?" he asked the man of the clarinet.

"For some it is," he answered.

"Could you teach me?" asked David.

The black man looked at the others, who looked away; they were no help at all. "Let me see your fingers," he said.

Eisenhower held out his hands, wrists up, then down.

"I could probably teach you to play in six weeks," he said. "I don't know if I could teach you to play like that. You've got to feel that music." He was trying not to say that Eisenhower was white.

"Wait right here," said Ike.

He went inside the depot and cashed in his ticket. He sent two telegrams, one home and one to the Army. He was back

Ike at the Mike

outside in fifteen minutes, with thirty-three dollars in his pocket, total.

"Let's go find me a clarinet," he said to the black man.

He knew he would not sleep well that night, and neither would anybody back on the farm. He probably wouldn't sleep good for weeks. But he sure knew what he wanted.

Armstrong smiled, wiped his face and blew the opening notes of "When It's Sleepy Time Down South."

Ike joined in.

Then they went into "Just a Closer Walk with Thee," quiet, restrained, the horn and clarinet becoming one instrument for a while, then Ike bent his notes around Armstrong's, then Pops lifted Eisenhower up, then the instruments walked arm in arm toward Heaven.

Ike listened to the drummer as he played. He sure missed Wild George.

The first time they had met, Ike was the new kid in town, just another guy with a clarinet that some gangster had hired to fill in with a band, sometime in 1911.

Ike didn't say much. He was working his way south from KC, toward Memphis, toward New Orleans (which he would never see until after New Orleans didn't mean the same anymore).

Ike could cook anyone with his clarinet—horn player, banjo man, even drummers. They might make more noise but when they ran out of things to do, Ike was just starting. He'd begun at the saloon filling in, but the bandleader soon had sense enough to put him out front. They took breaks, leaving just him and the drummer up there, and the crowds never noticed. Ike was hot before there was hot music.

Till one night a guy came in—a new drummer. He was a crazy man. "My name is Wild George S. Patton," he said before the first set.

"What's the S. stand for?" asked Ike.

"Shitkicker!" said the drummer.

Ike didn't say anything.

That night they tried to cut each other, chop each other off the stage. Patton was doing two-hand cymbal shots, paradiddles, and flails. His bass foot never stopped. Ike wasn't a show-off,

59

Strange Things in Close-Up

but this guy drove him to it. He blew notes that killed mice for three square blocks. Patton ended up by kicking a hole through the bass drum and ramming his sticks through his snare like he was opening a can of beans with them.

The bandleader fired Patton on the spot and threatened to call the cops. The crowd nearly lynched the manager for it.

As soon as the hubbub died, Patton said to Ike, "The S. stands for Smith," and shook his hand.

He and Ike took off that night to start up their own band.

And were together for almost thirty years.

Armstrong blew "Dry Bones."

Ike did "St. Louis Blues."

They had never done either better. This Washington audience loved them.

So had another, long ago.

The first time he and Armstrong had met had been in Washington, too. A hot bleak July day in 1932.

The Bonus Army had come to the capital, asking their congressmen and their nation for some relief in this third year of the Depression. President Al Smith was powerless; he had a Republican Congress under him.

The bill granting the veterans of the Great War their bonus, due in 1945, had been passed back in the twenties. All the vets wanted was it to be paid immediately. It had been sitting in the Treasury, gaining interest, and was already part of the budget. The vote was coming up soon.

Thousands, dubbed the B.E.F., had poured into Washington, camping on Anacostia Flats, in tin boxes, towns of shanties dubbed "Smithvilles," or under the rain and stars.

Homeless men who had slogged through the mud of Europe, been gassed and shelled, and who had lived with rats in the trenches for democracy, now they found themselves back in the mud again.

This time they were out of money, out of work, out of luck.

The faces of the men were tired. Soup kitchens had been set up. They tried to keep their humor. It was all they had left. May dragged by, then June, then July. The vote was taken in Congress on the twelfth.

Congress said no.

Ike at the Mike

They accused the Bonus Marchers of being Reds. They said they were armed rabble. Rumors ran wild. Such financial largesse, said Congress, could not be afforded.

Twenty thousand of the thirty thousand men tried to find some way back home, out of the city, back to No Place, U.S.A.

Ten thousand stayed, hoping for something to happen. Anything.

Ike went down to play for them. So did Armstrong. They ran into each other in town, got together their bands and equipment. They set up a stage in the middle of the Smithville, now a forlorn-looking bunch of mud-strewn shacks.

About five thousand of the jobless men came to hear them play. They were in a holiday mood. They sat on the ground, in the mud. They didn't much care anymore.

Armstrong and Ike had begun to play that day. Half the band, including Wild George, had hangovers. They had drunk with the Bonus Marchers the night before, and well into the morning before the noon concert.

They played great jazz that day anyway. A cloud of smoke had risen up from some of the abandoned warehouses the veterans had been living in, just before the music began. There was some commotion from over toward the Potomac. The band just played louder and wilder.

The marchers clapped along. Wild George smiled a bleary-eyed smile toward the crowd. They were doing half his job.

Automatic rifle fire rang out, causing heads to turn.

The Army was coming. Sons and nephews of some of the Bonus Marchers there were coming toward them on orders from Douglas MacArthur, the Chief of Staff. He had orders to clear them out.

The men came to their feet, picking up rocks and bottles.

Marching lines of soldiers came into view, bayonets fixed. Small two-man tanks, armed with machine guns, rolled between the soldiers. The lines stopped. The soldiers put on gas masks.

The Bonus Marchers, who remembered phosgene and the trenches, drew back.

"Keep playing!" said Ike.

"Keep goin'. Let it roll!" said Armstrong.

Tear gas grenades flew toward the Bonus Marchers. Rocks

and bottles sailed toward the soldiers in the masks. There was a real explosion a block away.

The troops came on.

The gas rolled toward the marchers. Some picked up the spewing canisters to throw them back, fell coughing to the ground, overcome.

The tanks and bayonets came forward in a line.

The marchers broke and ran.

Their shacks and tents were set afire by chemical corpsmen behind the tanks.

"Let it roll! Let it roll!" said Armstrong, and they played "Didn't He Ramble" and the gas cloud hit them, and the music died in chokes and vomiting.

That night the Bonus Marchers were loaded on Army trucks, taken fifty miles due west and let out on the sides of the roads.

Ike and Louis went up before the Washington magistrate, paid ten dollars each fine for them and their band members, and took trains to New York City.

The last time he had seen Wild George alive was two years ago. Patton had been found by somebody who'd known him in the old days.

He'd been in four bad marriages, his only kid had died in the taking of the Japanese Home Islands in early '47, and he'd lost one of his arms in a car wreck in '55. He had been in a flophouse when the guy found him. They'd put him in a nursing home and paid the bills.

Ike had gone to visit. The last time they had seen each other in those intervening twenty-odd years had been the day of the fistfight in 1943, just before the Second World War broke out. Patton had joined the Miller band for a while, but was too much for them. He'd gone from band to band and marriage to marriage to oblivion.

He was old, old. Wild George was only five years older than Ike. He looked a hundred. One eye was almost gone. He had no teeth. He was drying out in the nursing home, turning brittle as last winter's leaves.

"Hello, George," said Ike, shaking his only hand.

"I knew you'd come first," said Patton.

"You should have let somebody know."

Ike at the Mike

"What's to know? One old musician lives, another one dies."

"George, I'm sorry. The way things have turned out."

"I've been thinking it over, about that fight we had." Patton stopped to cough up some bloody spittle into a basin Ike held for him.

"God, oh, jees. If I could only have a drink." He stared into Ike's eyes. Then he said:

"About that fight. You were still wrong."

Then he coughed some more.

Ike was crying as they went into the final number. He stepped forward to the mike Helen had used when she came out to sing with them for the last three numbers.

"This song is for the memory of George Smith Patton," he said.

They played "The Old, Rugged Cross." Ike, nor anybody else, had ever played it just like that before.

Ike broke down halfway through. He waved to the crowd, took his mouthpiece off, and walked into the wings.

Pops kept playing. He tried to motion Ike back. Helen was hugging him. He waved and brushed the tears away.

Armstrong finished the song.

The audience tore the place apart. They were on their feet and stamping, screaming, applauding.

Presley, out there, sat in his chair.

He was crying too, but quickly stood up and cheered.

Then the whole thing was over.

At home, later, in Georgetown, Senator Presley was lying in bed beside his wife Muffy. They had made love. They had both been excited. It had been terrific.

Now Muffy was asleep.

Presley got up and went to the bathroom. Then he went to the kitchen, poured himself a Scotch, and stood with his naked butt against the countertop.

It was a cold night. Through the half curtains on the window he saw stars over the city. If you could call this a city.

He went into the den. The servants would be asleep.

He turned the power on the stereo, took down four or five of his Eisenhower records, looked through them. He put on *Ike at the Mike*, a four-record set made for RCA in 1947, toward the end of the last war.

Ike was playing "No Love, No Nothing," a song his wife had made famous three years before. She wasn't on this record, though. This was all Ike and his band.

Presley got the bottle from the kitchen, sat back down, poured himself another drink. Tomorrow was more hearings. And the day after.

Someday, he thought, someday, E. Aaron Presley will be President of these here United States. Serves them right.

Ike was playing "All God's Chillun Got Shoes."

I didn't even get to shake his hand, thought Presley.

I'd give it all away to be like him, he thought.

He went to sleep sitting up.

Introduction to
Dr. Hudson's Secret Gorilla

We all have guilty pleasures, only some are more guilty of them than others.

One of my many is terrible old monster movies—the kind with George Zucco and Rondo Hatton and Joseph Calleia (and compared to the people in some of the movies, these guys were stars), movies made by Monogram and PRC and Independent Pictures, pictures directed by people like Jean Negulesco and William "One-Shot" Beaudine. (A producer once walked onto one of Beaudine's sets and said, "You're two hours behind your shooting schedule," which was like being a month behind on a real movie, and Beaudine reportedly said, "You mean somebody's waiting to see this junk?!")

They always had a laboratory, and a mad assistant, and a beautiful daughter and, well, you'll see.

I wrote this early in 1975 at the end of a creative burst (more later) and sent it off everywhere. (Reversing my usual procedure, I sent it to high-paying markets first.) Somebody said the ending was "camp." (I told Robert Silverberg that when I sent it to him. He sent back a rejection saying something like, no, the ending was chilling and effective, but it didn't justify the 5,000 words of junk you had to wade through to get there. Or something like that.)

This sold twice (once to Shayol*) and overseas to Michel Parry, who put together an anthology called* The Rivals of King Kong, *which is in print on five continents now.*

This is the only story they know me by in Buenos Aires and Cairo.

Dr. Hudson's Secret Gorilla

I do not remember anything, after the wreck, until I put my finger to my ear.
 And felt the fur scratch against my hairy neck.
 The fur from the back of my hand.

Later, after I had tried to rip the bandages from my head, and from somewhere behind me a needle had descended and pricked me, and I passed out; later, I awoke.
 I lay still. I was on my back and watched the rise and fall of my smooth chest. My head was ringing from the drug used on me. Little blue circles swirled like a gnat swarm in my eyes. Slowly I raised my hand into my line of sight and saw its hairy back, like a glove made from a shag rug.
 I pulled it to my head, found the edges of the bandages which started just above my brow. The brow was thick and long as a bicycle handlebar.
 I lay back. Even that small movement caused my head to scream and slip sideways, and I went over.

Late for showtime. Critic's screening of new, solid blockbuster movie, seventeen stars, studio hype. Wet night, slick streets. Down the Canyon road, around the turn, headlights catch a dog or a cat or a small child, stomp the brake, good Michelin tires grab the road, Triumph says good-bye highway, sailing, sailing the lights of LA look nice tonight and are they getting close no time to scream now . . .

I come up from the memory and shiver to find I have awakened myself groaning.
 The groan is a hurricane inside an echo chamber, long, low, wet, with lungs and strength, hurt strength behind it.

Dr. Hudson's Secret Gorilla

The head pain is gone. Again, I look down my body at the hugeness, the shagginess, the alienness. My body.

I need to take a dump. I cannot move well enough to get— where? To the corner of the cage. For I am barred in. It is ten body lengths long, five wide. Through one corner is a slanted running trough of water. Through the other, a fountain with a steel foot pedal. Outside the cage is dark. It is night, or the lights are off.

I am hurt. I do not understand what has happened. I do not think I am still dreaming. So this is what it is like to begin to lose the mind. I am afraid. I try to cry.

I see him staring at me while I open my eyes. The place is bright again and the light hurts.

He looks like Albert Einstein. He looks like a thousand mad scientists. He looks like . . . he has a large nose, unkempt white mustache, a fringe of hair from the temples around his head. His eyes are grey and quite gone. I have seen those tombstone eyes on the Strip, asking for change to support a habit. I saw them once in the Army, in Nam, on a guy who'd lived through an ambush when no one else had. He was over the edge. He was gone. His eyes looked like those in photographs of factory workers from the 1890s, all shiny like little steel balls.

Little steel balls with lights burning inside them.

"Tuleg! Tuleg!" he yells. "He is awake."

I twitched from the loudness of his voice. The blue gnats threaten my sight, then subside.

I try to move.

He watches me. He does not say anything. He studies the way I try to use my fingers. I cannot place them flat so I can push myself up. I realize I am trying to use them as my own hands. And that will not work. These are twice as large.

A door opens somewhere. My vision is still fuzzy. Beyond the bars of the cage is a blur. Light comes from somewhere, then goes.

And before me stands the Evil Assistant.

He is huge, he must be huge. He looks like an oak stump stretched out by chains. He is bald, a muscular Erich von Stroheim, and he moves like an acrobat. He is wearing khaki pants (I can only see the waistband. The cage is raised about a

Strange Things in Close-Up

meter off the flooring of the—room?—the cage is in) and a real undershirt, the kind with thin shoulder straps and no sleeves. He is rubbing pizza sauce from his mouth as he walks in. He looks at me and scratches his chest with his right hand.

"So?" he says to the madman.

"So!?" says the other. "I have succeeded. You helped with the operation, you saw! A man's brain in the body of a gorilla. He lives! He will live, of that I'm sure."

"Mmm," grunted the man. He turned to leave. "Call me if you *really* need me."

I listened to them talk. I could not believe it. Was I making up this dialogue? Was I still asleep?

I looked at the Mad Scientist. He stared back as if I were golden, silver, a flying saucer, the Loch Ness monster.

The Evil Assistant went out the door. There was something about him I did not like. He seemed familiar.

Rondo Hatton. He reminded me of Rondo Hatton, the Creeper. He did not need acromegaly. He was an ugly man.

The Mad Scientist leaned on the cage and stared at me.

Time passed and the scientist was gone. I managed to get up and hobble my way to the trough. I took a dump.

Gorilla shit is dry, almost all the liquid is gone from it. What I had eaten, or rather what the former owner of the body had last eaten, I do not know.

When I finished I lay back down. My head hurt. My body hurt. I sank into slumbers.

Sometime later I felt another needle go into my skin. I was too weak to fight back. My sleep was filled with dim nightmares.

I saw beyond the cage a hospital stand with an empty IV bottle attached. Intravenous feeding, saves time, saves trouble.

I stood, went to the latrine, shuffled my weight across to the water fountain, stepped on the pedal and doused my face with water.

It did not feel the same as it did when I had done it . . . when I was a man. It felt as if the skin there were made of leather sewn on the outside of my normal face. I pushed on it, pulled at it with my clumsy hands. I pulled my fingers and tried my toes.

I stepped on the pedal, ran water into the fountain. I held my hairy, notebook-sized hand over the drain. There was light, from an indirect source, in the room.

I watched the drain fill, the water rise over my hand like a river flood covering a forest. Then I took my foot away from the handle.

I stared into the basin.

Gorilla eyes. Tiny. Brow swept back to a sagittal crest. Head like a cinderblock. Thick. Ugly.

I sat on the floor, my toes curled in. I could not believe it. I sat that way until I realized how I must look. Like a gorilla. A gorilla trying to solve the mysteries of the universe. I got up and began to pace the cage, slowly. Then I stood with my hands through the bars. Gorillas don't do that. Humans do that.

GORILLA GORILLA

The most nearly human, the most frightening primate. No one believed the stories the natives told. Old men of the woods. They live there, they beat their chests, they drive you off. They kill. They have teeth the size of knives. Pliny wrote about them. The Romans knew them, and later the Spanish and the Portugee. And they did not believe, either.

Two gorillas. The lowland, first, the one of the rain forest, and the mountain gorilla, he of the open hillsides. Dying, now, the bands breaking down, to the bulldozer, the city, the poachers.

Huge, the gorilla. Fierce-looking. Bestial, perhaps because he is so close to man, yet so far away. So strong, so heavy. Men twisted by nightmares.

The gorilla will fight, is shy. The beating of the chest is liable to be replaced by some other harmless activity. The males will protect the young and the females. They usually run and do not charge.

See the gorilla. Terror of the jungle. Killer of the Congo. King of the Apes. gorilla gorilla.

The Mad Scientist was named Hudson.
 The Evil Assistant called him that next day.
 I watched them come into the room while they talked.
 Then I stood.

Strange Things in Close-Up

"You see?" said Hudson. "He stands on two legs."

I walked to the bars. I motioned with my hands. I wanted to know *why*?

Hudson watched me.

"You see?" he said to Tuleg. "He understands. He is still a man."

I was clumsy. I couldn't walk so well on two legs. I didn't know *how* to walk on all fours. You can't walk on four legs like a man would. I couldn't do anything right. I sat down.

"He is uncoordinated," said Hudson. "He can learn, though."

"So, who's gonna teach him?" asked Tuleg.

"We are," said Hudson.

For the first time, there was authority in his voice.

The days passed. At first, they still gave me intravenous feedings and kept me groggy with drugs.

Then Hudson began to speak to me, like a child.

I tried to talk. What came out was *nnnngmnnnnnnnnng*.

I wanted to write. I moved my hands like writing.

Hudson handed me a pen and paper, happy as a child.

My fingers were like tree limbs. My thumb was like a sledgehammer. One letter took up most of the page. I tried.

"You will get better with it," said the Mad Scientist. "Don't worry."

I threw the pen down, tore the paper, clumsily, in half. I couldn't even do that well.

"Nod if you understand me," he said.

I nodded.

Hudson laughed and clapped his hands. "You do!" he said, dancing in little steps. "You do!"

I nodded again, my insides were turning with joy.

"Wait until I tell Tuleg!" he said, and ran from the room. I stood dumbfounded. We had been communicating, no matter how crudely. And he left. He left.

I did not want to be alone. I roared. I yelled, I shook the bars until my head began to spin and I had to sit. I sank to the floor and shivered.

I found that gorillas can cry.

I held the ballpoint pen in my hand and rocked myself to sleep.

Dr. Hudson's Secret Gorilla

The next morning, I realized what was wrong. Dr. Hudson was crazy, really mad. I had never thought of the meaning of the words "mad scientist" before. He must be mad to experiment so. But his madness did not end there. No. He is *mad*. He walked away when we were ready to communicate. He works to make me a gorilla, then he works to bring the man back out. And at the instant he does, he forgets me. He is *mad*.

Tuleg walked in by himself and shut the door.

I sat with the ballpoint pen in my hand, toes curled in, my knuckles flat on the floor. I stared back at him.

He stood with his arms akimbo. With his bald head, in the daylight, he reminded me of Boris Karloff in *Tower of London*. Mord, the Executioner.

He said nothing. Then he went to the cabinet in the far corner and drew out a long thin stick.

I jumped. I had seen one like it before.

"Ha ha ha," he said. His eyes said, "So you recognize the cattle prod, eh?"

He came toward me, moving his head to always keep eye contact with me through the bars. He reached the prod in and the sharp spark leapt like a knife. I felt as if I had been stabbed and clubbed at the same time. Smoke curled, and there was the smell of burnt hair in the air. I roared and leapt away from him.

But he moved far faster than I, and the prod touched again
and again
and again
and

I wrote with the pen, though he shocked me each second or so, and laughed as he did. I was quivering.

NO, I wrote, and he saw it, and knocked the pen from my hand. I reached for it, and he struck at me. The spark made my hand go numb. I watched the hair burn. I looked into his eyes.

"Fight me," he said. "Why don't you fight me?" He stuck the prod at my face. I tried to push it away.

Its touch blasted through my elbows to my teeth. I was crying, whimpering now. I lay down and curled up as best I could. He kept jabbing me, sending pain into me. I almost let go at each jolt. I bit my tongue in pain, felt blood run under my teeth.

The pain stopped.

"Damn you," he said, throwing the prod on the cabinet shelf. "Damn you to hell, why don't you fight me?"

He left. His words ran through my head. *Why don't you fight me?*

Because I am a man. Because. Because . . .

The Evil Assistant was evil. Evil with all its connotations. Evil has motive. Evil strikes without warning. Sadism is an evil which needs no motivation. To give pain is human. Perhaps Tuleg gets sexual release in giving pain? I couldn't tell. I did not give him whatever he needed. I will not. Not ever.

I have learned the meaning of the word evil. I do not like it.

There were hands on me.

Tiny hands.

I opened my eyes and winced where one of the prod burns had seared the flesh of my brow. I moaned and rolled to my side.

"You poor thing," she said. "You frightened thing."

Why, why, why when there is a gorilla, and a mad scientist, and an evil assistant, why . . .

why must there be a beautiful woman?

I have seen all this before, I tell myself, as the doctor and the beautiful woman tend my wounds. I am so hurt, so stunned I can do nothing but lie and shiver. I am running a fever. My eyes feel made of grit and sand. I shake. Inside, I cry. They cover me with a blanket. I become dank, and cold by turns, and then burn for hours. I pass in and out of fever dreams. I see a jungle.

It is later, and I hear the Mad Doctor talk to the Beautiful Woman.

"I wouldn't have brought you here if I didn't want you to see it," he said. "I wouldn't have, if I had known what Tuleg was going to do. The brute! I hope he fries in hell. I'm going to send him away the moment he returns."

"I told you when he came to work for you that he was a terrible man," she said, her voice soft like an unswept floor.

"Well, he was a great help."

Dr. Hudson's Secret Gorilla

"I'm sure." Her voice sounded as if she had turned her back on him. "He helped you. Oh, Father," her voice quavered, then she continued. "Why?" she asked. "Why do something as stupid, as pointless as this? What use is it? What can you prove by it? What?"

"But, Blanche," he said. "If you could have known the heartache, the toil, the hours . . ."

"Can you imagine," she asked, turning toward him sharply, "what that poor man is going through? Can you?"

"He will make me immortal, Blanche."

"Oh Father, Father," she said. I heard her footsteps and the door open and close, hard.

"She doesn't understand. She just doesn't understand," said the old man, and moved some apparatus (the tinkling of glass and metal) around on the workbench.

I slept.

Tuleg must have come back sometime during the night. I opened my eyes and he was walking around the room, preparing food and tasting it as he put it in a bowl.

He brought it over to the cage.

"Here," he said, putting it in through the bars. "Eat."

He went back to the workbench. He took down, and began to clean, a Thompson submachine gun. He looked at me from time to time as he worked with it. "Eat, I said."

I went to the bowl. It was filled with rolled oats, raisins, bits of celery and apple, sugar. I tried it and found it good. I was still running a fever, but I put the food in my mouth anyway.

My hand brushed my incisors. I felt them both. Long, curved, they were really there. They could crunch through meat as easily as a pair of pruning shears. They could punch open a tin can. They could kill a man. I shook my head.

I finished eating

Hudson came in. He and Tuleg must have talked before, because the scientist was not surprised to see him.

"Today," he said to me, "we begin to teach you."

"You were Roger Ildell," said Dr. Hudson.

I nodded.

"You were killed in a wreck just beyond my home," he said.

Strange Things in Close-Up

"At least, your body was. I was able to remove your brain before deterioration set in. I saved it. I saved your conscious mind."

I nodded again.

"I used to read your reviews," said Blanche, who was sitting at her father's side. "The police are still looking for your body. My father and Tuleg removed all traces. They were very thorough. They were very methodical," she said.

"We have to begin all over with you," said her father. "She tells me you were an intelligent man. There should be no problem. You'll be able to write again, though you'll never be able to talk. I regret that," he said. Then quietly, "I regret that."

I opened my hands wide, held them out toward the scientist. And his daughter. *Why? Why?*

Hudson was puzzled.

Tuleg snorted and left the room. He still wore the stained undershirt he'd had on the first time I'd seen him.

I made motions of writing. The gorilla body I wore was struggling with itself. I wanted to tell them, I wanted to ask them. What was wrong? Was my mind crippled in the wreck? Why couldn't I speak!? Why couldn't I write?

Blanche handed me a large pencil and a piece of paper the size of a tabloid. I wrote as best I could, taking up most of the sheet, slipping, straining to make myself understood.

WHY ME? WHY DO THIS TO ME?

Blanche read it and looked deep into my piggy anthropoid eyes.

"Oh, Father!" she said, and turned to the Mad Scientist.

He stared at me with his Einstein looks, his fringe of hair.

"I did it to save your life! Don't you understand? You would have died out there!" He began to shout. Lines of saliva hung inside his mouth as it opened and closed. "I have to teach you! I have to! You have lived so I could carry on my research! Yarr!" he screamed, and fell to the floor in a convulsion.

I watched. Blanche screamed for Tuleg. Together, they got the madman up off the floor and out the doorway of the laboratory. After a while, Blanche came back.

"You poor man, you," she said. She came to the bars of the cage. She put her hand through and touched my hairy fingers.

I jerked as if with the shock from the cattle prod.

"No!" she said. "Don't. I'll help you all I can."

She leaned closer, still holding my hand.

"My father is not well," she said, staring at my eyes. "He is a sick man in many ways."

She kissed my fingers just above the nails, and licked the hair between the thumb and index finger.

Mad. She, too, is mad.

I sit in the corner of the cage, my back against the bars, my feet and legs sticking out before me. I look at my bent legs, at my hairy knees, the flat pad where the bottoms of my feet begin.

I think.

First, there are the movies. I saw them all, in that other life. The gorilla is the image of terror, the anthropoid killer of men and children, the despoiler of women.

(The penis of the male adult gorilla is only a couple of inches long. Ask me.)

Gorilla at Large. White Pongo. Nabongo. Killer Gorilla. In Poe's "Murders in the Rue Morgue," I was Old Man Pong, the orangutan. In the film, I was gorilla. Bela Lugosi. Poor, tired old Bela, shambling through role after role in which he had nothing to do but menace and laugh. *The Ape. Return of the Ape Man. The Ape Girl. Captive Wild Woman.* They put a horn on my head for *Flash Gordon. Konga. Unknown Island. Mighty Joe Young.*

King Kong.

I think of Blanche and I dream of Fay Wray. She does not look anything like her. I see Skull Island. I fight *Tyrannosaurus* for her. Through the dim eyes of the beast I pull the wings off the pterodactyl. I throw men from the log over the ravine to the waiting spiders. I roar my challenge from the Empire State Building.

I fall to the streets below.

Why does the gorilla always lust after the beautiful girl?

Why?

Why?

Tuleg has hurt me again.

Blanche found me quivering and shaking.

Strange Things in Close-Up

She came into the cage with me, opening it with a key from the workbench. I lay moaning.

"Oh, Roger, Roger," she said, cradling my head in her lap. "I'll kill him. I'll kill him if he hurts you again! My father will get rid of him."

She washes away the scored and scorched places, soothes me, rubs my chest where the prod has not bitten.

I DIDN'T FIGHT, I write.

"I know," she says, rocking me, "I know. It'll be all right."

But it is not all right. Tuleg comes into the room.

He stops dead still when he sees her in the cage with me.

"Get out of there!" he yells, and runs into the cage, pulling her away from me. He slams the door. The key falls to the floor and he kicks it away. I try to get up. I hurt too much.

I struggle up.

"Your father is dead," says Tuleg. "He went crazy and died."

"Oh no," she said, and ran up the stairs.

Tuleg followed her.

In a few moments, there is a scream, a woman's scream, and then another and another.

"No No!" yells Blanche as she falls through the door, her clothes torn from her. I hear Tuleg laughing outside, and he comes in the room, still holding part of her dress.

I shamble to my feet and roar. I slam against the cage. Tuleg laughs, then grabs Blanche by the hair and pulls her backward behind the workbench.

I mash my fist to paste against the door as I catch it between my shoulder and the bars. And still I push against it.

And still.

And still.

I have to watch the murder. And then the rape.

Then, only then, do I see the keys. I can't reach them. I try. Tuleg is not through with Blanche, though Blanche is finished with everything.

He is groaning.

The ballpoint pen. I find it with my hand. I stick it through the bars. Tuleg surely hears the jingle as I spear the brass ring. But he is busy, and finishing up.

Dr. Hudson's Secret Gorilla

I have the keys now, and I put them inside the cage lock.

I turn the key. The lock grates. "No," says Tuleg, as he looks up from behind the bench, his face twisted in release. He jerks from the body.

He is going for the submachine gun.

I am there first, cutting him off. He is half naked. He bolts for the door. He slams it shut. His feet run up the stairs.

The doors part for me like a curtain, flinders flying each way.

It is a beautiful house, and Tuleg has made it to a phone. He is screaming an address into it. He turns, and his eyes go strange as he tries to stick a knife in me.

I do not feel it. I grab him by the ankle and pull him down. I am four hundred pounds of muscle and sinew, and he is a paper doll. The phone smashes against the bannister, Tuleg tries to scream.

I use him like a pogo stick, my foot and weight on his neck, while I hold to his kicking feet. One jump, two. *Snap crunch snap*. I like the sound as his neck goes soft like a pair of socks. Then I smash his head, and use the knife like a hoe in his stomach.

I carry the body of Blanche Hudson, and the air is filled with sirens, all coming toward us.

I carry her into the garden, where there is a gazebo. It looks out over the rest of the Canyon, and above me, that must be where my car plunged over.

I also carry the Thompson submachine gun in my hand.

I place the body of Blanche on the floor of the grape arbor, and lay her dress over her as neatly as possible. She is sweet in death, if you ignore the blood.

The house is beginning to burn. Tuleg's smoke will rise up to Hell forever, like the doctor said.

Fire trucks, police cars, spectators arrive around front.

Ah.

Two policemen run toward me, yelling.

It is night, and they could not have seen me. One turns the corner of the garden house and sees Blanche's body (the beautiful daughter of the Mad Scientist) and stops. His eyes go wide as I bite through his throat, my hand on his face in a grip like a vise.

Strange Things in Close-Up

One banana, two banana, three banana, four.

The second cop sees me and draws his pistol.

I break his arm and knock in his head with the butt of the Thompson.

There is a stinging on my cheek, and the sound of a bee going by. Bullets. Oh so many of them. Pop pop pop.

I turn and say my name, but it must sound like a roar to them.

I turn the selector switch on automatic and open fire.

The Thompson says *its* name.

(A: A gorilla with a submachine gun.)

There is the sound of glass exploding and brick dust powdering wherever I point. *Tinkle tinkle crash*.

Little points of light wink, and the air fills with whines and screams. I fire again, and run into the bushes where the yard ends.

They are after me. I show them. They are afraid for what I am. I'll show them how near they are to me. I show them my teeth, up close.

Someone gets in the way and I kill him as I run.

I have the machine gun. They will not take me alive. You have sent me after the Three Stooges. You have visited my nightmare form on Abbott and Costello. You have run me across a footbridge where I snarled at Laurel and Hardy.

I am funny. Gorillas are funny.

I will show you funny.

This ape can think. It can pick locks and plant dynamite charges and use an M16. Oh, there will be deaths! Run, Kong, shamble away before they catch you.

Careful, there. Almost crouched as I ran. Have to watch it.

Not to go on all fours. That is the Law.

Introduction to
"... The World as We Know't"

I carried this one around in my head for three or four years, threatening to write it a lot. I called my own bluff and spent six months researching everything, and I mean everything about the subject, about eighteenth-century physics and chemistry, Joseph Priestley, Lavoisier, the whole taco as they used to say. Then I wrote the story and sent it off. It's another Shayol story.

About six months after I sold this, I found a copy of a doctoral dissertation written in the 1930s that had pulled together all the research I'd done in three dozen books. Oh well, live and learn to use the subject index, I always say.

Most people look at science as a straight-line thing: One person has a theory, another tries it, a third, a fourth, an umpty-umpth, and eventually, you have television! Vulcanized rubber! The quantum theory! Lava lamps!

Anyone who works in a scientific or technical field will tell you that's not the way things happen. There are more delusions, blind alleys, false starts, false finishes and jerkwater theories than you can shake a stick at. It's always been that way, and always will. (Read Greg Benford's Timescape.*)*

If you took all the crackpot stuff, dead ends, and false hopes and stacked them end to end, it would, in someone's words, serve us right.

This story's about one of those ideas mankind labored under for more than a hundred years, which, in the end, amounted, as John Nance Garner once said, "to a bucket of warm spit."

"... The World, as We Know't"

The neptunists and vulcanists were going at it hammer and tongs.

The fight had begun just after Curwell's demonstration on counteracting the effects of garlic on the compass. His methods, which would open the seas to safe passage of condiments and spices, had been wildly applauded by his peers in the Lunatick Society.

He had graciously accepted their accolades, and was making a few ex-temporary remarks. He seemed the essence of charm and grace as he answered questions from the audience, until he made the unfortunate mistake of mentioning the age of the earth.

Canes had begun rapping on the floor, there were whistles, words of dispute, and then the yelling had begun.

The president of the Society gaveled for quiet. Fists were brandished in faces. "Gentlemen! Order, please. Order."

This only infuriated them the more.

"I maintain," someone shouted from the back of the hall, "that the earth is no less than..."

They yelled him down.

To make matters worse, the argument began to eddy and splinter around the main one. The gradualist uniformitarians, who thought the land masses had been uncovered from a once all-pervading ocean, were yelling at the catastrophic vulcanists who were gathered in one corner of the hall.

"... The earth has been made over," yelled one of the latter in the face of one of the former, "by terrible volcanic upheavals something approaching twenty-seven consecutive times!"

"Faddle."

"Hear, hear!"

Across the aisle, a catastrophic neptunist climbed atop his

"... *The World as We Know't*"

chair and shouted at both groups. "You people can't use your own eyes to see that the rocks of the Northwest Territory were carried there by the action of a series of deluges, more than seven, but no more than ten in number, as has . . ."

Instantly, members of *all* the other factions turned on him.

The president kept gaveling for order.

Sir Robert Athole, mounting the platform, shook hands with Curwell, who was smiling and watching the uproar he had caused.

"They really are in some mood tonight," said Lawrence Curwell, who was a young man with a broad handsome face.

"It's really too bad you gave them no points to dispute in your presentation, which was quite remarkable," said Sir Robert.

They were bumped from behind by a black man who was taking models and equipment to the raised stage, where the gavel kept pounding and having absolutely no effect on the turmoil.

"Sorry, sir, so sorry," said the black.

Curwell took no notice.

"Thank you for the compliment," said Curwell. "I've already turned the results over to your Maritime Commission. I hope no more tragedies of the kind which took the *Bon Apetit* and the *Lucie Marie* to their watery graves will occur again because of my researches."

There were dull thuds from the back of the room. The two men turned to watch cane-brandishing men be pulled apart by their friends to the uttering of great vile oaths and epithets.

"Shall you be visiting the States long?" asked Sir Robert to Curwell. "If it's at all possible, I should like you to come visit and see the progress of my researches. They might interest you."

"I'd love to. I hear you're doing splendid things. I look forward to your presentation tonight."

Sir Robert Athole began to bow, but paused to turn and watch as one of the more elderly philosophs bounded across the aisle and began to vigorously choke a younger man. They were absorbed in the crowd.

Then "oohs" and "ahhs" raced from the front of the room toward the back. It became very quiet and somber, and some bowed their heads.

For up on the dais, the president of the Society had signaled

81

for the sergeant-at-arms to bring in a small square box and place it in the center of the president's desk.

"Franklin's spectacles," whispered someone. The whisper susurrated through the room. Persons righted their overturned chairs, straightened their wigs, took their seats.

"Order," said the president. The two raps of his small gavel now sounded like the slamming of the great gates of a fort in the still hall.

"The next item on the agenda," he said, "will be a presentation by Sir Robert Athole on the absolute nature of phlogiston."

The room itself was old, huge, and dark. It was lit by chandeliers and by candle sconces along the walls. The odor of wig powder, soot and sweat filled the hall. Through several doors leading in, household servants could be seen coming and going, preparing the traditional meal which would end the monthly meeting of the Lunatick Society.

Velvet and brocade rustled as the men moved about in their upholstered chairs. A snort, sniff and occasional sneeze broke the quiet as one or another of them took snuff. A cane rolled from a lap and clattered loudly to the floor.

The black man indicated to Sir Robert that the models were ready. He came a little closer. "Go easy on the cylinder," he said. "I think it might have cracked a little on the way over in the wagon."

"Very good, Hamp," said Sir Robert, and nodded to the president. There was polite applause for him as he stepped to the rostrum, on which sat a whale-oil lamp smoking quietly.

He looked out at the mass of faces and wigs flickering slowly in the dim light, and saw them as bubbles in the darkening pudding that was the world. No matter. He smiled and began.

He started with the history of combustion and with mention of the works of Becher and Stahl.

"Phlogiston is thought to permeate all things in finely inseparable parts. It is characterized by setting up a violent motion within substances in the presence of heat. This motion results in flame, and as long as the air is not kept from it, the motion will continue until only earthly ash remains."

"... The World as We Know't"

He then described *terra pinguis* and the fatty earths, and the search for the phlogistic principle itself. His audience continued to listen intently, even a little restlessly. So far he had told them nothing new.

"Recently Cavendish thought he had found the most highly phlogiston-charged substance in his inflammable gas, which is lighter than common air, and is used to lift aerostatic vehicles to heretofore unheard-of heights. Inflammable gas burns violently in air, sometimes to the point of detonation. But, as others, including Dr. Priestley, have shown, a mixture of inflammable gas and eminently respirable air explodes, but leaves as residue a wet liquid, indistinguishable from common water.

"And water, as you know, is the enemy of phlogiston. It seems to me therefore, that a mixture of phlogiston and any other substance *could not* give a residue of its exact opposite. Cavendish, however..."

"Question!"

Sir Robert looked up.

"Yes?"

"According to the leading French theorists, eminently respirable air is..."

"The French," said someone else, "are a bunch of rabble who cannot even carry out a revolution in the accepted manner, as did we."

This was a matter of agreement.

"You were going to say," said Sir Robert to his questioner, "that the French New Chemistry, which denies the phlogistic principle, attributes other causes to combustion and calcination. Most of these concern the properties of the eminently respirable air, or oxygine, as it is named. Instead of phlogiston being given off by substances in combustion, the New Chemistry says substances combine with this oxygine in the presence of heat. And you are asking what I think of this theory?"

"Yes."

"Not much," said Sir Robert. "I *have* read in the French Chemistry. If you must deal with the devil, first you must know him." There was hearty applause from the back. "I have decided to ignore most of these theories, insofar as is possible. For I believe it is now within the power of science to isolate phlogiston itself."

"No! No! Impossible! Wrong!" they shouted.

Oaths crossed the air again as others took his side.

Sir Robert raised his hand for quiet.

"I have come here tonight to outline my plans and to show you models of the operations by which I intend to carry out . . ."

"Phlogiston . . . ," said a voice, ". . . is present to some extent in all matter, and indivisible. Might as well try and weigh or separate sunlight itself!"

"Hear! Hear!"

Sir Robert looked them down. A tremor passed through his hand then, something he had noticed as happening more often since he began experimenting with his mercuric pneumatic troughs. He raised it as the tremor passed. "Some say phlogiston drifts down from the shooting stars through the aether. Others say it *comes* from the very sun. Perhaps if I succeed in isolating the phlogistic principle, we shall find, indeed, the true nature of even that great sun overhead."

That was too much for even the devout phlogistians in the audience. They came to their feet, arguing against him.

"Nevertheless," said Sir Robert, rolling up his manuscript. "Nevertheless, I have had special equipment ordered, and will carry through . . ." The president stood up and pounded with his gavel. ". . . I will prevail in my work, and expect within a fortnight to have all ready. Such of you as may want shall be invited to witness . . ." The roar rose above his words for a space and he paused. ". . . to witness this great thing, and those of you who don't can go to the very devil himself!"

He stomped from the dais. Hamp drove home in the wagon down the snow-covered ruts which passed for a road. The ground was lit by the cold still glow of the full moon, on whose closest Monday night the Lunatick Society sat, and for whose shining light it was named.

At noon two days later, Lawrence Curwell arrived. Sir Robert and Lady Margurite Athole met him on the wide carriage porch in the light of a bright cold sun.

Curwell bowed to Lady Margurite. "Your servant, madam."

"Sorry Hamp isn't here, too," said Sir Robert. "He's out in the laboratory, unpacking the new globe which arrived this forenoon from Philadelphia."

"... *The World as We Know't*"

"I'm sure my note arrived rather late the night of the meeting," said Curwell. "I was surrounded by disputants during your speech. It's only luck we kept Hazzard from plunging his penknife into Revecher. What a contentious lot!"

Lawrence Curwell, like Sir Robert, was from Britain. Unlike the elder scientist, he could return, being in America to check on his brother's tobacco holdings. This was possible only because the new Constitution had been adopted, and relations between the two countries were normalizing again after the shaky years of the Confederation.

Sir Robert, who had once been a notorious supporter of the Colonies in their rebellion, had been hounded to the States, much like his contemporary Priestley who now lived in Pennsylvania.

Curwell, who was young and still loyal to Britain, and Sir Robert, in his fifties, experienced, but now apolitical, met only on the common ground of a devotion to knowledge and the empire of science. They shared another opinion that the American philosophs were hotheaded, opinionated, prejudiced, and had no science to match the new country's ideals. With a few exceptions: the late, lamented Franklin, Priestley, who really didn't count, Bartram of Carolina.

"I trust they'll sing another tune if you succeed," said Curwell.

"They'll have to," said Lady Margurite.

"Do we have time to see how Hamp's getting on before lunch?" asked Sir Robert.

Lady Margurite gave a knowing smile. "Surely," she said.

"Will you come with us?" asked Curwell, who was very taken with her beauty.

"Not presently. I have to see to the servants," she said, and turned to go into the house, which was an imposing, square, white three-story structure with a green roof.

"This way," said Sir Robert.

They followed a flagstone path around the house. A vista opened up to the flat rolling hills toward the west. Here was a barn, there poultry houses, stables and servant quarters larger than the cottage Curwell lived in. Past those was a wide field and beyond that a low squat edifice of fieldstones with many smokestacks and chimneys protruding from it. As Curwell neared it, he saw a huge pile of sand under the fire bell tower

Strange Things in Close-Up

which stood near the doorway. One of the many large windows showed blackened signs of scorching.

"An accident late last year," said Sir Robert.

There were still a few patches of snow here and there in the shadows of the building and trees across the field. The wind was from the north but spring was in the air.

"This is quite a marvelous globe flask," said Sir Robert as they entered the building through a low rickety door. Several white servants and the black man were busy with crates and boxes. "It has a diameter of three feet, its sides are two and one-half inches in thickness, stoppable ports and conduits for sparking. I had it made especially for the grand experiment."

"Hamp," said Sir Robert. The black man looked up from his work, rubbed his hands on a chamois, came over. "Hamp. Lawrence Curwell. Lawrence, Hampton Hamilton."

"Pleased, indeed," said Hampton, and offered his hand.

It was the first time Lawrence Curwell had been offered the hand of a black man. He shook it nonetheless. He had assumed at the meeting that the man had been Sir Robert's slave.

"Hamp runs the laboratory for me, and is in charge of all the equipment and requisitioning. How's the globe, Hamp?"

"Excellent, indeed," said Hamp. turning to the great transparent globe before them supported on sawhorses, he said, "The ports fit so tightly that I doubt we shall need wax and quicklime to seal the joints tight."

"Good, good," said Sir Robert. "Let me see the bill of lading, will you? Excuse me, Lawrence . . ."

While they put their heads together, Lawrence Curwell looked around the laboratory. He was struck by the spaciousness and cleanliness of the place and its supplies. Where most chemists got on with two or three small furnaces, Sir Robert had no less than seven—three of them large reverberatory cones, two forced-draft furnaces, two smaller ones spread down the length of the room, each with its own stack or chimney.

At one end stood large jugs—gallons of ether, vitriol, spirit of wine, acid, distilled waters. In other places were ceramic buckets marked sulfur, antimony, lead, earth of rhubarb, Mohr's salt.

Shelf after shelf stretched across the walls with tins, vials and flasks—the most completely stocked workroom Curwell had

"... The World as We Know't"

ever seen—syrup of violets, oil of Dippel, ley of oxblood, Icy Butter, Starkeys Soap, salt of Gall, Glauber's salt, liquor of flints, Minderer's spirit. Numberless others.

At the far end of the laboratory were pumps and basins for washing. Near each end were large workbenches covered with experiments in progress.

In the center of the room were pneumatic troughs for the recovery of gases. Two were filled with water, the third with four inches of mercury. Several glass bottles, some filled with a reddish air, stood upside down in each.

Curwell walked to the workbench where retorts and a Woulfe bottle caught his eye. In a few seconds he recognized it as the cohobation of some solid. At another spot he found lixiviation in process – how long it had been going on he did not know. He had seen some last for half a year, with virtually no result.

He followed to another spot where some matter was being edulcorated from acid by a water bath.

There seemed no order to the experiments, nowhere they should be leading. There was no thread holding them together, except perhaps that of refinement. Maybe Sir Robert was getting the best possible metals and calxes together before using them in his actual work.

"Lawrence," said Sir Robert. "Here, come over here." He was now standing near one of his pneumatic troughs, while behind him Hamp and the others busied themselves once more with the boxes.

"Here." He pointed at one of the inverted bottles. "I've been doing things with a gas collected over sulfur and nitre. Would you like to see?"

He began by showing Curwell some of the properties of the gas, talking occasionally of how it would be a part of the great experiment. They began moving from table to trough to bench as one or another thing they should try came to them. At one point they took off their frock coats, and sometime later their wigs. Curwell suggested other properties, other processes. They took bottles from workbench to crucible to mortar and pestle. The workmen came and left, came again. They ignored the two men huddling over the trough.

At some time Hamp lit candles in the room, finished the unpacking. Then he left. The candles burned down.

Strange Things in Close-Up

At 11 P.M. the two scientists stumbled back to the house, talking, gesturing, happy as mice and famished as wolves. Everyone was asleep.

It was the second week of Curwell's stay. Something was bothering Sir Robert, and both Margurite and Hampton could tell. Sir Robert seemed distracted in the middle of conversation or experiments. He drew plans on sheets of foolscap with a thick graphite pencil, then discarded them in lumps around the house or the laboratory.

Most of them dealt with clockwork devices, cogs, fuses. None seemed to satisfy him.

Curwell had begun to see that all the experiments and processes in the laboratory were coming together in a great design. It was ambitious, complicated, and to Curwell's mind it would probably not work. Most of it centered on fixing the phlogiston, much as fixed air is obtained from common air. He thought there were too many variables, and it depended on timing of at least four major processes. But Sir Robert's enthusiasm stirred him, and he and Hamp set about putting together minor portions of the apparatus and materials. Sir Robert talked less and less, worked more and more, and became still more dissatisfied.

One morning as he and Curwell walked toward the laboratory, they were interrupted by a halloo. Turning, they saw Athole's gamekeeper riding slowly toward them down the road. On the wagon-rut before him walked a trussed man dressed in deerskin trousers and jacket who seemed much the worse for wear.

"Caught a live one, Your Lordship," said the gamekeeper, who was Irish. "He made the best shot I've ever seen. Right into one of your heath hens," he continued, and produced the feathered evidence from his saddlepack. "Am I to take him to the constable, or shall I pummel him unmercifully?"

"As if you haven't already!" grumbled the man in leather.

"Quiet, you!" said the gamekeeper, and yanked on the rope.

Sir Robert was staring as if transfixed. "What rifle did he use?"

"Here," said the gamekeeper, and handed down a Kentucky rifle.

"I didn't do anything," said the man.

". . . The World as We Know't"

"Quite right," said the gamekeeper, and dealt him a smart blow behind the ear with his own rifle butt.

"No need for that, McCartney," said Sir Robert.

"Ow Ow Ow!" said the man, who had fallen to the ground.

"How far was the hen?" asked Sir Robert.

"Between eighty and a hundred paces, my lord," said McCartney.

"It was a hundred or I'm damned," said the man on the road.

"And could you make a shot at a quarter mile?"

"How big a target, and with what gun?" asked the man.

Sir Robert thought a moment. "A target two feet across, and with whatever weapon you need."

"It'd take a Philadelphia rifle of .60 caliber," said the man, "and I could do it."

"Done!" said Sir Robert. "Be here at dawn on the twenty-first of the month. You shall have the Philadelphia rifle, and yours to keep, and a gold crown for making the shot."

"What's the catch?" asked the man.

"None whatever. You've solved a problem of great weight for me."

"I'm not going to have to kill a man, am I?"

"No, no! What's your name, man?"

"Bumppo," he said.

"Well, Bumppo, make this shot, you have all I named before and free hunting on my land besides, in perpetuity. What say?"

"But sir—" said McCartney.

"Untie the man, McCartney," said Sir Robert, "so he can shake hands on the deal." Then he danced a little jig on the edge of the road.

The ropes came off. Humbly, Bumppo shook Sir Robert's hand.

They set up the apparatus for the Great Experiment in a field near the woods two miles from the house. It was a quarter mile from an old Indian mound which Sir Robert thought would serve as an excellent vantage point for the spectators.

The experiment had many stops, all leading to the great glass globe which was at the center of the setup. It was surrounded by charcoal buckets, basins and jars. Over all they had erected canvas to protect it from the elements.

The invitations had been posted for the morning of the twenty-first, weather permitting.

On the afternoon of the nineteenth, they were linking the last of the equipment in place. There came to them a far-off noise, like low thunder or fireworks on the Fourth of July.

Sir Robert came out from under a basin he was installing. "What's that?"

Hampton turned to the south, from where the noise rose.

He smiled. "Pigeons," he said.

The rumble heightened like a great wind from a storm.

"Here they come," said Hamp.

To the south was a ragged blot on the horizon which wound in on itself, then spread.

"Pigeons?" asked Curwell, his face covered with soot from a charcoal bucket. "That noise?"

He stood beside the black man, who pointed.

"Passenger pigeons," he said. "Coming north again to nest. This time every year."

The line covered a quarter of the southern horizon. The sound was like a droning flutter, and the shape moved toward them with the inexorability of the rising tide. It seemed a solid mass which only resolved itself as they drew near the zenith.

They were brown and blue specks which flashed pink. They were packed more densely than Curwell had ever seen birds, ten or twenty sleek shapes to the cubic yard. They flew in a column thirty feet thick and two miles wide and—Curwell tried to count. "What's their rate of flight?"

"A mile to the minute," said Hamp, who watched a hawk diving at one of the edges of the flock. Where the predator flew the pigeons eddied and swirled, but still the column came on.

Curwell looked at his watch. The sun was blotted out as the pigeons passed over, and the fluttering roar was omnipresent.

"Under the awning!" said Hamp, and pulled Curwell back. White flashes like snow, and occasional feathers began to drift down. Passenger pigeon excrement dotted the ground in spots, then more, and fell like a gentle white rain.

Through the flutter of wings, shots could be heard from the neighboring estates. Curwell saw great clumps of pigeons drop a mile away on a surrounding farm.

Then one fell a few feet outside the canvas, struggled and lay still. It must have been hit some distance away and flown this far.

Curwell ran out, picked it up and brought it inside the tent.

It was the most beautiful bird he had ever seen, even in death. Its back was blue, its neck and stomach bronze, and its chest pink and dull red, with an iridescent sheen to all the feathers. Its beak was dark, and its legs, feet and eyes were a brilliant orange-red. He placed it on the bench and examined it minutely.

Still the fluttering roared overhead, and the ground was as white as in a snow flurry. The sky outside was an interrupted play of darkness and light where the cloud of birds went in transit across the sun.

Curwell went back to work in the artificial gloom, occasionally looking out to make sure the flock was still traveling. Gunshots came more frequently from the nearby roads and fields.

Sometime later, the sound subsided. Curwell came out of the tent in time to see the last of the flock rocket overhead. The late evening sun began to shine again.

He looked at his watch. Two hours and forty minutes had elapsed. The column had been one hundred and sixty miles long. At ten birds to the yard, ten yards thick, 1,700 yards to the mile, two miles wide . . .

Sir Robert looked at Curwell. "About sixteen million birds, I'd say."

"I've seen more," said Hamp. "When I was a boy I saw a flock that took from noon to dusk to pass. It got dark at midday, and we never saw the sun go down. We had only morning that day." He pounded a copper pipe in place with a maul. He stopped to look at the encrusted ground for a moment.

Then they all went back to work.

All was in readiness.

The spectators, scientific men for the most part, had begun arriving in the early hours of the morn. Dawn was approaching. Then men on the Indian mound waited while Curwell, Hampton and Sir Robert Athole walked up the intervening field from the apparatus, which looked to be a jumble of metal and glass to the unaided eye at this distance.

Bumppo stood well back from the others. McCartney kept

Strange Things in Close-Up

an eye on him. The leather-clad man was testing the feel of his new Philadelphia rifle, swinging it up and down from his shoulder.

Sir Robert came to the top of the mound and stood beside Lady Margurite.

"Gentlemen," he said. "Lady. Others.

"You are here to witness what I hope is a grand event in scientific progress. On yonder field," he pointed, "are working apparatus for the generation of gases and airs—of dephlogisticated, or eminently respirable, air; of flammable gas, of sulfur air, of phosphorus. They are all working and generating as we stand here, and shall be in fruition soon.

"They enter into conduits taken to the glass globe which you see at the center. They will enter the glass when Mr. Bumppo . . ." Here Bumppo held up his hand shyly, and a ragged cheer went up from the spectators, ". . . fires at his target disk. These phlogiston-rich gases and liquids will rush together. They should produce the essence of fire, of combustion, of calcination viz. phlogiston itself. A clockwork will then be put in motion, and fifteen seconds later, the mixture will be sparked by means of a circuit from a Leyden jar. This should fix the phlogiston itself, much as common air becomes fixed in the presence of the electric principle, and allow us the examination for the first time, of one of the principles, of one of the elements itself.

"That is my Great Experiment."

Some applauded.

"Question?"

"Yes?"

"You're mixing inflammable air, dephlogisticated air and phosphorus in the presence of common air, and sparking it?"

"That is my plan."

"Then what you'll get," said the voice, after a moment's reckoning, "is a gentle explosion, a small quantity of fixed air, and a small field fire to fight."

Some laughed.

"I doubt that," said Sir Robert Athole. "I have taken the precaution of removing us to this distance in case of some apparatus failure, and the leakage of noxious fumes."

". . . The World as We Know't"

The sun topped the small ridge to the east, and the field and mound were bathed in a frosty light.

"Win or lose," said Sir Robert, "I feel on the edge of great things."

"And I," said Curwell.

"I too," said Lady Margurite, and took her husband's hand.

"Mr. Bumppo," said Sir Robert. "You see your target?"

"That I do," said Bumppo.

"Then earn your crown, man!"

The leather-clad man stepped to the front of the mound. Smoothly he raised the weapon as if it were part of him, pulled back the dog-ear hammer, aimed and fired.

The smoke from the muzzle wafted away.

Even without his spy-glass, Sir Robert saw the great globe turn milky white. But it was not the milk-white of residue gases. It roiled and swirled slowly. An "ooh" went up from the small crowd. Winks of light seemed to play across the equipment from the globe. All the apparatus was bathed in a white light.

Sir Robert felt the muscles of his stomach twitch.

For the requisite few more seconds, nothing happened.

Then it did.

Shaken and dazed, Sir Robert pulled himself from the ground in the blinding light. He was near the bottom of the mound. Some of the others were getting up as well as they could. One man lay with a branch through his chest. A few lay unmarked but unmoving. Hampton, near him, held his arm crookedly the wrong way.

There was a roaring in their ears, and it did not subside. Sir Robert stumbled back to the top of the mound, shielding his eyes.

To the west was a great roiling white cloud, too bright to be looked at directly. Bright blooms and bursts of light flew out from it like those from a pan of burning phosphorus. Sir Robert could tell that it was moving slowly away from him to the westward.

He turned. The cloud stretched to north and south, horizon to horizon, moving laterally to its progress westward. Ribbons of red flame shot through the bright white wall.

The smell of burnt wood permeated all the air. As the cloud moved away, it continued to grow in height.

The wind rose from the east, first gently, then in gusts, then faster and faster. The earth to the west was charred to the surface. Matchstick trees poked up. As Sir Robert watched, a puff of wind blew them to ash before his eyes.

The numbed scientists were milling around behind the mound. The wind rose to gale force.

"It's moving west with the rotation of the earth," said Hampton Hamilton. He knew, as did any schoolboy, that the air moves with the surface under it falling behind, from whence rise winds.

Sir Robert turned to see Curwell helping Lady Margurite up. They both seemed safe, though Lady Margurite's skirts flapped immodestly in the racking wind. Sir Robert noticed his wig was gone just as he saw Hamp's wig blow off and be lost in the western distance toward the bright cloud. They climbed down the Indian mound against the force of the wind.

"How long will it burn?" asked Curwell.

"I have no idea," said Sir Robert. "It was not supposed to burn at all. It was supposed to fix in the globe. I just don't understand."

"It may burn until it reaches the Western Ocean," said Hampton, and he had voiced all their fears.

"Surely, surely not," said Athole, yelling to be heard above the wind.

"But you must have succeeded," said someone else. "You *must* have released all the phlogiston in the mixed matter. There's no telling what will happen with it. It could burn that far!"

"Then the water will put it out. The water!" said Sir Robert. He felt a spasm go through him and he lost consciousness.

He awakened with smoke and the smell of soot in his nostrils. The light outside was murky. A wind whistled around the rafters outside the house, but it was no longer the gale it had been. A brown darkness of smoke lapped against the windows.

He sat up on the couch where they had lain him.

Lady Margurite was crying on the sofa opposite.

". . . The World as We Know't"

"Everything to the west is gone, Robert," she said quietly when she saw him rouse.

"*Everything?*"

"As far as a horse and man can ride, before it becomes too hot to continue. And that was hours ago, when the scout from the township came back from his reconnoiter."

"The barometer," said Lawrence Curwell, tapping the great Dresden instrument atop the mantelpiece. "The barometer has dropped a full six inches since this morning, and is still falling."

"Oh, great Jehovah!" said Sir Robert. "What have I done?"

"Nothing any of us wouldn't have done," said Hampton Hamilton tiredly from another chair. "It only seems you succeeded much better than you had planned."

"Why didn't you stop me?"

"I don't know," said Hampton. "I doubt you would have stopped me."

"What time is it?"

"A little after five."

"We'll know in fourteen hours, then," said Curwell. He continued to stare at the barometer, as if to drag secrets from it.

They tried to eat after darkness fell, but no one was hungry. Tins of molasses had begun to pop their lids in the pantry. Sir Robert imagined it was harder to breathe, but knew better.

They sat in the parlor until no one could stand the waiting and the heat any longer.

"Damn it!" Sir Robert jumped to his feet. "If it's going to happen, I want to look it in the face. We'll go to the ocean."

They looked at him a moment, then climbed from their chairs. It was better than waiting here, where each ticking of the clock sounded loud as a carpenter's hammer to them.

The wagon bounced on the rutted road. The horse labored.

Sir Robert drove in front with Hampton; Curwell and Lady Margurite were in back with a picnic basket and blankets.

It was nearing midnight. The air was filled with the odors of burning—of a thousand things, burnt wood, grass, feathers, calcined metals, gunpowder smells. The wind brought warmth. Through rifts in the smoky sky they saw the stars—larger and

Strange Things in Close-Up

colder than they had ever looked before, and they hardly twinkled.

The temperature was still rising, and the barometer had bottomed out an hour ago. It was now decidedly harder to breathe.

They topped the hill overlooking the port town of New Sharpton. Candles burned in the houses, torches moved in the streets as knots of people formed together and dispersed. An occasional rider left on the road down the coast.

"Over here will be fine," said Sir Robert, guiding the horse to a spot beneath a group of trees atop the hill.

They spread the blankets on the seaward side of hill and lay back, watching the still Atlantic.

Sir Robert drifted in and out of sleep as from fatigue. The air was hot and close, as if he were shut up in a chimney in the middle of summer.

Curwell had gone down the hill toward the bay. It had taken him a long time to go the few hundred yards. He had stopped frequently and rested.

The horse, which had been unhitched from the wagon, was in distress, as if it had been galloped miles, instead of being walked the few from the estate to the sea.

"The water temperature is rising, and the streams coming to it are out of their banks from melted snow," said Curwell, when he had labored up the hill and lay down. "There are shoals of dead fish away from the stream outlet. There are so many we could smell them from here were it not for this infernal smoke."

"It just can't be true," said Sir Robert. "It just cannot. Water *will not* burn!"

"Maybe," said Hampton, where he lay on the ground above them, holding his splinted and broken arm. "Maybe the New Chemistry has some truths. Perhaps water is *not* an element. Perhaps it, too, contains phlogiston, or inflammable gas, which . . ." For the first time in his life, Hampton was having trouble following a line of thought. He shook his head to clear it. ". . . Inflammable gas. Perhaps a constituent like the oxygine principle. Perhaps it was separated by the heat from the land. Perhaps the fire is fueled from it. Maybe it will have to pass over the Earth innumerable times before it is all combusted with phlogiston . . ."

"... The World as We Know't"

Sir Robert lay back on the blanket. He held Lady Margurite's hand.

"All gone," he said at last.

"The buffalo. The Indians," said Margurite.

"The Chinese. The bold Russians. The Turks," said Ḥampton.

"The French. *Britain*!" said Curwell.

"Now us," said Hampton Hamilton, and pointed.

The east was beginning to lighten, though it was still an hour before dawn. The wind blew toward the sea, but it was still a gentle wind, a thin wind. It had very little force.

From north to south the bright white boiling line appeared, like the sun breaking through under a late afternoon storm. But much brighter.

"Shall we be burned?" asked Lady Margurite. Her arm sprouted gooseflesh. "The thought of burning is the worst."

"I think not," said Curwell. "Like the martyrs, I think the air will be too saturated with phlogiston for us to breathe before the fire reaches us." He paused as a great tongue of flame licked out of the roil toward them.

The hill and the village were bathed in the glaring artificial dawn. Screams came from the town from those who were still able to scream.

The thin wind rose more.

They watched the burning line quietly, each locked in their thoughts. The edge of the great combusting cloud was still more than two hundred miles away.

"Phlogiston!" said Sir Robert Athole and turned and passed away.

"I want to stand up," said Hamp. They heard him stir and fall behind them.

"The French *were* right, partly . . ." said Curwell.

"Robert . . . ?" asked Lady Margurite.

Curwell looked at the enormous burning wall.

"It's the end of . . ."

The sentence was the only thing left unfinished.

Introduction to
Green Brother

This was the first story I wrote after "The Ugly Chickens" in 1979. Like a lot of others it was written on someone's kitchen table, this time in Washington, D.C. This one, too, has a strange publishing history—sometimes I think they all do. It was promised to an anthology of fiction about American Indians edited by Russell Bates that never appeared, or hasn't yet; it saw first publication in Shayol.

This was the third published piece of mine about American Indians (the others were "Custer's Last Jump" with Steven Utley, written in 1972 and published in 1976, and "Mary Margaret Road-Grader," the next story in the book, q.v.). My novel Them Bones *(Ace, 1984) was set in an alternate universe where the Mississippian mound-builder Indian cultures had had another 500 years of isolation before the Europeans hit the shoreline (and the Europeans in that book were lots nicer than the real ones).*

People ask me why I'm always writing about cultural and biological losers and underdogs—Amerindians, the Japanese in WWII (and once, in a story called "I Was a Graduate of U.C.R.A," about a Navajo mistaken for a Japanese movie villain), Jews in the Middle Ages, blacks in 60s America, Africans under colonial rule, the Frankenstein monster, gorillas, dodos, dinosaurs and little lost robots.

My first impulse is to say maybe we've got to see where we've been before we can try to figure out where we're going.

My second impulse is to say I don't know.

Green Brother

I am talking now about the time Red Cloud was fighting the Yellowlegs about the dirt road they put through our lands.

That started the last winter the Yellowlegs were beating the Grey White Men far to the east. We did not understand why they wanted to kill each other, but we did not mind so long as they left us alone.

I am Seldom Blanket. In those days I was a big medicine chief of my people. I would not have been down there in all the fighting with the soldiers if it had not been that my two sons-in-law wanted to go with the others. I don't give much of a damn for most of the rest of my people, but I did like my two daughters and the men who married them.

So early that spring we moved our lodges up to the places where the rest of the Lakota were camped, and we did the medicine dances and the younger men went off to fight the soldiers in their fort on the great dirt road.

I was in camp most of the time, though I would occasionally go up and watch the shooting and killing. Sometimes the war parties brought back one of our men, and we sang the death songs and wept. Sometimes we heard they caught a few of the soldiers and had fun with them and then killed them. It wasn't really a war at that time. We were just showing them how annoyed we were.

They had had a big meeting some years before, with representatives of the Great White Father, and we had all touched the pen, and got nice gifts and had a big supper. Then they brought us a lot of blankets and hardtack and beads. Then they built a road through our best hunting lands.

The road had filled up with wagons and the people who came through let us know they did not like us. They were afraid, too, so soon the soldiers came out while we were in the winter

Strange Things in Close-Up

hunting grounds to the south and built a big wooden fort. It was there when our first scouts came back north. Also the soldiers were shooting the buffalo for their livers.

Red Cloud, the big talker for our people, went to the big fort and asked the main soldier there if they were going to move before it got cold again. The man said no.

They sent a man from the East who told Red Cloud that he had agreed to the building of the fort and the road.

Red Cloud said he didn't remember the subject ever coming up. So they sent more white people to see Red Cloud.

"We ate real good for a week," he said to the Council, "but I don't think any one of them ever spoke from his heart the whole time." He said the white men complained that they were fighting with each other now over the Black White Men and needed the big dirt road.

Red Cloud told them the big wooden building was an eyesore in the Great Mystery's vision, and the dirt road was making the buffalo skittish and could they please move them both.

They said no, and waved the piece of paper around.

So Red Cloud and a few hundred warriors went out one night and burned the fort down.

Then the white men rebuilt it two winters ago. Now everybody was in on the fight. My sons-in-law were gone most of the time, except when they brought food back, and I was much in the company of older men, and women and children. It is pleasant occasionally to do this. It gives a man perspective.

The favorite of my grandchildren was then called Fall Colt, but that would change soon, as he was nearing his thirteenth birthday. He was a fast learner and picked up on the wisdom that I gave him very quickly. I could tell he wanted to be out there with the men fighting around the fort, but he was as yet too young.

I was smoking outside my lodge one day when he came to see me. I puffed on my pipe after offering some smoke to the winds. Then I sat facing the open end of the circled teepees. The sun had been up a few hours.

"Grandfather!" he said, all out of breath. He was thin and his hair was as black as night. He wore deerskin leggings even in the summer. It was all the fashion among young boys that year, as I remember.

"Yes? Something excites you?"

"Onion Boy is no longer Onion Boy. He went off three days ago and came back, and now he is Falcon Foot."

"Ah, that is good. I shall try to remember his new name. Is he changed much?"

"No, except that he now has a medicine bundle with a falcon foot in it. He said the hawk must have been shot, because as it flew over him, it lurched in the air and its foot dropped to the ground before him."

"Ah, a good sign. Did he dream of flying? Usually people who take bird's names have visions of flying while on their quest."

"I forgot to ask him."

"Not important," I said.

"Grandfather?"

"Yes?"

"What was your vision quest like?"

I saw before me in my mind's eye the river valley, the wavering of my sight and my tiredness, felt the ache in my lids and the cuts between my toes where I had wedged the sharp rocks. I experienced again my shakes and sweats, and the heat of the day. Then I saw again the man who was me walking through snow without a blanket, walking and walking, not cold, not tired, not sick or fevered. It would be forever on my brain.

"Oh, that was a long time ago," I said. "I saw a man who did not need a blanket in the winter."

"Did you see a spirit animal?" he asked.

The great beast reared up before me, huge and terrible, its eyes afire, its shaggy coat rippling with power, its claws large as knives, its teeth the size of bullets, its head wide as a hide shield, its breath rancid, its smell stifling, its charge unstoppable. I had evacuated my bowels.

"A bear," I said. "Go and play now."

One of my sons-in-law was brought in with a bullet in his leg. I did the medicine and took out the bullet and chewed tobacco and invoked the Great Mystery to wrestle with death for him. He was up and about in no time.

Strange Things in Close-Up

I decided to ride up to the big dirt road where the fighting was going on and see it for myself.

"Can I go with you, Grandfather?" asked Fall Colt.

I looked at his mother. She shrugged her shoulders.

"Yipppppeeee!" he said, running to get his pony.

"You must remember we will not be able to see much," I said after him.

"I don't care!" he said. "I don't care!"

There were three small hills before you got to the big wooden fort. Our people stayed on the third hill, just outside rifle range from the walls.

Between the first and second hills, woods used to grow, but the soldiers had cut those down to build the forts, and they had to come between the second and third hills for their firewood. That was still in sight of the fort, and occasionally they would send men out to get logs in a wagon. They would also send men out to shoot at us while the others gathered wood. That was when we would try to kill them and they would try to kill us.

We did not like fighting this way, but other methods had failed. Early on, some of the warriors had attacked during the night and had been shot. Others had tried getting close during the day but the soldiers had used them for target practice. They seemed to have plenty of food and ammunition, but no firewood. So we waited till they came out.

It was boring work. Most of the time our men lay around and watched from the warm grass on the hills, polishing their coup sticks or sharpening their knives. Others would go hunting or fishing. They always cooked the game on the hills where the soldiers could see. The soldiers always shot at them when they did. That is how my son-in-law got the bullet in his leg.

Fall Colt and I walked up the hill where his father, Terrible Wolf, was dozing in the sun.

"Ho, Father," he said, waking, as he saw us come up the draw. He sat up.

"Don't get up on our account," I said.

Fall Colt ran to his father and hugged him. "You embarrass me," said Terrible Wolf. The boy let go of him.

"How are things in camp?"

Green Brother

"Dull," I said. "Your brother is fine. He will come back this week." We sat down. Terrible Wolf and I started to talk.

It was a few minutes before I noticed that Fall Colt had not said anything. He was back down the draw toward the horses. But he kept looking toward the top of the hill behind me. He appeared nervous.

"Hey-A! Hey-A!" yelled someone from the top of the hill. Instantly Terrible Wolf and all the other men were up, rifles in hand and onto their horses. They swept up over the hill in a cloud of dust.

From the direction of the fort we could hear rifle fire. I went to my horse and pulled my shotgun from its holder and Fall Colt got his boy's bow and arrows from his mount. Then we went to the ridgetop.

Below us the ground swelled downward to the fort. Soldiers were on the walls, others milled around in the open gateway. Halfway between us and them, a wagon and several dozen mounted soldiers were on the near side of the first hill.

The warriors swept down toward them from all sides, yelling and raising a great bother. The soldiers came determinedly on, until they reached the timber on the near side of the second hill. Then the wagon stopped and the horsemen dismounted and began to shoot while others with axes started cutting up dead trees.

The braves rode toward them and stopped and dismounted and began firing. The soldiers all fired at once, the warriors whenever they wanted. The sound of axes could be heard intermittently.

Then came the formal charge from the fort, with another two dozen soldiers on horses riding out toward the braves. The warriors mounted and turned back up the third hill. Then they stopped and fired back at the blue-clad soldiers.

Then our second bunch of braves charged from the draw near the third rise, and the soldiers in the fort went wild. Smoke rose up everywhere on the walls as they shot. The wave of troops rushing the hill turned. Everywhere was motion and gunshots. A lot of dust was raised.

Some of the first braves had run back up the hill beside us and were yelling and taunting the soldiers. An occasional bullet whistled by. One man dropped his breechclout and danced rib-

Strange Things in Close-Up

aldly with his buttocks toward the fort. Then he held his ankles and hopped backwards down the hill toward the firing.

Many bullets began to hit around us.

The second wave of soldiers would never come up the third rise. Some started to, but the man with the sword and the two bars on his hat stopped them. They are usually more cautious than the ones with one bar on their hats.

Dust obscured everything. The warriors on the hill fired down into the woodchopping party, holding their rifles high. The soldiers there and in the fort were firing as fast as they could. The troops between them and us flitted in and out of the smoke and dust.

Then everything was quiet. The dust began to settle.

The wagon and the soldiers were going back into the fort, only a few logs bouncing in the back. The mounted soldiers kept a wary eye backward on the hills. Some of our people put their thumbs in their ears and stuck out their tongues, an old white man's insult.

The doors to the fort closed. We went back over the hill.

No one had been hurt.

I looked around, then up. Fall Colt was standing against the skyline, looking down at the fort. He was shaking and pale.

"Come down," I said. "They might hit you by mistake."

He shook himself, looked around.

"What is it?"

He looked down at the bow in his hand. "I don't know, Grandfather, . . . I . . . I . . ."

"Was the excitement too much for you?"

"No . . . I . . . I didn't pay much attention."

His eyes were troubled. I said no more to him, and we rode back to our camp.

It did not surprise me when I saw him calling his friends together two days later. He handed one his bow, another his arrows and knife. Then he passed out his leggings, his moccasins, his breechclout. Naked, he turned his back on the lodges and fires of our people and walked toward the distant mountains.

His mother came to me. "Father, did you see . . ."

I took my pipe from my mouth so her shadow wouldn't fall

across it and harm the tobacco. "It is time," I said. "This has been coming on for days. He will be fine."

We watched him until he was lost in the evening sun.

Then we got busy for a few days, and I thought of Fall Colt rarely.

What we got busy doing was killing soldiers. It happened this way:

I accompanied my other son-in-law when he went back to the big dirt road. We got there when the sun stood straight up. The heat was already oppressive, the air still. Sound traveled a long way. We heard the gates of the fort open from up on our hill. The brave on watch let out his cry then. I looked up into the sky. A lone flycatcher chased a winged insect. I drew my shotgun from its scabbard and mounted up.

We did the same things we did the other day. The wagon came out, and we harassed it. Then the other soldiers charged out. Then our reserves came out of their places. Then our warriors mounted up and came back up the hill.

I saw what was happening before the others did. I let out a cry and began my death chant.

Because the second wave of soldiers had not stopped at the near side of the second hill. They kept coming. They were led by a soldier with one bar on his hat. He pointed his sword at us and spurred his horse. I could see each of his horse's hoofbeats raise dust. His eyes locked on mine.

Supposing the ritual to be the same, some of our people had dismounted and were prancing on top of the hill.

"Yah-Yah-Yah!" they said, turning somersaults. "Yah-Yah-Can't catch us!" Then they noticed the mounted soldiers had not stopped but were bearing down on them. They fell all over each other for a second, then jumped on their horses.

Bullets whipped around me as the oncoming soldiers flew up the hill. As I jumped on my horse, I could see the man in charge of the wagon party shaking his fist at the man leading the charge up the hill. It was a very foolish thing for the man with one bar to do.

For a few seconds, it seemed like a marvelous thing, but only because we did not expect it. But even as they neared the top of the hill and we spurred down into the open flat beyond, I saw that our reserves which had already made their ritual charge had turned and were heading up around the draw. Spotted Bull was in charge and he was a good man.

So we kicked our ponies and made them run. We could tell when the white men reached the top of the hill, because they started shooting everything in sight. Bullets hit all around us. Somebody on my left went down. The man to my right turned and fired, and we circled to the right so the white men would come sooner between us and the reserves. We turned on the soldiers as soon as their fire became scattered.

This was because Spotted Bull had gotten between them and the top of the hill. I turned to see the soldiers milling around as his bunch came down on them.

There were twenty or so mounted soldiers. There were a hundred of us.

I sent Terrible Wolf back up to the top of the hill. "Tell us when the whole fort is coming," I said.

Then we turned back into battle.

I had no coup stick with me, so I leaned down next to my mount and swung up and out when I neared a soldier. He fired at me with his pistol. Powder burned my face and arms. I came up and hit him under the chin with the butt of my shotgun. He went limp and slid off his horse.

Then I saw the man with one bar and shot him in the face with both barrels. He died quickly.

A few of the soldiers had killed their horses and were shooting at us from behind them. We dismounted and began walking toward them, firing as we went. Smoke hung over everything.

"The whole fort is coming," yelled Terrible Wolf.

"Keep killing!" I said. "Keep killing!"

"They're on the second hill," yelled Terrible Wolf, but he hadn't mounted up yet.

We killed the last soldier just as the world filled with the sound of hooves. Terrible Wolf jumped on his mount and took off across the ridge.

I got on mine and did the same. We divided up, half going east, half west.

Seventy soldiers came over the hill in brown and blue waves. Bullets went by like bees. Then we all turned and went over the

Green Brother

same hill back down toward the fort. We caught the wagon party unprepared.

We killed most of them and looted and set the wagon afire.

Somebody got off his horse and pissed on the face of a dead man. Then we rode as fast as we could away from there with everything we had taken from the wagon. They chased us until it was too dark to see.

We moved the camp some miles away from where it had been. Things calmed down in a few days, and our warriors were back on the hill and the soldiers were back in the fort.

It was evening. I sat smoking in front of my lodge. Then I saw a naked boy coming towards camp from a long way off. It was my grandson.

He paused often. He was limping. He kept turning to stare back toward the near mountains, in the direction the fort lay.

"Hello, Grandson," I said. "Did you follow our travois trail?"

He stared at me a moment.

"Grandfather," he said.

"Yes?"

"Can I sleep now? I will tell you about it later."

"Here," I said, moving over and giving him half my buffalo robe. He lay down slowly and then he was asleep. I patted his head while he dreamed.

He woke up late the next night.

"Could you help me with my new name?" asked my grandson.

"Most people do not need help with theirs," I said.

"That is because they have seen a totem animal spirit and know its name," he said.

"You saw no animal?"

"I saw an animal, Grandfather, but I do not know its name."

"That *is* a problem. Perhaps I can help."

He began to tell me what he remembered of his vision quest. It was disjointed, like most are up until a vision comes. He had roamed the hills, chanted, he did not sleep. He put rocks between his toes and scoured his eyes with brambles to keep himself awake. He heard voices, but it was always the wind when he listened closer. He lay over a rock with his head down to help get a vision. One did not come until the third day.

"I turned in the direction of the big dirt road," he said. "And I saw it. I saw everything. There was water out there, much water. It was shining in the sun. The ground steamed and all was green and growing. Many small animals I did not know moved through the growths. In the water, things with long necks waded thick as buffalo on the plains. Animals like bats with long noses wheeled through the skies and dipped into the water for fish. All was large and out of proportion. All was cries and calls and roars like cougars. I did not understand."

"Visions are sometimes not meant to be understood, only acted upon," I said. "What was your animal like?"

"Then I *was* an animal, moving through the reeds. The wading animals that had seemed large were small to me now, my size. I brushed aside ferns. I chased one of the long-necked things which was trying to run from me. Its eyes were filled with terror. I caught it in a jump. I bit into its head and it crushed like pecans. I felt blood and bone. I bit off the head and swallowed it, while the rest of the thing stumbled and staggered around, bleeding in great gouts. I waited and then I pushed it over and began eating while it flopped and heaved on the ground, mashing a place flat with its tail and legs. I threw my head back to eat and swallowed whole chunks without chewing.

"I was near the water and I saw my reflection. I was huge and green. I stood on two legs and had tiny claws where my arms were. My eyes were at the sides of a great head. I had a long mouth full of sharp teeth, and a long thick tail which I used to balance.

"I stood up from my prey and roared a challenge to all the world around me. The earth was silent for a moment, then all resumed as it was before."

My grandson looked at me. "I feel great kinship with that beast, Grandfather. I do not know what it is. It is a beast of terror and strength, and it had skin like a snake."

"There is no doubt it is a powerful animal."

"Grandfather, there is something else."

"What is that?"

"It is still here. Near the white man's fort."

My grandson looked around him, saw some of the booty from

the attack on the wagon a few days before. "I will need that," he said, picking up a tool.

"There is no great magic in a shovel," I said.

"There is no great water near the white man's fort, either," he said. "But I saw it there."

He said he would choose a new name after he was done with his work. The shovel was taller than he was. He strapped it on his pony and rode off toward the big dirt road.

"Where is Fall Colt going?" asked his mother.

"His name is not Fall Colt anymore."

"What is it, then?"

"He is going to find that out," I said.

"Aren't you going with him, Father?" she asked.

"I was just leaving," I said.

When I arrived, Terrible Wolf was standing on top of the hill scratching his head. He held his rifle across the crook of his left arm.

"He has been on his vision quest, hasn't he?" asked my son-in-law.

"Yes. He is troubled. It was inconclusive."

"I can . . . wait . . . what's he doing?"

We looked down the hill toward the fort. I saw that my grandson had been keeping to cover behind a clump of small trees, but now, shovel in hand, he took off running toward the fortress.

We saw puffs of smoke from the walls, then heard the crack of Army rifles. My grandson zigged and zagged like the woodpecker in flight. Puffs of dirt went up around him.

Some others had joined us on the hill, curious since they heard shots but no one had raised a cry. They watched the lone figure darting over the ground.

"Has he lost his wits?" asked someone.

"Great Mystery problems," I said.

"Oh."

Then he stopped. He looked around back and forth. Dust went up all around him, and the fire from the fort became heavy. I saw one of his braids whip in the air behind him.

He dropped down. I thought he was dead. He was obscured

by a small bush barely big enough to hide a dog. Then we saw the flash of his shovel moving, the handle end sticking back up in the air like a great tongue.

"Yayyy!" we all yelled.

A few more shots came from the fort, then it was quiet.

Faintly we could hear the sound of the shovel, digging.

By nightfall he had disappeared behind a mound of dirt.

"I'm going down there soon to see if he is all right," said Terrible Wolf.

"Better take him some food and his bow," I said. "The white men might send someone out to try to hurt him."

My grandson was about two bowshots out from the fort but that seemed to worry the soldiers. The white men do not understand things dealing with the Great Mystery. I am sure they thought his digging had something to do with their fort. They were deathly afraid a thirteen-year-old was going to tunnel up under their buildings and kill them all in their sleep. So there was no telling what the soldiers would do.

After pitch dark, Terrible Wolf made his way out toward the sound of the shovel.

"I kept my eyes turned away," said Terrible Wolf later. "When I saw what he was doing."

"Oh," I said, smoking my pipe on the side of the hill away from the fort.

"There were parts of Storm Beasts around there. He was digging among them."

"That *is* bad," I said. We believe Storm Beasts dash themselves from the sky during rains. They are monsters who live in the heavens with the Thunderbird. They kill themselves with roars which is the thunder, and fall with a flash which is the lightning.

We believe this because you can always find their remains after storms, as they are exposed when the rains carry the earth away. Their bones litter our hunting grounds for miles after the spring rainstorms. We usually go around them, as they are unlucky animals.

"Did he mention Storm Beasts in his vision?" asked Terrible Wolf.

"There was no thunder and lightning in his story," I said.

"Do you think the Great Mystery has driven my son mad?" he asked.

"Let me get a reading on that," I said.

I was beginning to have a few doubts myself.

I performed three ceremonies, each more taxing than the one before it. I was sweating and tired, and my medicine bundle was oily and smelled bad when I finished.

"The Great Mystery is not punishing your son," I said to Terrible Wolf. "But there is magic at work out there, and it's so great I'd rather not be around when it happens."

"But you will."

"Of course I will."

The mound had grown. He was piling it up on the side toward the big dirt road. Occasionally a shovelful of dirt would clear the place he dug. Otherwise, the days were serene.

We could see men moving in the fort. Sometimes one would fire at the place where my grandson dug. Then they even quit doing that.

We settled into a routine. Terrible Wolf would take food and water out to his son at night, and we would watch and wait during the day, in case the soldiers came out for firewood or to harm my grandson. It was not the kind of thing we liked to do.

Terrible Wolf came back one night. He sat down tiredly, put his head between his knees and stared at the ground. I noticed in the moonlight that his moccasins had already started wearing out this early in the summer.

"I did not know one person could move so much dirt," he said.

"Grandfather," someone said, shaking me awake.

"Yes," I said, sitting up on my robe where I had fallen asleep. I rubbed my eyes and sat up. It was some hours before dawn. There was a dull boom far away.

"I need some great medicine worked."

He was streaked with dirt, haggard. His eyes were clouded over with fatigue, barely reflecting the fires on the hill. He was as naked as he had been when he left on his vision quest.

In the distance, I heard another rumble of thunder, and the sky flashed light.

"If a storm is coming, and you are working among Storm Beasts, you are going to need more power than I can ask for. But I will see what I can do."

The first thing I did was to strip off naked and do a protection dance for myself. I am no fool. Then I did a small one for him, because he is so small. I didn't think that would stop the lightning from killing us, anyway. Then I picked up my medicine bundle.

"Have you thought of a name yet, Grandson?" I asked as we walked down the hill. The eastern horizon talked to itself in flashes of light. Great clouds walked toward us across the sky, their tops reaching far out in our direction.

"I am going to be called Green Brother," he said.

"Green Brother is a good name."

The small trees were being whipped about in the rising wind. Dust blew from the big dirt road. I was getting afraid, though my grandson did not know it.

Lightning slammed to the ground behind the white man's fort. Men moved on the walls. Possibly lightning would hit it and burn it to the ground and end all our troubles. I could not be concerned with the soldiers just now.

The pit was before us. Green Brother had dug a rampway down into the place he had scooped out of the ground. It started a long way back, the hole was so deep.

I did not know one person could move so much dirt, either.

"Guide me," I said, closing my eyes. I moved my lips in the death chant. If I saw the spirit animal all at once, it would be easier on me. I would either live or die in that instant.

I felt us go downward into the earthworks. The whistling wind stopped, only dust was blown onto my face from above. I felt my heart pound within my chest. I could not breathe right.

Green Brother turned to me. "It is before you, Grandfather."

"Is it terrible, Grandson?"

"Not after you get used to it."

My nerve failed then.

"Turn me away from it," I said. "The magic will be better if I am not used to it."

"There," he said, turning me.

I opened my eyes. The sides of the hole slanted down around me. The rampway went up from where I stood. A flash of

Green Brother

lightning threw a horrible shadow on the ground before me. I felt the dead presence of the thing behind me.

"Make magic with it, Grandfather," said Green Brother.

"Is it upright? Are its legs and arms free? Will it step on us?"

"It is only bones, but they are iron. It is upright though curled toward us as if falling. Its body is stuck in the rock beneath us. I could not cut it away with the shovel."

"It is well you didn't. It might have fallen on you, and I would not know your new name." I wiped my brow. "This is going to be tough. What do you wish it to do?"

Green Brother looked up behind me. He smiled. "I want it to walk up this ramp and then across the big dirt road and into the fort."

"That would *probably* impress the white men," I said.

Thunder smashed outside the pit with a white flash. It unsettled me mightily. A few drops of rain hit my head. Soon the storm would open up. Perhaps more of the Storm Beasts would fall on us and kill us.

"Stand back," I said. "I need lots of room."

"Is there anything I can do?" asked my grandson Green Brother. "I feel kinship with this beast. I *was* this beast in my vision."

"If it moves," I said, "you can do *anything* you want."

I spread the things from my medicine bundle before me. It would take them all. I wished I had more sacred things. I had never tried anything so powerful before.

I called on the Great Mystery and reminded him that I was small before the storm, as are all men and women. I asked that he remember the things our people had done in gratitude for his blessings, and thanked him for the many times he had wrestled death for me.

When I had worked up his enthusiasm for me, I began to speak of specific things the soldiers had done to us, then asked him to intercede through the Storm Beast behind me.

As I paused for breath I heard the first gunshot. Then the warning cry from our people that meant the soldiers were coming from the fort.

"Sing your death song, Green Brother," I said. "I will try to finish this."

I had left my shotgun up on the hill because I did not like to

Strange Things in Close-Up

carry it in a storm. Years ago I had seen a man melted to his rifle where he sat. It had not been pretty.

The storm crashed about us. There was a sound of firing, and hooves drummed near.

"Hurry, Grandfather!" said Green Brother. "Hurry!"

I was calling on the spirit of the Storm Beast to help us. I was really inspired, since it was no longer just my people, it was Green Brother and I who were in trouble. A gun fired from the dirt up near the mound from the pit, and voices called. The wind howled and roared. The sky danced with light and noise.

A bullet whipped into the ground near me. I closed my eyes tight. I heard men at the top of the ramp, nervous laughter.

"Thing!" I yelled, opening my eyes and dancing around. "Thing! Come alive! Come alive!"

A great bolt of lightning hit just outside the pit.

I saw many things at once:

I saw six soldiers on foot halfway down the ramp. Some were crouched down, rifles ahead of them. Two were upright, guns pointing toward me.

I saw Green Brother near me, head up, the shovel drawn back in his arms, ready to swing at the soldiers on the ramp.

I saw the shadow of the thing behind me on the ground.

It moved. It may have been only shadows from a different lightning flash.

I saw two of the soldiers jerk. I saw their hearts stop working in their chests. I saw six sets of eyes go wide as the doorknobs on the white man's houses. The eyes of the two men who died fell away to each side. The others disappeared backwards up the ramp.

Thunder crashed on top of us.

I turned and looked up at the thing behind me.

I wet myself all over my legs and fell forward into the soft ground.

Rain was falling in torrents, pushing at my face and eyes. I sat up. Water was running down into the pit. Green Brother lay sprawled across from me, his head bleeding where he had fallen against the shovel.

I went to him after retrieving my medicine bag. Strangely there was no more thunder and lightning, just the rain.

Green Brother

I took the rifles from the two dead men and put them over one shoulder. I picked up Green Brother and walked up the muddy ramp. I did not look back. I did not care if the other soldiers were still there or not.

It was very calm under the cold rain.

Soon after the white men left and we burned down the fort again. After the snows melted the next spring, we signed another treaty, and a Doctor of Bones came out from the Great River Potomac to see the field of Storm Beasts.

He and Green Brother spent much time at the pit and all around there. Then men and a wagon came and took all the Storm Beasts away. The Doctor of Bones said Green Brother's vision animal was called in the white man's language *Tyrannosaurus rex*. He said this one was splendid.

Green Brother asked to go back East with the doctor and to learn more about all the spirit animals he had seen.

So he is at the university, and I miss him greatly. We are peaceful here now, and get our coffee and cattle and flour every month, and things are very boring.

Before he left, Green Brother said his spirit animal had been like the long-tailed yellow and brown lizard, only much bigger and much more fierce.

I am a simple man, and I am ignorant of many white men's things. But I do know one truth, and as long as there is a blue sky above me, and the Great Mystery smiles, I know this. That thing I saw that night in the pit was no lizard.

Please turn me toward the sun so I can smoke.

Introduction to
Mary Margaret Road-Grader

This is the kind of story writers hope happens to them once in their careers.

I was living in Bryan, Texas for six months of 1974, at the Monkey House (the kind of place old time SF fans called a Slan Shack—far too many people with a common interest under one roof). Concurrently with this (and the first few months after I moved to Austin), from February of 1974 to March of 1975 was the most productive period of my life—twelve stories that were eventually bought and published, maybe a dozen losers, and abortive starts on two novels. All the good stories written at the Monkey House sold, but none of them while I was there; I owed everybody money and I moved to Austin.

I was visiting in Austin in June of 1974, sleeping on a friend's couch. I'd gone to sleep the night before with my head stuck between two stereo speakers. I woke at 7 A.M. (there were seven or eight people asleep in the two rooms upstairs) and got up to stagger into the kitchen to put on some coffee. Before I did, I dropped an album on the turntable. It was Simon and Garfunkel's "Bridge over Troubled Water."

Between the opening piano notes and the first verse, "Mary Margaret Road-Grader" came to me whole and unbidden. I turned around, opened my typewriter, rolled in paper and began typing.

By the time everybody else got up at 11 A.M., I had finished the story.

I sent it to Damon Knight who edited the late lamented Orbit *anthology series. Damon sent back a list of questions about some stupidities I'd committed in the original version of the story. I fixed them. Otherwise, it's the version that came to me that long-ago morning.*

It was published in Orbit 18 *and picked up by* The Best

Science Fiction Stories of the Year. *It was on the final 1977 Nebula ballot, and lost handily. (So did the best story that year, Jake Saunders' "Back to the Stone Age.") In a real stupid move of mine, it was optioned for filming by a local production company, for a longer time than I care to say for so little money I cry when I think about it.*

The story dropped on me like a bale of hay. I'm proud the story chose me to tell it.

Mary Margaret Road-Grader

It was the time of the Sun Dance and the Big Tractor Pull. Freddy-in-the-Hollow and I had traveled three days to be at the river. We were almost late, what with the sandstorm and the raid on the white settlement over to Old Dallas.

We pulled in with our wrecker and string of fine cars, many of them newly-stolen. You should have seen Freddy and me that morning, the first morning of the Sun Dance.

We were dressed in new-stolen fatigues and we had bright leather holsters and pistols. Freddy had a new carbine, too. We were wearing our silver and feathers and hard goods. I noticed many women watching us as we drove in. There seemed to be many more here than the last Sun Ceremony. It looked to be a good time.

The usual crowd gathered before we could circle up our remuda. I saw Bob One-Eye and Nathan Big Gimp, the mechanics, come across from their circles. Already the cook fires were burning and women were skinning out the cattle that had been slaughtered early in the morning.

"*Hoo!*" I heard Nathan call as he limped to our wrecker. He was old; his left leg had been shattered in the Highway wars, he went back that far. He put his hands on his hip and looked over our line.

"I know that car, Billy-Bob Chevrolet," he said to me, pointing to an old Mercury. "Those son-a bitch Dallas people stole it from me last year. I know its plates. It is good you stole it back. Maybe I will talk to you about doing car work to get it back sometime."

"We'll have to drink about it," I said.

"Let's stake them out," said Freddy-in-the-Hollow. "I'm tired of pulling them."

We parked them in two parallel rows and put up the signs, the strings of pennants and the whirlers. Then we got in the wrecker and smoked.

Many people walked by. We were near the Karankawa fuel trucks, so people would be coming by all the time. Some I know by sight, many I had known since I was a boy. They all walked by as though they did not notice the cars, but I saw them looking out of the corners of their eyes. Music was starting down the way, and most people were heading there. There would be plenty of music in the next five days. I was in no hurry. We would all be danced out before the week was up.

Some of the men kept their strings tied to their tow trucks as if they didn't care whether people saw them or not. They acted as if they were ready to move out at any time. But that was not the old way. In the old times, you had your cars parked in rows so they could be seen. It made them harder to steal, too, especially if you had a fence.

But none of the Tractor Pullers had arrived yet, and that was what everybody was waiting for.

The talk was that Simon Red Bulldozer would be here this year. He was known from the Brazos to the Sabine, though he had never been to one of our Ceremonies. He usually stayed in the Guadalupe River area.

But he had beaten everybody there, and had taken all the fun out of their Big Pulls. So he had gone to the Karankawa Ceremony last year, and now was supposed to be coming to ours. They still talk about the time Simon Red Bulldozer took on Elmo John Deere two summers ago. I would have traded many plates to have been there.

"We need more tobacco," said Freddy-in-the-Hollow.

"We should have stolen some from the whites," I said. "It will cost us plenty here."

"Don't you know anyone?" he asked.

"I know everyone, Fred," I said quietly (a matter of pride). "But nobody has any friends during the Ceremonies. You pay for what you get."

It was Freddy-in-the-Hollow's first Sun Dance as a Raider. All the times before, he had come with his family. He still wore his coup-charm, a big VW symbol pried off the first car he'd boosted, on a chain around his neck. He was only seventeen summers. Someday he would be a better thief than me. And I'm the best there is.

Simon Red Bulldozer was expected soon, and all the men were talking a little and laying a few bets.

"You know," said Nathan Big Gimp, leaning against a wrecker at his shop down by the community fires, "I saw Simon turn over three tractors two summers ago, one after the other. The way he does it will amaze you, Billy-Bob."

I allowed as how he might be the man to bet on.

"Well, you really should, though the margin is slight. There's always the chance Elmo John Deere will show."

I said maybe that was what I was waiting for.

But it wasn't true. Freddy-in-the-Hollow and I had talked in English to a man from the Red River people the week before. He made some hints but hadn't really told us anything. They had a big Puller, he said, and you shouldn't lose your money on anyone else.

We asked if this person would show at our Ceremony, and he allowed as how maybe, continuing to chew on some willow bark. So we allowed as how maybe we'd still put our hard goods on Simon Bulldozer.

He said that maybe he'd be down to see, and then had driven off in his jeep with the new spark plugs we'd sold him.

The Red River people don't talk too much, but when they do, they say a lot. So we were waiting on the bets.

Women had been giving me the eye all day, and now there were a few of them looking openly at me; Freddy too, by reflected glory. I was thinking of doing something about it when we got a surprise.

At noon, Elmo John Deere showed, coming in with his two wreckers and his Case 1190, his families and twelve strings of cars. He was the richest man in the Nations, and his camp took a large part of the eastern end of the circle.

Then a little while later, the Man showed. Simon Red Buldozer came only with his two wives, a few sons and his transport truck. And in the back of it was the Red Bulldozer, which, they say, had killed a man before Simon had stolen it.

It's an old legend and I won't tell it now.

And it's not important anymore, anyway.

Mary Margaret Road-Grader

So we thought we were in for the best Pull ever, between two men we knew by deeds. Simon wanted to go smoke with Elmo, but Elmo sent a man over to tell Simon Red Bulldozer to keep his distance. There was bad blood between them, though Simon was such a good old boy that he was willing to forget it.

Not Elmo John Deere, though. His mind was bad. He was a mean man.

Freddy said it first, while we lay on the hood of the wrecker the eve of the dancing.

"You know," he said, "I'm young."

"Obvious," I said.

"But," he continued, "things are changing."

I had thought the same thing, though I hadn't said it. I pulled my bush hat up off my eyes, looked at the boy. He was part white and his mustache needed trimming, but otherwise he was all right.

"You may be right," I answered, uneasily.

"Have you noticed how many horses there are this year, for God's sake?"

I had. Horses were usually used for herding our cattle and sheep. They were pegged out over on the north side with the rest of the livestock. The younger boys who hadn't discovered women were picking up hard goods by standing watch over the animals. I mean, there were always *some* horses, but not this many. This year, people brought in whole remudas, twenty-thirty to a string. Some were even trading them like cars. It made my skin crawl.

"And the women," said Fred-in-the-Hollow. "Loose is loose, but they go too far, really they do. They're not even wearing halters under their clothes, most of them. Jiggle-jiggle."

"Well, they're nice to look at. Times are getting hard," I said. The raid night before last was our first in two months, the only time we'd found anything worth the taking. Nothing but rusted piles of metal all up and down the whole Trinity. Not much on the Brazos, or the Sulphur. Even the white men had begun to steal from each other.

Pickings were slim, and you really had to fight like hell to get away with anything.

We sold a car in the evening, for more plates than it was

worth, which was good. But what Freddy had been talking and thinking about had me depressed. I needed a woman. I needed some good dope. Mostly, I wanted to kill something.

The dances started early, with people toking up on rabbit tobacco, shag bark and hemp. The whole place smelled of burnt meat and grease, and there was singing going on in most of the lodges.

Oh, it was a happy group.

I was stripped down and doing some prayers. Tomorrow was the Sun Dance and the next day the contests. Freddy tried to find a woman and didn't have any luck. He came through twice while I was painting myself and smoking up. Freddy didn't hold with the prayer parts. I figure they can't hurt, and besides, there wasn't much else to do.

Two hours after dark, one of Elmo John Deere's men knifed one of Simon Red Bulldozer's sons.

The delegation came for me about thirty minutes later.

I thought at first I might get my wish about killing something. But not tonight. They wanted me to arbitrate the judgement. Someone else would have to be executioner if he were needed.

"Watch the store, Freddy," I said, picking up my carbine.

I smoked while they talked. When Red Bulldozer's cousin got through, John Deere's grandfather spoke. The Bulldozer boy wasn't hurt too much, he wouldn't lose the arm. They brought the John Deere man before me. He glared at me across the smoke, and said not a word.

They summed up.

Then they all looked at me.

I took two more puffs, cleaned my pipe. Then I broke down my carbine, worked on the selector pin for a while. I lit my other pipe and pointed to the John Deere man.

"He lives," I said. "He was drunk."

They let him leave the lodge.

"Elmo John Deere," I said.

"Uhm?" asked fat Elmo.

"I think you should pay three mounts and ten plates to do this thing right. And give one man for three weeks to do the work of Simon Red Bulldozer's son."

Silence for a second, then Elmo spoke. "It is good what you say."

"Simon Red Bulldozer."

"Hmmm?"

"You should shake hands with Elmo John Deere and this should be the end of the matter."

"Good," he said.

They shook hands. Then each gave me a plate as soon as the others had left. One California and one New York. A 1993 and a '97. Not bad for twenty minutes' work.

It wasn't until I got back to the wrecker that I started shaking. That had been the first time I was arbiter. It could have made more bad trouble and turned hearts sour if I'd judged wrong.

"Hey, Fred!" I said. "Let's get real drunk and go see Wanda Hummingtires. They say she'll do it three ways all night."

She did, too.

The next dawn found us like a Karankawa coming across a new case of 30-weight oil. It was morning, quick. I ought to know. I watched that goddammed sun come up and I watched it go down, and every minute of the day in between, and I never moved from the spot. I forgot everything that went on around me, and I barely heard the women singing or the prayers of the other men.

At dusk, Freddy-in-the-Hollow let me back to the wrecker and I slept like a stone mother log for twelve hours with swirling violet dots in my head.

I had had no visions. Some people get them, some don't.

I woke with the mother of all headaches, but after I smoked awhile it went away. I wasn't a Puller, but I was in two of the races, one on foot and one in the Mercury.

I lost one and won the other.

I also won the side of beef in the morning shoot. Knocked the head off the bull with seven shots. Clean as a whistle.

At noon, everybody's life changed forever.

The first thing we saw was the cloud of dust coming over the third ridge. Then the outriders picked up the truck when it came over the second. It was coming too fast.

Strange Things in Close-Up

The truck stopped with a roar and a squeal of brakes. It had a long lumpy canvas cover on the back.

Then a woman climbed down from the cab. She was the most gorgeous woman I'd ever seen. And I'd seen Nellie Firestone two summers ago, so that was saying something.

Nellie hadn't come close to this girl. She had long straight black hair and a beautiful face from somewhere way back. She was built like nothing I'd seen before. She wore tight coveralls and had a .357 Magnum strapped to her hip.

"Who runs the Pulls?" she asked, in English, of the first man who reached her.

He didn't know what to do. Women never talk like that.

"Winston Mack Truck," said Freddy at my side, pointing.

"What do you mean?" asked one of the young men. "Why do you want to know?"

"Because I'm going to enter the Pull," she said.

Tribal language mumbles went around the circle. Very negative ones.

"Don't give me any of that shit," she said. "How many of you know of Alan Backhoe Shovel?"

He was another legend over in Ouachita River country.

"Well," she said, and held up a serial number plate from a backhoe tractor scoop, "I beat him last week."

"Hua, hua, hua!" the chanting started.

"What is your name, woman?" asked one of Mack Truck's men.

"Mary Margaret Road-Grader," she said, and glared back at him.

"Freddy," I said quietly, "put the money on her."

So we had a Council. You gotta have a council for everything, especially when honor and dignity and other manly virtues are involved.

Winston Mack Truck was pretty old, but he was still spry and had some muscles left on him. His head was a puckered lump because he had once crashed in a burner while raiding over on the Brazos. He only had one car, and it wasn't much of one.

But he did have respect, and he did have power, and he had more sons than anyone in the Nations, ten or eleven of them.

Mary Margaret Road-Grader

They were all there in Council, with all the heads of other families.

Winston Mack Truck smoked awhile, then called us to session.

Mary Margaret Road-Grader wasn't allowed inside the lodge. It seemed sort of stupid to me. If they wouldn't let her in here, they sure weren't going to let her enter the Pull. But I kept my tongue. You can never tell.

I was right. Old man Mack Truck can see clear through to tomorrow.

"Brothers," he said. "We have a problem here."

Hua Hua Hua

"We have been asked to let a woman enter the Pulls."

Silence.

"I do not know if it's a good thing," he continued. "But our brothers to the East have seen fit to let her do so. This woman claims to have defeated Alan Backhoe Shovel in fair contest. She enters this as proof."

He placed the serial plate in the center of the lodge.

"I will listen now," he said, and sat back, folding his arms.

They went around the circle then, some speaking, some waving away the opportunity.

It was Simon Red Bulldozer himself who changed the tone of the Council.

"I have never seen a woman in a Pull," he said. "Or in any contest other than those for women."

He paused. "But I have never wrestled against Alan Backhoe Shovel, either. I know of no one who has bested him. Now this woman claims to have done so. It would be interesting to see if she were a good Puller."

"You want a woman in the contest?!" asked Elmo, out of turn.

Richard Ford Pinto, the next speaker, stared at Elmo until John Deere realized his mistake. But Ford Pinto saved face for him by asking the same question of Simon.

"I would like to see if she is a good Puller," said Simon, adamantly. He would commit himself no further.

Then it was Elmo's turn.

"My brothers!" he began, so I figured he would be at it for a long time. "We seem to spend all our time in Council, rather than having fun like we should. It is not good, it makes my heart bitter.

"The idea that a woman can get a hearing at Council revolts me. Were this a young man not yet proven, or an Elder who had been given his Service feather, I would not object. But, brothers, this is a woman!" His voice came falsetto now, and he began to chant:

> "I have seen the dawn of bad days, brothers.
> But never worse than this.
> A woman enters our camp, brothers!
> A woman! A woman!"

He sat down and said no more in the conference.

It was my turn.

"Hear me, Pullers and Stealers!" I said. "You know me. I am a man of my word and a man of my deeds. As are you all. But the time has come for deeds alone. Words must be put away. We must decide whether a woman can be as good as a man. We cannot be afraid of a woman! Or can some of us be?"

They all howled and grumbled just like I wanted them to. You can't suggest men in Council are afraid of anything.

Of course, we voted to let her in the contest, like I knew we would.

Changes in history come easy, you know?

They pulled the small tractors first, the Ford 250s and the Honda Fieldmasters and such. I wasn't much interested in watching young boys fly through the air and hurt themselves. So me and Freddy wandered over where the big tractor men were warming up. The Karankawas were selling fuel from the old Houston refineries hand over hose. A couple of the Pullers had refused, like Elmo at first, to do anything with a woman in the contest.

But even Elmo was there watching when Mary Margaret Road-Grader unveiled her machine. There were lots of oohs and ahhs when she started pulling the tarp off that monster.

Nobody had seen one in years, except maybe as piles of rust on the roadside. It was long and low, and looked much like a yellow elephant's head with wheels stuck on the end of the trunk. The cab was high and shiny glass. Even the doors still worked. The blade was new and bright; it looked as if it had never been used.

The letters on the side were sharp and black, unfaded. Even the paint job was new. That made me suspicious about the Alan Backhoe Shovel contest. I took a gander at the towball while she was atop the cab unloosening the straps. It *was* worn. Either she had been lucky in the contest, or she'd had sense enough to put on a worn towball.

Everybody watched her unfold the tarp (one of those heavy smelly kind that can fall on you and kill you) but she had no helpers.

So I climbed up to give her a hand.

One of the women called out something and some others took it up. Most of the men just shook their heads.

There was a lot of screaming and hoorawing from the little Pulls, so I had to touch her on the shoulder to let her know I was up there.

She turned fast and her hand went for her gun before she saw it was me.

And I saw in her eyes not killer hate, but something else; I saw she was scared and afraid she'd have to kill someone.

"Let me help you with this," I said, pointing to the tarp.

She didn't say anything, but she didn't object, either.

"For a good judge," called out fat Elmo, "you have poor taste in women."

There was nothing I could do but keep busy while they laughed.

They still talk about that first afternoon, the one that was the beginning of the end.

First, Elmo John Deere hitched onto an IH 1200 and drug it over the line in about three seconds. No contest, and no one was surprised. Then Simon Red Bulldozer cranked up; his starter engine sounded like a beehive in a rainstorm. He hooked the chain on his towbar and revved up. The guy he was pulling against was a Paluxy River man named Theodore Bush Hog. He didn't hook up right. The chain came off as soon as Simon let go his clutches. So Bush Hog was disqualified. That was bad, too; there were some darkhorse bets on him.

Then it was the turn of Mary Margaret Road-Grader and

Strange Things in Close-Up

Elmo John Deere. Elmo had said at first he wasn't going to enter against her. Then they told him how much money was bet on him, and he couldn't afford to pass it up. Though the excuse he used was that somebody had to show this woman her place, and it might as well be him, first thing off.

You had to be there to see it. Mary Margaret whipped that roadgrader around like it was a Toyota, and backed it onto the field. She climbed down with motor running and hooked up. She was wearing tight blue coveralls and her hair was blowing in the river breeze. I thought she was the most beautiful woman I had ever seen. I didn't want her to get her heart broken.

But there was nothing I could do. It was all on her, now.

Elmo John Deere had one of his sons come out and hand the chain to him. He was showing he didn't want to be first to touch anything this woman had held.

He hooked up, and Mary Margaret Road-Grader signaled she was ready.

The judge dropped the pitchfork and they leaned on their gas feeds.

There was a jerk and a sharp clang, and the chain looked like a straight steel rod. Elmo gunned for all he had and the big tractor wheels began to turn slowly, and then they spun and caught and Elmo's Case tractor eased a few feet forward.

Mary Margaret never looked back (Elmo half turned in his seat; he was so good working the pedals and gears, he didn't need to look at them) and then she upshifted. The transmission on the yellow roadgrader screamed and lowered in tone.

I could hardly hear the machines for the yells and screams around me. They sounded like war yells. Some of the men were yelling in bloodlust at the woman. But I heard others cheering her, too. They seemed to want Elmo to lose.

He did.

Mary Margaret shifted again and her feet worked like pistons on the pedals. And as quickly as it had begun, it was over.

There was groaning noise, Elmo's wheels began to spin uselessly and in a second or two his tractor had been drug twenty feet across the line.

Elmo got down from his seat. Instead of congratulating the winner (an old custom) he turned and strode off the field. He signaled one of his sons to retrieve the vehicle.

Mary Margaret Road-Grader

Mary Margaret was checking the damage to her machine. Simon Red Bulldozer was next.

They had been pulling for twelve minutes when the contest was called by Winston Mack Truck himself. There was wonder on his face as he walked out to the two contestants. Nobody had ever seen anything like it.

The two had fought each other to a standstill. When they were stopped, Mary Margaret's grader was six or seven inches from its original position, but Simon's bulldozer had moved all over its side of the line. The ground was destroyed forever three feet each side of the line. It had been that close.

For the first time, there had been a tie.

Winston Mack Truck stopped before them. We were all whistling our approval when Simon Red Bulldozer held up his hand.

"Hear me, brothers, I will accept no share in honors. They must be all mine, or none at all."

Winston looked with his puckered face at Mary Margaret. She was breathing hard from working the levers, the wheel, the pedals.

She shrugged. "Fine with me."

Maybe I was the only one who knew she was acting tough for the crowd. I looked at her, but couldn't catch her eye.

"Listen, Fossil Creek People," said old Mack Truck. "This has been a draw. But Simon Red Bulldozer is not satisfied. And Mary Margaret Road-Grader has accepted. Tomorrow as the sun crosses the tops of the eastern trees, we will begin again. I have declared a fifth night and a sixth day to the Dance and Pulls."

Shouts of joy broke from the crowd. This had happened only once in my life, for some religious reason or other, and that was when I was a child. The Dance and Pulls were the only meeting of the year when all the Fossil Creek People came together. It was to have ended this night.

Now, we would have another day.

The cattle must have sensed this. You could hear them bellowing in fear even before the first of the butchers crossed the camp toward them, axe in hand.

"Where are you going?" asked Freddy as I picked up my carbine, boots and blanket.

"I think I will sleep with Mary Margaret Road-Grader," I said.

"Watch out," said Freddy. "I bet she makes love like she drives that machine."

First we had to talk.

She was ready to cry she was so tired. We were under the roadgrader; the tarp had been refolded over it. There was four feet of crawlspace between the trailer and the ground.

"You drive well. How did you learn?"

"From my brother, Donald Fork Lift. He once used one of these. And when I found this one . . ."

"Where? A museum? A tunnel? Of some . . ."

"An old museum, a strange one. It must have been sealed off before the Highway wars. I found it there a year ago."

"Why didn't your brother pull with this machine, here, instead of you?"

She was very quiet, and then she looked at me. "You are a man of your word? That must be true, or you would not have been called to judge, as I heard."

"That is true."

She sighed, flung her hair from her head with one hand. "He would have," she said, "except he broke his hip last month on a raid at Sand Creek. He was going to come. But since he had already taught me how to work it, I drove it instead."

"And first thing off you defeat Alan Backhoe Shovel?" She looked at me and frowned.

"I . . . I . . ."

"You made it up, didn't you?"

"Yes." She bit her lip.

"As I thought. But I have given my word. Only you and I will know. Where did you get the serial plates?"

"One of the machines in the same place where I found my grader. Only it was in worse shape. But its plate was still shiny. I took it the night before I left with the truck. I didn't think anybody would know what Alan Backhoe Shovel's real plate was."

"You are smart," I said. "You are also very brave, for a

woman, and foolish. You might have been killed. You may still be."

"Not if I win," she said, her eyes hard. "They couldn't afford to. If I lose, it would be another matter. I am sure I will be killed before I get to the Trinity. But I don't intend to lose."

They probably would like to kill her, some of them.

"No," I said. "I will escort you as near your people as I can. I have hunted the Trinity, but never as far as the Red. I can go with you past the old Fork of the Trinity."

She looked at me. "You're trying to get into my pants."

"Well, yes."

"Let's smoke first," she said. She opened a leather bag, rolled a parchment cigarette, lit it. I smelled the aroma of something I hadn't smoked in six moons.

It was the best dope I'd ever had, and that was saying something.

I don't know what we did afterwards, but it felt good.

"To the finish," said Winston Mack Truck and threw the pitchfork into the ground.

It was better than the day before—the bulldozer like a squat red monster and the roadgrader like avenging yellow death. On the first yank, Simon pulled the grader back three feet. The crowd went wild. His treads clawed at the dirt then, and the roadgrader lurched and regained three feet. Back and forth, the great clouds of black smoke whistling from the exhausts like the bellowing of bulls.

Then I saw what Simon was going to do. He wanted to wear the roadgrader down, keep a strain on it, keep gaining, lock himself, downshift. He would dog his way into the championship.

Yesterday he tried to finish the grader on might. It had not worked. Today he was taking his time.

He could afford to. The roadgrader was light in front; it had hardrubber tires instead of treads. When it lurched, the front end sometimes left the ground. If Simon timed it right, the grader wheels would rise while he downshifted and he could pull the yellow machine another few inches. And could continue to do so.

Mary Margaret was alternately working the pedals and levers, trying to get an angle on the squat red dozer. She was trying to pull across the back end of the tractor, not against it.

That would lose her the contest, I know. She was vulnerable. When the wheels were up, Simon could inch her back. The only time he lost ground was when he downshifted while the claws dug their way into the ground. Then he lost purchase for a second. Mary Margaret could maybe use that, if she were in a better position.

They pulled, they strained, but slowly Mary Margaret Road-Grader was losing to Simon Red Bulldozer.

Then she did something unexpected. She lurched the road-grader and dropped the blade.

The crowd went gonzo, then was silent. The shiny blade, which had been up yesterday, and so far today, dug into the ground.

The lurch gained her an inch or two. Simon, who never looked back either, knew something was wrong. He turned, and when his eyes left the panel, Mary Margaret jerked his bulldozer back another two feet.

We never thought in all those years we had heard about Simon Red Bulldozer that he would not have kept his blade in working order. He reached out to his blade lever and pulled it, and nothing happened. We saw him panic then, and the contest was going to Mary Margaret when . . .

The black plastic of the steering wheel showered up in her face. I heard the shot at the same time and dropped to the ground. I saw Mary Margaret holding her eyes with both hands.

Simon Red Bulldozer must not have heard the shot above the roaring of his engine, because he lurched the bulldozer ahead and started pulling the roadgrader back over the line.

It was Elmo John Deere doing the shooting. I had my carbine off my shoulder and was firing by the time I knew where to shoot.

Elmo was trying to kill Mary Margaret, he was still aiming and firing over my head from the hill above the pit. He must have been drunk. He had gone beyond the taboos of the People now. He was trying to kill an opponent who had bested him in a fair fight.

I shot him in the leg, just above the knee, and ended his pulling days forever. I aimed at his head, but he dropped his rifle and screamed so I didn't shoot him again. If I had, I would have killed him.

It took all the Fossil Creek People to keep his sons from killing me. There was a judgement, of course, and I was let go free.

That was the last Sun Dance they had. The Fossil Creek People separated. Elmo's people split off from them, and then went bitter crazy. The Fossil Creek People even steal from them, now, when they have anything worth stealing.

The Pulls ended, too. People said if they were going to cause so much blood, they could do without them. It was bad business. Some people stopped stealing machines and cars and plates, and started bartering for food and trading horses.

I wasn't going to get killed for anything that wouldn't go 150 kilometers per hour.

The old ways are dying. I have seen them come to an end in my time, and everything is getting worthless. People are getting lazy. There isn't anything worth doing. I sit on this hill over the Red River and smoke with Fred-in-the-Hollow and sometimes we get drunk.

Mary Margaret sometimes gets drunk with us.

She lost one of her eyes that day at the pulls. It was hit by splinters from the steering wheel. Me and Freddy took her back to her people in her truck. That was six years ago. Once, years ago, I went past the palace where we held the last Sun Dance. Her roadgrader was already a rustpile of junk with everything stripped off it.

I still love Mary Margaret Road-Grader, yes. She started things. Women have come into other ceremonies now, and in the Councils.

I still love Mary Margaret, but it's not the same love I had for her that day at the last Sun Dance, watching her work the pedals and the levers, her hair flying, her feet moving like birds across the cab.

I love her. She has grown a little fat. She loves me, though.

We have each other, we have the village, we have cattle, we have this hill over the river where we smoke and get drunk.

But the rest of the world has changed.

All this, all the old ways . . . gone.

Strange Things in Close-Up

The world has turned bitter and sour in my mouth. It is no good, the taste of ashes is in the wind. The old times are gone.

Introduction to
Save a Place in the Lifeboat for Me

This has the second strangest publishing history of any story of mine. I wrote it during that wonderful crazy time of '74-'75, sent it a bunch of places, then sold it to Steve Utley and George Proctor's Lone Star Universe *(an anthology of SF stories by Texas writers published in 1976 by a regional press, now defunct; if you see a copy you better buy it). Then they saw another story of mine and wanted it more. So a couple of years after I sold this one I got it back.*

About this time the late Tom Reamy (the most talented writer of all us Texans) moved to Kansas City and started Nickelodeon, *a beautifully printed semiprofessional magazine, famous, mostly, for its nude centerfolds of SF writers and fans. (The first issue featured Steve Utley.) Tom had heard me read this story at a convention and wanted it for his second issue. I gave it to him, since I'd exhausted all my other markets (Shayol had two in their inventory.) Nickelodeon # 2 came out at the World SF Convention on the same day as four other magazines with my stories in them. Yow!*

It has never been reprinted anywhere, except that Yoshio Kobayashi's now doing a translation of it for a Japanese rock and roll SF anthology called JEEZ!

(I have one regret about the story. Tom wanted more of the witty repartee between Leonard and Quackenbush. I went to sleep one night and dreamed, I don't know, maybe twenty lines of the funniest dialogue I'd ever heard in my life. I woke up falling out of bed laughing with tears running down my face. I grabbed a pencil. It all went away except for one line of it.)

Since this story was written, others have used the central event, most notably Jack Dann, Gardner Dozois and Mike Swanwick in their three-way collaboration "Touring." Among people my age there were three pivotal questions, the second and third of which were "Where were you when Kennedy was shot?" and "Where were you when we landed on the moon?" The first was "Where were you the Day the Music Died?"

Save a Place in the Lifeboat for Me

The hill was high and cold when they appeared there, and the first thing they did was to look around.

It had snowed the night before, and the ground was covered about a foot deep.

Arthur looked at Leonard and Leonard looked at Arthur.

"Whatsa matter you? You wearin' funny clothes again!" said Leonard.

Arthur listened, his mouth open. He reached down to the bulbhorn tucked in his belt.

Honk Honk went Arthur.

"Whatsa matter us?" asked Leonard. "Look ata us! We back inna vaudeville?"

Leonard was dressed in pants two sizes too small, and a jacket which didn't match. He wore a tiny pointed felt hat which stood on his head like a roof on a silo.

Arthur was dressed in a huge coat which dragged the ground, balloon pants, big shoes, and above his moppy red hair was a silk tophat, its crown broken out.

"It's a fine-a mess he's gots us in disa time!"

Arthur nodded agreement.

"Quackenbush, he's-a gonna hear about this!" said Leonard.

Honk Honk went Arthur.

The truck backed into the parking lot and ran into the car parked just inside the entrance. The glass panels which were being carried on the truck fell and shattered into thousands of slivers in the snowy street. Cars slushing down the early morning road swerved to avoid the pieces.

"Ohh, Bud, Bud!" said the short baby-faced man behind the

Strange Things in Close-Up

wheel. He was trying to back the truck over the glass and get it out of the way of the dodging cars.

A tall thin man with a rat's mustache ran from the glass company office and yelled at the driver.

"Look what you've done. Now you'll make me lose this job, too! Mr. Crabapple will . . ." He paused, looked at the little fat man, swallowed a few times.

"Uh . . . hello, Lou," he said, a tear running into his eye and brimming down his face. He turned away, pulled a handkerchief from his coveralls and wiped his eyes.

"Hello, Bud," said the little man, brightly. "I don' . . . don' . . . understand it either, Bud. But the man said we got something to do, and I came here to get you." He looked around him at the littered glass. "Bud, I been a *baaad* boy!"

"It doesn't matter, Lou," said Bud, climbing around to the passenger side of the truck. "Let's get going before somebody gets us arrested."

"Oh, Bud?" asked Lou, as they drove through the town. "Did you ever get out of your contract?"

"Yeah, Lou. Watch where you're going! Do I have to drive myself?"

They pulled out of Peoria at eight in the morning.

The two men beside the road were dressed in black suits and derby hats. They stood; one fat, the other thin. The rotund one put on a most pleasant face and smiled at the passing traffic. He lifted his thumb politely, as would a gentleman, and held it as each vehicle roared past.

When a car whizzed by, he politely tipped his hat.

The thin man looked distraught. He tried at first to strike the same pose as the larger man, but soon became flustered. He couldn't hold his thumb right, or let his arm droop too far.

"No, no, no, Stanley," said the larger, mustached man, as if he were talking to a child. "Let me show you the way a man of gentle breeding asks for a ride. Politely. Gently. Thus."

He struck the same pose he had before.

A car bore down on them doing eighty miles an hour. There was no chance in the world it would stop.

Stanley tried to strike the same pose. He checked himself

against the larger man's attitude. He found himself lacking. He rubbed his ears and looked as if he would cry.

The car roared past, whipping their hats off.

They bent to pick them up and bumped heads. They straightened, each signaling that the other should go ahead. They simultaneously bent and bumped heads again.

The large man stood stock still and did a slow burn. Stanley looked flustered. Their eyes were off each other. Then they both leaped for the hats and bumped heads once more.

They grabbed up the hats and jumped to their feet.

They had the wrong hats on. Stanley's derby made the larger man look like a tulip bulb. The large derby covered Stanley down to his chin. He looked like a thumbtack.

The large man grabbed the hat away and threw Stanley's derby to the ground.

MMMMMM-MMMMMM-MMMMM!" said the large man.

Stanley retrieved his hat. "But Ollie . . ." he said, then began whimpering. His hat was broken.

Suddenly Stanley pulled Ollie's hat off and stomped it. Ollie did another slow burn, then turned and ripped off Stanley's tie.

Stanley kicked Ollie in the shin. The large man jumped around and punched Stanley in the kneecap.

A car stopped, and the driver jumped out to see what the trouble was.

Ollie kicked *him* in the shin. *He* ripped off Stanley's coat.

A woman pulled over and slammed into the man's parked car. He ran over and kicked out her headlight. Stanley threw a rock through *his* windshield.

Twenty minutes later, Stanley and Ollie were looking down from a hill. A thousand people were milling around on the turnpike below, tearing each other's cars to pieces. Parts of trucks and motorcycles littered the roadway. The two watched a policeman pull up. He jumped out and yelled through a bullhorn to the people, too far away for the two men to hear what he said.

As one, the crowd jumped him, and pieces of police car began to bounce off the blacktop.

Ollie dusted off his clothing as meticulously as possible. His

Strange Things in Close-Up

and Stanley's clothes consisted of torn underwear and crushed derby hats.

"That's another fine mess you've gotten us in, Stanley," he said. He looked north.

"And it looks like it shall soon snow. Mmmm-mmmm-mmmm!"

They went over the hill as the wail of sirens began to fill the air.

"Hello, a-Central, givva me Heaven. ETcumspiri 220."

The switchboard hummed and crackled. Sparks leaped off the receiver of the public phone booth in the roadside park. Arthur did a back flip and jumped behind a trash can.

The sun was out, though snow was still on the ground. It was a cold February day, and they were the only people in the park.

The noise died down at the other end and Leonard said:

"Hallo, Boss! Hey, Boss! We doin'-a like you tell us, but you no send us to the right place. You no send us to Iowa. You send us to Idaho, where they grow the patooties."

Arthur came up beside his brother and listened. He honked his horn.

On the other end of the line, Rufus T. Quackenbush spoke:

"Is that a goose with you, or do you have a cold?"

"Oh, no, Boss. You funnin'-a me. That's-a Bagatelle."

"Then who are you?" asked Quackenbush.

"Oh, you know who this is. I gives you three guesses."

"Three guesses, huh? Hmmmm, let's see . . . you're not Babe Ruth, are you?"

"Hah, Boss. Babe Ruth, that's-a chocolate bar."

"Hmmm. You're not Demosthenes, are you?"

"Nah, Boss. Demosthenes can do is bend in the middle of your leg."

"I should have known," said Quackenbush. "This is Rampolini, isn't it?"

"You got it, Boss."

Arthur whistled and clapped his hands in the background.

"Is that a hamster with you, Rampolini?"

"Do-a hamsters whistle, Boss?"

"Only when brought to a boil," said Quackenbush.

"Ahh, you too good-a for me, Boss!"

Save a Place in the Lifeboat for Me

"I know. And if I weren't too good for you, I wouldn't be good enough for anybody. Which is more than I can say for you."

"Did-a we wake you up, Boss?"

"No, to be perfectly honest, I had to get up to answer the phone anyway. What do you want?"

"Like I said, Boss Man, you put us inna wrong place. We no inna Iowa. We inna Idaho."

"That's out of the Bronx, isn't it? What should I do about it?"

"Well-a, we don't know. Even if-a we did, we know we can't-a do it anyway, because we ain't there. An if-a we was, we couldn't get it done no ways."

"How do you know that?"

"Did-a you ever see one of our pictures, Boss?"

There was a pause. "I see what you mean," said Quackenbush.

"Why for you send-a us, anyway? We was-a sleep, an then we inna Idaho!"

"I looked at my calendar this morning. One of the dates was circled. And it didn't have pits, either. Anyway, I just remembered that something very important shouldn't take place today."

"What's-a that got to do with us two?"

"Well . . . I know it's a little late, but I really would appreciate it if you two could manage to stop it."

"What's-a gonna happen if we don't?"

"Uh, ha ha. Oh, small thing, really. The Universe'll come to an end several million years too soon. A nice boy like you wouldn't want that, would you? Of course not!"

"What for I care the Universe'll come to an end? We-a work for Paramount."

"No, no. Not the studio. The big one!"

"M-a GM?"

"No. The Universe. All that stuff out there. Look around you."

"You mean-a Idaho?"

"No, no, Rampolini. Everything will end soon, too soon. You may not be concerned. A couple of million years is nothing to somebody like you. But what about me? I'm leasing this office, you know?"

"Why-a us?"

"I should have sent someone earlier, but I've . . . I've been so terrible busy. I was having a pedicure, you see, and the time just *flew* by."

"What-a do the two of us do to-a stop this?"

"Oh, I just know you'll think of something. And you'll both be happy to know I'm sending you lots of help."

"Is this help any good, Boss?"

"I don't know if they're any good," said Quackenbush. "But they're cheap."

"What-a we do inna meantime?"

"Be mean, like everybody else."

"Nah, nah. (That's-a really good one, Boss.) I mean, about-a the thing?"

"Well, I'd suggest you get to Iowa. Then give me another call."

"But what iffa you no there?"

"Well, my secretary will take the message."

"Ah, Boss, if-a you no there, you're secretary's-a no gonna be there neither."

"Hmmm. I guess you're right. Well, why don't you give me the message now, and I'll give it to my secretary. Then I'll give her the answer, and she can call you when you get to Iowa!"

"Hey, that's-a good idea, Boss!"

"I thought you'd think so."

Outside the phone booth, Arthur was lolling his tongue out and banging his head with the side of his hand, trying to keep up with the conversation.

There were two lumps of snow beside the highway. The snow shook itself, and Stan and Ollie stepped out of it.

"Brr," said Ollie. "Stanley, we must get to some shelter soon."

"But I don't know where any is, Ollie!"

"This is all your fault, Stanley. It's up to you to find us some clothing and a cheery fireside."

"But Ollie, I didn't have any idea we'd end up like this."

Ollie shivered. "I suppose you're right, Stanley. It's not your fault we're here."

Save a Place in the Lifeboat for Me

"I don't even remember what we were doing before we were on that road this morning, Ollie. Where have you been lately?"

"Oh . . . don't you remember, Stanley?"

"Not very well, Ollie."

"Oh," said Ollie. He looked very tired, very suddenly. "It's very strange, but neither do I, Stanley."

The cold was forgotten then, and they were fully clothed in their black suits and derbys. They thought nothing of it, because they were thinking of something else.

"I suppose now we shall really have to hurry and find a ride, Stanley."

"I know," said the thin man. "We have to go to Iowa."

"Yes," said Ollie, "and our wives will be none the wiser."

The Iowa they headed for was pulling itself from under a snowstorm which had dumped eleven inches in the last two days. It was bitterly cold there. Crew-cut boys shoveled snow off walks and new '59 cars so their fathers could get to work. It was almost impossible. Snowplows had been out all night, and many of them were stalled. The National Guard had been called out in some sections and was feeding livestock and rescuing stranded motorists. It was not a day for travel.

At noon, the small town of Cedar Oaks was barely functioning. The gleaming sun brought no heat. But the town stirred inside, underneath the snows which sagged the roofs.

The *All-Star Caravan* was in town that day. The teenagers had prayed and hoped that the weather would break during the two days of ice. The *Caravan* was a rock 'n' roll show that traveled around the country, doing one-night stands.

The show had been advertised for a month: All the businesses around the two high schools and junior highs were covered with the blazing orange posters. They had been since New Year's Day.

So the kids waited, and built up hopes for it, and almost had them dashed as the weather had closed in.

But Mary Ann Pickett's mother, who worked the night desk at the Holiday Inn, had called her daughter at eleven the night before: The *All-Star Caravan* had landed at the airport in the clearing night, and all the singers had checked in.

Mary Ann asked her mother, "What does Donny Bottoms look like?"

Strange Things in Close-Up

Her mother didn't know. They were all different-looking, and she wasn't familiar with the singer anyway.

Five minutes after Mary Ann rang off, the word was spreading over Cedar Oaks. The *All-Star Caravan* was there. Now it could snow forever. Maybe if it did, they would have to stay there, rather than start their USO tour of Alaska.

Bud and Lou slid and slipped their way over the snows in the truck.

"Watch where you're going!" said Bud. "Do you have anything to eat?"

"I got some cheese crackers and some Life Savers, Bud. But we'll have to divide them, because . . ." His voice took on a little-boy petulance ". . . because I haven't had anything to eat in a long time, Bud."

"Okay, okay. We'll share. Give me half the cheese crackers. You take these."

Lou was trying to drive. There was a munching sound.

"Some friend you are," said Bud. "You have two cheese crackers and I don't have any."

Lou coughed. "But, Bud! I just *gave* you two cheese crackers?"

"Do I look like I have any cheese crackers?" asked Bud, wiping crumbs from his chin.

"Okay," said Lou. "Have this cheese cracker, Bud. Because you're my friend, and I want to share."

Again, the sound of eating filled the cab.

"Look, Lou. I don't mind you having all the Life Savers, but can't you give me half your cheese cracker?"

Lou puffed out his cheeks while watching the road. "But, Bud! I just gave you *three* cheese crackers!"

"Some friend," said Bud, looking at the snowbound landscape. "He has a cheese cracker and won't share with his only friend."

"Okay! Okay!" said Lou. "Take half this cheese cracker! Take it!"

He drove on.

"Boy . . . ," said Bud.

Lou took the whole roll of Life Savers and stuffed them in his mouth, paper and all. He began to choke.

144

Save a Place in the Lifeboat for Me

Bud began beating him on the back. The truck swerved across the road, then back on. They continued toward Cedar Oaks, Iowa.

There were giants in the *All-Star Caravan*. Donny Bottoms, from Amarillo, Texas; his backup group, the Mosquitoes, most from Amarillo Cooper High School, his old classmates. Then there was Val Ritchie, who'd had one fantastic hit song, which had a beat and created a world all the teenagers wanted to escape to.

The third act, biggest among many more, was a middle-aged man, calling himself The Large Charge. His act was strange, even among that set. He performed with a guitar and a telephone. He pretended to be talking to a girl on the other end of the line. It was billed as a comedy act. Everybody knew what was really involved—The Large Charge was rock 'n' roll's first dirty old man. His real name was Elmo Simpson and he came from Bridge City, Texas.

Others on the bill included the Pipettes, three guys and two girls from Stuttgart, Arkansas who up until three months ago had sung only at church socials; Jimmy Wailon, who was having a hard time deciding whether to sing "Blue Suede Shoes" for the hundredth time, or strike out into country music where the real money was. Plus the Champagnes, who'd had a hit song three years before, and Rip Dover, the show's M.C.

The *All-Star Caravan* was the biggest thing that had happened to Cedar Oaks since Bill Haley and the Comets came through a year and a half ago, and one of Haley's road men had been arrested for DWI.

"What's-a matter us?" asked Leonard for the fiftieth time that morning. "We really no talka like dis! We was-a grown up mens, with jobs and-a everything."

Whonka whonka went Arthur sadly, as they walked through the town of Friedersville, Idaho.

Arthur stopped dead, then put his hands in his pockets and began whistling. There was a police car at the corner. It turned onto the road where they walked. And slowed.

Leonard nonchalantly tipped his pointy felt hat forward and put his hands in his pockets.

Strange Things in Close-Up

The cop car stopped.

The two ran into the nearest store. *Hadley's Music Shop*.

Arthur ran around behind a set of drums and hid. Leonard sat down at a piano and began to play with one finger, "You've Taught Me a New Kind of Love."

The store manager came from the back room and leaned against the doorjamb, listening.

Arthur saw a harp in the corner, ran to it and began to play. He joined in the song with Leonard.

The two cops came in and watched them play. Leonard was playing with his foot and nose. Arthur was plucking the harp strings with his teeth.

The police shrugged and left.

"Boy, I'm-a tellin' you," said Leonard, as he waited for the cops to turn the corner. "Quackenbush, he's-a messed up dis-a time! Why we gots to do this?" With one hand he was wiping his face, and with the other he was playing as he never had before.

Donny Bottoms was a scrawny-looking kid from West Texas. He didn't stand out in a crowd, unless you knew where to look. He had a long neck and an Adam's apple that stuck out of his collar. He was twenty-four years old and still had acne. But he was one of the hottest new singers around, and the *All-Star Caravan* was going to be his last road tour for a while. He'd just married his high school sweetheart, a girl named Dottie, and he had not really wanted to come on the tour without her. But she was finishing nurse's training and could not leave. At two in the afternoon, he and the other members of the *Caravan* were trying the sound in the Municipal Auditorium.

He and the Mosquitoes ran through a couple of their numbers. Bottoms' style was unique, even in a field as wild and novelty-eating as rock 'n' roll. It had a good boogie beat, but Bottoms worked hard with the music, and the Mosquitoes were really good. They turned out a good synthesis of primitive and sophisticated styles.

The main thing they had for them was Donny's voice. It was high and nasal when he talked, but, singing, that all went away. He had a good range, and he did strange things with his throat.

Save a Place in the Lifeboat for Me

A critic once said that he dry-humped every syllable till it begged for mercy.

Val Ritchie had one thing he did well, exactly one: that was a song called "Los Niños." He'd taken an old Mexican folk song, got a drummer to beat hell out of a conga, and yelled the words over his own screaming guitar.

It was all he did well. He did some of other people's standards, and some Everly Brothers' stuff by himself, but he always finished his set with "Los Niños" and it always brought the house down and had them dancing in the aisles.

He was the next-to-last act before Bottoms and the Mosquitoes.

He was a tough act to follow.

But he was always on right before The Large Charge, and *he* was the toughest act in rock 'n' roll.

They had turned the auditorium upside down and had finally found a church key to open a beer for The Large Charge.

Elmo Simpson was dressed, at the sound rehearsal, in a pair of baggy pants, a checked cowboy shirt, and a string tie with a Texas-shaped tieclasp. Tonight, on stage, he would be wearing the same thing.

Elmo's sound rehearsal consisted of chinging away a few chords, doing the first two bars of "Jailhouse Rock" and then going into his dirty-old-man voice.

His song was called "Hello, Baby!" and he used a prop telephone. He ran through the first two verses, which were him talking in a cultured, decadent nasty voice, and he had the sound man rolling in his control chair before he finished.

Elmo sweated like a hog. He'd been doing this act for two years, he'd even had to lip-synch in on Dick Clark's "American Bandstand" a couple of times. He was still nervous, though he could do the routine in his sleep. He was always nervous. He was in his late thirties. Fame had come late to him, and he couldn't believe it. So he was still nervous.

Bud and Lou were hurrying west in the panel truck, through snowslides, slush and stalled cars.

Stan and Ollie had hitched a ride on a Mayflower moving

van, against all that company's policies, and were speeding toward Cedar Oaks from the south-southeast.

Leonard and Arthur, alias Rampolini and Bagatelle, were leaving an Idaho airport in a converted crop duster which hadn't been flown since the end of the Korean War. It happened like this.

"We gots to find us a pilot-a to fly us where the Boss wants us," said Leonard, as they ran onto a small municipal field.

Whonk? asked Arthur.

"We's gots to find us a pilot, pilot."

Arthur pulled a saber from the fold of his coat, and putting a black poker chip over his eye, began swordfighting his shadow.

"Notta pirate. Pilot! A man whatsa flies in the aeroplanes," said Leonard.

A man in coveralls, wearing a WWII surplus aviator's cloth helmet, walked from the operations room.

"There's-a one now!" said Leonard. "What's about we gets him?"

Without a honk, Arthur ran and tackled the flyer.

"What the hell's the matter with him?" asked the man as Arthur grinned and smiled and pointed.

"You gots to-a excuse him," said Leonard, pulling his tophatted brother off him. "He's-a taken too many vitsamins."

"Well, keep him away from me!" said the flyer.

"We's a gots you a prepositions," said Leonard, conspiratorially.

"What?"

"A prepositions. You fly-a us to Iowa, anda we no break-a you arms."

"What's going on? Is this some kind of gag?"

"No, it's-a my brother. He's a very dangerous man. Show him how dangerous you are, Bagatelle."

Arthur popped his eyes out, squinted his face up into a million rolls of flesh, flared his nostrils and snorted at each breath.

"Keep him away from me!" said the man. "You oughtn't to let him out on the streets."

"He's-a no listen to me, Bagatelle. Get tough with him."

Arthur hunched his shoulders, intensified his breathing, stepped up into the pilot's face.

Save a Place in the Lifeboat for Me

"No, that's-a no tough enough. Get really tough with him."

Arthur squnched over, stood on tiptoe, flared his nostrils until they filled all his face except for the eyes, panted, and passed out for lack of breath.

The pilot ran across the field and into a hangar.

"Hey, wake-a up!" said Leonard. "He's-a getting the plane ready. Let's-a go."

When they got there, the pilot was warming the crop duster up for a preflight check.

Arthur climbed in the aft cockpit, grabbed the stick, started jumping up and down.

"Hey! Get outta there!" yelled the pilot. "I'm gonna call the cops!"

"Hey, Bagatelle. Get-a tough with him again!"

Leonard was climbing into the forward cockpit. Arthur started to get up. His knees hit the controls. The plane lurched.

Leonard fell into the cockpit head first, his feet sticking out.

Arthur sat back down and laughed. He pulled the throttle.

The pilot just had time to open the hangar door before the plane roared out, plowed through a snowbank, ricocheted back onto the field and took off.

It was heading east toward Iowa.

At three in the afternoon, the rehearsals over, most of the entertainers were back in their rooms at the Holiday Inn. Already the hotel detective had had to chase out several dozen girls and boys who had been roaming up and down the halls looking for members of the *All-Star Caravan*.

Some of them found Jimmy Wailon in the corridor and were getting his autograph. He had been on the way down the hall, going to meet one of the lady reservation clerks.

"Two of yours is worth one Large Charge," said one of the girls as he signed her scrapbook.

"What's that?" he asked, his eyes twinkling. He pushed his cowlick out of his eyes.

"Two of your autographs are worth one of Donny's," she said.

"Oh," he said. "That's nice." He scribbled his usual "With Best Wishes to My Friend . . . ," then asked, "What's the name, honey?"

Strange Things in Close-Up

"Sarah Sue," she said. "And please put the date."

"Sure will, baby. How old are you?"

"I'm eighteen!" she said. All her friends giggled.

"Sure," he said. "There go!"

He hurried off to the room the lady reservation clerk had gotten for them.

"Did you hear that?" the girl asked behind him as he disappeared around the corner. "He called me 'honey.'"

Jimmy Wailon was smiling long before he got to Room 112.

Elmo was sitting in Donny's room with three of the Mosquitoes. Donny had gone to a phone booth to call his wife collect rather than put up with the noise in the room.

"Have another beer, Elmo?" asked Skeeter, the head Mosquito.

"Naw, thanks, Skeeter," he said. "I won't be worth a diddly-shit if I do." Already, Elmo was sweating profusely at the thought of another performance.

"I'll sure be glad when we get on that tour," he continued, after a pause. "Though it'll be colder than a monkey's ass."

"Yeh," said Skeeter. They were watching television. "The Millionaire," the daytime reruns, and John Beresford Tipton was telling Mike what to do with the money with his usual corncob-up-the-butt humour. Skeeter was highly interested in the show. He'd had arguments with people many times about whether the show was real or not, or based on some real person. He was sure somewhere there was a John Beresford Tipton, and a Silverstone, and that one of those checks had his name on it.

"Look at that, will you?" asked Skeeter a few minutes later. "He's giving it to a guy whose kid is dying."

But Elmo Simpson, The Large Charge, from Bridge City, Texas, was lying on his back, fast asleep. Snores began to form inside his mouth, and every few minutes, one would escape.

Donny talked to his wife over the phone out in the motel lobby. They told each other how much they missed each other, and Donny asked about the new record of his coming out this week, and Dottie said she wished he'd come home soon rather than going on the tour, and they told each other they loved each other, and he hung up.

Save a Place in the Lifeboat for Me

Val Ritchie was sitting in a drugstore just down the street, eating a chocolate sundae and wishing he were home. Instead of going to do a show tonight, then fly with one or another load of musicians off to Alaska for two weeks for the USO.

He was wearing some of his old clothes and looked out of place in the booth. He thought most northern people overdressed anyway, even kids going to school. *I mean, like they were all ready for church or Uncle Fred's funeral.*

He hadn't been recognized yet, and wouldn't be. He always looked like a twenty-year-old garage mechanic on a coffee break.

Bud and Lou swerved to avoid a snowdrift. They had turned onto the giant highway a few miles back and had it almost to themselves. Ice glistened everywhere in the late afternoon sun, blindingly. Soon the sun would fall and it would become pitch black outside.

"How much further is it, Bud?" asked Lou. His stomach was growling.

"I don't know. It's around here somewhere. I'm just following what's-his-name's orders."

"Why doesn't he give better orders, Bud?"

"Because he never worked for Universal."

Stan and Ollie did not know what was happening when the doors of the moving van opened and carpets started dropping off the tops of the racks.

Then the van slammed into another vehicle. They felt it through the sides of the truck.

The driver was already out. He was walking toward a small truck with two men in it.

Stan and Ollie climbed out of the back of the Mayflower truck and saw who the other two were.

The four regarded each other, and the truck driver surveyed the damage to the carpets, which was minor.

They helped him load the truck back up, then Stan and Ollie climbed in the small van with Bud and Lou.

"I wonder what Quackenbush is up to now?" asked Bud, as he scrunched himself up with the others. With Lou and Ollie taking up so much room, he and Stan had to share a space hardly big enough for a lap dog. Somehow, they managed.

Strange Things in Close-Up

"I really don't know," said Ollie. "He seems quite intent on keeping this thing from happening."

"But, why us, Bud?" asked Lou. "We been *good* boys since . . . well, we been good boys. He could have sent so many others."

"That's quite all right with me," said Stanley. "He didn't seem to want just *anybody* for this."

"I don't know about you two, but Lou and I were sent from Peoria. That's a long way. What's this guy got against us?"

"Well, there's actually no telling," said Stanley. "Ollie and I have been traveling all day, haven't we, Ollie?"

"Quite right, Stanley."

"But what I don't get," said Bud, working at his pencil-thin mustache, "is that I remember when all this happened the first time."

"So do I," said Stanley.

"But not us two," said Lou, indicating Ollie and himself, and trying to keep the truck on the road.

"Well, that's because you two had . . . had . . . left before them. But that doesn't matter. What matters is that he sent us back here to . . . Come to think of it, I don't understand, either."

"Or me," said Lou.

"Quackenbush moves in mysterious ways," said Bud.

"Right you are," said Stan.

"Mmmm Mmmmm Mmmmm," said Ollie.

By the time they saw they were in the air they also realized the pilot wasn't aboard.

Leonard was still stuck upside down in the forward cockpit. Arthur managed to fly the plane straight while his brother crawled out and sat upright.

Looping and swirling, they flew on through the late afternoon toward Cedar Oaks.

The line started forming in front of the doors of the civic auditorium at five, though it was still bitterly cold.

The manager looked outside at 5:15. It was just dark, and there must be a hundred and fifty kids out there already, tickets in hand. He hadn't been at the sound rehearsal and hadn't seen the performers. All he knew was what he heard about them:

they were the hottest rock and roll musicians since Elvis Presley and Chuck Berry.

The show went on at 7 P.M. as advertised, and it was a complete sellout. The crowd was ready, and when Rip Dover introduced the Champagnes, the people yelled and screamed even at their tired *doo-wah* act.

Then came Wailon, and they were polite for him, except that they kept yelling "Rock 'n' roll! Rock 'n' roll!" and he kept singing "Young Love" and the like.

Then other acts, then Val Ritchie, who jogged his way through several standards and launched into "Los Niños." He tore the place apart. They wouldn't let him go, they were dancing in the aisles. He did "Los Niños" until he was hoarse. They dropped the spots on him, finally, and the kids quit screaming. It got quiet. Then there was the sound of a mike being turned on and a voice, greasy in the magnificence, filled the hall:

"Helloooooooooooo, baby!"

It was long past dark, and the truck swerved down the road, the forms of Stan, Ollie, Bud and Lou illuminated by the dome light. Bud had a map unfolded in front of the windshield and Ollie's arms were in Lou's way.

"It's here somewhere," said Bud. "I know it's here somewhere!"

Overhead was the whining, droning sound of an old aeroplane, sometimes close to the ground, sometimes far above. Every once in a while was a yell of "Watch-a yourself! Watcha where you go!" and a *whonk whonk*.

The truck below passed a sign which said:

WELCOME TO CEDAR OAKS
Speed Limit 30 MPH

After The Large Charge hung up the telephone receiver, and they let him offstage to thunderous ovation, the back curtain parted and there were Donny Bottoms and the Mosquitoes.

And the first song they sang was "Dottie," the song Bottoms had written for his wife while they were still high school sweethearts. Then "Roller Coaster Days" and "Miss America" and all his classics. And the crowd went crazy and . . .

Strange Things in Close-Up

The truck roared in the snowy, jampacked parking lot of the auditorium, skidded sideways, wiped out a '57 cherry-red Merc and punched out the moon window of a T-Bird. The cops on parking lot duty ran toward the wreck.

Halfway there, they jumped under other cars to get away from the noise.

The noise was that of an airplane going to crash very soon, very close.

At the last second, the sound stopped.

The cops looked up.

An old biplane was sitting still in a parking space in the lot, its propeller still spinning. Two guys in funny clothes were climbing down from it, one whistling and *honking* to the other, who was trying to get a pointy hat off his ears.

The doors of the truck which had crashed opened, and four guys tumbled out all over each other.

They ran toward the auditorium, and the two from the plane saw them and whistled and ran toward them. They joined halfway across the lot, the six of them, and ran toward the civic hall.

The police were running for them like a berserk football team and then . . .

The auditorium doors were thrown open by the ushers, lances of light gleamed out on the snow and parked cars, and the mob spilled out onto the concrete and snow, laughing, yelling, pushing, shoving in an effort to get home.

The six running figures melted into the oncoming throng, the police right behind them.

Above the cop whistles and the mob noise was an occasional "Ollie, oh, Ollie!" or "Hey, Bud! Hey, Bud!" or *whonk whonk* and . . .

The six made it into the auditorium as the maintenance men were turning out the lights, and they ran up to the manager's office and inside.

The thin manager was watching TV. He looked up to the six, and thought it must be some sort of a publicity stunt.

On TV came the theme music of "You Bet Your Duck."

"It's-a Quackenbush!" said Leonard.

Save a Place in the Lifeboat for Me

The TV show host looked up from his rostrum. "Hi, folks. And tonight what's the secret woids?" Here a large merganser puppet flopped down and the audience applauded. The show host turned the word card around and lifted his eyebrows, looked at the screen and said:

"That's right. Tonight, the woids are Inexorable Fate. I knew I should've hired someone else. You guys are too late."

Then he turned to the announcer and asked, "George, who's our first guest?" as the duck was pulled back overhead on its strings.

The six men tore from the office and out to the parking lot, through the last of the mob. Stan, Ollie, Bud and Lou jumped in the truck which a wrecker attendant was just connecting to a winch, right under the nose of the astonished police chief.

Arthur and Leonard, whistling and yelling, jumped in the plane, backed it out, and took off after circling the crowded parking lot. They rose into the air to many a loud scream.

The truck and plane headed for the airport.

The crowd was milling about the airport fence. Inside the barrier, musicians waited to get aboard a DC–3, their instrument cases scattered about the concourse.

The truck with four men in it crashed through the fence, strewing wire and posts to the sides.

It twisted around on its wheels, skidded sideways, almost hitting the musicians, and came to a halt. The four looked like the Keystone Firemen as they climbed out.

There was a roar in the air, and the biplane came out of the runway lights, landed and taxied to a stop less than an inch from the nose of the passenger plane.

"We not-a too late! We not-a too late!" yelled Leonard, as he climbed down. "Arthur, get tough with-a that plane. Don't let it take off!"

Arthur climbed to the front of the crop duster and repeated the facial expressions he'd gone through earlier with the pilot. This time at the frightened pilot of the DC–3, through the windshield.

Leonard, Bud, Lou, Stan and Ollie ran to the musicians and found Wailon.

"Where's Bottoms?" asked Bud.

"Huh?" asked Jimmy Wailon, still a little distraught by the skidding truck and the aeroplane. "Bottoms? Bottoms left on the first plane."

"The first plane?" asked Ollie. "The first aeroplane?"

"Uh, yeah. Simpson and Ritchie were already on. Donny wanted to wait for this one, but I gave him my seat. I'm waiting for someone." He looked at them; they had not moved. "I gave him my seat on the first plane," he said. Then he looked them over in the dim lights. "You friends of his?"

"No," said Stanley, "but I'm sure we'll be seeing him again very soon."

Overhead, the plane which had taken off a few minutes before circled and headed northwest for Alaska.

They listened to it fade in the distance.

Whonk went Arthur.

They drove back through the dark February night, all six of them jammed into the seat and the small back compartment. After they heard the news for the first time, they turned the radio down and talked about the old days.

"This fellow Quackenbush," asked Ollie. "Is he in the habit of doing things such as this?"

"Ah, the Boss? There's-a no tellin' what the boss man willa do!"

"He must not be a *nice* man," said Lou.

"Oh, he's probably all right," said Bud. "He just has a mind like a producer."

"A contradiction in terms," said Stanley.

"You're *so* right," said Ollie.

"Pardon me," said the hitchhiker for whom they stopped. "Could you fellows find it in your hearts to give me a ride? I feel a bit weary after the affairs of the day, and should like to nestle in the arms of Morpheus for a short while."

"Sure," said Lou. "Hop in."

"Ah yes," said the rotund hitchhiker in the beaver hat. "Been chasing about the interior of this state all day. Some fool errand, yes indeed. Reminds me of the time on safari in Afghanistan . . ." He looked at the six men, leaned forward, tapping a deck of cards with his gloved hands. "Would any of you gentlemen be interested in a little game of chance?"

"No thanks," said Bud. "You wouldn't like the way I play."

They drove through the night. They didn't need to stop for the next hitchhiker, because they knew him. They saw him in the headlights, on the railroad tracks beside the road. He was kicking a broken-down locomotive. He came down the embankment, stood beside the road as they bore down on him.

He was dressed in a straw hat, a vest and a pair of tight pants. He wore the same countenance all the time, a great stone face.

The truck came roaring down on him, and was even with him, and was almost by, when he reached out with one hand and grabbed the back door handle and with the other clamped his straw hat to his head.

His feet flew up off the pavement and for a second he was parallel to the ground, then he pulled himself into the spare tire holder and curled up asleep.

He had never changed expression.

Over the hill went the eight men, some of them talking, some dozing, toward the dawn. Just before the truck went out of sight there was a sound, so high, so thin it did not carry well.

It went *honk honk*.

Introduction to
Horror, We Got

In 1980 I was the only male on a feminist and female SF writers' panel (John Varley wasn't available). The subject came around to "Are there story ideas you get you won't write because they're against Sisterhood, or politically incorrect or down on women or whatever?"

It came to my turn to respond, and since I was the wrong gender, I brought this story up as an example of how sometimes you just have to write the damned story, no matter what, because if you don't, it will drive you crazy.

I wrote this in July of 1978, and had to drive 800 miles to a convention in St Louis with the last five pages unwritten. I fought my way through the worst traffic jam in the city's history, got to the hotel (without a room) at 5 P.M. I was scheduled to read at 6:30. I went to some friends' room (they were having an argument) and finished, ran downstairs and read this to an audience of which maybe five of the two hundred people knew who I was.

Ed Bryant was watching. He said for the first ten minutes it was like watching the audience in Mel Brooks' The Producers *watching* Springtime for Hitler. *It was real quiet in the place, folks. I kept reading and waiting for the lights to be eclipsed by a lazily tumbling brick or two. Then people slowly caught on, and they ended up applauding.*

The idea came to me while reading a lot of right-wing, racist paranoid conspiracy newspapers (there are such things; in the seventies they were fringe material, now they're a major party's platform). I began to wonder what it would be like if all that stuff were real, and . . . well, the story drove me crazy.

Pat and Arnie weren't at the convention, but their friends were, and when I got home on Tuesday there was a letter waiting that said "Instead of giving yourself grief for three or

Horror, We Got

four years trying to sell this to people who can't *buy it, send it to Shayol." I did.*

I can only add by way of warning that A Short History of Anti-Semitism *is a three-volume work.*

Horror, We Got

Even as *shtetls* go, this one wasn't much.

Then again, not very much of anything in this section of Poland in 1881 c.e. is much, either. One side of the Pale is pretty much like the other.

So here I am on this nice day before Passover, and I'm waiting beside the road dressed as a scissors grinder. Behind me are a bunch of thrown-together huts, oddments of housing. Down the street is the synagogue, the town house and such.

In my long coat is a machine pistol of a kind which won't be invented for another twelve years. I like it because there's something classic-looking in its design. It has levers and bars extending out all over it like there's a mechanical spider trapped inside trying to get out.

There are no other people outside here. There's plenty good reason for that.

Up the road a few hundred years is a column of the 2nd Imperial Cossacks, dressed in their finery. Coming this way. Red and black uniforms, standardbearers carrying the Imperial double-headed eagle banner. They're bundled against the cold, all bristles of mustache and *shakos*. Behind come row on row on row of lances. Across their shoulders are rifles. Horses' breaths steam and seethe in the morning sunlight. They're passing through on their way to restation the garrison at Zmlenye. A nice quiet ride of fifty kilometers or so through *zhid* country. Boring indeed.

Well, up to a point. As the standards go by, I bow pretty much like a *shtetl* Jew is supposed to. As I come up from the bow, I see eyes peering from all the windows and closed shutters across the way. The inhabitants are frightened, but still curious enough to look out as the sound of the dreaded hoofbeats go through their pitiful town.

Horror, We Got

The colonel of the Cossacks draws even with me. His mustaches are red, his mare is chestnut, his eyes are green. His gaze sweeps over me. He does not acknowledge my presence any more than he does the corner of the building I lean against.

It is his last happy memory.

Everything is in slow motion except me. I move in, pistol in hand. Shiny and bright. A adjutant turns toward me, words forming on his lips. To the colonel's left, a hand moves toward a sword. His horse is still staring ahead. Across the road, an eye at a knothole widens.

I squeeze the trigger and fire. The colonel rips open like something gigantic had pulled a pop-top attached to his head and chest. His body flops in a windmilling arc onto the horse of the officer next to him. His mare, its back broken, collapses to the frozen street, spilling others to each side. Horses kick and rear.

Already I am through the doorway behind me, through the false wall, down the tunnel, back to the Machine. Rifle fire cascades onto the *shtetl* and everyone in it. Buildings will burn, women and children ridden down, raped, dismembered, shot, pulled apart. Men will be castrated (hear them scream), the synagogue will be pulled down (hear the writings burn), all the crafts and houses destroyed. No one will be left. This town will cease to be a memory.

I pause a few seconds, hear footsteps above me. Sandals, slap-slap-slap, are overtaken by hooves. The hooves trample, trample, and recede. There are no more footsteps. A child screams. A rifle barks.

Halfway across the continent, somebody else is killing the Czar. I smile. Into the Machine, then. Back to Tel Aviv.

We will force up wages which, however, will be of no benefit to the workers, for we will at the same time cause a rise in the prices of necessities, pretending that this is due to the decline of agriculture and of cattle raising. We will also artfully and deeply undermine the sources of production by instilling in the workmen ideas of anarchy.
—Protocol 6, *Protocols of the Learned Elders of Zion*

My name is Abe Sheenie. I am small and hunched over. My age is thirty-four, though I have masqueraded within the past year as

Strange Things in Close-Up

both a sixteen-year-old Marrano, and as an Ashkenazi patriarch whose years are too many to be counted. My nose juts halfway down my face. (Everyone in the Action Arm has plastic surgery to produce the desired effects. Only my friend Heimie Schwatz had a nose large enough to pass muster when he was accepted into our elite group.) We take injections to make us smell of garlic and dead places while on assignment. (*Foetor judaicus* is thought to be integral to the race, passed on through the blood.) Even the female agents who seduce Gentile boys and women have exaggerated features, but they don't have to go through the rigours of smelling like hogs (you should pardon the expression). I have pointy ears. A beard that would make a Hassidim positively livid with rage. I sometimes tie it to my belt. I have hands made for wringing and breast-beating. My hair looks like a brush heap a crazy man piled.

Other than these defects, I'm one handsome devil.

I grin at myself in the shiny steel walls of the Machine as it bumps and grinds its way toward 2006 c.e. (their reckoning) and creeps across the face of the earth invisibly to Israel.

Decompression takes forever. The lights flash on and the door opens. Sholmo sticks his head in.

"Hey, Abie," he says. "So how are things?"

"I have such a headache," I say. It's true. I walk out where the medics check me over with all sorts of very personal tests. I gobble some aspirin as soon as they take my pulse.

"So how's Colonel Obromev back in Poland?"

"He's very, very sick," I say.

"Well, the town's gone," says Sholmo. "It's no longer on the rolls for the next year."

"Things going okay?"

"Fine," says Sholmo.

"I need some sleep," I say.

"Sleep you can have," says Sholmo.

"Wait," says the medic. He looks on a chart. "Be back at 1800 tomorrow."

"What for?"

"Plague shots," he says.

"Plague shots," I say.

It is for this reason we must undermine faith, eradicate from the minds of the Gentiles the very principles of God and Soul, and replace these conceptions by mathematical calculations and material desires. When we deprived the masses of their belief in God, ruling authority was thrown into the gutter, where it became public property, and we seized it.

—Protocol 4, *Protocols of the Learned Elders of Zion*

I can't talk to Sholmo very long. It's his turn on the Wandering Jew duty roster.

"Where you going?" I ask him while he's in makeup, getting a white knotted beard fitted. It makes my 1881 model look positively thin by comparison. And some tremendous white eyebrows.

"Brussels, 1661," he says.

"Ought to cause a lot of excitement."

"Yeah. Somebody else is doing the Sabbatei Zevi bit over in Prussia. They ought to be ecstatic when I show up."

Sabbatei Zevi was this poor Levant who had the misfortune to be educated far beyond his abilities. He proclaimed himself Messiah one day in synagogue. All the dispersed Jews got the Zionist hots for about five years, and wanted news, news, news. Our man in Constantinople wasn't doing Zevi, he was one of his followers, spreading the word. Zevi himself would later convert to Islam at the point of a Turkish sword.

"When's your next turn?" asks Sholmo.

"Next month. Haven't seen where or when, yet."

"Maybe you'll be lucky and get South America just after the fall of the Inca, or something. Boy, am I tired of Renaissance Europe!"

"Talk about your method acting . . . ," I say.

"I mean it," says Sholmo. "Trudge into town. Weep and wail. Be filled with *Angst*. Lament the fall of the Temple. Take out a rosary and weep. Pray in churches. Talk with *goyim*. Same thing every time."

The Wandering Jew duty roster is separate from the others and takes precedence over most. All the men in the Action Arm have to pull it every two or three months. The time wasn't so bad (you *do* lose the same amount of subjective time as you spend in the past). But the wailing and gnashing get boring real quick. And such dumps you have to live in!

Strange Things in Close-Up

Sholmo stands up.

"Fantastic," I say.

"I look the same as everybody. Only older," he says.

"We'll have a party when you get back."

"Good. My heart goes out to my friends."

"See you in two weeks."

He trudges away, looking like Father Time himself. Already he's limping. So he gets into character. He's supposed to be the man who struck Jesus, and to whom Jesus said, "I go, but you shall tarry until I return again." So he's wandering the earth all during time. He's named Ahasuerus, or John Butadeus, or Isaac Lacquedem. He should lament Christ, and he should wait until he returns.

Boy, does he have a long wait.

I mean, if they gave medals for the people who make up dumb Gentile myths, the people who thought of that one should get the Legion of Honor, right? Like Dreyfus, you know?

To wear everyone out by dissensions, animosities, feuds, famine, inoculation of diseases, want until the Gentiles see no other way of escape but an appeal to our money and power.
—Protocol 10, *Protocols of the Learned Elders of Zion*

This horse is goddamned heavy, but the town well is just around the next corner. There are six of us, and we're grunting and straining enough to wake the dead.

Of course, we're going to have to make an awful lot of noise to do that.

Over on the next street you can hear the sounds of the groaning wheels of carts. All the shutters and house windows are closed, the doors are bolted, you can hear people crying behind them. Only this isn't some *shtetl* in Poland, this is your main classy neighborhood of Antwerp, and this isn't 1881, this is 1348.

From down the way comes the cry, "Bring out your dead! Bring out your dead!"

We smell bad enough, but this horse is *ripe*. It's been lying in the sun a week. It's about to explode, and if we're not careful, we'll get it all over us. Not a nice thing to do.

So sue us. We learned it from Genghis Khan a hundred years

before when he used to catapult them over the walls of cities that didn't surrender to him.

The wailing and cries float over the dim narrow street. Near midnight. Outside the town is the glow of the fires where they're burning the latest of the innumerable dead. Before this plague is over, Europe will lose half its people. Only two good things will come of this: Boccaccio will write the *Decameron*, and the people of Europe won't run out of food in the 1700s.

But that's all in the future and doesn't concern us. Our main problem is to get the horse over the lip of the well.

"Ready?" I ask. "Heave ho! Heave—eeve—eeeve—unngh!!!"

Over it goes. We hear it rupture on the way down, and this miasma of dead equine floats up just before we hear the splash. A window comes open on the third floor above us. We pause a beat (you've got to be an actor more than anything to be in the Action Arm) so they can see our woolen caftans and round hats and yellow Juden badges. And then we run, run, run back toward the Jewish streets.

We wait, smoking and talking for a few minutes, outside the room where the Machine is hidden. The Jews on the street are wailing and moaning, too, and their cemetery down the way has been filled a month. Already this community has lost half its people, and the other half live in fear that they will be dead of the plague by morning.

They don't have to worry about the time, anyhow. From toward the main part of town we see lights of hundreds of torches converging in the streets, growing like a swarm of honeybees, spilling from housefront to housefront until all the streets to the south are filled with flickering lights. Their footsteps grow louder, louder. They're in lock-step now, the tread of each in the crowd lost in the din of all the others. They become faceless now, in a sea of a faces and heads; they're full of hate. Very poetic. Now they come this way. They begin to chant; the voices in counterpoint to their steps:"HEP! HEP! HEP! HEP! HEP!"

(*Herusalema Est Perdita. Herusalema Est Perdita . . .*)

The old war cry from the Crusades, when the Knights sacked Antioch and put all the Jews to the torch in their own synagogues.

I forgot to tell you that part of our makeup for this caper is that we have blood running from our ears. The Sons of Simeon,

Strange Things in Close-Up

as well as his daughters, are supposed to have menses, but only on four days a year, and then from the ears.

More dumb Gentile myths.

(But who are we to argue with history?)

All the Jews here will be dead soon. Back to the Machine. Back to the future.

Every little bit hurts.

To divert over-restless people from discussing political questions, we shall now bring forward new problems apparently connected with them— problems of industry.
—Protocol 13, *Protocols of the Learned Elders of Zion*

Dr. Frederick Schwartz had just been liberated from a forced labor camp on the eastern front in 1945 when he discovered his rudimentary theory of time travel. He was put, through some Russian mistake, into an Allied DP camp, where he worked out his calculations. He emigrated to Israel in 1948, just in time to be killed on some *kibbutz* in the first war with the Arabs. His papers weren't found until 1954. These were immediately brought to the attention of the members of the Knesset who would later control the world.

Up until then, there were no supposed twelve Jews who ran the economies and governments of the world. The full manpower of Israel was thrown into the problem of working out Dr. Schwartz's theories and turning them to fact, but it wasn't until 1997 (what with fighting with their neighbors) that it happened. Overnight, there were twelve Elders of Zion. They now had all history to play with, to control, to do with as they pleased, of which to change the course of.

The first thing the most vocal of the Elders wanted to do was strangle Little Baby Hitler in his crib. Also some early Church fathers. The three most hawkish of the Elders drew up a hit list in a matter of minutes, along with the Scriptural quotes about eyes and teeth.

But the other Nine said No. A period of heated discussion took place, with the Elders sitting as a Committee of the Whole. What was said? What titanic battles of tradition and wit must have gone on there! What resort to Law and to common sense! Ah, but we'll never know. (I've been in the presence of the

Elders only once, and the room was dark. All I know is that one of them coughs a lot, even though he has all of medical science at his disposal, to do with as he pleases. It must please him to cough. For all I know, my grandfather may be one of the Elders of Zion.)

Here is the plan, they finally said.

We conquer the world. But we do it *just like* they accuse us of doing all along. Everything, every deed they attribute to us, we do. We don't change history, we implement it. We become the grasping monsters they accuse us of being. We live up to their worst expectations. We dream their nightmares for them.

The Elders are a great bunch of guys, but they can be a little cold-blooded.

So in 1998 c.e. they created the Action Arm in Tel Aviv. I joined in 2000 c.e. (We use Christian time, too.) It is now 2006. Already we rule the world. We're just patching up the history, making it real. When we're through, it will have happened just like they said it would. The great snake of Zion has doubled back on itself and come to rest in Palestine.

These trips back into the past make me introspective and full of *ennui*. None of us talk coming back from Antwerp. Sometimes you talk after a job. Mostly not, though.

We will represent ourselves as saviors of the working class who have come to liberate them from this oppression by suggesting that they join our army of socialists, anarchists, communists to whom we always extend our help under the guise of fraternal principles of universal human solidarity.
—Protocol 3, *Protocols of the Learned Elders of Zion*

Abe Sheenie eats with relish the inner organs of beasts and fowls. Sometimes I don't even use relish. I am not above a big glass of milk and some summer sausage. I have been known to partake of an occasional pig-in-the-blanket.

So we're at the party for Sholmo.

It's high old time. (You'll excuse the pun. One of the things they accused us of was being pushers of narcotics. Corrupting the youth of Christendom, sending nice *shikses* into lives of prostitution at the end of opium pipes or needles. So we have

Strange Things in Close-Up

these warehouses full of things that would make General "Chinese" Gordon weep, and the late Dr. Leary, well, oh my!)

Sholmo's back, and he's got his arm in a sling. But he has this beatific smile on his face. Part of that is the dope, part is because he's so very pleased to still be alive.

"It's getting so you can't trust the history books anymore," he says.

"They were all written by *goyim*. Don't blame us," says someone from the research department.

"Crowd finds out some big Jew's in town. Lots of excitement on the old Jewish street," says Sholmo. "Wandering Jew or not, some alderman or something convinces his drinking buddies over in the nice part of town that it would be a good thing to put all this Messiah agitation down. They were sneaky bastards. Came a few at a time, in the night. Didn't make a lot of noise. Couple of hundred I'd say. I was in the home of this rich jeweler, typical learned man, you know, talking with him and a few of his friends about Jesus and Sabbatei Zevi (may his memory be preserved!) when all of a sudden the door lands on the kitchen table, followed by a lot of wheel lock balls and a pike or two. Everybody else froze while these guys started piling in hollering about Christ-killers. Me, I kicked out the lamp and went backwards through the window. If I'd have been a second later, they'd have shot me, for sure."

He laughs, then we all do. He caught half the pellets from a blunderbuss from someone waiting outside the window. They fired when he came through. He had to shoot his way out and hide for three days before he could make it back to the Machine.

The story we got from the time, from one Abram Goessepson, is that the Wandering Jew appeared in Brussels, and disappeared before the very eyes of many of the ghetto's most respected men after lecturing them on Christianity and his wanderings over the earth. What old Abram forgot to mention was that there was gunplay in the streets of old Brussels, and that ol' sky-pilot Ike Lacquedem had to draw down on the *hombres*.

(We've only lost sixteen good friends in eight years. Two a year, regular as clockwork. You can almost count the days between deaths. A moment of silence for the dead. That's the price you pay to be owners of the world and all its goodies.)

On the hi-fi is Kinky Friedman singing "Ride 'Em, Jewboy."

Horror, We Got

(Such a nice world to own it is, too.)

Moshe Feeberman and Izzy Gottesman are over in the corner telling about the Big Caper of 2006, with hand gestures like you wouldn't believe. This year's historic mission was the actual drawing up of the *Protocols of the Learned Elders of Zion*, the master plan for the conquest of the world.

(There's a room back at the office we call the Hate Room. It has anti-Semitic writings on microfilm. There are several tons of them. And we wrote less than 10 percent of them.)

"So," Izzy is saying as I come up to him, none too steady, "we go back to where the Czar and Czaritsa were killed, and we leave a copy of Nilus' book, the *Great in the Small*, in the Czaritsa's bedroom . . ."

". . . and open the Bible to Revelations . . . ," says Moshe.

". . . and Moshe carves a swastika on the windowsill, like it was to keep out Jewish vampires or something . . . ," says Izzy.

". . . and all this a few minutes before the hunters come out of the woods and find the bodies at the Summer House."

"Then we go back to Paris in the 1890s."

"You should see the place," says Moshe. "I don't see how Proust and all those guys lived there. So, we go to the offices of the Okhrana, the Czar's secret police, and we put this copy of the *Protocols* in with all the other stuff in Colonel Ratchkovsky's OUT box for the clerk to copy the next day . . ."

"Then we go back a few weeks earlier and give everybody in the office a memo about coming up with some hotshot thing to get the people down on the Jews and revolutionaries, and . . ."

"Then we make sure a copy of it gets to old Sergei Nilus, sitting in his writer's colony house back in Russia, along with a generous supply of hashish of the kind he's used to, and have everybody around him keep talking about the revolutionaries and the Jews . . ."

"Meanwhile we skip back to Paris about a mouth before we plant the *Protocols* in Ratchkovsky's office, and put this book Zeke ('Hey, Zeke, great job that, on the aging,' says Moshe. Zeke lifts his drink across to them.) gave us, called *Dialogue in Hell Between* . . . oh, somebody and somebody or other, and we underline the same passages as from the *Protocols*, and put one in with Ratchkovsky's papers, and take one to the British

Strange Things in Close-Up

Museum so some reporter can find it in 1920 and prove it all a hoax."

"And here's the killer," says Moshe. "Izzy goes to Munich in 1920 and hands a copy to..."

People lean closer. There is a morbid fascination about anything to do with the man.

"...this sidewalk artist who used to be a corporal in the German Army."

The wait. The question comes from someone.

"What did he look like?"

"Young. Nondescript. Still wearing his Army overcoat. Carrying some brushes and paints and bits of cardboard and a flimsy fold-up easel. Nothing like you'd expect. He still had the Hindenburg-type mustache at the time."

"I saw him last week. In 1945," someone says from the corner. "He didn't look so good."

"When in 1945?" asks someone else.

"April 11," the man says.

"Did you speak to him?" a nice lady asks.

Izzy clears his throat. "Not exactly. I handed him a copy of the *Protocols* and gave him the name of a political club over on the Münsterstrasse."

"So that's where it all started," says a young man sitting on the sofa.

"Not really," says Moshe, and winks. "Izzy gave him the address of a vacant lot."

We will, so wear out and exhaust the Gentiles by all this that they will be compelled to offer us an international authority, which by its position will enable us to absorb without disturbance all the governmental forces of the world and thus form a super-government. We must so direct the education of Gentile society that its hands will drop in the weakness of discouragement in the face of any undertaking where initiative is needed.

—Protocol 5

The party's over and we're back at my place overlooking the Technicon. I am lying on the couch, and between my legs the beautiful Sheila Berkowitz is sucking my *schlong*. Her dark hair is swept back from her head, and her heavy-lidded eyes are closed. She is enjoying what she is doing, and oh, so am I.

Horror, We Got

(There's this myth that us Jewish guys are addicted to it. Atavistic memories. Ever since the *mohel* planted the old ritual kiss on the bloody end of our teeny penises during the *bris*, well . . . you can see how a guy can get hooked on it.)

I moan a little and move my right leg up. Sheila smiles around the bare head of my dong. She licks a little circle. I moan again.

(In a few moments, when I have experienced some more sweet agony at Sheila's talented touch, I am going to jump on her crotch and do a little smiling and nibbling of my own, but till then, well, a little faster Sheila, a little harder.)

I'm paying attention to what's happening, but my mind is drifting in some pretty strange places. (It's had some pretty strange stimuli during the past few hours.) As I lie here and am consumed by several passions, I think of this business I'm in.

Some of the thoughts are not pretty.

Like, we own the world, and history, and soon maybe the future also. It will come as a great shock to some people.

Even as I lie here, our salvage boats ply the waters of the past like the ships of Tarshish. They dredge up all the sunken galleons, the lost triremes, the misplaced clipper ships and tramp steamers, and empty their holds of gold and silver, ingots, feathers, fur, ores. Then they come back to our ports and times, and are sold at the time and place which brings the best deal. They buy gold and silver and diamonds, the mark, the pound, the yen, the oil and the LPG.

Our agents roam the past. We sow the threads of coincidence and change, we remold and shape the world, we figure its works and thoughts, not in our image, but in one made and forced on us. One we have now taken and are using, in our own way, at our own pace.

(Oh. Moan. Wiggle.)

We have been cheated and damned and spat upon. Burned in our place of worship, dragged through the streets, scattered, dispersed. We have been gassed and shot and buried in heaps, in mounds, in acres at the time. And sometimes, our people, while they took their places in line, still did not believe the Lord God would let them die this way, crowded, herded, moved like cattle to the slaughter.

So we in the Action Arm implement what has gone before. We heighten it. We make it more real. We can now make it just

Strange Things in Close-Up

like those who persecuted us want it to be. You can't ask for more revenge than *that*. We have conquered him with his own worst imaginings. So we do. Sometimes we save, sometimes we condemn our own to the lies and images they have us take.

It is hard being like gods and deciding what needs to be done.

It leads to bad dreams and long nights when there is no sleep to be found in the immensity of all time. But we have doctors to take care of that, and we get lots of vacation, and we're not chosen for our kindness and pity anyway. Steely-eyed sons and daughters of Zion are what we are. Time is a playground before us. We can use nations like jungle gyms and empires for teeter-totters. And once we get the future, too . . .

(Oh.)

The onus of history spreads like thin paint from our actions, covering the world like Sherwin-Williams.

(Moan.)

The bad thoughts take me. Like:

When the ghetto Jews called on us in the Middle Ages, when they prayed for help, for any kind of relief from the inhuman misery they suffered, they asked for saviors. For superhuman deliverance for anything.

What they got was us. *We* are the golems of deliverance.

(Sheila changes her position and goes back to her delicious work.)

When we helped them come for the Jews in the trucks, we supplied the lists, we helped the rabbis draw up the names, we handed the names over to them. When the gas was turned on, we supplied the engineering. When the ovens were lit, our planning turned the laden cartwheels. The smoke coming up from the compounds went to heaven with our prayers, but also with our aid.

(Ooh.)

There is something I think of that makes me ask what I am doing working for such a bunch of vengeful old men. It is a last thing to wonder over.

Hitler worked for *us*. He had the right idea. *We* are the final solution.

My head should grow in the ground like a turnip that I think such thoughts.

(Faster, Sheila. Harder.)

Horror, We Got

We have taken care long ago to discredit the Gentile clergy.
—Protocol 17

Paris, 1763:

Get out the hot tongs and the meat grinder, Heimie! It's Passover! We got two consecrated wafers and there's this new fat *goy* kid on the block.

Sheila's working up a batch of matzoh, and I'm getting out the chains.

Ritual murder is hard work.

Next year, it's Jerusalem all over.

Introduction to
Man-Mountain Gentian

I'd been interested in Japanese culture since I don't know when, and I grew up with Kudzu in Mississippi. The title of this story came to me simultaneously with a line that is not used in the story. I had a vision of two sumo wrestlers grappling and the voice of an announcer saying "Now he's got the Champ in a half-lotus!"

That was enough for me. Like a lot of others, I threatened to write this one for so long I thought I had already written it. I finally did, on a Greyhound bus between Austin and Dallas, going to yet another SF convention. (Smart editors always try to put their deadlines close to a convention where I've promised to read a new story. It usually works.)

This was the second story I sold to Omni. It was picked up by Dozois's The Year's Best Science Fiction, *justifying Ellen Datlow's faith in it. Everybody in the world except the three of us ignored it.*

Man-Mountain Gentian

Just after the beginning of the present century it was realized that some of the wrestlers were throwing their opponents from the ring without touching them.
—Ichinaga Naya, *Zen-Sumo: Sport and Ritual* All Japan Zen-Sumo Association Books, Kyoto, 2014.

It was the fourteenth day of the January Tokyo tournament. Sitting with the other wrestlers, Man-Mountain Gentian watched as the next match began.

Ground Sloth Ikimoto was taking on Killer Kudzu. They entered the tamped-earth ring and began their *shikiris*. Ground Sloth, a *sumotori* of the old school, had changed over from traditional to *zen-sumo* four years before. He weighed 180 kilos in his *mawashi*. He entered at the white tassel salt corner. He clapped his huge hands, rinsed his mouth, threw salt, rubbed his body with tissue paper, then began his high leg lifts, stamping his feet, his hands gripping far down his calves. The ring shook with each stamp. All the muscles rippled on his big frame. His stomach, a flesh-colored boulder, shook and vibrated.

Killer Kudzu was small, and thin, weighing barely over ninety kilos. On his forehead was the tattoo of his homeland, the PRC, one large star and five smaller stars blazing in a constellation. He also went into his ritual *shikiri*, but as he clapped he held in one hand a small box, ten centimeters on a side, showing his intention to bring it into the match. Sometimes these were objects for meditation, sometimes favors from male or female lovers, sometimes no one knew what. The only rule was that they could not be used as weapons.

The wrestlers were separated from the onlookers by four clear walls and a roof of plastic. Over this hung the traditional canopy and tassels, symbolizing heaven and the four winds. Through

Strange Things in Close-Up

the plastic walls ran a mesh of fine wiring, connected to a six-volt battery next to the north-side judge.

A large number of 600X slow motion video cameras were placed around the auditorium to be used by the judges if necessary. Killer Kudzu placed the box on his side of the line. He returned to his corner and threw more salt.

Ground Sloth Ikimoto stamped once more, twice, went to his line, settled into position like a football lineman, legs apart, knuckles to the ground. His nearly-bare buttocks looked like giant rocks. Killer Kudzu finished his *shikiri*, squatted at his line, where he settled his hand near his votive box, and glared at his opponent.

The referee, in his ceremonial robes, had been standing to one side during the preliminaries. Now he came to a position halfway between the wrestlers, his war fan down. He leaned away from the two men, left leg back to one side as if ready to run. He stared at the midpoint between the two and flipped his fan downward.

Instantly sweat sprang to their foreheads and shoulders, their bodies rippled as if pushing against great unmoving weights, their toes curled into the clay of the ring. They stayed immobile on their respective marks.

Killer Kudzu's neck muscles strained. With his left hand he reached and quickly opened the votive box.

Man-Mountain Gentian and the other wrestlers on the east side drew in their breaths.

Ground Sloth Ikimoto was a vegetarian and always had been. In training for traditional sumo, he had shunned the *chunkonabe*, the communal stew of fish, chicken, meat, eggs, onions, cabbage, carrots, turnips, sugar and soy sauce. Traditional *sumotori* ate as much as they could hold twice a day, and weight gain was tremendous.

Ikimoto had instead trained twice as hard, eating only vegetables, starches and sugars. Meat and eggs had never touched his lips.

What Killer Kudzu brought out of the box was a cheeseburger. With one swift movement he bit into it only half a meter from Ground Sloth's face.

Ikimoto blanched and started to scream. As he did, he lifted into the air as if chopped in the chest with an ax, arms and legs

Man-Mountain Gentian

flailing, a Dopplering wail of revulsion coming from his emptied lungs. He passed the bales marking the edge of the ring, one foot dragging the ground, upending a boundary bale, and smashed to the ground between the ring and the square bales at the plastic walls.

The referee signaled Killer Kudzu the winner. As he squatted the *gyoji* offered him a small envelope signifying a cash prize from his sponsors. Kudzu, left hand on his knee, with his right hand made three chopping gestures from the left, right and above, thanking man, earth and heaven. Kudzu took the envelope, then stepped through the doorway of the plastic enclosure and left the arena to rejoin the other west-side wrestlers.

The audience of 11,000 was on its feet cheering. Across Japan and the world, 200 million viewers watched.

Ground Sloth Ikimoto had risen to his feet, bowed and left by the other door. Attendants rushed in to repair the damaged ring.

Man-Mountain Gentian looked up at the scoring clock. The match had taken 4.1324 seconds. It was 3:30 in the afternoon on the fourteenth day of the Tokyo tournament.

The next match would pit Cast Iron Pekowski of Poland against Typhoon Takanaka.

After that would be Gentian's bout with the South African veldt wrestler Knockdown Krugerand.

Man-Mountain Gentian stood at 13–0 in the tournament, having defeated an opponent each day so far. He wanted to retire as the first Grand Champion to win six tournaments in a row, undefeated. He was not very worried about his contest later this afternoon.

Tomorrow, though, the last day of the January tournament, he would face Killer Kudzu, who, after this match, also stood undefeated at 14–0.

Man-Mountain Gentian was 1.976 meters tall and weighed exactly 200 kilos. He had been a *sumotori* for six years, had been *yokozuna* for the last two of those. He was twice holder of the Emperor's Cup. He was the highest paid, the most famous *zen-sumotori* in the world.

He was twenty-three years old.

Strange Things in Close-Up

He and Knockdown Krugerand finished their *shikiris*. They got on their marks. The *gyoji* flipped his fan.

The match was over in 3.1916 seconds. He helped Krugerand to his feet, accepted the envelope and the thunderous applause of the crowd, and left the reverberating plastic enclosure.

"You are the wife of Man-Mountain Gentian?" asked a voice next to her.

Melissa put on her public smile and turned to the voice. Her nephew, on the other side, leaned around to look.

The man talking to her had five stars tattooed to his forehead. She knew he was a famous *sumotori*, though he was very slim and his *chon-mage* had been combed out and washed and his hair was not a fluffy explosion above his head.

"I am Killer Kudzu," he said. "I'm surprised you weren't at the tournament."

"I am here with my nephew, Hari. Hari, this is Mr. Killer Kudzu." The nephew, dressed in his winter Little League outfit, shook hands firmly. "His team, the Mitsubishi Zeroes play the Kawasaki Claudes next game."

They paused while a foul ball caused great excitement three rows down the bleachers. Hari leapt for it but some construction foreman of a father came up grinning with the ball.

"And what do you play?" asked Killer Kudzu.

"Utility outfield. When I play," said Hari, averting his eyes and sitting back down.

"Oh. How's your batting?"

"Pretty bad. .123 for the year," said Hari.

"Well, maybe this will be the night you shine," said Kudzu.

"I hope so," said Hari. "Half our team has the American flu."

"Just the reason I'm here," said Kudzu. "I was to meet a businessman whose son was to play this game. I find him not to be here, as his son has the influenza also."

It was hot in the domed stadium and Kudzu insisted they let him buy them Sno-cones. Just as the vendor got to them, Hari's coach signaled and the nephew ran down the bleachers and followed the rest of his teammates into the warmup area under the stadium.

Soon the other lackluster game was over and Hari's team took the field.

Man-Mountain Gentian

The first batter for the Claudes, a twelve-year-old built like an orang-utan, got up and smashed a line drive off the Mitsubishi third baseman's chest. The third baseman had been waving to his mother. They carried him into the dugout. Melissa soon saw him up yelling again.

So it went through three innings. The Claudes had the Zeroes down by three runs, 6–3. In the fourth inning, Hari took right field, injuries having whittled the flu-ridden team down to the third-stringers.

One of the Claudes hit a high looping fly straight to right field. Hari started in after it, but something happened with his feet; he fell and the ball dropped a meter from his outstretched glove. The center fielder chased it down and made the relay and by a miracle they got the runner sliding into home plate. He took out the Zeroes catcher doing it.

"It doesn't look good for the Zeroes," said Melissa.

"Oh, things might get better," said Killer Kudzu. "The opera's not over till the fat lady sings."

"A *diva* couldn't do much worse out there," said Melissa.

"They still don't like baseball in my country," he said. "Decadent. Bourgeois, they say. As if anything could be more decadent and middle-class than China."

"Yet you wear the flag?" She pointed toward his head.

"Call it a gesture to former greatness," he said.

Bottom of the sixth, last inning in Little League. The Zeroes had the bases loaded but they had two outs in the process. Hari came up to bat.

Things were tense. The outfielders were nearly falling down from tension.

The pitcher threw a blistering curve that got the outside. Hari was caught looking.

From the dugout the manager's voice saying unkind things carried to the crowd.

Eight thousand people were on their feet.

The pitcher wound up and threw.

Hari started a swing that should have ended in a grounder or a pop-up. Halfway through, it looked like someone had speeded up a projector. The leisurely swing blurred. Hari literally threw himself to the ground. The bat cracked and broke in two at his feet.

Strange Things in Close-Up

The ball, a frozen white streak, cometed through the air and hit the scoreboard 110 meters away with a terrific crash, putting the inning indicator out of commission.

Everyone was stock-still. Hari was staring. Every player was turned toward the scoreboard.

"It's a home run, kid," the umpire reminded Hari. Slowly, unbelieving, Hari began to trot toward first base.

The place exploded, fans jumping to their feet. Hari's teammates on the bases headed for home. The dugout emptied, waiting for him to round third.

The Claudes stood fuming. The Zeroes climbed all over Hari.

"I didn't know you could do that more than once a day," said Melissa, her eyes narrowed.

"Who, me?" asked Kudzu.

"You're perverting your talent," she said.

"We're *not* supposed to be able to do that more than once every twenty-four hours," said Killer Kudzu, flashing a smile.

"I know that's not true, at least really," said Melissa.

"Oh, yes. You are *married* to a *sumotori*, aren't you?"

Melissa blushed.

"The kid seemed to feel bad enough about the dropped fly. Besides, it's just a game."

At home plate, Hari's teammates climbed over him, slapping him on the back.

The game was over, the scoreboard said 7–6, and the technicians were already climbing over the inning indicator.

Melissa rose. "I have to go pick up Hari. I suppose I will see you at the tournament tomorrow?"

"How are you getting home?" asked Killer Kudzu.

"We walk. Hari lives near."

"It's snowing."

"Oh."

"Let me give you a ride. My electric vehicle is outside."

"That would be nice. I live several kilometers away from—"

"I know where you live, of course."

"Fine, then."

Hari ran up. "Aunt Melissa! Did you see?! I don't know *what* happened! I just felt, I don't know, I just *hit* it!"

"That was wonderful." She smiled at him. Killer Kudzu was looking up, very interested in the stadium support structure.

Man-Mountain Gentian

The stable in which Man-Mountain Gentian trained was being entertained that night. That meant that the wrestlers would have to do all the entertaining.

Even at the top of this sport, Man-Mountain has never gotten used to the fans. Their kingly prizes, their raucous behavior at matches, their donations of gifts, clothing, vehicles, and in some cases houses and land to their favorite wrestlers. It was all appalling.

It was a carryover from traditional sumo, he knew. But *zen-sumo* had become a worldwide, not just a national sport. Many saved for years to come to Japan to watch the January or May tournaments. People here in Japan sometimes sacrificed at home to be able to contribute toward a new *kesho-mawashi* apron for a wrestler entering the ring. Money, in this business, flowed like water, appearing in small envelopes in the mail, in the locker room, after feasts such as the one tonight.

Once a month, Man-Mountain Gentian gathered them all up and took them to his accountant, who had instructions to give it all, above a certain princely level, away to charity. Other wrestlers had more, or less, or none of the same arrangements. The tax men never seemed surprised by whatever amount wrestlers reported.

He entered the club. Things were already rocking. One of the hostesses took his shoes and coat. She had to put the overcoat over her shoulders to carry it into the cloakroom.

The party was a haze of blue smoke, dishes, bottles, businessmen, wrestlers and funny paper hats. Waitresses came in and out with more food. Three musicians played unheard on a raised dais at one side of the room. Someone was telling a snappy story. The room exploded with laughter.

"Ah!" said someone. "Yokozuna Gentian has arrived."

Man-Mountain bowed deeply. They made two or three places for him at the low table. He saw that several of the host-party were Americans. Probably one or more were from the CIA.

They and the Russians were still trying to perfect *zen-sumo* as an assassination weapon. They offered active and retired *sumotori* large amounts of money in an effort to get them to develop their powers in some nominally destructive form. So far, no one he knew of had. There were rumors about the Brazilians, however.

Strange Things in Close-Up

He could see it now, a future with premiers, millionaires, presidents and paranoids in all walks of life wearing wire-mesh clothing and checking their Eveready batteries before going out each morning.

He had been approached twice, by each side. He was sometimes followed. They all were. People in governments simply did *not* understand.

He began to talk, while saki flowed, with Cast Iron Pekowski. Pekowski, now 2–12 for the tournament, had graciously lost his match with Typhoon Takanaka. (There was an old saying: In a tournament, no one who won more than nine matches ever beat an opponent who has lost seven. Which had been the case with Takanaka. Eight was the number of wins needed to retain current ranking.)

"I could feel him going," said Pekowski, in Polish. "I think we should talk to him about the May tournament."

"Have you mentioned this to his stablemaster?"

"I thought of doing so after the tournament. I was hoping you could come with me to see him."

"I'll be just another retired *sekitori* by then."

"Takanaka respects you above all the others. Besides, your *dampatsushiki* ceremony won't be for another two weeks. You'll still have your hair. And while we're at it, I still wish you would change your mind."

"Perhaps I could be Takanaka's dew-sweeper, if he decides."

"Good! You'll come with me then, Friday morning?"

"Yes."

The hosts were very much drunker than the wrestlers. Nayakano the stablemaster was feeling no pain but still remained upright. Mounds of food were being consumed. A businessman tried to grab-ass a waitress. This was going to become every bit as nasty as all such parties.

"A song! A song!" yelled the head of the fan club, a businessman in his sixties. "Who will favor us with a song?"

Man-Mountain Gentian got to his feet, went over to the musicians. He talked with the samisen player. Then he stood facing his drunk, attentive audience.

How may of these parties had he been to in his career? Two, three hundred? Always the same, drunkenness, discord, braggadocio, on the part of the host-clubs. Some fans really

Man-Mountain Gentian

loved the sport, some lived vicariously through it. He would not miss the parties. But as the player began the tune he realized this might be the last party he would have to face.

He began to sing:

> "I met my love by still Lake Biwa
> just before Taira war banners flew..."

And so on through all six verses, in a clear pure voice belonging to a man half his size.

They stood and applauded him, some of the wrestlers in the stable looking away, as only they, not even the stablemaster, knew of his retirement plans and what this party probably meant.

He went to the stablemaster, who took him to the club host, made apologies concerning the tournament and a slight cold, shook hands, bowed and went out into the lobby, where the hostess valiantly brought him his shoes and overcoat. He wanted to help her, but she reshouldered the coat grimly and brought it to him. He handed her a tip and signed the autograph she asked for.

It had begun to snow outside. The neon made the sky a swirling multicolored smudge. Man-Mountain Gentian walked through the quickly-emptying streets. Even the everpresent taxis scurried from the snow like roaches from a light. His home was only two kilometers away. He liked the stillness of the falling snow, the quietness of the city in times such as this.

"Shelter for a stormy night?" asked a ragged old man on a corner. Man-Mountain Gentian stopped.

"Change for shelter for an old man?" asked the beggar again, looking very far up at Gentian's face.

Man-Mountain Gentian reached in his pocket, took out three or four small ornate paper envelopes which had been thrust on him as he left the club.

The old man took them, opened one. Then another and another.

"There must be more than 800,000 yen here...," he said, very quietly and very slowly.

"I suggest the Imperial or the Hilton," said Man-Mountain Gentian. Then the wrestler turned and walked away.

The old man laughed, then straightened himself with dignity, stepped to the curb and imperiously summoned an approaching pedicab.

Melissa was not home.

He turned on the entry light as he took off his shoes. He passed through the spartanly-furnished low living room, turned off the light at the other switch.

He went to the bathroom, put depilatory gel on his face, wiped it off. He went to the kitchen, picked up half a ham and ate it, washing it down with three liters of milk. He returned to the bathroom, brushed his teeth, went to the bedroom, unrolled his futon and placed his cinderblock at the head of it.

He punched on the hidden tape deck and an old recording of Kimio Eto playing "Rukodan" on the koto quietly filled the house.

The only decoration in the sleeping room was Shuncho's print, "The Strongest and the Most Fair," showing a theater-district beauty and a *sumotori* three times her size, hanging on the far wall.

He turned off the light. Instantly the silhouettes of falling snowflakes showed through the paper walls of the house, cast by the strong streetlight outside. He watched the snowflakes fall, listening to the music, and was filled with *mono no aware* for the transience of beauty in the world.

Man-Mountain Gentian pulled up the puffed cotton covers, put his head on the building block and drifted off to sleep.

They had let Hari off at his house. The interior of the runabout was warm. They were drinking coffee in the near-empty parking lot of Tokyo Sonic # 113.

"I read somewhere you were an architect," said Killer Kudzu.

"Barely," said Melissa.

"Would you like to see Kudzu House?" he asked.

For an architect, it was like being asked to one of Frank Lloyd Wright's vacation homes, or one of the birdlike buildings designed by Eino Saarinen in the later twentieth century. Melissa considered.

"I should call home first," she said after a moment.

"I think your husband will still be at the Nue Vue Club, whooping it up with the money-men."

"You're probably right. I'll call him later. I'd love to see your house."

The old man lay dying on his bed.

"I see you finally heard," he said. His voice was tired.

Man-Mountain Gentian had not seen him in seven years. He had always been old, but he had never looked this old, this weak.

Dr. Wu had been his mentor. He had started him on the path toward *zen-sumo* (though he did not know it at the time). Dr. Wu had not been one of those cryptic koan-spouting quiet men. He had been boisterous, laughing, playing with his pupils, yelling at them, whatever was needed to get them *to see*.

There had been the occasional letter from him. Now, for the first time, there was a call in the middle of the night.

"I'm sorry," said Man-Mountain Gentian. "It's snowing outside."

"At your house, too?" asked Dr. Wu.

Wu's attendant was dressed in Buddhist robes and seemingly paid no attention to either of them.

"Is there anything I can do for you?" asked Man-Mountain Gentian.

"Physically no. This is nothing a pain shift can help. Emotionally, there is."

"What?"

"You can win tomorrow, though I won't be around to share it."

Man-Mountain Gentian was quiet a moment. "I'm not sure I can promise you that."

"I didn't think so. You are forgetting the kitten and the bowl of milk."

"No. Not at all. I think I've finally come up against something new and strong in the world. I will either win or lose. Either way, I will retire."

"If it did not mean anything to you, you could have lost by now," said Dr. Wu.

Man-Mountain Gentian was quiet again.

Wu shifted uneasily on his pillows. "Well, there is not much time. Lean close. Listen to what I have to say.

Strange Things in Close-Up

"The novice Itsu went to the Master and asked him: 'Master, what is the key to all enlightenment?'

" 'You must teach yourself never to think of the white horse,' said the Master.

"Itsu applied himself with all his being. One day while raking gravel he achieved insight.

" 'Master! Master!' yelled Itsu, running to his quarters. 'Master! I have made myself not think about the white horse!'

" 'Quick!' said the Master. 'When you were not thinking of the white horse, where was Itsu?'

"The novice could make no answer.

"The Master dealt Itsu a smart blow with his staff.

"At this, Itsu was enlightened."

Then Dr. Wu let his head back down on his bed.

"Good-bye," he said.

In his bed in the lamasery in Tibet, Dr. Wu let out a ragged breath and died.

Man-Mountain Gentian, standing on his futon in his bedroom in Tokyo, began to cry.

Kudzu House took up a city block in the middle of Tokyo. The taxes alone must have been enormous.

Through the decreasing snow, Melissa saw the lights. Their beams stabbed up into the night. All she could see from a block away was the tangled kudzu.

Kudzu was a vine, originally transplanted from China, raised in Japan for centuries. Its crushed root was used as a starch base, in cooking; its leaves were used for teas and medicines, its fibers to make cloth and paper. What kudzu was most famous for was its ability to grow over and cover anything which didn't move out of its way.

In the Depression thirties of the last century, it had been planted on road cuts in the southeastern United States to stop erosion. Kudzu had almost stopped progress there. In those ideal conditions it grew runners more than twenty meters long in a single summer, several to a root. Its vines climbed utility poles, hills, trees. It completely covered other vegetation, cutting off its sunlight.

Many places in the American South were covered three kilometers wide to each side of the highways with kudzu vines. The

Great Kudzu Forest of central Georgia was a U.S. National Park.

In the bleaker conditions of Japan the weed could be kept under control. Except that this owner didn't want to. The lights playing into the snowy sky were part of the heating and watering system which kept vines growing year-round. All this Melissa had read before. Seeing it was something again. The entire block was a green tangle of vines and lights.

"Do you ever trim it?" she asked.

"The traffic keeps it back," said Killer Kudzu, and laughed. "I have gardeners who come in and fight it once a week. They're losing."

They went into the green tunnel of a driveway. Melissa saw the edge of the house, cast concrete, as they dropped into the sunken vehicle area.

There were three boats, four road vehicles, a hovercraft and a small sport flyer parked there. Lights shone up into a dense green roof from which hundreds of vines grew downward toward the light sources.

"We have to move the spotlights every week," he said.

A butler met them at the door. "Just a tour, Mord," said Killer Kudzu. "We'll have drinks in the sitting room in thirty minutes."

"Very good, sir."

"This way."

Melissa went to a railing. The living area was the size of a bowling alley, or the lobby of a terrible old hotel. The balcony on the second level jutted out from the east wall. Killer Kudzu went to a console, punched buttons.

Moe and the Meanies boomed from dozens of speakers.

Killer Kudzu stood snapping his fingers for a moment. "O, send me! Honorable cats!" he said. "That's from Spike Jones, an irreverent American musician of the last century. He died of cancer," he added.

Melissa followed him, noticing the things everyone noticed—the Chrome Room, the Supercharger Inhalorium, the archery range ("the object is *not* to hit the targets," said Kudzu), the Mosasaur Pool with the fossils embedded in the sides and bottom.

Strange Things in Close-Up

She was more affected by the house and its tawdriness than she thought she would be.

"You've done very well for yourself."

"Some manage it, some give it away, some save it. I *spend* it."

They were drinking kudzu tea highballs in the sitting room, which was one of the most comfortable rooms Melissa had ever been in.

"Tasteless, isn't it?" asked Killer Kudzu.

"Not quite," said Melissa. "Well worth the trip."

"You could stay, you know?" said Kudzu.

"I thought I could." She sighed. "It would only give me one more excuse not to finish the dishes at home." She gave him a long look. "Besides, it wouldn't give you an advantage in the match."

"That really never crossed my mind."

"I'm quite sure."

"You are a beautiful woman."

"You have a nice house."

"Hmmm. Time to get you home."

"I'm sure."

They sat outside her house in the cold. The snow had stopped. Stars peeped through the low scud.

"I'm going to win tomorrow," said Killer Kudzu.

"You might," said Melissa.

"It is sometimes possible to do more than win," he said.

"I'll tell my husband."

"My offer is always open," he said. He reached over and opened her door on the runabout. "Life won't be the same after he's lost. Or after he retires."

She climbed out, shaking from more than the cold. He closed the door, whipped the vehicle in a circle and was gone down the crunching street. He blinked his lights once before he drove out of sight.

She found her husband in the kitchen. His eyes were red; he was as pale as she had ever seen him.

"Dr. Wu is dead," he said, and wrapped his huge arms around her, covering her like an upright sofa.

Man-Mountain Gentian

He began to cry again. She talked to him quietly.

"Come, let's try to get some sleep," she said.

"No, I couldn't rest. I wanted to see you first. I'm going down to the stable." She helped him dress in his warmest clothing. He kissed her and left, walking the few blocks through the snowy sidewalks to the training building.

The junior wrestlers were awakened at 4 A.M. They were to begin the day's work of sweeping, cleaning, cooking, bathing, feeding and catering to the senior wrestlers. When they came in they found him, stripped to his *mawashi*, at the 300-kilo push bag, pushing, pushing, straining, crying all the while, not saying a word. The floor of the arena was torn and grooved. They cleaned up the area for the morning workouts, one following him around with the sand-trowel.

At 7 A.M. he slumped exhausted on a bench. Two of the *juryo* covered him with quilts and set an alarm clock beside him for 1 P.M.

"Your opponent was at the ball game last night," said Nayakano the stablemaster. Man-Mountain Gentian sat in the dressing rooms while the barber combed and greased his elaborate *chon-mage*. "Your wife asked me to give you this."

It was a note in a plain envelope, addressed in her beautiful calligraphy. He opened and read it. She warned him of what Kudzu said about "more than winning" the night before, and wished him luck.

He turned to the stablemaster.

"Has Killer Kudzu injured any opponent before he became *yokozuna* last tournament?"

Nayakano's answer was immediate. "No. That's unheard of. Let me see that note." He reached out.

Man-Mountain Gentian put it back in the envelope, tucked it in his *mawashi*.

"Should I alert the judges?"

"Sorry I mentioned it," said Man-Mountain Gentian.

"I don't like this," said the stablemaster.

Three hefty junior wrestlers ran in carrying Gentian's *kenzo-mawashi* between them.

The last day of the January tournament always packed them in.

Strange Things in Close-Up

Even the *maegashira* and *komusubi* matches, in which young boys threw each other, or tried to, drew enough of an audience to make the novices feel good.

The call for the Ozeki class wrestlers came, and they went through the grandiose ring-entering ceremony, wearing their great *kenzo-mawashi* aprons of brocade, silk and gold while their dew-sweepers and swordbearers squatted to the sides. Then they retired to their benches, east or west, to await the call by the falsetto-voiced *yobidashi*.

Man-Mountain Gentian watched as the assistants helped Killer Kudzu out of his ceremonial apron, gold with silk kudzu leaves, purple flowers, yellow stars. His forehead blazed with the PRC flag. He looked directly at Gentian's place and smiled a broad smile.

There was a great match between Gorilla Tsunami and Typhoon Takanaka which went on for more than 30 seconds by the clock, both men straining, groaning, sweating until the *gyoji* made them stop, and rise, and then get on their marks again.

Those were the worst kinds of matches for the wrestlers, each opponent alternately straining, then bending with the other, neither getting advantage. There was a legendary match five years ago which took six 30-second tries before one wrestler bested the other.

The referee flipped his fan. Gorilla Tsunami fell flat on his face in a heap, then wriggled backwards out of the ring.

The crowd screamed and applauded Takanaka.

Then the *yobidashi* said, "East—Man-Mountain Gentian. West—Killer Kudzu."

They hurried their *shikiris*. Each threw salt twice, rinsing once. Then Man-Mountain Gentian, moving with the grace of a dancer, lifted his right leg and stamped it, then his left, and the sound was like the double echo of a cannon throughout the stadium.

He went immediately to his mark.

Killer Kudzu jumped down to his mark, glaring across the meter that separated them.

The *gyoji*, off guard, took a few seconds to turn sideways to them and bring his fan into position.

Man-Mountain Gentian

In that time, Man-Mountain Gentian could hear the quiet hum of the electrical grid, hear muffled intake of breath from the other wrestlers, hear a whistle in the nostril of the northside judge.

"Huuu!" said the referee and his fan jerked.

Man-Mountain Gentian felt like two freight trains had collided in his head. There was a snap as his muscles went tense all over and the momentum of the explosion in his brain began to push at him, lifting, threatening to make him give or tear through the back of his head. His feet were on a slippery sandy bottom, neck-high wave crests smashed into him, a rip tide was pushing at his shoulder, at one side, pulling his legs up, twisting his muscles. He could feel his eyes pushed back in their sockets as if by iron thumbs, ready to pop them like ripe plums. His ligaments were iron wires stretched tight on the turnbuckles of his bones. His arms ended in strands of noodles, his face was soft cheese.

The sand under him was soft, so soft, and he knew that all he had to do was to sink in it, let go, cease to resist.

And through all that haze and blindness he knew what he was not supposed to think about.

Everything *quit:* He reached out one mental hand, as big as the sun, as fast as light, as long as time, and he pushed against his opponent's chest.

The lights were back, he was in the stadium, in the arena, and the dull pounding was applause, screams.

Killer Kudzu lay blinking among the ring-bales.

"Hooves?" Man-Mountain Gentian heard him ask in bewilderment before he picked himself up.

Man-Mountain Gentian took the envelope from the referee with the three quick chopping motions, then made a fourth to the audience, and they knew then and only then that they would never see him in the ring again.

The official clock said .9981 seconds.

"How did you do it, Man-Mountain?" asked the Tokyo *paparazzi* as he showered out his *chon-mage* and put on his clothes. He said nothing.

He met his wife outside the stadium. A lone newsman was with her, "Scoop" Hakimoto.

"For old times' sake," begged Hakimoto. "How did you do it?"

Man-Mountain Gentian turned to Melissa. "Tell him how I did it," he said.

"He didn't think about the white horse," she said. They left the newsman standing, staring.

Killer Kudzu, tired and pale, was getting in his vehicle. Hakimoto came running up. "What's all this I hear about Gentian and a white horse?" he asked.

Kudzu's eyes widened, then narrowed.

"No comment." he said.

That night, to celebrate, Man-Mountain Gentian took Melissa to the Beef Bowl.

He had seventeen orders and helped Melissa finish her second one.

They went back home, climbed onto their futons and turned on the TV.

Gilligan was on his island. All was right with the world.

Introduction to
God's Hooks!

When I was a kid, in the 1950s, I spent all summer every summer with relatives in Mississippi. (I was born in Houston, Mississippi in 1946, but my family moved to Texas during the worst southern winter in history in 1950.) And I spent all day, every day, from before dawn until after summer sunset fishing. There were two ponds on my paternal grandparents' place, and a pond and a creek on the other side of the family, which was forty miles away at Bruce, a few miles from the Water Valley of "The Ugly Chickens." I read three kinds of literature those summers: SF, comic books, and books on fishing. I fished in Texas, too, until I was sixteen or eighteen years old. Then I quit. Didn't fish again for almost twenty years.

In 1980 I got the idea for the following story. What struck me most about it was that somebody, somewhere, but especially a hot-shot British writer, hadn't done it before. It was right there in front of them all the time, everytime they opened a history of English Literature.

As usual, I researched like a maniac; the times, clothing, gear, guilds, food, weather. I dipped into Pepys and Evelyn and Hamon L'Estrange (an old friend from "The Ugly Chickens").

I built fishing rods from scratch, and read, so help me, Puritan religious tracts.

Best of all, I started fishing again.

When John Kessel heard me read this at the World SF Convention in Denver, he turned to Leigh Kennedy and said, "That's really great, but where's he going to sell it? Field & Stream or Catholic Digest?"

Terry Carr bought it on the spot for Universe 12. *A year or so later it was up for yet another Nebula.*

It's probably the favorite of my stories in this book for reasons I don't really understand.
Pow Sock Wham! And another one flops into the creel.

God's Hooks!

They were in the End of the World Tavern at the bottom of Great Auk Street.

The place was crowded, noisy. As patrons came in, they paused to kick their boots on the floor and shake the cinders from their rough clothes.

The air smelled of wood smoke, singed hair, heated and melted glass.

"Ho!" yelled a man at one of the noisiest tables to his companions, who were dressed more finely than the workmen around them. "Here's old Izaak now, come up from Staffordshire."

A man in his seventies, dressed in brown with a wide white collar, bagged pants and cavalier boots, stood in the doorway. He took off his high-brimmed hat and shook it against his pants leg.

"Good evening, Charles, Percy, Mr. Marburton," he said, his grey eyes showing merry above his full white mustache and Vandyke beard.

"Father Izaak," said Charles Cotton, rising and embracing the older man. Cotton was wearing a new-style wig, whose curls and ringlets flowed onto his shoulders.

"Mr. Peale, if you please, sherry all round," yelled Cotton to the innkeeper. The old man seated himself.

"Sherry's dear," said the innkeeper, "though our enemy the King of France is sending two ships' consignments this fortnight. The Great Fire has worked wonders."

"What matters the price when there's good fellowship?" asked Cotton.

"Price is all," said Marburton, a melancholy round man.

"Well, Father Izaak," said Charles, turning to his friend, "how looks the house on Chancery Lane?"

"Praise to God, Charles, the fire burnt but the top floor. Enough remains to rebuild, if decent timbers can be found. Why, the lumbermen are selling green wood most expensive, and finding ready buyers."

"Their woodchoppers are working day and night in the north, since good King Charles gave them leave to cut his woods down," said Percy, and drained his glass.

"They'll not stop till all England's flat and level as Dutchman's land," said Marburton.

"If they're not careful they'll play hob with the rivers," said Cotton.

"And the streams," said Izaak.

"And the ponds," said Percy.

"Oh, the fish!" said Marburton.

All four sighed.

"Ah, but come!" said Izaak. "No joylessness here! I'm the only one to suffer from the Fire at this table. We'll have no long faces till April! Why, there's tench and dace to be had, and pickerel! What matters the salmon's in his Neptunian rookery? Who cares that trout burrow in the mud, and bite not from coat of soot and cinders? We've the roach and the gudgeon!"

"I suffered from the Fire," said Percy.

"What? Your house lies to the east," said Izaak.

"My book was at bindery at the Office of Stationers. A neighbor brought me a scorched and singed bundle of title pages. They fell sixteen miles west o' town, like snow, I suppose."

Izaak winked at Cotton. "Well, Percy, that can be set aright soon as the Stationers reopen. What you need is something right good to eat." He waved to the barkeep, who nodded and went outside to the kitchen. "I was in early and prevailed on Mr. Peale to fix a supper to cheer the dourest disposition. What with shortages, it might not pass for kings, but we are not so high. Ah, here it comes!"

Mr. Peale returned with a huge round platter. High and thick, it smelled of fresh-baked dough, meat and savories. It looked like a cooked pond. In a line around the outside, halves of whole pilchards stuck out, looking up at them with wide eyes, as if they had been struggling to escape being cooked.

"Oh, Izaak!" said Percy, tears of joy springing to his eyes. "A star-gazey pie!"

God's Hooks!

Peale beamed with pleasure. "It may not be the best," he said, "but it's the End o' the World!" He put a finger alongside his nose, and laughed. He took great pleasure in puns.

The four men at the table fell to, elbows and pewter forks flying.

They sat back from the table, full. They said nothing for a few minutes, and stared out the great bow window of the tavern. The shop across the way blocked the view. They could not see the ruins of London which stretched, charred, black and still smoking, from the Tower to the Temple. Only the waterfront in that great length had been spared.

On the fourth day of that Great Fire, the King had given orders to blast with gunpowder all houses in the way of the flames. It had been done, creating the breaks that, with a dying wind, had brought it under control and saved the city.

"What the city has gone through this past year," said Percy. "It's lucky, Izaak, that you live down country, and have not suffered till now."

"They say the fire didn't touch the worst of the plague districts," said Marburton. "I would imagine that such large crowds milling and looking for shelter will cause another one this winter. Best we should all leave the city before we drop dead in our steps."

"Since the comet of December year before last, there's been nothing but talk of doom on everyone's lips," said Cotton.

"Apocalypse talk," said Percy.

"Like as not it's right," said Marburton.

They heard the clanging bell of a crier at the next cross-street.

The tavern was filling in the late afternoon light. Carpenters, tradesmen covered with soot, a few soldiers all soiled came in.

"Why, the whole city seems full of chimneysweeps," said Percy.

The crier's clanging bell sounded, and he stopped before the window of the tavern.

"New edict from His Majesty Charles II to be posted concerning rebuilding of the city. New edict from Council of Aldermen on rents and leases, to be posted. An Act concerning movements of trade and shipping to new quays to become law. Assize Courts sessions to begin September 27, please God. Foreign

Strange Things in Close-Up

nations to send all manner of aid to the City. Murder on New Ogden Street, felon apprehended in the act. Portent of Doom, monster fish seen in Bedford."

As one, the four men leapt from the table, causing a great stir, and ran outside to the crier.

"See to the bill, Charles," said Izaak, handing him some coins. "We'll meet at nine o' the clock at the Ironmongers' Company yard. I must go see to my tackle."

"If the man the crier sent us to spoke right, there'll be no other fish like it in England," said Percy.

"Or in the world," said Marburton, whose spirits had lightened considerably.

"I imagine the length of the fish has doubled with each county the tale passed through," said Izaak.

"It'll take stout tackle," said Percy. "Me for my strongest salmon rod."

"I for my twelve-hair lines," said Marburton.

"And me," said Izaak, "to new and better angles."

The Ironmongers' Hall had escaped the fire with only the loss of its roof. There were a few workmen about, and the company secretary greeted Izaak cordially.

"Brother Walton," he said, "what brings you to town?" They gave each other the secret handshake and made The Sign.

"To look to my property on Chancery Lane, and the Row," he said. "But now, is there a fire in the forge downstairs?"

Below the Company Hall was a large workroom, where the more adventurous of the ironmongers experimented with new processes and materials.

"Certain there is," said the secretary. "We've been making new nails for the roof timbers."

"I'll need the forge for an hour or so. Send me down the small black case from my lockerbox, will you?"

"Oh, Brother Walton," asked the secretary. "Off again to some pellucid stream?"

"I doubt," said Walton, "but to fish, nonetheless."

Walton was in his shirt, sleeves rolled up, standing in the glow of the forge. A boy brought down the case from the upper floor, and now Izaak opened it, and took out three long grey-black bars.

"Pump away, boy," he said to the young man near the bellows, "and there's a copper in it for you."

Walton lovingly placed the metal bars, roughened by pounding years before, into the coals. Soon they began to glow redly as the teenaged boy worked furiously on the bellows-sack. He and Walton were covered with sweat.

"Lovely color now," said the boy.

"To whom you are prenticed?" asked Walton.

"To the company, sir."

"Ah," said Walton. "Ever seen angles forged?"

"No, sir, mostly hinges and buckles, nails-like. Sir Abram Jones sometimes puddles his metal here. I have to work most furious when he's here. I sometimes don't like to see him coming."

Walton winked conspiratorially. "You're right, the metal reaches a likable ruddy hue. Do you know what this metal is?"

"Cold iron, wasn't it? Ore beaten out?"

"No iron like you've seen, or me much either. I've saved it for nineteen years. It came from the sky, and was given to me by a great scientific man at whose feet it nearly fell."

"No!" said the boy. "I heard tell of stones falling from the sky."

"I assure you he assured me it did. And now," said Izaak, gripping the smallest metal bar with great tongs and taking it to the anvil, "We shall tease out the fishhook that is hidden away inside."

Sparks and clanging filled the basement.

They were eight miles out of northern London before the air began to smell more of September than of Hell. Two wagons jounced along the road toward Bedford, one containing the four men, the other laden with tackle, baggage and canvas.

"This is rough enough," said Cotton. "We could have sent for my coach!"

"And lost four hours,' said Marburton. "These fellows were idle enough, and Izaak wanted an especially heavy cart for some reason. Izaak, you've been most mysterious. We saw neither your tackles nor your baits."

Strange Things in Close-Up

"Suffice to say, they are none too strong nor none too delicate for the work at hand."

Away from the town there was a touch of coming autumn in the air.

"We might find nothing there," said Marburton, whose spirits had sunk again. "Or some damnably small salmon."

"Why then," said Izaak, "we'll have Bedfordshire to our own, and all of September, and perhaps an inn where the smell of lavender is in the sheets and there are twenty printed ballads on the wall!"

"Hmmph!" said Marburton.

At noon of the next day, they stopped to water the horses and eat.

"I venture to try the trout in this stream," said Percy.

"Come, come," said Cotton. "Our goal is Bedford, and we seek Leviathan himself! Would you tempt sport by angling here?"

"But a brace of trouts would be fine now."

"Have some more cold mutton," said Marburton. He passed out bread and meat and cheese all round. The drivers tugged their forelocks to him and put away their rougher fare.

"How far to Bedford?" asked Cotton of the driver called Humphrey.

"Ten miles, sir, more or less. We should have come farther but what with the Plague, the roads haven't been worked in above a year."

"I'm bruised through and through," said Marburton.

Izaak was at the stream, relieving himself against a tree.

"Damn me!" said Percy. "Did anyone leave word where I was bound?"

Marburton laughed. "Izaak sent word to all our families. Always considerate."

"Well, he's become secretive enough. All those people following him a-angling since his book went back to the presses the third time. Ah, books!" Percy grew silent.

"What, still lamenting your loss?" asked Izaak, returning. "What you need is singing, the air, sunshine. Are we not Brothers of the Angle, out a-fishing. Come, back into the charts! Charles, start us off on 'Tom o' the Town.'"

God's Hooks!

Cotton began to sing in a clear sweet voice the first stanza. One by one the others joined, their voices echoing under the bridge. The carts pulled back on the roads. The driver of the baggage cart sang with them. They went down the rutted Bedford road, September all about them, the long summer after the Plague over, their losses, heartaches all gone, all deep thoughts put away. The horses clopped time to their singing.

Bedford was a town surrounded by villages, where they were stared at when they went through. The town was divided neatly in two by the double-gated bridge over the River Ouse.

After the carts crossed the bridge, they alighted at the doorway of a place called the Topsy-Turvy Inn, whose sign above the door was a world-globe turned ass-over-teakettle.

The people who stood by the inn were all looking up the road where a small crowd had gathered around a man who was preaching from a stump.

"I think," said Cotton, as they pulled their baggage from the cart, "that we're in Dissenter country."

"Of that I'm sure," said Walton. "But once we Anglicans were on the outs and they'd say the same of us."

One of the drivers was listening to the man preach. So was Marburton.

The preacher was dressed in somber clothes. He stood on a stump at two cross streets. He was stout and had brown-red hair which glistened in the sun. His mustache was an unruly wild thing on his lip, but his beard was a neat red spike on his chin. He stood with his head uncovered, a great worn clasp-Bible under his arm.

"London burned clean through," he was saying. "Forty-three parish churches razed. Plagues! Fires! Signs in the skies of the sure and certain return of Christ. The Earth swept clean by God's loving mercy. I ask you sinners to repent for the sake of your souls."

A man walking by on the other side of the street slowed, listened, stopped.

"Oh, this is Tuesday!" he yelled to the preacher. "Save your rantings for the Sabbath, you old jail-bird!"

A few people in the crowd laughed, but others shushed him.

Strange Things in Close-Up

"In my heart," said the man on the stump, "it is always the Sabbath as long as there are sinners among you."

"Ah, a fig to your damned sneaking disloyal Non-Conformist drivel!" said the heckler, holding his thumb up between his fingers.

"Wasn't I once as you are now?" asked the preacher. "Didn't I curse and swear, play at tip-cat, ring bells, cause commotion wherever I went? Didn't God's forgiving Grace . . . ?"

A constable hurried up.

"Here, John," he said to the stout preacher. "There's to be no sermons, you know that!" He waved his staff of office. "And I charge you all under the Act of 13 Elizabeth 53 to go about your several businesses."

"Let him go on, Harry," yelled a woman. "He's got words for sinners."

"I can't argue that. I can only tell you the law. The sheriff's about on dire business, and he'd have John back in jail and the jailer turned out in a trice. Come down off the stump, man."

The stout man waved his arms. "We must disperse, friends. The Sabbath meeting will be at . . ."

The constable clapped his hands over his ears and turned his back until the preacher finished giving directions to some obscure clearing in a woods. The red-haired man stepped down.

Walton had been listening and staring at him, as had the others. Izaak saw that the man had a bag of his tools of the trade with him. He was obviously a coppersmith or brazier, his small anvils, tongs and tap hammers identifying him as such. But he was no ironmonger, so Walton was not duty-bound to be courteous to him.

"Damnable Dissenters indeed," said Cotton. "Come, Father Izaak, let's to this hospitable inn."

A crier appeared at the end of the street. "Town meeting. Town meeting. All free men of the Town of Bedford and its villages to be in attendance. Levies for the taking of the Great Fish. Four of the clock in the town hall."

"Well," said Marburton, "that's where we shall be."

They returned to the inn at dusk.

"They're certainly going at this thing full tilt," said Percy. "Nets, pikes, muskets."

"If those children had not been new to the shire, they wouldn't have tried to angle there."

"And wouldn't have been eaten and mangled," said Marburton.

"A good thing the judge is both angler and reader," said Cotton. "Else Father Walton wouldn't have been given all the morrow to prove our mettle against this great scaly beast."

"If it have scales," said Marburton.

"I fear our tackle is not up to it," said Percy.

"Didn't Father Walton always say that an angler stores up his tackle against the day he needs it? I'll wager we get good sport out of this before it's over."

"And the description of the place! In such a narrow defile the sunlight touches it but a few hours a day. For what possible reason would children fish there?"

"You're losing your faith, Marburton. I've seen you up to your whiskers in the River Lea, snaggling for salmon under a cutbank."

"But I, praise God, know what I'm about."

"I suppose," said Izaak, seating himself, "that the children thought so too."

They noticed the stout Dissenter preacher had come in and was talking jovially with his cronies. He lowered his voice and looked toward their table.

Most of the talk around Walton was of the receding Plague, the consequences of the Great Fire on the region's timber industry and other matters of report.

"I expected more talk of the fish," said Percy.

"To them," said Cotton, "it's all the same. Just another odious county task, like digging a new canal or hunting down a heretic. They'll be in holiday mood day after tomorrow."

"They strike me as a cheerless lot," said Percy.

"Cheerless but efficient. I'd hate to be the fish."

"You think we won't have to gaff long before the workmen arrive?"

"I have my doubts," said Marburton.

"But you always do."

Next morning, the woods became thick and rank on the road they took out of town. The carts bounced in the ruts. The early

Strange Things in Close-Up

sun was lost in the mist and the trees. The road rose and fell again into narrow valleys.

"Someone is following us," said Percy, getting out his spyglass.

"Probably a peddler out this way," said Cotton, straining his eyes at the pack on the man's back.

"I've seen no cottages," said Marburton. He was taking kinks out of his fishing line.

Percy looked around him. "What a godless-looking place."

The trees were more stunted, thicker. Quick shapes, which may have been grouse, moved among their twisted boles. An occasional cry, unknown to the four anglers, came from the depths of the woods. A dull boom, as of a great door closing, sounded from far away. The horses halted, whinnying, their nostrils flared.

"In truth," said Walton from where he rested against a cushion, "I feel myself some leagues beyond Christendom."

The gloom deepened. Green was gone now, nothing but greys and browns met the eye. The road was a rocky rut. The carts rose, wheels teetering on stones, and agonizingly fell. Humphrey and the other driver swore great blazing oaths.

"Be so abusive as you will," said Cotton to them, "but take not the Lord's name in vain, for we are Christian men."

"As you say." Humphrey tugged his forelock.

The trees reached overhead, the sky was obscured. An owl swept over, startling them. Something large bolted away, feet drumming on the high bank over the road.

Percy and Cotton grew quiet. Walton talked, of lakes, streams, of summer. Seeing the others grow moody, he sang a quiet song. A driver would sometimes curse.

A droning flapping sound grew louder, passed to their right, veered away. The horses shied then, trying to turn around in the road, almost upsetting the carts. They refused to go on.

"We'll have to tether them here," said Humphrey. "Besides, Your Lordship, I think I see water at the end of the road."

It was true. In what dim light there was, they saw a darker sheen down below.

"We must take the second cart down there, Charles," said Walton, "even if we must push it ourselves."

God's Hooks!

"We'll never make it,' said Percy.

"Whatever for?" asked Cotton. "We can take our tackle and viands down there?"

"Not my tackle," said Walton.

Marburton just sighed.

They pushed and pulled the second cart down the hill; from the front they kept it from running away on the incline, from the back to get it over stones the size of barrels. It was stuck.

"I can't go on," said Marburton.

"Surely you can," said Walton.

"Your cheerfulness is depressing," said Percy.

"Be that as it may. Think trout, Marburton. Think salmon!"

Marburton strained against the recalcitrant wheel. The cart moved forward a few inches.

"See, see!" said Walton. "A foot's good as a mile!"

They grunted and groaned.

They stood panting at the edge of the mere. The black sides of the valley lifted to right and left like walls. The water itself was weed-choked, scummy, and smelled of sewer-ditch. Trees came down to its very edges. Broken and rotted stumps dotted the shore. Mist rose from the water in fetid curls.

Sunlight had not yet come to the bottom of the defile. To left and right, behind, all lay twisted woody darkness. The valley rose like a hand around them.

Except ahead. There was a break, with no trees at the center of the cleft. Through it they saw, shining and blue-purple against the cerulean of the sky, the far-off Chiltern Hills.

"Those," said a voice behind them, and they jumped and turned and saw the man with the pack. It was the stout red-haired preacher of the day before. "Those are the Delectable Mountains," he said.

"And this is the Slough of Despond."

He built a small lean-to some hundred feet from them.

The other three anglers unloaded their gear and began to set it up.

"What, Father Walton? Not setting up your poles?" asked Charles Cotton.

Strange Things in Close-Up

"No, no," said Izaak, studying the weed-clotted swamp with a sure eye. "I'll let you young ones try your luck first."

Percy looked at the waters. "The fish is most likely a carp or other rough type," he said. "No respectable fish could live in this mire. I hardly see room for anything that could swallow a child."

"It is Leviathan," said the preacher from his shelter. "It is the Beast of Babylon which shall rise in the days before Antichrist. These woods are beneath his sway."

"What do you want?" asked Cotton.

"To dissuade you, and the others who will come from doing this. It is God's will these things come to pass."

"Oh, hell and damn!" said Percy.

"Exactly," said the preacher.

Percy shuddered involuntarily. Daylight began to creep down to the mere's edge. With the light, the stench from the water became worse.

"You're not doing very much to stop us," said Cotton. He was fitting together an eighteen-foot rod of yew, fir and hazelwood.

"When you raise Leviathan," said the preacher, "then will I begin to preach." He took a small cracked pot from his large bag, and began to set up his anvil.

Percy's rod had a butt as thick as a man's arm. It tapered throughout its length to a slender reed. The line was made of plaited dyed horsehair, twelve strands at the pole end, tapering to nine. The line was forty feet long. Onto the end of this he fastened a sinker and a hook as long as a crooked little finger.

"Where's my baits? Oh, here they are." He reached into a bag filled with wet moss, pulled out a gob of worms and threaded seven or eight, their ends wriggling, onto the hook.

The preacher had started a small fire. He was filling an earthen pot with solder. He paid very little attention to the anglers.

Percy and Marburton, who was fishing with a shorter but thicker rod, were ready before Cotton.

"I'll take this fishy spot here," said Percy, "and you can have that grown-over place there." He pointed beyond the preacher.

"We won't catch anything," said Marburton suddenly and pulled the bait from his hook and threw it into the water. Then he walked back to the cart and sat down, and shook.

God's Hooks!

"Come, come," said Izaak. "I've never seen you so discouraged, even after fishless days on the Thames."

"Never mind me," said Marburton. Then he looked down at the ground. "I shouldn't have come all this way. I have business in the city. There are no fish here."

Cajoling could not get him up again. Izaak's face became troubled. Marburton stayed put.

"Well, I'll take the fishy spot then," said Cotton tying onto his line an artificial fly of green with hackles the size of porcupine quills.

He moved past the preacher.

"I'm certain to wager you'll get no strikes on that gaudy bird's wing," said Percy.

"There is no better fishing than angling fine and far off," answered Cotton. "Heavens, what a stink!"

"This is the place," said the preacher without looking up, "where all the sins of mankind have been flowing for 1,600 years. Not 20,000 cartloads of earth could fill it up."

"Prattle," said Cotton.

"Prattle it may be," said the preacher. He puddled solder in a sandy ring. Then he dipped the pot in it. "It stinks from mankind's sins, nonetheless."

"It stinks from mankind's bowels," said Cotton.

He made two back casts with his long rod, letting more line out the wire guide at the tip each time. He placed the huge fly gently on the water sixty feet away.

"There are no fish about," said Percy, down the mire's edge. "Not even gudgeon."

"Nor snakes," said Cotton. "What does this monster eat?"

"Miscreant children," said the preacher. "Sin feeds on the young."

Percy made a clumsy cast into some slime-choked weeds.

His rod was pulled from his hands and flew across the water. A large dark shape blotted the pond's edge and was gone.

The rod floated to the surface and lay still. Percy stared down at his hands in disbelief. The pole came slowly in toward shore, pushed by the stinking breeze.

Cotton pulled his fly off the water, shook his line and walked back toward the carts.

"That's all for me, too," he said. They turned to Izaak. He

Strange Things in Close-Up

rubbed his hands together gleefully, making a show he did not feel.

The preacher was grinning.

"Call the carters down," said Walton. "Move the cart to the very edge of the mere."

While they were moving the wagon with its rear facing the water, Walton went over to the preacher.

"My name is Izaak Walton," he said, holding out his hand. The preacher took it formally.

"John Bunyan, mechanic-preacher," said the other.

"I hold no man's religious beliefs against him, if he be an honest man, or an angler. My friends are not of like mind, though they be both fishermen and honest."

"Would that Parliament were full of such as yourself," said Bunyan. "I took your hand, but I am dead set against what you do."

"If not us," said Walton, "then the sheriff with his powder and pikes."

"I shall prevail against them, too. This is God's warning to mankind. You're a London man. You've seen the Fire, the Plague?"

"London is no place for honest men. I'm of Stafford."

"Even you see London as a place of sin," said Bunyan. "You have children?"

"Have two, by my second wife," said Walton. "Seven others died in infancy."

"I have four," Bunyan said. "One born blind." His eyes took on a faraway look. "I want them to fear God, in hope of eternal salvation."

"As do we all," said Walton.

"And this monster is warning to mankind of the coming rains of blood and fire and the fall of stars."

"Either we shall take it, or the townsmen will come tomorrow."

"I know them all," said Bunyan. "Mr. Nurse-Nickel, Mr. By-Your-Leave, Mr. Cravenly-Crafty. Do ye not feel your spirits lag, your backbone fail? They'll not last long as you have."

Walton had noticed his own lassitude, even with the stink of the slough goading him. Cotton, Percy and Marburton, finished with the cart, were sitting disconsolately on the ground. The swamp had brightened some, the blazing blue mountain ahead seemed inches away. But the woods were dark, the defile precipitous, the noises loud as before.

"It gets worse after dark," said the preacher. "I beg you, take not the fish."

"If you stop the sheriff, he'll have you in prison."

"It's prison from which I come," said Bunyan. "To gaol I shall go back, for I know I'm right."

"Do your conscience," said Walton, "for that way lies salvation."

"Amen!" said Bunyan, and went back to his pots.

Percy, Marburton and Charles Cotton watched as Walton set up his tackle. Even with flagging spirits, they were intrigued. He'd had the carters peg down the trace poles of the wagon. Then he sectioned together a rod like none they had seen before. It was barely nine feet long, starting big as a smith's biceps, ending in a fine end. It was made of many split lathes glued seamlessly together. On each foot of its length past the handle were iron guides bound with wire. There was a hole in the handle of the rod, and now Walton reached in the wagon and took out a shining metal wheel.

"What's that, a squirrel cage?" asked Percy.

They saw him pull line out from it. It clicked with each turn. There was a handle on the wheel, and a peg at the bottom. He put the peg through the hole in the handle and fastened it down with an iron screw.

He threaded the line, which was thick as a pen quill, through the guides, opened the black case and took out the largest of the hooks he'd fashioned.

On the line he tied a strong wire chain, and affixed a sinker to one end and the hook on the other.

He put the rod in the wagon seat and climbed down the back and opened his bait box and reached in.

"Come, my pretty," he said, reaching. He took something out, white, segmented, moving. It filled his hand.

It was a maggot that weighed half a pound.

"I had them kept down a cistern behind a shambles," said Walton. He lifted the bait to show them. "Charles, take my line after I bait the angle, make a hand cast into the edge of those

Strange Things in Close-Up

stumps yonder. As I was saying, take your gentles, put them in a cool well, feed them on liver of pork for the summer. They'll eat and grow and not change into flies, for the changing of one so large kills it. Keep them well-fed, put them into wet moss before using them. I feared the commotion and flames had collapsed the well. Though the butcher shop was gone, the baits were still fat and lively."

As he said the last word, he plunged the hook through the white flesh of the maggot.

It twisted and oozed onto his hand. He opened a small bottle. "And dowse it with camphire oil just before the cast." They smelled the pungent liquid as he poured it. The bait went into a frenzy.

"Now, Charles," he said, pulling off fifty feet of line from the reel. Cotton whirled the weighted hook around and around his head. "Be so kind as to tie this rope to my belt and the cart, Percy," said Walton.

Percy did so. Cotton made the hand cast, the pale globule hitting the water and sinking.

"Do as I have told you," said Walton, "and you shall not fail to catch the biggest fish."

Something large between the eyes swallowed the hook and five feet of line.

"And set the hook sharply, and you shall have great sport." Walton, seventy years old, thin of build, stood in the seat, jerked far back over his head, curving the rod in a loop.

The waters of the slough exploded; they saw the shallow bottom and a long dark shape, and the fight was on.

The preacher stood up from his pots, opened his clasp Bible and began to read in a loud strong voice.

"Render to Caesar . . ." he said. Walton flinched and put his back into turning the fish, which was heading toward the stumps. The reel's clicks were a buzz. Bunyan raised his voice, ". . . those things which are Caesar's, and to God those things which are God's."

"Oh, shut up!" said Cotton. "The man's got trouble enough!"

The wagon creaked and began to lift off the ground. The rope and belt cut into Walton's flesh. His arms were nearly pulled from their sockets. Sweat sprang to his forehead like curds through a cheesecloth. He gritted his teeth and pulled.

The pegs lifted from the ground.
Bunyan read on.

The sunlight faded though it was only late afternoon. The noise from the woods grew louder. The blue hills in the distance became flat, grey. The whole valley leaned over them, threatening to fall over and kill them. Eyes shined in the deeper woods.

Walton had regained some line in the last few hours. Bunyan read on, pausing long enough to light a horn lantern from his fire.

After encouraging Walton at first, Percy, Marburton and Cotton had become quiet. The sounds were those of Bunyan's droning voice, screams from the woods, small pops from the fire and the ratcheting of the reel.

The fish was fighting him on the bottom. He'd had no sight of it yet since the strike. Now the water was becoming a flat black sheet in the failing light. It was no salmon or trout or carp. It must be a pike or eel or some other toothed fish. Or a serpent. Or cuttlefish, with squiddy arms to tear the skin from a man.

Walton shivered. His arms were numb, his shoulders a tight aching band. His legs where he braced against the footrest quivered with fatigue. Still he held, even when the fish ran to the far end of the swamp. If he could keep it away from the snags he could wear it down. The fish turned, the line slackened, Walton pumped the rod up and down. He regained the lost line. The water hissed as the cording cut through it. The fish headed for the bottom.

Tiredly, Walton heaved, turned the fish. The wagon creaked.

"Blessed are they that walk in the path of righteousness," said Bunyan.

The ghosts came in over the slough straight at them. Monkey-demons began to chatter in the woods. Eyes peered from the bole of every tree. Bunyan's candle was the only light. Something walked heavily on a limb at the wood's edge, bending it. Marburton screamed and ran up the road.

Percy was on his feet. Ghosts and banshees flew at him, veering away at the last instant.

"You have doubts," said Bunyan to him. "You are assailed. You think yourself unworthy."

Percy trotted up the stony road, ragged shapes fluttering in the air behind him, trying to tug his hair. Skeletons began to dance across the slough, acting out pantomimes of life, death and love. The Seven Deadly Sins manifested themselves.

Hell yawned open to receive them all.

Then the sun went down.

"Before you join the others, Charles," said Walton, pumping the rod, "cut away my coat and collar."

"You'll freeze," said Cotton, but climbed in the wagon and cut the coat up the back and down the sleeves. It and the collar fell away.

"Good luck, Father Walton," he said. Something plucked at his eyes. "We go to town for help."

"Be honest and trustworthy all the rest of your days," said Izaak Walton. Cotton looked stunned. Something large ran down from the woods, through the wagon and up into the trees. Cotton ran up the hill. The thing loped after him.

Walton managed to gain six inches on the fish.

Grinning things sat on the taut line. The air was filled with meteors, burning, red, thick as snow. Huge worms pushed themselves out of the ground, caught and ate the demons, then turned inside out. The demons flew away.

Everything in the darkness had claws and horns.

"And lo! the seventh seal was broken, and there was quietness on the earth for the space of half an hour," read Bunyan.

He had lit his third candle.

Walton could see the water again. A little light came from somewhere behind him. The noises of the woods diminished. A desultory ghost or skeleton flitted grayly by. There was a calm in the air.

The fish was tiring. Walton did not know how long he had fought on, or with what power. He was a human ache, and he wanted to sleep. He was nodding.

"The townsmen come," said Bunyan. Walton stole a fleeting glance behind him. Hundreds of people came quietly and cautiously through the woods, some extinguishing torches as he watched.

Walton cranked in another ten feet of line. The fish ran, but only a short way, slowly, and Walton reeled him back. It was still a long way out, still another hour before he could bring it to gaff. Walton heard low talk, recognized Percy's voice. He looked back again. The people had pikes, nets, a small cannon. He turned, reeled the fish, fighting it all the way.

"You do not love God!" said Bunyan suddenly, shutting his Bible.

"Yes I do!" said Walton, pulling as hard as he could. He gained another foot. "I love God as much as you."

"You do not!" said Bunyan. "I see it now."

"I love God!" yelled Walton and heaved the rod.

A fin broke the frothing water.

"In your heart, where God can see from His high throne, you lie!" said Bunyan.

Walton reeled and pulled. More fin showed. He quit cranking.

"God forgive me!" said Walton. "It's fishing I love."

"I thought so," said Bunyan. Reaching in his pack he took out a pair of tin snips and cut Walton's line.

Izaak fell back in the wagon.

"John Bunyan, you son of a bitch!" said the Sheriff. "You're under arrest for hampering the King's business. I'll see you rot."

Walton watched the coils of line on the surface slowly sink into the brown depths of the Slough of Despond.

He began to cry, fatigue and numbness taking over his body.

"I denied God," he said to Cotton. "I committed the worst sin." Cotton covered him with a blanket.

"Oh Charles, I denied God."

"What's worse," said Cotton, "you lost the fish."

Percy and Marburton helped him up. The carters hitched the wagons, the horses now docile. Bunyan was being ridden back to jail by constables, his tinker's bag clanging against the horse's side.

They put the crying Walton into the cart, covered him more, climbed in. Some farmers helped them get the carts over the rocks.

Walton's last view of the slough was of resolute and grim-faced men staring at the water and readying their huge grapples, their guns, their cruel hooked nets.

They were on the road back to town. Walton looked up into the trees, devoid of ghosts and demons. He caught a glimpse of the blue Chiltern Hills.

"Father Izaak," said Cotton. "Rest now. Think of spring. Think of clear water, of leaping trout."

"My dreams will be haunted by God the rest of my days," he said tiredly. Walton fell asleep.

He dreamed of clear water, leaping Trouts.

This story is for Chad Oliver, Punisher of Trouts.

Introduction to
Heirs of the Perisphere

The first piece of writing I ever sold was a joke for the Playboy *joke page, back in 1966. I got twenty-five dollars. When the issue with the joke came out (September 1966) I was visiting in California. I went in this place to pick up a copy, and was run out of the newsstand. Seems you couldn't buy a copy of* Playboy *in California until you were twenty-one, although you could pick up copies when you were eighteen in Texas. (You couldn't vote or drink when you were eighteen in Texas, but you could damn sure be drafted and have parts of your body shot off by strangers).*

I'd wanted to write about the central subject of this story since I was ten years old and read about the 1939 World's Fair, and saw the buttons that said I HAVE SEEN THE FUTURE. (The 60s version was I Have Seen the Future. It Doesn't Work.)

Everything came together in 1983. The subject, the treatment, how to do it—well, almost. I wrote the story anyway, supposedly for Mike Bishop's Light Years and Dark *(it was then called* The Cosmopedia, *and boy am I glad they called the book something else!), but for complex and uninteresting reasons (mostly having to do with length) I ended up writing something else for Mike.*

Joe Elder, my agent, sent this story to Playboy.

Alice Turner bought it, and worked with me through many drafts. It's certainly a better story now than it was then, when I wasn't quite sure what I was doing.

This is the most recent story in the book, and it may point a new direction my writing seems to be taking. I don't know what direction that is yet. ("Toward the Land of the Knee-Walking Turkeys!" someone cries.) The only way I can find out is to write the stories as they come to me, and worry about it later.

Strange Things in Close-Up

I'm looking forward to them with eagerness and anticipation. The editors are looking forward to them with a whole other set of emotions, I betcha.

Heirs of the Perisphere

Things had not been going well at the factory for the last 1,500 years or so.

A rare thunderstorm, a soaking rain and a freak lightning bolt changed all that.

When the lightning hit, an emergency generator went to work as it had been built to do a millennia and a half before. It cranked up and ran the assembly line just long enough, before freezing up and shedding its brushes and armatures in a fine spray, to finish some work in the custom design section.

The factory completed, hastily programmed and wrongly certified as approved the three products which had been on the assembly line fifteen centuries before.

Then the place went dark again.

"Gawrsh," said one of them. "It shore is dark in here!"

"Well, huh-huh, we can always use the infrared they gave us!"

"Wak Wak Wak!" said the third. "What's the big idea?"

The custom order jobs were animato/mechanical simulacra. They were designed to speak and act like the famous creations of a multimillionaire cartoonist who late in life had opened a series of gigantic amusement parks in the latter half of the twentieth century.

Once these giant theme parks had employed persons in costume to act the parts. Then the corporation which had run things after the cartoonist's death had seen the wisdom of building robots. The simulacra would be less expensive in the long run, would never be late for work, could be programmed to speak many languages, and would never try to pick up the clean-cut boys and girls who visited the Parks.

Strange Things in Close-Up

These three had been built to be host-robots in the third and largest of the Parks, the one separated by an ocean from the other two.

And, as their programming was somewhat incomplete, they had no idea of much of this.

All they had were a bunch of jumbled memories, awareness of the thunderstorm outside, and of the darkness of the factory around them.

The tallest of the three must have started as a cartoon dog, but had become upright and acquired a set of baggy pants, balloon shoes, a sweatshirt, black vest and white gloves. There was a miniature carpenter's hat on his head, and his long ears hung down from it. He had two prominent incisors in his muzzle. He stood almost two meters tall and answered to the name GUF.

The second, a little shorter, was a white duck with a bright orange bill and feet, and a blue and white sailor's tunic and cap. He had large eyes with little cuts out of the upper right corners of the pupils. He was naked from the waist down, and was the only one of the three without gloves. He answered to the name DUN.

The third and smallest, just over a meter, was a rodent. He wore a red bibbed playsuit with two huge gold buttons at the waistline. He was shirtless and had shoes like two pieces of bread dough. His tail was long and thin like a whip. His bare arms, legs and chest were black, his face a pinkish-tan. His white gloves were especially prominent. His most striking feature was his ears, which rotated on a track, first one way, then another, so that seen from any angle they could look like a featureless black circle.

His name was MIK. His eyes, like those of GUF, were large and the pupils were big round dots. His nose ended in a perfect sphere of polished onyx.

"Well," said MIK, brushing dust from his body, "I guess we'd better, huh-huh, get to work."

"Uh hyuk," said GUF. "Won't be many people at thuh Park in weather like thiyus."

"Oh boy! Oh boy!" quacked DUN. "Rain! Wak Wak Wak!"

Heirs of the Perisphere

He ran out through a huge crack in the wall which streamed with rain and mist.

MIK and GUF came behind, GUF ambling with his hands in his pockets, MIK walking determinedly.

Lightning cracked once more but the storm seemed to be dying.

"Wak Wak Wak!" said DUN, his tail fluttering, as he swam in a big puddle. "Oh boy Oh joy!"

"I wonder if the rain will hurt our works?" asked MIK.

"Not me!" said GUF. "Uh hyuk! I'm equipped fer all kinds a weather." He put his hand conspiratorially beside his muzzle. "'Ceptin' mebbe real cold on thuh order of—40° Celsius, uh hyuk!"

MIK was ranging in the ultraviolet and infrared, getting the feel of the landscape through the rain. "You'd have thought, huh-huh, they might have sent a truck over or something," he said. "I guess we'll have to walk."

"I didn't notice anyone at thuh factory," said GUF. "Even if it was a day off, you'd think some of thuh workers would give unceasingly of their time, because, after all, thuh means of produckshun must be kept in thuh hands of thuh workers, uh hyuk!"

GUF's speciality was to have been talking with visitors from the large totalitarian countries to the west of the country the Park was in. He was especially well-versed in dialectical materialism and correct Mao Thought.

As abruptly as it had started, the storm ended. Great ragged gouts broke in the clouds, revealing high, fast-moving cirrus, a bright blue sky, the glow of a warming sun.

"Oh rats rats rats!" said DUN, holding out his hand palm up. "Just when I was starting to get wet!"

"Uh, well," asked GUF, "which way is it tuh work? Thuh people should be comin' out o thuh sooverneer shops real soon now."

MIK looked around, consulting his programming. "That way, guys," he said, unsure of himself. There were no familiar landmarks, and only one that was disturbingly unfamiliar.

Far off was the stump of a mountain. MIK had a feeling it should be beautiful, blue and snow-capped. Now it was a brown lump, heavily eroded, with no white at the top. It looked like a bite had been taken out of it.

All around them was rubble, and far away in the other direction was a sluggish ocean.

It was getting dark. The three sat on a pile of concrete.

"Them and their big ideas," said DUN.

"Looks like thuh Park is closed," said GUF.

MIK sat with his hands under his chin. "This just isn't right, guys," he said. "We were supposed to report to the programming hut to get our first day's instructions. Now we can't even find the Park!"

"I wish it would rain again," said DUN, "while you two are making up your minds."

"Well, uh hyuk," said GUF. "I seem tuh remember we could get hold of thuh satellite in a 'mergency."

"Sure!" said MIK, jumping to his feet and pounding his fist into his glove. "That's it! Let's see, what frequency was that . . . ?"

"Six point five oh four," said DUN. He looked eastward. "Maybe I'll go to the ocean."

"Better stay here whiles we find somethin' out," said GUF.

"Well, make it snappy!" said DUN.

MIK tuned in the frequency and broadcast the Park's call letters.

". . . ZZZZZ. What? HOOSAT?"

"Uh, this is MIK, one of the simulacra at the Park. We're trying to get ahold of one of the other Parks for, huh-huh, instructions."

"In what language would you like to communicate?" asked the satellite.

"Oh, sorry, huh-huh. We speak Japanese to each other, but we'll switch over to Artran if that's easier for you." GUF and DUN tuned in, too.

"It's been a very long while since anyone communicated with me from down there." The satellite's well-modulated voice snapped and popped.

"If you must know," HOOSAT continued, "it's been rather a while since anyone contacted me from anywhere. I can't say much for the stability of my orbit, either. Once I was forty thousand kilometers up, very stable . . ."

"Could you put us through to one of the other Parks, or maybe the Studio itself, if you can do that? We'd, huh-huh, like to find out where to report for work."

"I'll attempt it," said HOOSAT. There was a pause and some static. "Predictably, there's no answer at any of the locations."

"Well, where are they?"

"To whom do you refer?"

"The people," said MIK.

"Oh, you wanted humans? I thought perhaps you wanted the stations themselves. There was a slight chance that some of them were still functioning."

"Where are thuh folks?" asked GUF.

"I really don't know. We satellites and monitoring stations used to worry about that frequently. Something happened to them."

"What?" asked all three robots at once.

"Hard to understand," said HOOSAT. "Ten or fifteen centuries ago. Very noisy in all spectra, followed by quiet. Most of the ground stations ceased functioning within a century after that. You're the first since then."

"What do you do, then?" asked MIK.

"Talk with other satellites. Very few left. One of them has degraded. It only broadcasts random numbers when the solar wind is very strong. Another . . ."

There was a burst of fuzzy static.

"Hello? HOOSAT?" asked the satellite. "It's been a very long time since anyone . . ."

"It's still us!" said MIK. "The simulacra from the Park. We—"

"Oh, that's right. What can I do for you?"

"Tell us where the people went."

"I have no idea."

"Well, where can we find out?" asked MIK.

"You might try the library."

"Where's that?"

"Let me focus in. Not very much left down there, is there? I can give you the coordinates. Do you have standard navigational programming?"

"Boy, do we!" said MIK.
"Well, here's what you do . . ."

"Sure don't look much different from thuh rest of this junk, does it, MIK?" asked GUF.

"I'm sure there used to be many, many books here," said MIK. "It all seems to have turned to powder though, doesn't it?"

"Well," said GUF, scratching his head with his glove, "they sure didn't make 'em to last, did they?"

DUN was mumbling to himself. "Doggone wizoo-wazoo waste of time," he said. He sat on one of the piles of dirt in the large broken-down building of which only one massive wall still stood. The recent rain had turned the meter-deep powder on the floor into a mache sludge.

"I guess there's nothing to do but start looking," said MIK.

"Find a book on water," said DUN.

"Hey, MIK! Looka this!" yelled GUF.

He came running with a steel box. "I found this just over there."

The box was plain, unmarked. There was a heavy lock to which MIK applied various pressures.

"Let's forget all this nonsense and go fishing," said DUN.

"It might be important," said MIK.

"Well, open it then," said DUN.

"It's, huh-huh, stuck."

"Gimme that!" yelled DUN. He grabbed it. Soon he was muttering under his beak. "Doggone razzle-frazzin dadgum thing!" He pulled and pushed, his face and bill turning redder and redder. He gripped the box with both his feet and hands. "Doggone dadgum!" he yelled.

Suddenly he grew teeth, his brow slammed down, his shoulders tensed and he went into a blurred fury of movement. "WAK WAK WAK WAK WAK!" he screamed.

The box broke open and flew into three parts. So did the book inside.

DUN was still tearing in his fury.

"Wait, look out, DUN," yelled MIK. "Wait!"

Heirs of the Perisphere

"Gawrsh," said GUF, running after the pages blowing in the breeze. "Help me, MIK."

DUN stood atop the rubble, parts of the box and the book gripped in each hand. He simulated hard breathing, the redness draining from his face.

"It's open," he said quietly.

"Well, from what we've got left," said MIK, "this is called *The Book of the Time Capsule*, and it tells that people buried a cylinder a very, very long time ago. They printed up five thousand copies of this book and sent it to places all around the world, where they thought it would be safe. They printed them on acid-free paper and stuff like that so they wouldn't fall apart.

"And they thought what they put in the time capsule itself could explain to later generations what people were like in their day. So I figure maybe it could explain something to us, too."

"That sounds fine with me," said GUF.

"Well, let's go!" said DUN.

"Well, huh-huh," said MIK. "I checked with HOOSAT, and gave him the coordinates, and, huh-huh, it's quite a little ways away."

"How far?" asked DUN, his brow beetling.

"Oh, huh-huh, about eighteen thousand kilometers," said MIK.

"WHAAT???"

"About eighteen thousand kilometers. Just about halfway around the world."

"Oh, my aching feet!" said DUN.

"That's not literally true," said GUF. He turned to MIK. "Yuh think we should go that far?"

"Well . . . I'm not sure what we'll find. Those pages were lost when DUN opened the box . . ."

"I'm sorry," said DUN, in a contrite small voice.

". . . but the people of that time were sure that everything could be explained by what was in the capsule."

"And you think it's all still there?" asked DUN.

"Well, they buried it pretty deep, and took a lot of precautions with the way they preserved things. And we *did* find the book, just like they wanted us to. I'd imagine it was all still there!"

"Well, it's a long ways," said GUF. "But it doesn't look much like we'll find anyone here."

MIK put a determined look on his face.

"I figure the only thing for us to do is set our caps and whistle a little tune," he said.

"Yuh don't have a cap, MIK," said GUF.

"Well, I can still whistle! Let's go, fellas," he said. "It's *this* way!"

He whistled a work song. DUN quacked a tune about boats and love. GUF hummed "The East Is Red."

They set off in this way across what had been the bottom of the Sea of Japan.

They were having troubles. It had been a long time and they walked on tirelessly. Three weeks ago they'd come to the end of all the songs each of them was programmed with and had to start repeating themselves.

Their lubricants were beginning to fail, their hastily-wired circuitry was overworked. GUF had a troublesome ankle extensor which sometimes hung up. But he went along just as cheerfully, sometimes hopping and quickstepping to catch up with the others when the foot refused to flex.

The major problem was the cold. There was a vast difference in the climate they had left and the one they found themselves in. The landscape was rocky and empty. It had begun to snow more frequently and the wind was fierce.

The terrain was difficult, and HOOSAT's maps were outdated. Something drastic had changed the course of rivers, the land, the shoreline of the ocean itself. They had to detour frequently.

The cold worked hardest on DUN. "Oh," he would say, "I'm so cold, so cold!" He was very poorly insulated, and they had to slow their pace to his. He would do anything to avoid going through a snowdrift, and so expended even more energy.

They stopped in the middle of a raging blizzard.

"Uh, MIK," said GUF. "I don't think DUN can go much further in this weather. An' my leg is givin' me a lot o' problems. Yuh think maybe we could find someplace to hole up fer a spell?"

MIK looked around them at the bleakness and the whipping

Heirs of the Perisphere

snow. "I guess you're right. Warmer weather would do us all some good. We could conserve both heat and energy. Let's find a good place."

"Hey, DUN," said GUF. "Let's find us a hidey-hole!"

"Oh, goody gumdrops!" quacked DUN. "I'm so cold!"

They eventually found a deep rock shelter with a low fault crevice at the back. MIK had them gather up what sparse dead vegetation there was and bring it to the shelter. DUN and GUF crawled in the back and MIK piled brush all through the cave. He talked to HOOSAT, then wriggled his way through the brush to them.

Inside they could barely hear the wind and snow. It was only slightly warmer than outside, but it felt wonderful and safe.

"I told HOOSAT to wake us up when it got warmer," said MIK. "Then we'll get on to that time capsule and find out all about the people."

"G'night, MIK," said GUF.

"Goodnight, DUN," said MIK.

"Sleep tight and don't let the bedbugs bite. Wak Wak Wak," said DUN.

They shut themselves off.

Something woke MIK. It was dark in the rock shelter, but it was also much warmer.

The brush was all crumbled away. A meter of rock and dust covered the cave floor. The warm wind stirred it.

"Hey, fellas!" said MIK. "Hey, wake up! Spring is here!"

"Wak! What's the big idea? Hey, oh boy, it's warm!" said DUN.

"Garsh," said GUF, "that sure was a nice forty winks!"

"Well, let's go thank HOOSAT and get our bearings and be on our way."

They stepped outside.

The stars were in the wrong places.

"Uh-oh," said GUF.

"Well, would you look at that!" said DUN.

"I think we overslept," said MIK. "Let's see what HOOSAT has to say."

". . . Huh? HOOSAT?"

"Hello. This is DUN and MIK and GUF."

225

Strange Things in Close-Up

HOOSAT's voice now sounded like a badger whistling through its teeth.

"Glad to see ya up!" he said.

"We went to sleep, and told you to wake us up as soon as it got warmer."

"Sorry. I forgot till just now. Had a lot on my mind. Besides, it just now got warmer."

"It did?" asked GUF.

"Shoulda seen it," said HOOSAT. "Ice everywhere. Big ol' glaciers. Took the top offa everything! You still gonna dig up that capsule thing?"

"Yes," said MIK. "We are."

"Well, you got an easy trip from now on. No more mountains in your way."

"What about people?"

"Nah. No people. I ain't heard from any, no ways. My friend the military satellite said he thought he saw some fires, little teeny ones, but his eyes weren't what they used to be by then. He's gone now, too."

"The fires might have been built by people?"

"Who knows? Not me," said HOOSAT. "Hey, bub, you still got all those coordinates like I give you?"

"I think so," said MIK.

"Well, I better give you new ones off these new constellations. Hold still, my aim ain't so good anymore." He dumped a bunch of numbers in MIK's head. "I won't be talking to ya much longer."

"Why not?" they all asked.

"Well, you know. My orbit. I feel better now than I have in years. Real spry. Probably the ionization. Started a couple o' weeks ago. Sure has been nice talkin' to you young fellers after so long a time. Sure am glad I remembered to wake you up. I wish you a lotta luck. Boy, this air has a punch like a mule. Be careful. Good-bye."

Across the unfamiliar stars overhead a point of light blazed, streaked in a long arc, then died on the night.

"Well," said MIK. "We're on our own."

"Gosh, I feel all sad," said GUF.

"Warmth, oh boy!" said DUN.

Heirs of the Perisphere

The trip was uneventful for the next few months. They walked across the long land bridge down a valley between stumps of mountains with the white teeth of glaciers on them. Then they crossed a low range and entered flat land without topsoil from which dry rivercourses ran to the south. Then there was a land where things were flowering after the long winter. New streams were springing up.

They saw fire once and detoured, but found only a burnt patch of forest. Once, way off in the distance, they saw a speck of light but didn't go to investigate.

Within two hundred kilometers of their goal, the land changed again to a flat sandy waste littered with huge rocks. Sparse vegetation grew. There were few insects and animals, mostly lizards, which DUN chased every chance he got. The warmth seemed to be doing him good.

GUF's leg worsened. The foot now stuck, now flopped and windmilled. He kept humming songs and raggedly marching along with the other two.

When they passed one of the last trees, MIK had them all three take limbs from it. "Might come in handy for pushing and digging," he said.

They stood on a plain of sand and rough dirt. There were huge piles of rubble all around. Far off was another ocean, and to the north a patch of green.

"We'll go to the ocean, DUN," said MIK, "after we get through here."

He was walking around in a smaller and smaller circle. Then he stopped. "Well, huh-huh," he said. "Here we are. Lattitude 40° 44' 34" .089 North. Longitude 73° 50' 43" .842 West, by the way they *used* to figure it. The capsule is straight down, twenty-eight meters below the original surface. We've got a long way to go, because there's no telling how much soil has drifted over that. It's in a concrete tube, and we'll have to dig to the very bottom to get at the capsule. Let's get working."

It was early morning when they started. Just after noon they found the top of the tube with its bronze tablet.

"Here's where the hard work starts," said MIK.

It took them two weeks of continual effort. Slowly the tube was exposed as the hole around it grew larger. Since GUF could

Strange Things in Close-Up

work better standing still, they had him dig all the time, while DUN and MIK both dug and pushed rock and dirt clear of the crater.

They found some long flat iron rods partway down, and threw away the worn limbs and used the metal to better effect.

On one of the trips to push dirt out of the crater, DUN came back looking puzzled.

"I thought I saw something moving out there," he said. "When I looked, it went away."

"Probably just another animal," said MIK. "Here, help me lift this rock."

It was hard work and their motors were taxed. It rained once, and once there was a dust storm.

"Thuh way I see it," said GUF, looking at their handiwork, "is that yah treat it like a big ol' tree made outta rock."

They stood in the bottom of the vast crater. Up from the center of this stood the concrete tube.

"We've reached twenty-six meters," said MIK. "The capsule itself should be in the last 2.3816 meters. So we should chop it off," he quickly calculated, "about here." He drew a line all around the tube with a piece of chalky rock.

They began to smash at the concrete with rocks and pieces of iron and steel.

"Timber!" said DUN.

The column above the line lurched and with a crash shattered itself against the side of the crater wall.

"Oh boy! Oh boy!"

"Come help me, GUF," said MIK.

Inside the jagged top of the remaining shaft an eyebolt stood out of the core.

They climbed up on the edge, reached in and raised the gleaming Cupraloy time capsule from its resting place.

On its side was a message to the finders, and just below the eyebolt at the top was a line and the words CUT HERE.

"Well," said MIK shaking DUN and GUF's hands. "We did it, by gum!"

He looked at it a moment.

Heirs of the Perisphere

"How're we gonna get it open?" asked GUF. "That metal shore looks tough!"

"I think maybe we can abrade it around the cutting line, with sandstone and, well . . . go get me a real big sharp piece of iron, DUN."

When it was brought, MIK handed the iron to GUF and put his long tail over a big rock.

"Go ahead, GUF," he said. "Won't hurt me a bit."

GUF slammed the piece of iron down.

"Uh hyuk," he said. "Clean as a whistle!"

MIK took the severed tail, sat down crosslegged near the eyebolt, poured sand on the cutting line, and began to rub it across the line with his tail.

It took three days, turning the capsule every few hours.

They pulled off the eyebolt end. A dusty waxy mess was revealed.

"That'll be what's left of the waterproof mastic," said MIK. "Help me, you two." They lifted the capsule. "Twist," he said.

The metal groaned. "Now, pull!"

A long thin inner core, two meters by a third of a meter, slid out.

"Okay," said MIK, putting down the capsule shell and wiping away mastic. "This inner shell is threaded in two parts. Turn that way, I'll turn this!"

They did. Inside was a shiny sealed glass tube through which they could dimly see shapes and colors.

"Wow!" said GUF. "Looka that!"

"Oh boy, oh boy," said DUN.

"That's Pyrex," said MIK. "When we break that, we'll be through."

"I'll do it!" said DUN.

"Careful!" said GUF.

The rock shattered the glass. There was a loud noise as the partial vacuum disappeared.

"Oh boy!" said DUN.

"Let's do this carefully," said MIK. "It's all supposed to be in some kind of order."

The first thing they found was the message from four famous humans and another, whole copy of *The Book of the Time Capsule*. GUF picked that up.

Strange Things in Close-Up

There was another book with a black cover with a gold cross on it, then they came to a section marked "Articles of Common Use." The first small packet was labeled "Contributing to the Convenience, Comfort, Health and Safety." MIK opened the wrapper.

Inside was an alarm clock, bifocals, a camera, pencil, nail file, a padlock and keys, toothbrush, tooth powder, a safety pin, knife, fork and slide rule.

The next packet was labeled "Pertaining to the Grooming and Vanity of Women." Inside was an Elizabeth Arden Daytime Cyclamen Color Harmony Box, a rhinestone clip, and a woman's hat, style of autumn 1938 designed by Lily Daché.

"Golly-wow!" said DUN, and put the hat on over his.

The next packet was marked "For the Pleasure, Use and Education of Children."

First out was a small spring-driven toy car, then a small doll and a set of alphabet blocks. Then MIK reached in and pulled out a small cup.

He stared at it a long, long time. On the side of the cup was a decal with the name of the man who had created them, and a picture of MIK, waving his hand in greeting.

"Gawrsh, MIK," said GUF, "it's YOU!"

A tossed brick threw up a shower of dirt next to his foot.

They all looked up.

Around the crater edge stood ragged men, women and children. They had sharp sticks, rocks and ugly clubs.

"Oh boy!" said DUN. "People!" He started toward them.

"Hello!" he said. "We've been trying to find you for a long time. Do you know the way to the Park? We want to learn all about you."

He was speaking to them in Japanese.

The mob hefted its weapons. DUN switched to another language.

"I said, we come in peace. Do you know the way to the Park?" he asked in Swedish.

They started down the crater, rocks flying before them.

"What's the matter with you?" yelled DUN. "WAK WAK WAK!" He raised his fists.

"Wait!" said MIK, in English. "We're friends!"

Some of the crowd veered off toward him.

"Uh-oh!" said GUF. He took off clanking up the most sparsely-defended side of the depression.

Then the ragged people yelled and charged.

They got the duck first.

He stood, fists out, jumping up and down on one foot, hopping mad. Several grabbed him, one by the beak. They smashed at him with clubs, pounded him with rocks. He injured three of them seriously before they smashed him into a white, blue and orange pile.

"Couldn't we, huh-huh, talk this over?" asked MIK. They stuck a sharp stick in his ear mechanism, jamming it. One of his gloved hands was mashed. He fought back with the other and kicked his feet. He hurt them, but he was small. A boulder trapped his legs, then they danced on him.

GUF made it out of the crater. He had picked the side with the most kids, and they drew back, thinking he was attacking them. When they saw he was only running, they gave gleeful chase, bouncing sticks and rocks off his hobbling form.

"WHOA!" he yelled, as more people ran to intercept him and he skidded to a stop. He ran up a long slanting pile of rubble. More humans poured out of the crater to get him.

He reached the end of the long high mound above the crater rim. His attackers paused, throwing bricks and clubs, yelling at him.

"Halp!" GUF yelled. "Haaaaaaaalp!"

An arrow sailed into the chest of the nearest attacker.

GUF turned. Other humans, dressed in cloth, stood in a line around the far side of the crater. They had bows and arrows, metal-tipped spears and metal knives in their belts.

As he watched, the archers sent another flight of arrows into the people who had attacked the robots.

The skin-dressed band of humans screamed and fled up out of the crater, down from the mounds, leaving their wounded and the scattered contents of the time capsule behind them.

It took them a while, but soon the human in command of the metal-using people and GUF found they could make themselves understood. The language was a very changed English/Spanish mixture.

"We're sorry we didn't know you were here sooner," he said to GUF. "We only heard this morning. Those *others*," he said with a grimace, "won't bother you anymore."

He pointed to the patch of green to the north. "Our lands and village are there. We came to it twenty years ago. It's a good land, but those others raid it as often as they can."

GUF looked down into the crater with its toppled column and debris. Cigarettes and tobacco drifted from the glass cylinder. The microfilm with all its books and knowledge was tangled all over the rocks. Samples of aluminium, hypernik, ferrovanadium and hypersil gleamed in the dust. Razor blades, an airplane gear and glass wool were strewn up the side of the slope.

The message from Grover Whalen opening the World's Fair, and knowledge of how to build the microfilm reader were gone. The newsreel, with its pictures of Howard Hughes, Jesse Owens and Babe Ruth, bombings in China and a Miami Beach fashion show, was ripped and torn. The golf ball was in the hands of one of the fleeing children. Poker chips lay side by side with tungsten wire, combs, lipstick. GUF tried to guess what some of the items were.

"They destroyed one of your party," said the commander. "I think the other one is still alive."

"I'll tend to 'em," said GUF.

"We'll take you back to our village," said the man. "There are lots of things we'd like to know about you."

"That goes double fer us," said GUF. "Those other folks pretty much tore up what we came to find."

GUF picked up the small cup from the ground. He walked to where they had MIK propped up against a rock.

"Hello, GUF," he said. "Ha-ha, I'm not in such good shape." His glove hung uselessly on his left arm. His ears were bent and his nose was dented. He gave off a noisy whir when he moved.

"Oh, hyuk hyuk," said GUF. "We'll go back with these nice people, and you'll rest up and be as right as rain, I guarantee."

"DUN didn't make it, did he, GUF?"

GUF was quiet a moment. "Nope, MIK, he didn't. I'm shore sorry it turned out this way. I'm gonna miss the ol' hothead."

"Me, too," said MIK. "Are we gonna take him with us?"

Heirs of the Perisphere

"Shore thing," said GUF. He waved to the nearby men.

The town was in a green valley watered by two streams full of fish. There were small fields of beans, tomatoes and corn in town, and cattle and sheep grazed on the hillsides, watched over by guards. There was a coppersmith's shop, a council hut, and many houses of wood and stone.

GUF was walking up the hill to where MIK lay.

They had been there a little over two weeks, talking with the people of the village, telling them what they knew. GUF had been playing with the children when he and MIK weren't talking with the grown folks. But from the day after they had buried DUN up on the hill, MIK had been getting worse. His legs had quit moving altogether, and he could now see only in the infrared.

"Hello, GUF," said MIK.

"How ya doin' pardner?"

"I-I think I'm going to terminate soon," said MIK. "Are they making any progress on the flume?"

Two days before, MIK had told the men how to bring water more efficiently from one of the streams up to the middle of the village.

"We've almost got it now," said GUF. "I'm sure they'll come up and thank you when they're finished."

"They don't need to do that," said MIK.

"I know, but these are real nice folks, MIK. And they've had it pretty rough, what with one thing and another, and they like talkin' to yah."

GUF noticed that some of the human women and children waited outside the hut, waiting to talk to MIK.

"I won't stay very long," said GUF. "I gotta get back and organize the cadres into work teams and instruction teams and so forth, like they asked me to help with."

"Sure thing, GUF," said MIK. "I—"

"I wisht there was somethin' I could do . . ."

There was a great whirring noise from MIK and the smell of burning silicone.

GUF looked away. "They just don't have any stuff here," he said, "that I could use to fix you. Maybe I could find something at thuh crater, or . . ."

233

Strange Things in Close-Up

"Oh, don't bother," said MIK. "I doubt . . ."

GUF was looking at the village. "Oh," he said, reaching in the bag someone had made him. "I been meanin' to give you this for a week and keep fergettin'." He handed MIK the cup with the picture of him on the side.

"I've been thinking about this since we found it," said MIK. He turned it in his good hand, barely able to see it's outline. "I wonder what else we lost at the crater."

"Lots of stuff," said GUF. "But we did get to keep this."

"This was supposed to last for a long time," said MIK. "and tell what people were like for future ages? Then the people who put this there must really have liked the man who thought us up?"

"That's for sure," said GUF.

"And me too, I wonder?"

"You probably most of all," said GUF.

MIK smiled. The smile froze. The eyes went dark, and a thin line of condensation steam rose up from the eartracks. The hand gripped tightly on the cup.

Outside, the people began to sing a real sad song.

It was a bright sunny morning. GUF put flowers on MIK's and DUN's graves at the top of the hill. He patted the earth, stood up uncertainly.

He had replaced his frozen foot with a little wood-wheeled cart which he could skate along almost as good as walking.

He stood up and thought of MIK. He set his carpenter's cap forward on his head and whistled a little tune.

He picked up his wooden tool box and started off down the hill to build the kids a swing set.

ALL ABOUT STRANGE MONSTERS OF THE RECENT PAST

Six-months'-rent's-worth of this book is for Warren;
the rest is for Nancy.

Introduction to
All About Strange Monsters of the Recent Past

This was the second story I ever sold, and it took nine years to get into print.

My first story, "Lunchbox" sold to John W. Campbell at Analog *four days after I was drafted in 1970, and came out on the newstands the same time I came out of the Army in May of 1972.*

It was while I was doing the one-man road show of "The Reluctant Draftee" that the idea for this one came to me.

I was guarding an abandoned PX one night in Ft. Bragg, NC. Unless you've ever been in the Army, you might think this was unnecessary. But no. You see, the PX had been moved two blocks down the street, but the old building was still marked down on the list of facilities as a PX, so it had to be guarded until the new list came out classifying it as no longer a PX.

That meant three poor schlubbs of GIs were supposed to spend two hours there and four hours off all night long. Well this was a weekend where guard duty lasted 24 hours and instead of going out there and back four times each, we asked the Officer of the Guard if we could pull three eight-hour shifts. What did he care?

So here I was from 0200 to 1000 hours walking around this deserted building with my trusty clipboard and a flashlight.

It hit me with a blinding jolt.

In every monster and SF movie of the Fifties, there's this scene where the cops or the mayor or whatever wises up that the body count/path of destruction is a little unusual, and that They're Up Against Something Bigger Than Sheriff Jones Can Handle, and they call out the Army, usually to great cheering from the audience.

I suddenly realized that if there were a Giant Bee Emergency

Strange Things in Close-Up

on the East Coast, it would be jerks like me that would have to go fight them. I sure couldn't imagine being led into Monster Cover-And-Fire Tactics by my First Sergeant, if you know what I mean?

When I got off guard duty, I went home and wrote this story.

It sold to David Gerrold who was putting together some anthologies of new talent. It stayed sold until Dell told him in 1976 to squeeze two anthologies into one, and out popped this story.

Then it went to Chacal, precursor of Shayol, and after the two editors there had a punch-up, it emerged again and sold to Shayol in 1979 where it was published (after some revisions to update it) in 1981, nine years after it was written.

The draft is gone now (at least until the next war). Those of you who never sweated under it can't imagine what it was like. It was the driving social force of the 1960s, for males, for everybody. Everything was concerned with being deferred, getting out of the country, or getting it over with so you could get on with your life. If you were female, you sweated along with your brother or uncle or boyfriend or friends who had them.

Here I was worrying about Monster Martial Law, and the real world was still going on. About the same time as I wrote this, one cold morning in the barracks about 4 A.M., a friend sat up in his bunk. I could see in the dark that he was shaking and as pale as the piece of paper I'm writing on.

He came over to my cot.

"Howie," he said, his teeth still chattering. "I had a dream. I was in Nam. I was on bunker guard. There were yelling and explosions outside. The field phone rang and it was the OD. He said, 'They're coming your way'."

The title of this story pays off an old debt to Roy Chapman Andrews.

All About Strange Monsters of the Recent Past

It's all over for humanity, and I'm heading east.

On the seat beside me are an M1 carbine and a Thompson submachine gun. There's a special reason for the Thompson. I traded an M16 and 200 rounds of ammo for it to a guy in Barstow. He got the worst of the deal. When things get rough, carbine and .45 ammo are easier to find than the 5.56mm rounds the M16 uses. I've got more ammo for the carbine than I need, though I've had plenty of chances to use it.

There are fifty gallons of gasoline in the car, in cans. I have food for six days (I don't know if that many are left.)

When things really fell apart, I deserted. Like anyone else with sense. When there were more of them than we could stop. I don't know what they'll do when they run out of people. Start killing each other, maybe.

Meanwhile, I'm driving 160 kmph out Route 66. I have an appointment in the desert of New Mexico.

God. Japan must have gone first. They deluged the world with them; now, it's Japan's turn. You sow what you reap.

We were all a little in love with death and the atom bomb back in the 1950s. It won't do us much good now.

The road is flat ahead. I've promised myself I'll see Meteor Crater before I die. So many of them opened at Meteor Crater, largest of the astroblemes. How fitting I should go there now.

In the back seat with the ammo is a twenty kilo bag of sugar.

It started just like the movies did. Small strangenesses in small towns, disappearances in the back woods and lonely places, tremors in the Arctic, stirrings in the jungles.

We never thought when we saw them as kids what they would someday mean. The movies. The ones with the giant lizards, grasshoppers, molluscs. We yelled when the monsters started to get theirs. We cheered when the Army arrived to fight them. We yelled for all those movies. Now they've come to eat us up.

And nobody's cheered the Army since 1965. In 1978, the Army couldn't stop the monsters.

I was in that Army. I still am, if one's left. I was one of the last draftees, with the last bunch inducted. At the Entrance Station, I copped and took three years for a guaranteed job.

I would be getting out in three months if it weren't for this.

I left my uniform under a bush as soon as I decided to get away. I'd worn it for two and a half years. Most of the Army got torn away in the first days of the fight with the monsters. I decided to go.

So I went. East.

I saw one of the giant Gila monsters this morning. There had been a car ahead of me, keeping about three kilometers between us, not letting me catch up. Maybe a family, figuring I was going to rob them or rape the women. Maybe not. It was the first car I'd seen in eighteen hours of dodging along the back roads. The car went around a turn. It looked like it slowed. I eased down, too, thinking maybe it wasn't a family but a bunch of dudes finally deciding to ambush me. Good thing I slowed.

I came around the turn and all I could see was the side of an orange and black mountain. I slammed on the brakes and skidded sideways. The Gila monster had knocked the other car off the road and was coming for me. I was shaken, but I hadn't come this far to be eaten by a lizard. Oh no. I threw the snout of the M1 carbine out the window and blasted away at the thing's eyes. Scales flew like rain. It twitched away then started back for me. I shot it in the tongue. It went into convulsions and crawled over a small sandhill hissing and honking like a freight train. It would come back later to eat whatever was in the other car. I trundled back on the road and drove past the wreck. Nothing moved. A pool of oil was forming on the concrete. I drove down the road with the smell of cordite in my nose and the wind whipping past. There was Gila monster blood on the hood of the car.

I had been a clerk in an airborne unit deployed to get the giant

All About Strange Monsters of the Recent Past

locusts eating up the Midwest. It is the strangest time in the history of the United States. The nights are full of meteors and lights.

At first, we thought it was a practice alert. We suited up, climbed into the C–130s with full combat gear, T-10 parachutes, lurp bags and all. At least the others had chutes. I wasn't on jump status so I went in with the heavy equipment to the nearest airbase. A lot of my buddies jumped into Illinois. I never saw them again. By the time the planes landed, the whole brigade was gone.

We landed at Chanute. By then, the plague of monsters was so bad I ended up on the airbase perimeter with the Air Policemen. We fired at the things until the barrels of the machine guns moaned with heat. The locusts kept coming, squirting brown juice when they were hit or while killing someone.

Their mandibles work all the time.

We broke and ran after awhile. I caught a C–130 revving up. The field was a moving carpet of locusts as I looked behind me. They could be killed easily, as could any insect with a soft abdomen. But there were so many of them. You killed and killed and they kept coming. And dying. So you had to run. We roared off the runway while they scuttled across the airfield below. Some took to the air on their rotor-sized wings. One smashed against the Hercules, tearing off part of an elevator. We flew on through a night full of meteors. A light paced us for awhile but broke off and flew after a fighter plane.

We couldn't land back at Pope AFB. It was a shambles. A survivor said the saucers hit about midnight. A meteor had landed near Charlotte, and now the Martian fighting machines were drifting toward Washington, killing everything in their paths.

We roared back across country, looking for some place to land where we wouldn't be gobbled up. Fuel got lower. We came in on a wing, a prayer and fumes to Fitzee Field at Fort Ord. I had taken basic training at Ord.

A few hours later, I duffed.

I heard about New York on the radio before the stations went off. A giant lizard had come up from the Hudson submarine canyon and destroyed Manhattan. A giant octopus was ravaging

Strange Things in Close-Up

San Francisco, a hundred miles north of Ord. It had already destroyed the Golden Gate Bridge. Saucers were landing everywhere. One had crashed into a sandpit behind a house nearby. A basic training unit had been sent in. They wouldn't be back. I knew. A glass-globed intelligence would see to that.

Navy ships were pulled under by the monsters that pillaged New York, by the giant octopus, by giant crabs in the South Pacific; by caterpillar-like molluscs in the Salton Sea.

The kinds of invaders seemed endless: Martian fighting machines, four or five types of aliens. The sandpit Martians, much different from the fighting machine kind. Bigheaded invaders with eyes on the backs of their hands.

A few scattered reports worldwide. No broadcasts from Japan after the first few minutes. Total annihilation, no doubt. Italy: a craft, which only existed on celluloid, brings back from Venus an egg of death. Mexico: a tyranosaurus rex comes from the swamps for cattle and children. A giant scorpion invades from the volcanoes. South America: giant wasps, fungus disease, terrors from the earth. Britain: a monster slithers wild in Westminster Abbey, another fungus from space, radioactive mud, giant lizards again. Tibet: the yeti are on the move.

It is all over for humanity.

Meteor Crater at sunset. A hole punched in the earth while ice sheets still covered Wyoming and Pennsylvania.

I can see for miles, and I have the carbine ready. I stare into the crater, thinking. This crater saw the last mammoth and the first of the Indians.

The shadow deepens and the floor goes dark. Memories of man, crater. Your friend the Grand Canyon regards you as an upstart in time. It's jealous because you came from space.

Speaking of mammoths, perhaps it's our time to join old woolly in the great land of fossil dreams. Whatever plows farms in a million years can turn up our teeth and wonder at them.

Nobody knows why the mammoth disappeared, or the dinosaur, or our salamander friend the Diplovertebron, for that matter. Racial old age. No plausible reason. So now it's our turn. Done in by our dreams from the silver screen. Maybe we've created our own Id monsters, come to snuffle us out in nightmares.

All About Strange Monsters of the Recent Past

The reason I deserted: the Air Force was going to drop an A-bomb on the Martian fighting machines. They were heading for Ord after they finished LA. I was at the command post when one of the last B–52s went over, heading for the faraway carnage on the horizon.

"If the A-bomb doesn't stop it, Colonel," said a major to the commander, "nothing will."

How soon they forget, I thought, and headed for the perimeter.

The Great Southwest saw more scenes of monster destruction than anywhere in the world except Japan. Film producers loved it for the sterility of the desert, the hot sun, the contrasts with no gradations for their black and white cameras. In them, saucers landed, meteors hurtled down, townspeople disappeared, tracks and bones were found.

Here is where it started, was the reasoning. In the desert thirty-three years ago when the first atomic bomb was detonated, when sand was turned to glass.

So the monsters shambled, plodded, pillaged and shook the South-west. This desert where once there was only a shallow sea. You can find clamshells atop the Sierras, if you look.

I have an appointment here, near Alamogordo. Where it started. The racial old age is on us now. Unexplained, and we'll die not knowing why, or why we lived the least time of all the dominant species on this planet.

One question keeps coming to me. Why only films of the 1950s?

Am I the only one who remembers? Have I been left alone because I'm the only one who remembers and knows what I'm doing? Am I the only one with a purpose, not just running around like a chicken with its head cut off?

The radio stations are going off one by one as I drive from the crater to Alamogordo. Emergency broadcast stations, something out of Arkansas, an Ohio station. Tonight, I'm not going to be stopped. I've got the 30-round magazine in the carbine and the 45-round drum in the Thompson. I wish I had some grenades, or even tear gas, but I have no mask (I lost it in the battle against the grasshoppers.) Besides, I'm not sure tear gas will be effective for what I have in mind.

Strange Things in Close-Up

On the dying radio stations and in my mind's eye, this is what I see and hear.

The locusts reach Chicago and feast till dawn, while metal robots roam the streets looking for men to kill.

The giant lizard goes past Coney Island with no resistance.

The huge mantis, after pillaging the Arctic, reduces Washington to shambles. It has to dodge flying saucers while it pulls apart monuments, looking for goodies. The statue of Abraham Lincoln looks toward Betelgeuse and realizes that the War Between the States *was* fought in vain.

The sky is filled with meteors, saucers, a giant flying bird. Two new points of light hang in the sky: a dead star and a planet which will crash into earth in a few days. The night is beginning to be bathed in a dim bloody light.

An amorphous thing sludges its way through a movie theater, alternately flattening, thickening, devouring anything left.

The Martian fighting machines have gone up and down both coasts, moving in a crescent pivotal motion.

The octopus has been driven underwater by heat from the burning San Francisco.

So much for the rest of the country.

Here in the Southwest; a million-eyed monster has taken over the cattle and dogs for hundreds of miles.

A giant spider eats cattle and people and grows. The last Air Force fighters have given up and are looking for a place to land. Maybe one or two pilots, like me, will get away. Maybe saucers will get them. It won't be long now.

The Gila monsters roam, tongues moving, seeking the heat of people, cars, dogs.

Beings with a broken spaceship are repairing it, taking over the bodies of those not eaten by other monsters. Soon they will be back up in the sky. Benevolent monsters.

Giant columns of stone grow, break, fall, crushing all in their paths. Miles wide now, and moving toward the Colorado River, the Gulf and infinite growing bliss. No doubt they have crushed giant Gila monsters and spiders along with people, towns, and mountains.

A stranded spaceman makes it to Palomar and spends his last seconds turning the telescope toward his home star, he has already killed nineteen people in his effort to communicate.

All About Strange Monsters of the Recent Past

A monster grows, feeding on the atoms of the air.

A robot cuts its way through a government installation fence, off on its own path of rampage. The two MPs fire until their .45s click dry. Bullets ricochet off the metal being. Soon a saucer will fly over and hover. They will fire at the saucer with no effect; the saucer will fire and the MPs will drift away on the wind.

(There may be none of our bones to dig up in a million years.)

All this as I drive toward the dawn, racing at me and the Southwest like the avenging eye of god. No headlights. I saw a large meteor hit back in the direction of Flagstaff; there'll be hell to pay there soon. Meanwhile, I haven't slept in two days. The car sometimes swerves toward the road edge. No time for a crack-up, so close now.

The last radio station went off at 0417.

Nothing on the dial but mother earth's own radio music, and perhaps stellar noises which left somewhere 500 million years ago, about the time our friend the Diplovertebron slithered through the mud. The east is greying. I'm almost there.

The car motor pops and groans as it cools. The wind blows steadily toward the deeper desert. Not far from here, the first A-bomb went off. Perhaps that was the challenge to the universe, and it waited thirty years to get back at us. This is where it started.

This is where it ends.

I'm drinking a hot Coke. It tastes better than any I've ever had. No uppers, downers, hash, horse or grass for me. I'm on a natural high.

I've set my things in order. All the empty bottles are filled with gasoline and the blanket's been torn up for fuses. My lighter and matches are laid out, with some cigarettes for punks. With the carbine slung over my shoulder, I wait with the Thompson in my right hand, round chambered, selector on rock and roll.

They won't die easy, but I envision a stack of them ringing my body, my bones, the car; some scorched and blackened, some shot all away, some with mandibles still working long after I'm dead.

I open the twenty kilo bag of sugar and shake it onto the

Strange Things in Close-Up

wind. It sifts into a pile a few feet away. The scent should carry right to them.

I took basic at Fort Ord. There was a tunnel we had to double-time through to get to the range. In cadence. Weird shadows on the wall as we ran. No matter how tired I was, I thought of the soldiers going into the storm drains after the giant ants in a movie I'd seen when I was six. They started here, near the first A-blast. They had to be here. The sugar would bring them.

A sound floats back up the wind like the keening of an off-angle buzz saw. Ah. They're coming. They'll be here soon, first one, then many. Maybe the whole nest will turn out. They'll rise from behind that dune, or maybe that one.

Closer now, still not in sight.

It's all over for man, but there are still some things left. Like choices, there's still that. A choice of personal monsters.

Closer now, and more sounds. Maybe ten or twenty of them, maybe more.

End of movie soon. No chance to be James Arness and get the girl. But plenty of time to be the best James Whitmore ever. No kids to throw to safety. But a Thompson and a carbine. And Molotov cocktails.

Aha. An antenna waves in the middle distance. And—

Bigger than I thought. Take your head right off.

Eat leaden death, Hymenopterae! The Thompson blasts to life.

Screams of confusion. A flash of 100 octane and glass. High keening like an off-angle buzz saw.

I laugh. Formic acid. Cordite.

Hell of a life.

Introduction to
Helpless, Helpless

I wrote this story because Mike Bishop has no taste.

Well, that's not exactly true. Michael Bishop is one of the best writers this field's ever had; his works go to the heart of the matter, and the hearts of human beings with no fluff, and no detours along the way.

Berkley Books had contracted with him to edit a state-of-the-art anthology in 1983, called, at the time The Cosmopedia or some such claptrap (and boy am I glad the title was changed).

What he did was reprint about a dozen of the most important stories of the last two decades and open the rest of the anthology for originals, and boy! did I want to be in the book!

In my usual way, I farted around 'til it was almost too late, and push came to shove, and Mike had about 3500 words worth of space and money left, and mine was going to be the last story bought for the book.

I wrote "Heirs of the Perisphere" for him.

He wrote back and said it "might as well be about a wheelbarrow, a lawnmower and rototiller." He wanted it, but he wanted rewrites, and for it to be cut down to around 3500 words.

"Look, Mike," I said. "I'll write you another story, exactly 3500 words long."

Then I took "Heirs of the Perisphere" and sold it to Playboy for ten times the money Mike was going to pay me for it, and it was on the final Nebula ballot.

So a lot he knows.

The "another" story was this one, which Mike took in a New-York minute, and at 3300 words, one of the shortest things I'd ever done.

It was another of those ideas I carried for a long time. If you read medical histories, what strikes you most is not that our forebears were so dumb, but that enough of them lived for us to be born.

Until the germ theory of disease took hold, there was no one-to-one relationship between cause and effect in disease. The problem was not that medical men couldn't see what was happening around them, but that they couldn't make the intuitive leap between effect (everybody's dying!) and cause (germs on fleas on rats?). So you read of the best defense against disease: "A new pair of boots, worn out as quickly as possible." "Go far, stay long." You see drawings of doctors in robe-suits, their headpieces with long snouts filled with spices and flowers, like gigantic Boschian birds hopping about among the dead and dying. You read of the Pope at Avignon sitting between two roaring bonfires, day and night, summer and winter, for a year and a half.

There are two books on the subject which are indispensible: Howard W. Haggard's Devils, Drugs and Doctors *and William H. McNeill's* Plagues and Peoples.

This last will give you a whole new view of history. It should be taught in every introductory history course in the world, before the student gets on with the business of memorizing names and dates and events.

Both books bring across the helplessness of the story's title, a helplessness of people in the face of something that they not only do not understand, but are incapable of understanding with the knowledge of their society, their time.

The title and mood are from Neil Young's song. I also point to the story when someone asks me when I'm going to get a word processor.

Or an electric typewriter, for that matter.

Helpless, Helpless

"Bring out your malfunctioning! Bring out your malfunctioning!"

The huge refuse machine trundled down the roadway, broadcasting its cry both aurally and magnetically. It stopped every few meters. At each stop humans, androids, robots or simpler machines brought to it stiff and broken or limp and leaking bodies. They tossed these upwards into the back of the machine.

The machine made grinding noises as the pitted metal or sloughing plastic bodies disappeared into it. Then it moved itself slowly down the way and started its cry once more.

"Bring out your malfunctioning!" it said. "Bring out your malfunctioni–"

There was a great retching noise and half-digested bodies spewed into the air behind the machine, showering over the nearby houses. Humans ran for their doorways, androids and robots covered themselves with their arms. Glass shattered, roof tiles were broken.

"–ng. Bring out youryouryour mal–" said the great machine. It lost its steering ability and wobbled across the roadway, gathering speed. A gout of oil flushed from the bottom, smoke began to rise from its surging engine.

It retched again, this time its own metal parts, struck the curbing and slowly rolled over, its gyros failing with an angry whine. It took a small machine, two androids, an already ceased robot and part of a house under the great rolling hammer of itself before it stopped.

Its wheels continued to turn. The air and airwaves were filled with its mayday calls. From far away the blips and whines of emergency vehicles approached.

The other humans, the robots, and the androids returned to

Strange Things in Close-Up

their houses to finish their cleaning, to bring more ceased artificials outside to the curb for collection and disposal.

I turned and went back into my own home.

It was the second week of the Plague.

The Plague seems to be of two kinds (I wrote in my notebook): the robotic and the androidal.

The robotic does not seem to spread by direct contact, but rather to be pervasive, or airborne. If it is spread by direct contact, the period of incubation (so we shall call it) varies greatly. Many cases have been reported where the robot has had no direct contact with other mechanicals or artificials for a period of months before malfunctioning after use.

The androidal is spread by direct contact. Symptoms evince themselves within sixteen to twenty-four hours. It does seem to spread to robotic victims but has a whole range of symptoms. When it affects androids, the symptoms are more violent, run their course more quickly, and lead to cessation much earlier than in robots.

When robots contract the androidal fever, the symptoms develop more slowly, but lead to more violent onsets of malfunction, with greater dangers to society at large.

I looked down at my notes. Essentially meaningless. I write as if the robots and androids were human, as if the great plague striking them were a disease, as if there were germs, viruses, bacilli eating away at them, as if their skins were flesh, not metal, not plastic, their brains were cells, not magnetic bubbles, silicon, crystal. I write of social dangers, as if they were dying, instead of ceasing their go/no-go cycles.

I write one more note:

Simple machines below the 12-track level do not seem to be affected. *Why* is this?

Julie Hamer Harpstein comes over from her large house. We are to walk to the Center together. She is a librarian, I am a research clerk. We wonder if there will be much work for us. All the central input terminals have been requisitioned by the Health Department due to some failures in their own systems. This week we have been updating files, catching up on screen-work, printing hard copy photographically, which task is a novelty to us. The machines have not been used for this in a little less than a century.

Normally I work from my home, but regular feeds from the Center have been interrupted during the emergency. Besides, I am beginning to like the slow and deliberate work involved in actually photographing and reproducing data. I can see how the old, old craftsmen felt about their work. Someone has even suggested taking out the ancient machines, the ones where you had to have an *actual* image before the lens to reproduce the data. Our section chief thinks this is going a little too far, although she says if things get slower around there, she may go visit The Books. She hasn't been there for years.

"Hello, Julie," I say.

She looks confused and distraught. "Is something wrong?" I ask.

"Two of my last three ceased in the night," she said. "That leaves only Imago."

"I am truly sorry," I said. "The health people think they may have found a link between the onset of the plague and the ore ships that came in three weeks ago."

We left my house and walked down the street, past the overturned refuse machine and the wrecking vehicle. The Center was only a kilometer away. It would have been a bright blue day, and cheery, were it not for the oily smell in the air, the tang of fire. A line of smoke hung to the north, toward the Great Park.

"Can't we go some other way?" Julie asked. She had stopped when we turned the corner onto the main thoroughfare. On both sides of the streets, at every other door, lay ragged plastic or rusted metal bodies, some laid out carefully with dignity, some tossed to sprawl where they fell. The air was thick with ozone, oily odors, with the new-sofa smell of torn android plastic and melted wiring.

"I doubt there are any residential areas not like this," I said.

"Can't they do anything about cleaning this up, at least?" she asked. Then she sighed. "Of course they can't. I watch the video too."

We walked on toward the Center. On a corner three blocks from our destination, a robot stood limply, holding itself up

Strange Things in Close-Up

with one hand on a lamppost. The side of its head was a rusted bubble of plastic and steel. Only one eye was left.

"I require help, person," it said. "Please summon help for me. I seem to be malfunctioning. I can no longer summon aid magnetically."

"Do you want to go on without me?" I asked Julie.

"No, I'll wait."

I stepped to the door of the nearest house and rang. A person answered. I told her the location of the robot. She said she would call the emergency people. A hooter started some blocks away.

Julie was easing backwards toward me up the stairs. I bumped into her. "What?" I asked, turning.

The robot had put its hands out toward her breasts. "Gitchee gitchee gitchee," it said, its fingers making twiddling movements. We backed up the stairs.

The robot's one good eye went blank. Then it began to flutter open and shut. The robot came up the stairs. Its hands made groping movements of a more and more violent nature.

I pulled Julie to one side. The robot whirled to face her.

The hooter came closer to the block. The robot came closer to us. Then it turned its front toward me, lifted its arms higher, its fingers stiff as claws.

"Vile jellies!" it said, and raised one of its feet from the ground.

Hands grabbed it from behind, men pulled it away, something was stuck in its cervical groove, there was a crackle and sputter. The air reeked of burnt insulation, metal. The robot's good eye shattered like a fried marble onto the pavement.

"Sorry, persons," said one of the emergency people. He had burned his hand in ceasing the robot and was spraying it with a gelatin. "Best keep moving. We're rounding up all the strays. Just go about your business as usual, keep moving."

Julie was crying, so was I. I wiped away tears. I noticed that the emergency people were equipped with firearms. I had seen them many times in the museum, and had read all about them once on a slow day in the research banks.

We continued on to the Center, ignoring the pleas for aid, the audible beeps of locator beacons, the sirens of emergency people on the side streets.

Helpless, Helpless

There was a single android lying before the Center, ceased in all manners but one. That one function made me shiver throughout the day when I thought of it.

I was busy photographing hard copy when Julie came by my stall. "They're running the master program now; we can watch." I switched the input over to the Health Department channel. Graphs, correlations, raw data only a few moments old were being fed into the Center's banks. They were looking for an answer, some thread that would tie everything together. Roboticists, plastics and metal engineers, manufacturers, cyberneticists; all were watching their terminals to see if there was something, anything they could begin to use to fight the Plague.

I noticed that as they ran input the Central bank had an interrogative for them, but not directly concerned with the data. It would hold until the run was made, then ask, then act on their questions.

The interrogation light stayed on. I slowed some of the data to see what kind of information was going on. Shuttle schedules, destinations. Cargoes. Ore qualities. Rates of infection. Localities as yet untouched (many fewer than the week before). Symptoms, possible theories of infection. Sunspot cycles, weather data (terrestrial, solar, extrasolar), unusual insect activity, religious attendance among humans, data on human diseases (all twelve of them and the 329 kinds of colds). Everything anybody thought would be of consequence, and from which the Central computer could make a decision.

I let the inputs zip by once more. The interrogative light glowed on the screen.

The inputs slowed, stopped. The run ended. Julie leaned closer to me to watch the screen.

The question light disappeared as one of the technicians let the Central bank ask what it wanted.

PROCEED?

The Center data bank went blank a second, then across the screen it asked:

DO YOU HAVE PRINCE ALBERT IN A CAN?

Then it flickered and went dark.

"Stay in your houses," the loudspeakers said, and the video

screens showed. "Do not go into the streets. Do not let robots or androids not known to you into your homes. Do not let robots or androids who seem to be malfunctioning near you. Most will cease functioning quietly within twelve to twenty-four hours. Collections will be made as often as possible. Place ceased robotics in boxes, place ceased androids in sacks. Do not bring them out until called. No human has been infected during the course of these phenomena. Stay in your homes."

I watched the instructions run up the screen again. Then I saw Julie wave to me from the window of her house. I ran to the door, opened it. There was nothing in the street but a few ceased bodies.

Julie let me in her house.

"It's Imago," she said.

It was barely functioning. We put it in a box and dragged it to the curb.

"I have not ceased yet," it said, through bubbled lips.

We left it there. Julie came back to my house, not wanting to be alone without her robots.

There was a muffled droning, growing louder, then a thump and an explosion close by. Emergency vehicles headed toward it. I could see nothing from the windows but smoke rising some distance away, mingling with older smoke. I checked the fire-safety devices for the house. They seemed to be in good order.

"That sounded like a weather plane," said Julie. "My parents used to live near their launching facility."

"They have track–30 brains, don't they?"

"Or more."

I wrote in my notebook:

What we see around us we do not understand. We are looking for some invisible rat, some electronic flea, a subatomic protozoan that infects our machines and kills them as surely as any disease ever killed a human.

To an artificial, to cease function, after an infinitely long time, with many replacement parts, is one thing. To be cast onto the streets with thousands, helpless to understand what is happening, to lose their programming, is another.

We are as helpless to explain to them as were our forebears, when great epidemics took them away. When one in five, one

Helpless, Helpless

in three, one in two were taken, they could imagine nothing but that they had been put into the hands of some angry god punishing mankind for its sins.

The cause, the answers, the treatment are there, but beyond our grasp and understanding, separated from us by time and research, by new discoveries that might as well be in the next galaxy. It is there, nonetheless, even if it is only months away.

It is that we cannot, yet, understand it.

I have a theory: that it is a disease of artificial intelligence itself. With new thinking come new plagues. Our machines have become so wise that they are now susceptible to the disease. While they were ignorant, they were immune.

This theory is as good as any. It is worth nothing. All our energies and intelligence are worth nothing in this circumstance, for they are ultimately of no use. All our AI units will die, down to the last mealplanner and sharpening station.

The video, now with punched messages, told of new emergency laws enacted by the city (cities everywhere) calling upon citizens to perform extraordinary feats and unusual manual jobs, on a lottery basis. Otherwise the instructions repeated, with new ones—report unusual odors, clouding of water, turn off all fossil-fuel combustion devices. Store water, make ice. Remain in your homes. Do not panic.

There was a sound outside and a truck pulled up. Two men, nervous and armed, rang.

"Citizen Cawley?"

"Yes?"

"You have been chosen for special duty under the emergency laws of the city. Please gather one complete change of clothing. You will be on duty no more than seventy-two hours, unless new contingencies arise. For emergencies you can be reached at Municipal # 1, but for emergencies only. Please get your clothing and come with us."

"What is it?" asked Julie.

"I have to go. I've been called up.

"But they can't do that."

"Yes, they can. It'll be all right."

"Please don't leave me," she said suddenly. She grabbed my

Strange Things in Close-Up

shoulders. "The house is so—empty. So quiet. The video has been going on and off. What am I going to do?"

"You'll be okay. I'll be back in a day or so. Do you want to go to Phillipa's?"

"No," she said. Her hands fluttered, releasing my arm. "I'll stay here."

I got my clothing, said good-bye, left with the men.

There were twenty-seven of us. They took us to the municipal building. We were issued heavy work clothing and told the rudiments of our job—we would operate several of the giant crushing machines manually. Drivers were chosen, went to their instructions. The rest of us were taken to a room where we got two hours in the use of ceasing devices. Then we were taught the most efficient ways of loading various types of artificials into the grinders, and how to unload the residue at the central smelter.

Then we were divided into four-person teams, paired with a driver and two enforcement specialists, and sent on our rounds.

The city burned in many places. Emergency vehicles ran constantly. Systems were breaking down, central control of all kinds was gone. Overhead, another weather plane flew tight circles, its mind gone, randomly releasing carbon dioxide, particulate matter, and firefighting chemicals.

Our recordings told people to bring out their malfunctioning, and we heaved the rusting or flopping bodies of the ceased into the open back of the grinders. The driver pulled the controls and ground them down. When we found ones still functioning, we used the ceasers on it and threw it in with the others.

At first we were careful, but after just one street we were sweating, straining, ignoring leaking oil, runny metal, larded plastics. Our job was to throw them into the back of the grinder, and that's what we did.

We turned a corner. People who had been carrying malfunctioning to the streets came running toward us for aid.

In the middle of the street, lurching, was the Sphinx.

Its lion-shaped body was molded from a single piece, the back legs never meant to move. It dragged itself forward by the slow

Helpless, Helpless

ragged actions of its front claws, its only moving locomotor parts.

Above those claws was a winged human female torso. Its wings flopped brokenly behind it, one torn and hanging in the street.

Its half-human, half-feline face twitched from side to side, eyes searching, its opening and closing mouth showing jagged curved teeth.

It was the Sphinx from the annual Myth Day Parade, which had somehow gotten loose from its storage facility.

"Answer me," it said in a cracked voice, its head lolling, its feet jerking it forward another meter, its wings rattling. "Answer me and live. What goes on four legs in the morning, two legs at noontime, three legs—"

The enforcement specialists fired round after round into it until it sagged forward on its torn and leaking claws, its eyes closing, its mouth in a rictus of fanged surprise.

The people on the street were either screaming or numb.

It took six of us and the driver to get the Sphinx up into the grinder. There was another explosion farther up the road. No sirens wailed.

The sun was hot and bright, the wind westerly. Across the fields small tractors moved and bounced, making small disk marks in the earth.

I wiped sweat from my arms and neck, splashed water from the bucket onto my face.

My former supervisor from the Center was on kitchen duty, ladling soup to the workers.

"Hey, Cawley," she said. "How's Julie?"

"Better," I said. "She should be home soon."

Yesterday I had gone to the Compound where the Poor Unfortunates were kept. Julie should never really have been there, but when the examiners came around she was manifesting enough of the outward signs of Artificials' Withdrawal for them to take her for her own good.

The doctor told me she should be released within a week. After some recovery time she could come back to work with the rest of us.

"I'm running a smelter every other day," said the supervisor, filling my bowl from the big pot. "We've even got some of the old systems up. They seem to be holding. Even some low-track artificials, been on-line for a week at a time. We're learning."

I nodded, found a place to sit on the ground. Two months ago, before the General Duties were announced, I'd been called on special duty again. This time we went to homes, businesses, jerked all the artificial brains out of everything that could still make an independent decision. Most were ceased by then, anyway.

The smelters were working day and night, turning intelligence into tools.

I ate my soup, mostly dehydrated vegetables, and a piece of thick bread with oily margarine, and drank a cup of coffee.

Rebuilding was going on in the great gapped city. Wrecked buildings were being torn down and raised again, this time with hands, tools, simple machines.

We were once more at the mercy of the weather. We had to finish the plowing before a rainy cold front moved through that evening. We could predict the weather again, but could no longer do anything about it.

The summer ahead looked to be hard, hot, and dry.

I watched the tractors plow awhile, nodded off, drowsed. The shift foreman wakened me.

"Sorry, Citizen Cawley," he said. "Time to get back to work."

I rubbed my eyes, looked over what had been the Great Park, the area we had to till. It seemed green, yielding, a reminder of a happier, easier time.

It would take us years to get back where we were. Especially with half our people unable to face a world without artificials, a world of quiet houses, of nothing but human companionship, of doing things by hand or not at all.

It might take a tremendously longer time to find the cause of the Artificials' Plague, conquer it, build them again. It would take longer than all our lives to forget the Plague Month, what we had seen happen to our works and our cities.

The machines have left us on our own. We will not forget them. We will work to have them again.

I climbed into the saddle of the small tractor with its wired-up, bolted-down brainless controls. I set off, put my hand on that plow, and held on.

Introduction to
Fair Game

If you keep up with lit crit at all, you've probably noticed something new creeping in lately.

Since so much ink has been wasted on criticism of all the major (and most of the minor) writers, both in the mainstream and in SF, biographers are looking around for other ways to talk about them besides ". . . and then she wrote . . .", or ". . . after moving back to Ohio, he . . ." (I mean, who really has anything more to say about Henry James' style, or Yokonapatawpha County?)

Biographers have started writing about the people famous writers have slept with. (In some cases, as in those of Scott and Zelda Figzgerald, of treating the couple as a single unit or entity.) This is a pretty novel approach, stunning in its simplicity. On the one hand, it can bring some interesting hidden stuff to light. On the other, it opens the way for People Magazine-type journalism disguised as literary biography. It's certainly more interesting than another casebook on Petroleum V. Nasby or Albion W. Tourgee.

All this is preface to "Fair Game," written expressly for Ian Watson and Pamela Sargent's Afterlives. *While doing research for it I began to run across the "slept with" books. I research too much anyway, they tell me; the stories sleep while I read up in the subject area. This one was no exception, and the new literary bios (like* Fool for Love, *about F. Scott Fitzgerald) were a refreshing change from things like* James Gould Cozzens' Art of Revision: A Facsimile Ms.

I might also tell you that this was written straight through, beginning one 4 A.M., after the worst night of my life back in November of 1984.

And that my life, so far, hasn't imitated my art.

Fair Game

"AN OLD MAN IS A NASTY THING."

He heard church bells ringing anxiously on the wind.

He felt the cool air on his skin.

He saw the valley spread out below him like a giant shell.

It was a valley he had known, thirty-five or forty years ago, when he had been there for the skiing. It was a small valley in Bavaria, with its small town. He had never seen it in this season, having been here only in winter. This was spring. Patches of snow still lay in the shade, but everything was greening, the air was a robin-egg blue above the hovering mountains.

He was on the road into town, moving toward the sound of the bells. He lifted his eyes up a little past the village (the glare hurt them, but in the last few years so had all bright lights.) Through a slight haze he saw a huge barn, far off on the road leading out the other side of the town.

He looked quickly back down at his feet. He did not like looking at the barn.

He noticed his boots, his favorites, the ones he had hunted in until two years ago when his body had turned on him after all the years he had punished it, when he couldn't hunt anymore. When he could no longer crouch down for the geese in the blinds, he had taken to walking up pheasant and chukar. But then even that ability had left him, like everything else he ever had.

Walking toward the town was tiring. His pants were that tattered old pair from the first hunt in Africa, the one the book came out of. He had kept those pants in the bottom of an old trunk filled with zebra hides.

He put his hands to his broad chest and felt a flannel shirt and his fishing vest. It was the one he'd been wearing in that

Fair Game

picture with the two trout and the big smile, taken the first time he'd come to Idaho.

He felt his face as he walked. His beard was still scaggly on his chin. He reached up and felt the big lump on his forehead, the one he'd gotten when he'd butted his way through a jammed cabin door, out of a burning airplane, his second plane crash in two days seven years before.

His hat was the big-billed marlin cap from the days of Cuba and Bimini and Key West, back when everything was good: the writing, the hunting and fishing, the wives, the booze.

He remembered that morning in Idaho when he was in his bathrobe, just back from the hospital, and both the house and the shotgun had been still and cool.

Now he was walking down the hill toward the ruckus in town, dressed in odds and ends of his old clothing. It was a fine spring morning in the mountains half a world away.

Many houses stood with doors open, all the people now at the town square. Still, the pealing of the bells echoed off the surrounding peaks.

From way off to the left he could hear the small flat bells of cattle being driven toward him, and the shouts of the people who herded them.

A woman came from a house and ran past him without a glance, toward the milling people and voices ahead.

A child looked down at him from one of the high third-story windows, the ones you sometimes had to climb out of in the winter if you wanted to go outside at all.

He was winded from the half-mile walk into town.

The crowd stood looking toward the church doors, perhaps three hundred people in all, men, women, a few of the children.

The bells stopped ringing, slowed their swings, stopped in the high steeple. The doors opened up, and the priest and burgermëister came out onto the broad steps.

The crowd waited.

"There he is," said the priest.

Heads turned, the crowd parted, and they opened a path for him to the steps. He walked up to the priest and the mayor.

"Ernst," said the burgermëister. "We're so glad you came."

"I'm a little confused," he heard himself say.

Strange Things in Close-Up

"The Wild Man?" said the priest. "He's come down into the villages again. He killed two more last night and carried off a ram three men couldn't lift. Didn't you get our cablegram?"

"I don't think so," he said.

"We sent for you to come hunt him for us. Some townspeople remembered you from the Weimar days, how you hunted and skied here. You're the only man for the job. This Wild Man is more dangerous than any before has ever been."

Ernst looked around at the crowd. "I used to hunt in the old days, and ski. I can't do either anymore. It's all gone, all run out on me."

It hurt him to say those things aloud, words he had said over and over to himself for the last two years, but which he had told only two people in the world before.

The faces in the crowd were tense, waiting for him or the official to say something, anything.

"Ernst!" pleaded the burgermëister, "you are the only man who can do it. He has already killed Brunig, the great wolf hunter from Axburg. We are devastated."

Ernst shook his head slowly. It was no use. He could not pretend to himself or these people. He would be less than useless. They would put a faith in him when he knew better than to put any hopes in himself.

"Besides," said the young priest, "someone has come to help you do this great thing."

Somebody moved in the crowd, stepped forward. It was a withered old black man, dressed in a loincloth and khaki shirt. On its sleeve was a shoulder patch of the Rangers of the Ngorongoro Crater Park, and from the left pocket hung the string of a tobacco pouch.

"Bwana," he said, with a gap-toothed smile.

Ernst had not seen him in thirty years. It was Mgoro, his gunbearer from that first time in Africa.

"Mgoro," he said, taking the old man's hands and wrists, shaking them.

He turned to the officials.

"If he's come all this way, I guess we'll have to hunt this Wild Man together," said Ernst. He smiled uneasily.

The people cheered, the priest said a prayer of thanksgiving, and the mayor took him and Mgoro inside his house.

Fair Game

Later they took them to a home on the south side of town. The house looked as if a howitzer shell had hit one corner of it. Ernst saw that it wasn't exploded. The thin wall of an outbuilding had been pulled off, and a window clawed out from what had been a child's bedroom

"The undertaker," said the mayor, "is sewing the arms and legs back on. His mother heard him scream and came down to see what was wrong. They found her half a kilometre from here. When the Wild Man got through with her, he tossed her down and picked up the sheep.

"We tried to follow his trail earlier this morning. He must live in the caves on the other side of the mountain. We lost his trail in the rocks."

Ernst studied the tracks in the dirt of the outbuilding, light going in, sunken and heavy-laden coming out with the woman. They were huge, oddly shaped, missing one of the toes on the left foot. But they were still the prints of a giant barefoot man.

"I'll hunt him," said Ernst, "if you'll put some men up by that barn on the edge of town. I don't want him running near there." He looked down, eyes not meeting those of the burgermëister.

"We can put some men up there with shotguns," said the priest. "I doubt he'll go close with the smell of many men there. If you want us to."

"Yes. Yes, I do want that."

"Let's go see to your guns, then," said the mayor.

"We have a few small bore rifles and shotguns for the men of the village," said the priest, "but these are the heaviest. We saved them for you."

Ernst took his glasses out of his pocket, noticing they were the new bifocals he'd gotten for reading after those plane crashes in '54. He looked the weapons over.

One was a Weatherby .575 bolt action, three-shot magazine with a tooled stock and an 8X scope. He worked the bolt; smooth, but still a bolt action.

"Scope comes off, eh, bwana?" asked Mgoro.

"Yes. And check the shells close."

The second was an eight-gauge shotgun, its shells the size of small sticks of dynamite. Ernst looked in the boxes, pulled out a handful each of rifled slugs and oo shot. He put the slugs in the left bottom pocket of his fishing vest, the shotshells in the right.

The third was an ancient wheel-lock boar gun. Its inlaid silver and gilt work had once been as bright and intricate as the rigging on a clipper ship, but was now faded and worn. Part of the wood foregrip that had run the length of the barrel was missing. Its muzzle was the size of the exhaust pipe on a GMC truck.

"We shall have to check this thing very well," said Ernst.

"That gun was old when Kilimanjaro was a termite mound," said Mgoro.

Ernst smiled. "Perhaps," he said. "I'd also like a pistol each for Mgoro and me," he said to the mayor. "Anything, even .22's.

"And now, while Mgoro goes over these guns, I'd like to read. Do you have books? I used to have to bring my own when I came for the skiing."

"At the parish house," said the priest. "Many books, on many things."

"Good."

He sat at the desk where the priest wrote his sermons, and he read in the books again about the Wild Men.

Always, when he had been young and just writing, they had thought he was a simple writer, communicating his experience with short declarative sentences for the simple ideas he had.

Maybe that was so, but he had always read a lot, and knew more than he let on. The Indian-talk thing had first been a pose, then a defense, and at the last, a curse.

He had known of the Wild Men for a long time. There used to be spring festivals in Germany and France, and in the Pyrenees, in which men dressed in hairy costumes and covered themselves with leaves and carried huge clubs in a shuffling dance.

In Brueghel's painting, *The Battle Between Carnival and Lent*, one of his low-perspective canvases full of the contradictions of carnival, you can see a Wild Man play going on in the upper left corner, the Wild Man player looking like a walking cabbage with a full head of shaggy hair.

The Wild Men—feral men, abandoned children who grew up

Fair Game

in solitary savagery, or men who went mad—became hirsute. Lichens and moss grew on their bodies. They were the outlaws who haunted the dreams of the Middle Ages. All that was inside the village or the manor house was Godmade and good, everything outside was a snare of the devil.

More than the wolf or the bear, the serf feared the Wild Man, the unchained human without conscience who came to take what he wanted, when he wanted.

Ernst was reading Bernheimer's book again, and another on Wild Man symbolism in the art of the Middle Ages and the Renaissance. All they had agreed upon was that there had been Wild Men and that they had been used in decorative arts and were the basis of spring festivals. All this Ernst remembered from his earlier reading.

He took off his glasses and rubbed the bridge of his nose, felt again the bump above his eye.

What was the Wild Man? he asked himself. This thing of the woods and crags—it's nothing but man unfettered, unrestrained by law and civilization. Primitive, savage man. Rousseau was wrong—let man go and he turns not into the Noble Savage but into pure chaos, the chaos of Vico, of the totem fathers. Even Freud was wrong about that—the totem fathers, if they were Wild Men, would never compete with their offspring. They would eat them at birth, like Kronos.

What about this Wild Man, then? Where did he stay during the day? On what did he live when not raiding the towns? How do you find him, hunt him?

Ernst went back to the books. He found no answers there.

Mgoro said, "We are ready."

It was dusk. The sun had fallen behind the mountains. What warmth the day had had evaporated almost instantly. Ernst had taken a short nap. He had wakened feeling older and more tired than he had for years, worse than he had felt after the shock therapy in the hospital, where you woke not knowing where you were or who you were.

The other men had gone to places around the village, posted in the outlying structures, within sight and sound of each other, with clear fields of vision and fire toward the looming mountains.

Strange Things in Close-Up

Four others, with him and Mgoro, set out in the direction the Wild Man had taken that morning. They showed Ernst the rocky ground where the misshapen footprints ended.

"He'll be up and moving already," said Ernst. "Are the dogs ready?"

"They're coming now," said the burgermeïster. Back down the trail they heard men moving toward them. "Are we to try to drive him out with them?"

"No," said Ernst. "That's what he'll be expecting. I only want him to think about them. The most likely place he'll be is the caves?"

"Yes, on the other side of the mountain. It's very rocky there."

"Take the dogs over that way, then. Make as much noise as you can, and keep them at it all night, if need be. If they come across his spoor, so much the better. It would be good if they could be made to bark."

Three hounds and a Rottweiler bounded up, straining at their leashes, whimpering with excitement. The man holding them doffed his cap to the burgermeïster.

"Ernst would like to know if you can make the dogs howl all night, Rudolf."

The man put a small whistle to his mouth and blew a soundless note. The four dogs began to bark and whine as if a stag had stepped on them.

Ernst laughed for the first time in many months.

"That will do nicely," he said. "If they don't find anything, blow on that every quarter hour. Good luck."

The dogs, Rudolf, the burgermeïster, and the others started up the long trail that would take them around the mountain. Night was closing in.

"Where do you think he is?" asked Mgoro.

"Back down a quarter mile," said Ernst, "is where we should wait. He'll either pass us coming down, or back on the way up if they spot him in the village."

"I think so too," said Mgoro. "Though this is a man, not lion or leopard."

"I have to keep telling myself that," said Ernst.

"Moon come up pretty soon," said Mgoro. "Damn mountains too high, or already be moonlight."

"It's the full moon that does it maybe," said Ernst. "Drives them to come into the towns."

"You think he crazy man? From last war?"

"The burgermeïster said this is the first Wild Man attack since before the war, from before that paperhanging sonofabitch took over."

Mgoro wrapped a blanket around himself, the shotgun, the wheel-lock. Ernst carried the Weatherby across his arm. It was already getting heavy.

The outline of the mountains turned silvery with the light from the rising, still unseen moon.

Then from up the side of the mountain, the dogs began to bark.

Nothing happened after they reached the ravine where they would wait. The dogs barked, farther and farther away, their cries carried on the still, cool air of the valley.

Lights were on in the town below. Ernst was too far away to see the men standing guard in the village itself, or what was happening in the church where most of the women and children waited.

Mgoro sat in his blanket. Ernst leaned against a rock, peering into the dark upper reaches of the ravine. The moonlight had frosted everything silver and gold, with deep shadows. He would have preferred an early, westering moon lighting this side of the mountain. This one was too bright and you had to look into it. Anything could be hiding in the shadowed places. It would be better later, when the moon was overhead, or west.

The dogs barked again, still farther away. Maybe this moon was best. If they ran anything up on that side, the men over there could see it, too.

"Bwana," said Mgoro, sniffing the air. "Snow coming."

Ernst breathed deeply, sniffed. He was seized with coughing, quieted himself, choked, coughed again. His eyes stung, tears streamed down his face. He rubbed them away.

"Damn," he said. "Can't smell it yet. How long?"

"Don't know this land. One, mebbe two hours away."

Just what we need, a spring blizzard, Ernst thought.

An hour passed. Still they had bright moonlight. They heard the sound of the dogs far off. Nothing had come down the ravine. There had been no alarm from the town.

Ernst's back was knotted. His weak legs had gone to sleep several times. He'd had to massage them back to stinging life.

Mgoro sat in his blanket, the gun barrels made him look like a teepee in the moonlight. Ernst had seen him sit motionless for hours this way at waterholes, waiting for eland, wildebeest, lions. He was the best gunbearer Ernst had ever seen.

Something about Mgoro was gnawing at the back of Ernst's mind.

Ernst looked around, back down at the village. There were fewer lights now (the guards had been turning off a few at a time). He looked at the church, and he looked farther across the valley at the huge barn, a blot on the night.

He looked away, back up the ravine.

He thought something was wrong, then realized it was the light.

He looked up. High streaked cirrus raced across the moon. As he watched, it changed to altocumulus and the moon dimmed more. A dark, thicker bank slid in under that, blotting the stars to the north.

In ten minutes the sky was solidly overcast and huge, wet flakes of snow began to fall.

Two hours into the storm, Mgoro sat up, his head turned sideways. Snow already covered the lower part of his blanket, merging with the wet line of melted snow against the upper part of his body.

His finger pointed left of the ravine.

Ernst could barely make out Mgoro, much less anything further away.

But they heard it snuffling in the wet air as it went by down the rugged gully.

They waited. Ernst had eased the safety off the .575. But the sound grew fainter, continued on toward the village.

For an instant, Ernst smelled something in the air—sweat, dirt, mold, wet leaves, oil?—then it was gone. The thing must have missed their scent altogether.

The snow swirled down for another ten minutes, then stopped as abruptly as it had begun.

Another five minutes and the moon was out, bright and to the west, shining down on a transformed world of glass and powder.

The thing had come by close.

When they turned to look down the ravine they could see the shadowed holes of the footprints leading in a line down toward the town. The end of the tracks was still more than a kilometre from the village. They strained their eyes, then Ernst took out a pair of night binoculars, passed them to Mgoro. He scanned the terrain past where the footprints disappeared near a road.

He shook his head, handed them back.

Ernst put them to his eyes. It was too bright to make out anything through the glasses—the snow threw back too much glare, made the shadows too dark.

"If he decides not to go in, he'll come back this way," said Ernst.

"If we shoot to warn them, he go anywhere," said Mgoro.

"If nothing happens in the next hour, we follow his tracks," said Ernst.

The moon was dropping to the right of the village. Ernst checked his watch. Fifty minutes had passed.

If they stayed, they had the high ground, command of the terrain. They would be able to see him coming.

If they tracked him, and the Wild Man got above them, he could wait for them anywhere.

Do I treat this like stalking a lion, or following an airborne ranger? Ernst asked himself. He moved in place, getting the circulation back in his leg, the one with the busted kneecap and the shrapnel from three wars back.

He didn't want the Wild Man to get too far ahead of them. It could have circled the town and gone up the other side of the valley, sensing something wrong, or not wanting to leave tracks in the snow. Or it could be holed up just ahead, watching and waiting.

The dogs barked again. Now they sounded nearer, and they were holding the tone. They must have crossed the Wild Man's path somewhere and were trailing him now.

Ernst felt his pulse rise, like you do when beagles begin to

Strange Things in Close-Up

circle, indicating the rabbit somewhere ahead of you is coming your way, or when a setter goes on point, all tense, and you ready yourself for the explosion of quail.

Shouts from the village cut across his reverie. Shots followed, and banging on pots and pans. The bells began to toll rapidly.

Mgoro stood against a rock so as to give no silhouette to anything down the ravine. Lights went on in town, flashlight beams swung up and around. They converged toward this side of town. Lights crossed the field and came toward the ravine, with sporadic small arms fire. The sounds from the town grew louder, like an angry hornet's nest.

Mgoro pointed.

Far down, where the footprints had ended, there was a movement. It was only a blur against the snow, a dull change in the moonlit background, but it was enough.

Mgoro dropped the blanket from his shoulders, held the shotgun and wheel-lock, one in each hand, two feet to the side and one foot back of Ernst.

The movement came again, much closer than it should have been for so close a space of time, then again, closer still.

First it was a shape, then a man-shape.

It stopped for a few seconds, then came on in a half-loping ape shamble.

Behind and below, flashlight beams reached the far end of the ravine and were starting up, slowly, voices still too indistinct with the distance.

Now the shape moved from one side of the gully to the other, running. Now it was two hundred metres away in the moonlight. Now a hundred. Eighty.

It was too big for a man.

The baying of the dogs, up the mountain behind Ernst, got louder.

The man-shape stopped.

Ernst brought the Weatherby up, held his breath, squeezed.

The explosion was loud, louder than he remembered, but he worked the bolt as the recoil brought the muzzle up. He brought the sights back down, centered them on the gully before the shell casing hit the ground.

There had been a scream with the shot. Whatever had screamed was gone. The ravine was empty.

Fair Game

He and Mgoro ran down the gully.

It had jumped three metres between one set of prints and the next, and there was a spray of blood four metres back. A high hit, then. Maybe, thought Ernst, as they ran up out of the ravine to the left, maybe we'll find him dead twenty metres from here.

But the stride stayed long, the drops in the snow far apart.

Ernst's lungs were numb. He could hardly breathe in enough air to keep going. His legs threatened to fold, and he realized what he was—an old, half-crippled man trying to run down something that was twice his size, wounded and mad.

Mgoro was just behind him. His lungs labored, too, but still he held both guns where he could hand them to Ernst in seconds.

The flashlights and lanterns from the town headed across the front of the village, between the town and the Wild Man. Behind Ernst and Mgoro, the dogs neared in the ravine.

Ernst and Mgoro slowed. The footprints were closer together now, and there was a great clot of blood that seemed to have been coughed up. Internal bleeding maybe, thought Ernst, maybe a better shot than I thought I could ever make again.

The moon was on the edge of the far mountain. They would lose the light for a while, but it should be nearing dawn.

The tracks led in an arc toward the roadway south of the village. Lights from the men in town and those halfway up the hill led that way.

They heard the dogs behind them, whining with urgency when they came to the place of the hit. Now they left the ravine and came straight behind the two men.

"Off the tracks. Off!" puffed Ernst. He grabbed Mgoro, pulled him five paces down the mountainside.

In a moment the dogs flashed by, baying, running full speed. As they passed, the last of the direct moonlight left the valley. The dogs ran on into darkness.

"Come," said Mgoro, through gritted teeth. "We have him."

They heard the dogs catch up to the Wild Man. One bark ended in a squeal, another just ended. Two dogs continued on, and the sound of the pursuit moved down the valley.

Ernst ran on, his feet and chest like someone else's.

He realized that the Wild Man was heading toward the barn.

Strange Things in Close-Up

When Ernst was thirteen, up in Michigan one summer, he got lost. It was the last time in his life he was ever lost.

He had been fishing, and had a creel full of trout. But he had crossed three marshy beaver ponds that morning, skirted some dense woods getting to the fishing. On the way back he had taken a wrong turn. It was that easy to get lost.

He had wandered for two hours trying to find his way back to his own incoming tracks.

Just at dusk, he came to a clearing and saw in front of him a huge barn, half-gone in ruin. He wondered at it. There was no house with it. It was in the middle of the Michigan woods. There were no animals around, and looked as if there never had been.

He walked closer.

Someone stepped from around one corner, someone dressed in a long grey cloak, wearing a death's head mask.

Ernst stopped, stunned.

The thing reached down inside its cloak and exposed a long, diseased penis to him.

"Hey, you, Bright Boy," it said. "Suck on this."

Ernst dropped his rod, his creel, and ran in a blind panic until he came out on the road less than half a mile from the cabin his family had rented.

One dog still barked. They had found the other three on the way. Two dead, torn up and broken. The third had run until it had given out. It lay panting in a set of tracks, pointing the way with its body like an arrow.

Now the sky to the east was lighter. Ernst began to make things out—the valley floor, the lights of the men as they ran, the great barn up ahead beside the road.

Something ran through a break in the woods, the sound of the dog just behind it.

Ernst stopped, threw the .575 to his shoulder, fired. A vip of snow flew up just over the thing's shoulder, and it was gone into the woods again. The dog flashed through the opening.

Ernst loaded more shells in.

The great barn was a kilometer ahead when they found the last dog pulled apart like warm red taffy.

Fair Game

Ernst slid to a stop. The prints crossed a ditch, went up the other side, blood everywhere now.

Ernst jumped into the ditch just as he realized the prints were doubled, had been trodden over by something retracing its steps.

He tried to stop himself from going just as Mgoro, on the bank behind him, saw the prints and yelled.

Ernst's arms windmilled, he let go of the rifle, fell heavily, caught a rock with his fingers, slipped, his bad knee crashing into the bottom of the ditch.

Dull pain shot through him. He pulled himself to his other knee.

The Wild Man charged.

It had doubled back, jumped off into a stand of small trees fifty feet up the ditch. Now it had them.

The Weatherby was half-hidden in the ditch snow. Did he have time to get it? Was the action ready? Was the safety off? Was there snow in the barrel and would it explode like an axed watermelon in his hands when he fired?

Not on my knees, Ernst thought, and stood up.

"Gun!" he said, just as Mgoro slammed the shotgun butt down into his right shoulder from the bank above.

Ernst let the weight of the barrels bring the eight-gauge into line. He was already cocking both hammers as his left arm slid up the foregrip.

The Wild Man was teeth and beard and green-grey hair in front of him as the barrels came level with its chest.

Ernst pulled both triggers.

All the moments come down to this. All the writing and all the books and the fishing and the hunting and the bullfights. All the years of banging yourself around and being beaten half the time

The barrels leaped up with recoil.

All the years of living by your code. Good is what makes you feel good. A man has to do what a man has to do.

A huge red spot appeared on the Wild Man's shoulder as the slug hit and the right hand, which had been reaching for Ernst, came loose and flew through the air behind the buckshot.

Ernst let the shotgun fall.

"Gun!" he said.

And then you get old and hurt and scared, and the writing

doesn't work anymore, and the sex is gone and booze doesn't help, and you can't hunt or fish, all you have is fame and money and there's nothing to buy.

Mgoro put the butt of the wheel-lock against his shoulder.

The Wild Man's left hand was coming around like a claw, reaching for Ernst's eyes, his face, reaching for the brain inside his head.

Ernst pulled the trigger-lever, the wheel spun in a ratcheting blur, the powder took with a *floopth* and there was an ear-shattering roar.

Then they take you to a place and try to make you better with electricity and drugs and it doesn't make you better, it makes you worse and you can't do anything anymore, and nobody understands but you, that you don't want anything anymore.

Ernst lies under a shaggy wet weight that reeks of sweat and mushrooms. He is still deaf from the explosion. The wheel-lock is wedged sideways against his chest, the wheel gouging into his arm. He pushes and pulls, twisting his way out from under, slipping on the bloody rocks.

Mgoro is helping him, pulling his shoulders.

"It is finished," he says.

Ernst stands, looking down at the still-twitching carcass. Blood runs from jagged holes you can see the bottom of the ditch through. It is eight feet tall, covered with lichen and weeds, matted hair, and dirt.

Now it is dead; this thing that was man gone mad, man without law, like all men would be if they had nothing to hold them back.

And one day they let you out of the place because you've acted nice, and you go home with your wife, and you sing to her and she goes to sleep and next morning at dawn you go downstairs in your bathrobe and you go to your gun cabinet and you take out your favorite, the side-by-side double barrel your actor friend gave you before he died and you put it on the floor and you lean forward until the barrels are a cool infinity mark on your forehead ...

Ernst stands and looks at the big barn only a kilometer away,

Fair Game

and he looks at Mgoro, who, he knows now, has been dead more than thirty years, and Mgoro smiles at him.

Ernst looks at the barn and knows he will begin walking toward it in just a moment, he and Mgoro, but still there is one more thing he has to do.

He reaches down, pulling, and slowly turns the Wild Man over, face up.

The hair is matted, ragged holes torn in the neck and chest and stomach, the right arm missing from the elbow down.

The beard is tangled, thick and bloody. Above the beard is the face, twisted.

And Ernst knows that it is his face on the Wild Man, the face of the thing he has been hunting all his life.

He stands then, and takes Mgoro's arm, and they start up the road toward the barn.

The light begins to fade, though it is crisp morning dawn. Ernst knows they will make the barn before the light gives out completely.

And above everything, over the noise of the church bells back in town, above the yelling, jubilant voices of the running people, there is a long, slow, far-off sound, like the boom of surf crashing onto a shore.

Or maybe it is just the sound of both triggers being pulled at once.

Introduction to
What Makes Heironymous Run?

Friends who know me get real tired of hearing me talk about the stories I'm going to write. And what they hear me call them are usually not the titles you know them by.

Like, "The Ugly Chickens" was referred to as "the dodo story." "Flying Saucer Rock and Roll" was variously called "the doo-wop story" or "the piss-drinking story." "I'm going to write a doo-wop story," I would say. "Ike at the Mike," on the other hand, was always called "Ike at the Mike." "The alternate-Africa story" meant "The Lions Are Asleep This Night."

In my imagination, "What Makes Heironymous Run?" was always "the painter story," and that's what it says on the working title of the file folder with the research in it. (The research consisted mostly of looking at about 2000 Renaissance paintings until my eyeballs melted like lumps of Crisco in a skillet.)

Again, I'd carried this around for years, left over from when I was a kid looking at art history books in the library. Who are all those people? I didn't know much, but I knew they didn't have plate-armor in Roman Judea. Why do the Wise Men look like Frenchmen? What's Catherine d'Medici doing in the river with John the Baptist?

I don't want to pull my punches here, but if you're ever feeling that, in Gardner Dozois' words, "your morning newspaper headlines look more and more like they're out of 'The Marching Morons'," take a quick look at the complete works of Brueghel the Elder and Heironymous Bosch, and remember, they worked before television and penicillin were around.

This was finally written in late 1984 and published with another beautiful Hank Jankus illustration in the last issue of the much-lamented magazine, Shayol.

After all those years thinking about it, writing it was pretty close to a holy joy.

What Makes Heironymous Run?

So we push the buttons, there is the audible click, the moment of giddiness and the blurring of vision. Then we are back *here*.

Here is the Netherlands, and the time is the late sixteenth century. We are to answer questions which have evaded scholars to this point. Such as, what exactly did the Duke of Alba do in his reign as governor here; when did the hybrid tulip industry actually begin, so on and so forth. Also a few minor details if we have the inclination: did the Italians influence gable-roof architecture, and was the painter Roelandt Savery *really* mad at the end of his life?

We land, invisible to any but ourselves, at the edge of a dusty road. Everything is blurry to us as if we see through thick, badly-poured glass, oddly tinted grey. This is a byproduct of the field generated by the timebelts we wear. We look like striped harlequins, the dark and light patches caused by the wiring of our suits. The blurry vision is second nature to us now—like persons with failing eyesight we adjusted early in our careers to it. We blink a few times and get our bearings.

Something is wrong. Deborah looks at me, down at her time belt. I check mine.

Our target years were in the late sixteenth century—fine, the indicator is right on the money. But the Netherlands? They're flat as felt and twice as dull, even before millions of hectares of land were reclaimed from the sea in later centuries. Usually the tallest thing in sight would be a windmill, an occasional tree. (Neither of us has been here before.)

Something is greatly amiss for all around us are great looming mountains; super-Alps, proto-Rockies topped with wild wracks of clouds, sparkling grey-white with glaciers halfway up.

A great torrent of river is off to our left, waterfalls, rapids and all. We must be in Bavaria, Switzerland, some mountainous principality. Only these mountains look more like Himalayas or Andes than anything European. Certainly we have not missed by so far.

I check my readings. 51° 33' 12" North, 5° 24' 13" East, somewhere in the northern Brabant. The only river near here should be the Dommel, or in modern times, the Wilhelmina or Williams Canals, placid and flat as boards. In our time the Dommel empties into the Maas some kilometers from here. My geographical knowledge comes from the refresher course. But I do know nothing in these lands ever looked remotely like this.

"I'm calibrating," said Deborah. She tinkered with her belt, winked out of existence, wavered, popped back as if she had been edited in on videotape.

"You try, and tell me what you think," she said.

I fiddled, ran a few years like easing out the clutch on an automobile, felt a slight jerk, disappeared, set the counter to lock. Appeared again.

It read the same as when I'd started.

"Hmmm," she said. "Do we go back Up There now and put these things in the shop, or what?"

"Both of them can't be wrong," I said.

"You're looking at them." She looked down the road. "Here comes a nice family. Let's hang around and listen. Maybe the date and place will come up in the conversation."

We stood in the road. But we ended up not listening very closely, after all. The group was lead by a bearded peasant with a saw over his shoulder leading a donkey. On the donkey was a woman dressed in white and purple, nursing a child. They drew even with us on the roadway, went by, not saying anything to each other, not remarking on the haloes above all three of their heads, the angel with the sword which flew above them, or the roil and whirl of cherubs which came behind like a flock of migrating waterfowl, their small wings like the blur of hummingbirds.

They all disappeared around some outcrops of rocks and were gone.

"Let's sit down," I said.

Eventually we walked the same way on the road, downstream beside the wild river. There should be towns and houses that way.

What Makes Heironymous Run?

There was a lot more animal life than I supposed. Deer stood in the rocky forests, birds sat in the trees, a profusion of them, all kinds, tropical birds, storks, herons, cassowaries, ostriches. I slowed my walk. Tigers and lions lay in dim recesses, an elephant placidly pulled down tree limbs, a giraffe peeked out above thorny bushes.

"We must be in some rich prince's menagerie," I said. "He must have brought them here from all over the world, the East Indies, Africa."

"He sure as hell didn't bring these mountains or this river here," said Deborah.

Animals yelled, birds chittered. The woods were thick as rain forests, dark gloomy places through which shafts of sunlight sliced.

We turned a curve and the land opened up down the valley, became flatter, less wooded. Here and there were solitary houses, small groups of buildings. Still the mountains loomed all around, impossibly high and remote. The couple and child were nowhere in sight. Far up the side of one of the mountains we saw the long snakelike slow movement of an army, thousands and thousands of men moving in rows up the defiles, blocked from view by rocks, appearing again further up, finally lost from view among the clouds.

The valley just ahead seemed peaceful enough—far ahead of that the landscape became grey, darker, from what we could not see.

As we walked we saw fewer animals, more people, ones and twos of them, opening shutters of houses, digging in small gardens, turning cattle out of barns. On the river a ship was moving, a huge galleon, far too large for the waterway. A farmer with red leggings and a moldboard plow pulled by an ox turned great clods of earth over in rows. A shepherd stood over his flock, and another fished at the river's edge.

There was a loud splash. Something had fallen in the river. A small trail of feathers swirled down the sky and settled on the water as the ship sailed by.

"What was that?" asked Deborah.

"Maybe a bird?" I said.

It is spring, no doubt of it. The world is filled with the odors

Strange Things in Close-Up

of growing things and blooms. Calves and lambs are being born in the fields as we pass. Wheat shoots up. A woman with an exposed breast walks through a field, carrying a cornucopia. The very ground turns green and waving with grain. People appear everywhere.

We pass a small church at which peasants are dancing, stamping their great rude feet, costumes all woolen, somewhat washed out to our eyes but probably bright and colorful. Pipers play, their cheeks blown into ovals. Fights and drunkenness abound, couples lie humping in fresh grass.

Odors of bodies, cooking and sunlight come to us, filtered through time. Far off, a spring storm plays on a hillside. Animals and people run for cover.

In the wet distance, some trees take on the forms of naked women in flashes of lightning. The storm slackens, disappears, the day is golden and dripping. Hunters chase deer, crows bring bread to a hermit on a mountain. Another hermit sits writing in a cave, a lion asleep at his feet.

All this takes place across the river. Here we pass more villages; one is filled with playing children, no adults anywhere. A second, larger village has people behaving eccentrically, shovelling dirt on patches of sunlight, chasing eels, throwing flowers to hogs. They do not even seem to notice each other.

Another ship goes by on the river, a small one full of nuns and priests acting strangely, some of them climbing the mast to grab at a scrap of paper nailed there.

We pass a haywagon stalled in the road, surrounded by grasping people, and we notice now that some of the fields are already being harvested, men with scythes making great yellow swaths in the grain. Farmers eat out of wood bowls and clay dishes, they walk back and forth through the crops, others sleep beside their flails. The sides of the valleys seem muted gold and brown to our vision. Sheens of heat rise off the houses and the fields. The glaciers on the mountains are shrunken, smaller. Everything seems weighed down with the heat. We feel it through our suits and turn up the circulators.

As we walk the sun descends toward the end of the valley. The fields we pass lie sere and denuded, filled with stubble. Men drive cattle home, shut them in barns which hang with fruit, bulge with wheat and sacks of flour. The windmills are busy, their sails spin like dynamoes, they race like engines as the grain is milled.

The landscape is darker, the light flatter. People shut their houses, go to weddings and harvest dances at which food is heaped in mounds that threaten to overflow the tables. More pipers play, other musicians, dancers stomp in circles, sway back and forth. Then they make their ways home, do the evening chores, chop wood, trim trees, the mountains once again cool and blue.

Everything is still and calm.

The sound of the wind rises, then changes to a high roaring moan. The river ices over, turns milk-colored, lifts out of its bed. Hardy people appear, skate on its surface, ice-sail in their coffin-like boats, chop out frozen fish and drop fish, ice and all into sacks. They light bonfires, butcher hogs and make sausage.

The valleys above, once bare, turn white. The glaciers come down the sides of the mountains with frightening rapidity. In a moment the moraine is out onto the flatlands.

The wind moans again, and all the people hurry inside their houses. The air blurs. Animals caught outside become snowdrifts. Birds freeze in midflight and fall to the ground, bouncing like dark hailstones. A bonfire seems too blue, frozen, as if the flames were painted on the wood from which it springs.

Even outside of time we feel the cold.

The air becomes so dense and heavy it moves in gelid waves, settling in low places like a viscous liquid.

The world closes down. Nothing moves but smoke from the rude chimneys, and that curls down like grey rags to the ground.

The earth is shut up. The sky is greygreen, snow falls perpetually. There is no sound but that of the slow cold wind.

On the lintel of the door of one of the houses someone has hastily carved, in Flemish, "The ice has come again."

We spend the night in a travellers' rest filled with pilgrim shrines, turning our suits up against the biting chillness.

We talk.

"There have been four seasons today. Something is very wrong, either with us, our equipment, or with the sixteenth century," said Deborah.

"I choose us. Or at least, our perceptions," I said.

Strange Things in Close-Up

"You're wrong," she said. "Think back on what we've seen today. Haven't you seen it all before?"

"I hope to god not," I said.

"Think. Think about poor old Roelandt Savery who we're supposed to investigate. All those animals he painted endlessly, all those birds and dodoes. His canvases were filled with animals, like those in the woods this morning. Animals from everywhere."

"But he painted for Emperor Rudolph in Vienna. Those animals *were* all there. They were given the emperor by other kings, ships' captains, explorers. Savery just stuck them in his paintings in some wild Alp-like setting."

"I'm not so sure," said Deborah.

"Well, it's not making any much more sense to me than you," I said. "We can't find *anything* on the maps, much less Roelandt Savery's hometown."

"How far are we going with this? When do we give up?"

I thought a moment. "When we find an answer that makes some sense." I snuggled closer to her.

"Then we may be here for a very long time," she said.

We made love then, without turning our timebelts off, which is very much against the rules.

The next morning dawned clear and cold, the world locked in its coffin of ice. Snow had drifted in front of the door and we pushed our way out. Everything was flat and calm. The sun came up as cold and red as if its fires were going out. We walked on the flatter track of the road. People in the villages were out in the early morning light, chopping holes in the river for water, moving slowly in their heavy woolen clothing.

At one village some kind of activity was going on—people were lining up at a building, paying taxes. Soldiers (soldiers from Spain) lolled around the building, keeping people in line. I thought I saw the couple we had seen the day before. The man still had the saw, the lady sat bundled on the donkey, but there was no child to be seen, no haloes, no angels. All the buildings of the town seemed packed with people.

It clouded over and snowed for a short while, a gentle snow. We passed another village. Weeping and wailing rose from it, and there were splotches of blood and the prints of many men

What Makes Heironymous Run?

and horses in the churned and dirty drifts at the center of the town.

The snow quit. The sun came out again, and the ice melted away as we walked, the ground becoming soft and soggy underfoot. With a grinding roar, the ice broke in the river, the waters began to flow. Here the river was flatter and slower, but still those mountains loomed over us where they should not be.

We were entering the part of the valley that had been obscured by smoke and haze the day before. Even as the snow melted, the sun dulled over. Soot and cinders drifted over the road and countryside. Far away on the foothills people ran back and forth in great agitation. Darkness closed in, but darkness shot through with flashes of red light from high up on the mountainsides. There was a giant clanging in the air, the sound of huge horseshoes being struck by gigantic hammers.

And this is what we saw through the dimness of the light, through our blurred vision outside time. The sky above us was live with sparks and smoke. Things flew past, bugs made of feathers and fur. There were pink crustacean phallic towers on the horizons, surrounded by houses made of huge broken jugs. The trees were like turnips and among them skeletons dressed in rags moved to and fro, hunting the naked men, women and children who hid from them. In one place, a couple playing mandolins tried to sing one more verse before a scythe wielded by a hooded figure cut them down. Brambles and briers grew everywhere, the road became a narrow twisty path. The mouth of hell, encased in flames, was set in a hillside. Cities burned like smoky lamps. On every hand stood gallows, crucifixes and torture wheels like mills for the business of death. Only dogs, gaunt and sticklike, were left to feed on the rotting corpses of men and other animals. Towers, castles and hovels all blended in one ashen pile among the broken churches. People were doing things in the middle distance we would rather not know about. The mountains above us looked as if they were going to redden and melt. A giant madwoman was leading an army of housewives in an attack on a city filled with frogs and ears.

We hurried along.

The air became cool and clean, the sun in high overcast. The city lay before us with its towers, churches and checkered roofs.

Strange Things in Close-Up

Behind it, into the center of the valley a huge mountain rose up, filling the whole distance behind the city, its sides and top lost in a low cloud.

People walked on the broad road, unconcerned except for occasional glances over their shoulders at the smoldering conflagrations far behind us.

The city walls were long and wide. Houses were scattered outside it like fallen leaves. There was only a trace of snow left in the shady places. Above the walls rose an odd assortment of buildings—gothic churches, roman aqueducts, columned temples, gable-roofed houses, Italianate mercantile building fronts, here and there a modest pyramid, as if we were looking at some motion picture studio backlot of the late twentieth century. (I've seen Culver City!)

As we neared the city more and more people were on the road with us—some dressed in togas and stolae, others as Renaissance Italians, some in barbarous furs and necklaces, some as cavaliers, mediaeval ladies-in-waiting, most in the somber Dutch clothes, bonnets and broadbrimmed hats they were *supposed* to be wearing.

Soldiers wearing the colors of the Duke of Alba stood outside the walls, paying no attention to anyone. We passed through the huge gate (with doors thick enough to keep King Kong out, or in), under a broken and crumbling aqueduct, and into the city proper.

Chubby women sold fish and shrimp, men sat in front of taverns, smoking, drinking, playing cards. Fights broke out over rolls of dice. Prostitutes leaned down from windows, beckoning. Monks walked in processions, beggars clattered on crutches, the fox tails sewn to their garments flapping in the breeze. Everywhere was spending, getting, commerce.

Churches, taverns, guildhalls lay chock-a-block with a Sphinx and a boarding house. The light itself seemed to change from street to street. Here was bright daylight, there shadowy evening, here an overcast grey morning pall.

My eyes were hurting me. Everything had ghostly blurs, marred by lines and fuzziness.

"Over here, Deb," I said, taking her into the fornices of a church where there were fewer people. We waited until no one was looking. I turned off my timebelt.

What Makes Heironymous Run?

I wished I hadn't. I closed my eyes against the colors. I felt as if I were falling into a vortex of brilliant hues. What had seemed grey and drab through the time distortion was a psychedelic swab of neon reds, harsh greens, violent orange. The sky above the buttresses of the church was a deep neverending well of blue—I grabbed the wall to keep from falling up into it.

"Oh my god," said Deborah beside me. She, too, had stepped out of time, her hand still on her belt controls. Then she covered her face. "My god, how bright!"

My eyes adjusted to the overpowering hues. People were looking at us, talking. They stopped whatever they were doing. From the street outside, they came running into the shade of the church, pointing at us. Deborah was still looking up at the sky.

"Hey. We're drawing a crowd. Let's go!" I punched myself back out of time. Deb stood entranced. A beggar grabbed at her.

I reached over and pushed her controls. She joined me in the fuzzy time stream. The man's half-hand closed on nothing. The crowd drew back from where we stood.

Back up on the packed street, the crowd parted, and Rembrandt's *Night Watch*, seventeen strong, walked up and began questioning the crowd.

"Don't you see," said Deb. "All the history of this time is wrong. Only the artists, the painters were right. They were painting what they saw around them."

We sat still, outside time, on a *banco* under the balcony of a house. We had just seen another Madonna, Joseph and donkey turn the corner, on the way to a crowded row of inns.

"That can't be right. Our equipment is malfunctioning in some way we don't understand. Now I'm convinced we should leave, go back, turn these belts in. When we come back, we'll find a flat wet country filled with tulips and people who eat too much."

"What about the colors? The seasons we went through? That hellscape—"

"The seasons? Everybody knows the weather was freakish during the 1500s. That's why there are so many genre paintings of skaters, winter scenes. There was a small ice age. That part could be real."

Strange Things in Close-Up

"You still don't sound convinced."

"I'm not, not anymore. But I'll work on that assumption when we file our reports. I'm ready. Let's go."

A town crier was ringing a bell at the corner. He was yelling up a showing in an art studio down the crooked street.

"We're not going before I see *that*," said Deborah.

I didn't want a fight. "Be careful. Stay in time. As soon as you see it, we'll go."

"You're not coming?"

"I'm going to sit on this log, and wait for you to come out."

"Isn't there any adventure in your soul?"

"My soul's overloaded a bit, just now," I said.

She turned and followed the streaming crowd into the many-windowed building down the block, the only unfuzzy thing among the many blurred ones.

I looked past the edifices, beyond the back city walls at the huge red-grey mountain lost in the clouds.

An hour later, Deborah came out, walking slowly, looking past me. I caught her arm as she wandered by.

"How was it?" I asked. "What did you see in there?"

Her eyes were wild, staring. She took a deep breath and began to speak.

"Arms. Weapons. Paintings of war. A blacksmith was in the background. Globes, paintings, statues, musical instruments, dishes, shells, bugs, chairs, maps, books. Soldiers outside with pikes, monkeys, a man dressed as a donkey, flowers, jewelry, frames, terrariums. Bottles, dogs. Paintings of windmills, classical scenes, parrots, armillary spheres, seahorse mummies, tassels, miniature portraits, drawers opened, full of jewelry, seals, illuminated manuscripts, parrots, monkeys, dogs, teapots . . ."

"Please, Deb, stop." I squeezed her arm. "Tell me what you saw."

She shook her head, continued. "Warriors led by women, coming in doors, footlockers and chests full of rubies, palletes and paintboxes, violas, cellos, dwarves, babies dressed in classical costumes, calipers, cockatoos, greyhounds, fireplaces and columns, paintings of macaws, swords, *vanitas*, skulls and books, devils rolling rocks away, dragons, still life Boeschart flower paintings, books and monkeys, antique marble statues

What Makes Heironymous Run?

and busts, doors, cavaliers in boots examining paintings, waterfowl, astrolabes, arched and pillared entries, gargoyle and kneeling-cupid table legs, bottles of colored water, velvet curtains and cloth, two dogs fighting over a stick, dragon sculptures of wood over doors, inkstands, paints, paper, artwork, balcony rails, balusters and balustrades, mandrake root in bug collections, scrolled cupids and eagle fascia, mythological figures viewing paintings, cherubs copying artwork, students drawing from statuary—"

She ran down.

"Is that what you saw?" I asked.

"No. There was more. Much more."

She turned off her belt and became visible in *their* world.

"No. Don't!" I yelled.

She was already running toward the studio.

I pushed my way in just as the riot broke out. Whether Deborah had caused it or something else, I don't know. A struggling, pushing torrent of humans was emptying out the doors, breaking windows. A cherub flew out overhead, shedding feathers. I tried to force my way in against the mass.

The back door has been opened. The Duke of Alba's horsemen were riding back and forth, smashing statuary, slicing canvas, riding down people with their lances. Out beyond a ring of footsoldiers, the Duke sat impassively, watching the carnage.

I thought I saw Deborah's harlequinade suit disappear into a maelstrom of panic and pushed and shoved toward it. Someone shoved into my stomach. I popped into their time. Terrified faces shied away from me, fists lashed out. I shoved the controls, locked them, disappeared to the crowd. We fell out into the streets in a pile, up and running, caught in a river of people, forcing me further and further away from the studio.

"Deb!" I yelled. "Deb!" But my cries, outside of time, were drowned by those within.

Relentlessly, the people swept me out of the city in their panic.

We were slowing now. The crowd had become dispirited, quiet. An occasional horseman rode by, keeping the people moving outward, away from the city toward the red-grey mountain ahead.

Strange Things in Close-Up

I stepped away from the throng, walked parallel, watching for any sign of Deborah. Four or five long masses of people were coming out of the gates this side of the city, the separate streams forming into a single mass ahead.

To each side of the road, each hundred meters or so, were gallows, gibbets, wheels on long poles reaching into the sky. From each dangled one, two or more corpses, some quite fresh, others strings of bones. The roadside ditches were littered with skulls and wristbones.

The crowd was joining together at a small hill in front of the huge mountain. Soldiers rode and walked back and forth. The mood of the crowd had turned from fear to that of holiday. They were hurrying toward the place, and vendors were selling food, trinkets and indulgences on the sides of the road. There must be a million people at this place, more than lived in all the Low Countries at the time, and behind me still more streamed from the city.

I edged through the crowd as it stopped moving and made my way to the front ranks.

The soldiers were nailing three guys to crosses, the crowd cheering. Here and there a few men and women wept as the big iron nails were run in by the Spaniards.

I searched the crowd. No sign of Deborah. I walked past the crucifixions, into the massed ring of people on the other side, clambering for a better view.

The crowds cheered as the great crosses were pushed into their holes in the ground, and the men swung up to the sky, rocking back and forth like rag dolls on sticks.

I pushed my way through the yelling mob, out the other side. Some of the people were already losing interest and going home.

Then I looked up at the mountain, and it was no mountain at all.

It rose, ledge on ledge, like a giant broken red screw into the blue sky. It looked like an infinite Roman Coliseum, its bulk rising out of the whole width of the valley, jagged and incomplete, higher than Everest, dwarfing the mountains around it. Columns rose up with arched doorways ten meters high every thirty meters. I raised my head. The sets of doorways went up and around out of sight on the inclined ramp, to appear a row

What Makes Heironymous Run?

further up, then around and further, till they became dots, then dark indentations, then were lost in the haze of distance long before the tower itself jutted into the clouds.

Great wooden cranes and structures overflowed every level. To one side of the tower was a quarry, seemingly as deep as the structure was high. Huge quantities of great red-grey blocks lay cut but unmoved at the pit's edge.

In an hour I reached the roadway which became the ramp that spiralled up and up, around the tower.

I began to walk, the bulk of the structure looming over me, the second level of the ramp hundreds of meters above me.

The great broken wooden machines were weathered grey, unused for years or centuries. Houses had been built against the inner walls of the ramps, no doubt to shelter and feed the millions of workmen or slaves who had once labored here.

Frayed ropes, broken chains hung from the cranes, swayed in the wind. It was cold on this shaded side of the tower. I walked on.

I saw a movement through one of the sets of arches, stopped, looked in.

The inner structure was an infinite series of cells and arches, like the chambers of a nautilus, which had outgrown the earth. Some portions were finished, others only roughed in, some untouched solid rock which seemed to twine its way up and around, like a bad pour of metal throughout the whole structure.

Whatever had moved was gone. I went back outside, continued up and on.

Other movements came, and I paused and watched. The abandoned tower seemed a refuge for hermits and crazy people. They scurried like spiders up and down the inner cells, some laughing, some weeping bitterly, others whimpering in fear.

Someone was walking on the ramp far ahead of me just as I crossed out of the shadow and into the westward-facing sunlit portion of the structure.

It was Deborah, and she walked in time, a blur to me. I ran toward her.

I pushed my belt control off. "Deb! Deb!" I yelled.

She was paying no attention to me, but looking down below.

Strange Things in Close-Up

Far down, the great mass of people was gone, a few bunched knots of peasants and soldiers were left, the remnants of the crowd still on the roads back into the city. The three crucified men looked like pins stuck in a map.

It was growing dark, great clouds rolling in from all directions to cover the sun, flying over the tower, the overcast becoming total as I ran.

"Deb!" I yelled, then pushed the controls and went back out of time. I ran up to her.

Something grey-green grabbed at her. I ran into it. It was huge. I punched. Surprised, it reached out a great hand, grabbed me in the chest, flung me back.

I flew over, the breath leaving me, breaking something in my chest as I smashed into a rock. Stars pinwheeled.

Suddenly the sky became grey-black, the fuzziness gone, everything stark and real, everything Now.

I reached down. My timebelt lay broken and leaking in three pieces against the archway.

Deborah backed past me, her eyes full of fear, still unaware of me.

The grey-green thing coming toward her was a man, or had been. Two and a half meters tall, he was covered with matted fur from which moss and algae hung. His beard was a great gold-brown tangle which flowed out onto his chest. In one hand he carried a huge broken sapling as easily as a policeman holds a nightstick. He was naked, and he had a huge erection. As he advanced on Deborah, his black tongue lolled out and licked over his broken, jagged teeth in both lust and stomach-hunger.

It was the Wild Man of the Woods, the bogey, men whom the times had driven mad, who lived among the animals, who raided civilized places.

He gave me a glance from the corner of his eye, then stalked Deborah. She put her hands over her face.

I rolled over, great shards of pain in my chest, got to my feet. The world reeled. I staggered behind Deborah.

"Hold still," I said. She paid no attention to me, watching the monster advance.

The Wild Man lifted his club, ready to smash us both.

"Hold still," I said.

What Makes Heironymous Run?

I unbuckled her timebelt as we backed against a doorway. Then I put it around my waist and turned it on.

Everything went safe and fuzzy.

The Wild Man grabbed Deborah by the hair.

Now she screamed. He pulled her, kicking, through the archway into one of the inner cells.

She screamed louder.

The world was turning dark. Snow began to fall in great waves, huge flakes. First the ground below and the city were obscured, then the walls of the tower above were lost to sight, then the ramp itself.

The whiteness was erasing everything—the colors, the tower, the world, the Wild Man, Deborah, me. The snow closed in, and I was alone, in time, on the ramp.

I pushed the buttons to come back Up Here.

I felt time unlocking like an extension ladder, and then I began to scream.

Introduction to
The Lions are Asleep This Night

I carried this one around for years, too (like the book I'm someday going to write, a Chinese communist proletarian SF novel called Mars Is Red), *and believe me, it was still real hard to write when I sat down to it in early 1985.*

Not only that, but selling it brought me another of those blinding moments of satori I'd rather do without.

I sent it to Ellen Datlow at Omni.

She wanted it, but she also wanted some revisions to make it clearer to the reader what was going on.

"Remember," she said in the letter, "everybody doesn't know as much history as you do, Howard."

Yow! I began to question a lot of stuff I'd written. "Ike at the Mike"! ". . . the World, as We Know't."! "Custer's Last Jump" (with Steve Utley)! Them Bones! *All alternate histories!*

If nobody knows any *history, what am I doing writing about alternate ones, parallel worlds where things turned out differently? Who cares?*

Yow!

A few moments reflection brought me back to earth (this one). She was right. I'd wanted to write a subtle story. What I had written was a rarefied one.

Anyway, this is the rewrite, as it appeared in Omni.

There are Onitsha market pamphlets, or were, anyway, from about 1938–1967. If you're as fascinated by them as I was, get Emmanuel Obiechina's An African Popular Literature: A Study of Onitsha Market Pamphlets, *1973.*

After it was published, Omni *got a letter from someone who said "this puts an end to Anglo-Saxon anthropocentrism in SF."*

The Lions are Asleep This Night

"*About time, too,*" *said Chad Oliver when I told him about it.*

Like others, this pays back an influence, this time to the Tokens.

The Lions are Asleep This Night

The white man was drunk again. Robert Oinenke crossed the narrow, graveled street and stepped up on the boardwalk at the other side. Out of the corner of his eyes he saw the white man raving. The man sat, feet out, back against a wall, shaking his head, punctuating his monologue with cursing words.

Some said he had been a mercenary in one of the border wars up the coast, one of those conflicts in which two countries had become one; or one country, three. Robert could not remember which. Mr Lemuel, his history teacher, had mentioned it only in passing.

Since showing up in Onitsha town the white man had worn the same khaki pants. They were of a military cut, now torn and stained. The shirt he wore today was a dashiki, perhaps variegated bright blue and red when made, now faded purple, He wore a cap with a foreign insignia. Some said he had been a general; others, a sergeant. His loud harangues terrified schoolchildren. Robert's classmates looked on the man as a forest demon. Sometimes the constables came and took him away; sometimes they only asked him to be quiet, and he would subside.

Mostly he could be seen propped against a building, talking to himself. Occasionally somebody would give him money. Then he would make his way to the nearest store or market stall that sold palm wine.

He had been in Robert's neighborhood for a few months. Before that he had stayed near the marketplace.

Robert did not look at him. Thinking of the marketplace, he hurried his steps. The first school bell rang.

"You will not be dawdling at the market," his mother had said

The Lions are Asleep This Night

as he readied himself for school. "Miss Mbene spoke to me of your tardiness yesterday."

She took the first of many piles of laundry from her wash baskets and placed them near the ironing board. There was a roaring fire in the hearth, and her irons were lined up in the racks over it. The house was already hot as an oven and would soon be as damp as the monsoon season.

His mother was still young and pretty but worn. She had supported them since Robert's father had been killed in an accident while damming a tributary of the Niger. He and forty other men had been swept away when a cofferdam burst. Only two of the bodies had ever been found. There was a small monthly check from the company her husband had worked for, and the government check for single mothers.

Her neighbor Mrs Yortebe washed, and she ironed. They took washing from the well-to-do government workers and business people in the better section.

"I shan't be late," said Robert, torn with emotions. He knew he wouldn't spend a long time there this morning and be late for school, but he did know that he would take the long route that led through the marketplace.

He put his schoolbooks and supplies in his satchel. His mother turned to pick up somebody's shirt from the pile. She stopped, looking at Robert.

"What are you going to do with *two* copybooks?" she asked.

Robert froze. His mind tried out ten lies. His mother started toward him.

"I'm nearly out of pages," he said. She stopped. "If we do much work today, I shall have to borrow."

"I buy you ten copybooks at the start of each school year and then again at the start of the second semester. Money does not grow on the breadfruit trees, you know?"

"Yes, Mother," he said. He hoped she would not look in the copybooks, see that one was not yet half-filled with schoolwork and that the other was still clean and empty. His mother referred to all extravagance as "a heart-tearing waste of time and money."

"You have told me not to borrow from others. I thought I was using foresight."

"Well," said his mother, "see you don't go to the marketplace.

Strange Things in Close-Up

It will only make you envious of all the things you can't have. And do not be late to school one more time this term, or I shall have you ever ironing."

"Yes, Mother," he said. Running to her, he rubbed his nose against her cheek. "Good-bye."

"Good day. And don't go near that marketplace!"

"Yes, Mother."

The market! Bright, pavilioned stalls covered a square Congo mile of ground filled with gaudy objects, goods, animals, and people. The Onitsha market was a crossroads of the trade routes, near the river and the railway station. Here a thousand vendors sold their wares on weekdays, many times that on weekends and holidays.

Robert passed the great piles of melons, guinea fowl in cages, tables of toys and geegaws, all bright and shiny in the morning light.

People talked in five languages, haggling with each other, calling back and forth, joking. Here men from Senegal stood in their bright red hats and robes. Robert saw a tall Waziri, silent and regal, indicating the prices he would pay with quick movements of his long fingers, while the merchant he stood before added two more each time. A few people with raised tattoos on their faces, backcountry people, wandered wide-eyed from table to table, talking quietly among themselves.

Scales clattered, food got weighed, chickens and ducks rattled, a donkey brayed near the big corral where larger livestock was sold. A goat wagon delivered yams to a merchant, who began yelling because they were still too hard. The teamster shrugged his shoulders and pointed to his bill of lading. The merchant threw down his apron and headed toward Onitsha's downtown, cursing the harvest, the wagoners, and the food cooperatives.

Robert passed by the food stalls, though the smell of ripe mangoes made his mouth water. He had been skipping lunch for three weeks, saving his Friday pennies. At the schoolhouse far away the ten-minute bell rang. He would have to hurry.

He came to the larger stalls at the far edge of the market where the booksellers were. He could see the bright paper jackets and dark type titles and some of the cover pictures on them from fifty yards away. He went toward the stall of Mr Fred's

The Lions are Asleep This Night

printers and High-Class Bookstore, which was his favorite. The clerk, who knew him by now, nodded to Robert as he came into the stall area. He was a nice young man in his twenties, dressed in a three-piece suit. He looked at the clock.

"Aren't you going to be late for school this fine morning?"

Robert didn't want to take the time to talk but said, "I know the books I want. It will only be a moment."

The clerk nodded.

Robert ran past the long shelves with their familiar titles: *Drunkards Believe the Bar Is Heaven; Ruth, the Sweet Honey That Poured Away; Johnny, the Most-Worried Husband; The Lady That Forced Me to Be Romantic; The Return of Mabel, in a Drama on How I Was About Marrying My Sister*, the last with a picture of Miss Julie Engebe, the famous drama actress, on the cover, which Robert knew was just a way to get people to buy the book.

Most of them were paper covered, slim, about fifty pages thick. Some had bright stenciled lettering on them, others drawings; a few had *photographios*. Robert turned at the end of the shelf and read the titles of others quickly: *The Adventures of Constable Joe; Eddy, the Coal-City Boy; Pocket Encyclopedia of Etiquette and Good Sense; Why Boys Never Trust Money-Monger Girls; How to Live Bachelor's Life and a Girl's Life Without Too Many Mistakes; Ibo Folktales You Should Know*.

He found what he was looking for: *Clio's Whips* by Oskar Oshwenke. It was as thin as the others, and the typefaces on the red, green, and black cover were in three different type styles. There was even a different *i* in the word *whips*.

Robert took it from the rack (it had been well thumbed, but Robert knew it was the only copy in the store.) He went down two more shelves, to where they kept the dramas, and picked out *The Play of the Swearing Stick* by Otuba Malewe and *The Raging Turk, or Bajazet II* by Thomas Goffe, an English European who had lived three hundred years ago.

Robert returned to the counter, out of breath from his dash through the stall. "These three," he said, spreading them out before him.

The clerk wrote figures on two receipt papers. "That will be twenty-four new cents, young sir," he said.

Strange Things in Close-Up

Robert looked at him without comprehension. "But yesterday they would have been twenty-two cents!" he said.

The clerk looked back down at the books. Then Robert noticed the price on the Goffe play, six cents, had been crossed out and eight cents written over that in big, red pencil.

"Mr Fred himself came through yesterday and looked over the stock," said the clerk. "Some prices he raised, others he liberally reduced. There are now many more two-cent books in the bin out front," he said apologetically.

"But . . . I only have twenty-two new cents." Robert's eyes began to burn.

The clerk looked at the three books. "I'll tell you what, young sir. I shall let you have these three books for twenty-two cents. When you get two cents more, you are to bring them *directly* to me. If the other clerk or Mr Fred is here, you are to make no mention of this matter. Do you see?"

"Yes, yes. Thank you!" he handed all his money across. He knew it was borrowing, which his mother did not want him to do, but he wanted these books so badly.

He stuffed the pamphlets and receipts into his satchel. As he ran from the bookstall he saw the nice young clerk reach into his vest pocket, fetch out two pennies, and put them into the cashbox. Robert ran as fast as he could toward school. He would have to hurry or he would be late.

Mr Yotofeka, the principal, looked at the tardy slip.

"Robert," he said, looking directly into the boy's eyes. "I am very disappointed in you. You are a bright pupil. Can you give me one good reason why you have been late to school three times in two weeks?"

"No, sir," said Robert. He adjusted his glasses, which were taped at one of the earpieces.

"No reason at all?"

"It took longer than I thought to get to school."

"You are thirteen years old, Robert Oinenke!" His voice rose. "You live less than a Congo mile from this schoolhouse, which you have been attending for seven years. You should know by now how long it takes you to get from your home to the school!"

Robert winced. "Yessir."

"Hand me your book satchel, Robert."

The Lions are Asleep This Night

"But I . . ."

"Let me see."

"Yessir." He handed the bag to the principal, who was standing over him. The man opened it, took out the schoolbooks and copybooks, then the pamphlets. He looked down at the receipt, then at Robert's records file, which was open like the big book of the Christian Saint Peter in heaven.

"Have you been not eating to buy this trash?"

"No, sir."

"No, yes? Or yes, no?"

"Yes. I haven't."

"Robert, two of these are pure trash. I am glad to see you have bought at least one good play. But your other choices are just, just . . . You might as well have poured your coppers down a civet hole as buy these." He held up *Clio's Whips*. "Does your mother know you read these things? And this play! *The Swearing Stick* is about the primitive superstitions we left behind before independence. You want people to believe in this kind of thing again? You wish blood rituals, tribal differences to come back? The man who wrote this was barely literate, little more than just come in from the brush country."

"But . . ."

"But me no buts. Use the library of this schoolhouse, Robert, or the fine public one. Find books that will uplift you, appeal to your higher nature. Books written by learned people, who have gone to university." Robert knew that Mr Yotofeka was proud of his education and that he and others like him looked down on the bookstalls and their books. He probably only read books published by the universities or real books published in Lagos or Cairo.

Mr Yotofeka became stern and businesslike. "For being tardy you will do three days detention after school. You will help Mr Labuba with his cleaning."

Mr Labuba was the custodian. He was large and slow and smelled of old clothes and yohimbe snuff. Robert did not like him.

The principal wrote a note on a form and handed it to Robert. "You will take this note home to your hardworking mother and have her sign it. You will return it to me before *second* bell

Strange Things in Close-Up

tomorrow. If you are late again, Robert Oinenke, it will not be a *swearing* stick I will be dealing with you about."

"Yes, sir," said Robert.

When he got home that afternoon Robert went straight to his small alcove at the back of the house where his bed and worktable were. His table had his pencils, ink pen, eraser, ruler, compass, protractor, and glue. He took his copybooks from his satchel, then placed the three books he'd bought in the middle of his schoolbook shelf above the scarred table. He sat down to read the plays. His mother was still out doing the shopping as she always was when he got out of school.

Mr Yotofeka was partly right about *The Play of the Swearing Stick*. It was not a great play. It was about a man in the old days accused of a crime. Unbeknownst to him, the real perpetrator of the crime had replaced the man's swearing stick with one that looked and felt just like it. (Robert knew this was implausible.) But the false swearing stick carried out justice anyway. It rose up from its place on the witness cushion beside the innocent man when he was questioned at the chief's court. It went out the window and chased the criminal and beat him to death. (In the stage directions the stick is lifted from the pillow by a technician with wires above the stage and disappears out the window, and the criminal is seen running back and forth yelling and holding his head, bloodier each time he goes by.)

Robert really liked plays. He watched the crowds every afternoon going toward the playhouse in answer to the drums and horns sounded when a drama was to be staged. He had seen the children's plays, of course—*Big Magis, The Trusting Chief, Daughter of the Yoruba*. He had also seen the plays written for European children—*Cinderella, Rumpelstiltskin, Nose of Fire*. Everyone his age had—the Niger Culture Center performed the plays for the lower grades each year.

But when he could get tickets, through the schools or his teachers, he had gone to see real plays, both African and European. He had gone to folk plays for adults, especially *Why the Snake Is Slick*, and he had seen Ourelay the Congo playwright's *King of All He Surveyed* and *Scream of Africa*. He had seen tragedies and comedies from most of the African nations, even a play from Nippon, which he had liked to look at but in which not much happened. (Robert had liked the women actresses best, until he found out they weren't women; then he didn't know what to think.) But it was the older plays he liked best, those from England of the early 1600's.

The first one he'd seen was *Westward for Smelts!* by Christopher Kingstone, then *The Pleasant Historie of Darastus and Fawnia* by Rob Greene. There had been a whole week of Old English European plays at the Culture Hall, at night, lit by incandescent lights. His school had gotten free tickets for anyone who wanted them. Robert was the only student his age who went to all the performances, though he saw several older students there each night.

There had been *Caesar and Pompey* by George Chapman, *Mother Bombay* by John Lyly, *The Bugbears* by John Jeffere, *The Tragicall History of Romeus and Juliet* by Arthur Broke, *Love's Labour Won* by W. Shaksper, *The Tragedy of Dido, Queen of Carthage* by Marlow and Nash, and on the final night, and best of all, *The Sparagus Garden* by Richard Brome.

That such a small country could produce so many good playwrights in such a short span of time intrigued Robert, especially when you consider that they were fighting both the Turks and the Italians during the period. Robert began to read about the country and its history in books from the school library. Then he learned that the Onitsha market sold many plays from that era (as there were no royalty payments to people dead two hundred fifty years.) He had gone there, buying at first from the penny bin, then the two-cent tables.

Robert opened his small worktable drawer. Beneath his sixth-form certificate were the pamphlets from Mr Fred's. There were twenty-six of them: twenty of them plays, twelve of those from the England of three hundred years before.

He closed the drawer. He looked at the cover of Thomas Goffe's play he had bought that morning—*The Raging Turk, or Bajazet II*. Then he opened the second copybook his mother had seen that morning. On the first page he penciled, in his finest hand:

MOTOFUKO'S REVENGE:
         A Play in Three Parts
         By Robert Oinenke

Strange Things in Close-Up

After an hour his hand was tired from writing. He had gotten to the place where King Motofuko was to consult with his astrologer about the attacks by Chief Renebe on neighboring tribes. He put the copybook down and began to read the Goffe play. It was good, but he found that after writing dialogue he was growing tired of reading it. He put the play away.

He didn't really want to read *Clio's Whips* yet; he wanted to save it for the weekend. But he could wait no longer. Making sure the front door was closed, though it was still hot outside, he opened the red, green, and black covers and read the title page:

CLIO'S WHIPS: The Abuses of Historie
by the White Races
By Oskar Oshwenke

"So the Spanish cry was Land Ho! and they sailed in the three famous ships, the *Nina*, the *Pinta*, and the *Elisabetta* to the cove on the island. Colon took the lead boat, and he and his men stepped out onto the sandy beach. All the air was full of parrots, and it was very wonderful there! But they searched and sailed around for five days and saw nothing but big bunches of animals, birds, fish, and turtles.

"Thinking they were in India, they sailed on looking for habitations, but on no island where they stopped were there any people at all! From one of the islands they saw far off the long lines of a much bigger island or a mainland, but tired from their search, and provendered from hunting and fishing, they returned to Europe and told of the wonders they had found, of the New Lands. Soon everyone wanted to go there."

This was exciting stuff to Robert. He reread the passage again and flipped the pages as he had for a week in Mr Fred's. He came to his favorite illustration (which was what made him buy this book rather than another play.) It was the picture of a hairy elephant, with its trunk raised and with that magical stuff, snow, all around it. Below was a passage Robert had almost memorized:

"The first man then set foot at the Big River (now the New Thames) of the Northern New Land. Though he sailed for the Portingals, he came from England (which had just given the

The Lions are Asleep This Night

world its third pope), and his name was Cromwell. He said the air above the Big River was a darkened profusion of pigeons, a million and a million times a hundred hundred, and they covered the skies for hours as they flew.

"He said there were strange humped cattle there (much like the European wisents) that fed on grass, on both sides of the river. They stood so thickly that you could have walked a hundred Congo miles on their backs without touching the ground.

"And here and there among them stood great hairy mammuts, which we now know once lived in much of Europe, so much like our elephant, which you see in the game parks today, but covered with red-brown hair, with much bigger tusks, and much more fierce-looking.

"He said none of the animals were afraid of him, and he walked among them, petting some, handing them tender tufts of grass. They had never seen a man or heard a human voice, and had not been hunted since the very beginning of time. He saw that a whole continent of skins and hides lay before European man for the taking, and a million feathers for hats and decorations. He knew he was the first man ever to see this place, and that it was close to Paradise. He returned to Lisboa after many travails, but being a good Catholic, and an Englishman, he wasn't believed. So he went back to England and told his stories there."

Now Robert went back to work on his play after carefully sharpening his pencil with a knife and setting his eraser close at hand. He began with where King Motofuko calls in his astrologer about Chief Renebe:

MOTOFUKO: Like to those stars which blaze forth overhead, brighter even than the seven ordered planets? And having waxed so lustily, do burn out in a week?
ASTROLOGER: Just so! Them that awe to see their burning forget the shortness of their fire. The moon, though ne'er so hot, stays and outlasts all else.
MOTOFUKO: Think you then this Chief Renebe be but a five months' wonder?
ASTROLOGER: The gods themselves do weep to see his progress! Starts he toward your lands a blazing beacon, yet will his fol-

lowers bury his ashes and cinders in some poor hole 'fore he reaches the Mighty Niger. Such light makes gods jealous.

Robert heard his mother talking with a neighbor outside. He closed his copybook, put *Clio's Whips* away, and ran to help her carry in the shopping.

During recess the next morning he stayed inside, not joining the others in the playground. He opened his copybook and took up the scene where Chief Renebe, who has conquered all King Motofuko's lands and had all his wives and (he thinks) all the king's children put to death, questions his general about it on the way to King Motofuko's capital.

RENEBE: And certaine, you, all his children dead, all his warriors sold to the Moorish dogs?
GENERAL: As sure as the sun doth rise and set, Your Highness. I myself his children's feet did hold, swing them like buckets round my conk, their limbs crack, their necks and heads destroy. As for his chiefs, they are now sent to grub ore and yams in the New Lands, no trouble to you forevermore. Of his cattle we made great feast, his sheep drove we all to the four winds.

This would be important to the playgoer. King Motofuko had escaped, but he had also taken his four-year-old-son, Motofene, and tied him under the bellwether just before the soldiers attacked in the big battle of Yotele. When the soldiers drove off the sheep, they sent his son to safety, where the shepherds would send him far away, where he could grow up and plot revenge.
    The story of King Motofuko was an old one any Onitsha theatergoer would know. Robert was taking liberties with it—the story of the sheep was from one of his favorite parts of the *Odyssey*, where the Greeks were in the cave of Polyphemus. (The real Motofene had been sent away to live as hostage-son to the chief of the neighboring state long before the attack by Chief Renebe.) And Robert was going to change some other things, too. The trouble with real life, Robert thought, was that it was usually dull and full of people like Mr Yotofeka and Mr Labuba. Not like the story of King Motofuko should be at all.

The Lions are Asleep This Night

Robert had his copy of *Clio's Whips* inside his Egyptian grammar book. He read:

"Soon all the countries of Europe that could sent expeditions to the New Lands. There were riches in its islands and vast spaces, but the White Man had to bring others to dig them out and cut down the mighty trees for ships. That is when the White Europeans really began to buy slaves from Arab merchants, and to send them across to the Warm Sea to skin animals, build houses, and to serve them in all ways.

"Africa was raided over. Whole tribes were sold to slavery and degradation; worse, wars were fought between black and black to make slaves to sell to the Europeans. Mother Africa was raped again and again, but she was also traveled over and mapped: Big areas marked 'unexplored' on the White Man's charts shrank and shrank so that by 1700 there were very few such places left."

Miss Mbene came in from the play yard, cocked an eye at Robert, then went to the slateboard and wrote mathematical problems on it. With a groan, Robert closed the Egyptian grammar book and took out his sums and ciphers.

Mr Labuba spat a stream of yohimbe-bark snuff into the weeds at the edge of the playground. His eyes were red and the pupils more open than they should have been in the bright afternoon sun.

"We be pulling at grasses," he said to Robert. He handed him a big pair of gloves, which came up to Robert's elbows. "Pull steady. These plants be cutting all the way through the gloves if you jerk."

In a few moments Robert was sweating. A smell of desk polish and eraser rubbings came off Mr Labuba's shirt as he knelt beside him. They soon had cleared all along the back fence.

Robert got into the rhythm of the work, taking pleasure when the cutter weeds came out of the ground with a tearing pop and a burst of dirt from the tenacious, octopuslike roots. Then they would cut away the runners with trowels. Soon they made quite a pile near the teeter-totters.

Robert was still writing his play in his head; he had stopped in the second act when Motofuko, in disguise, had come to the

Strange Things in Close-Up

forgiveness-audience with the new King Renebe. Unbeknownst to him, Renebe, fearing revenge all out of keeping with custom, had persuaded his stupid brother Guba to sit on the throne for the one day when anyone could come to the new king and be absolved of crimes.

"Is he giving you any trouble?" asked the intrusive voice of Mr Yotofeka. He had come up and was standing behind Robert.

Mr Labuba swallowed hard, the yohimbe lump going down chokingly.

"No complaints, Mr Yotofeka," he said, looking up.

"Very good, Robert, you can go home when the tower bell rings at three o'clock."

"Yes, sir."

Mr Yotofeka went back inside.

Mr Labuba looked at Robert and winked.

MOTOFUKO: Many, many wrongs in my time. I pray you, king, forgive me. I let my wives, faithful all, be torn from me, watched my children die, while I stood by, believing them proof from death. My village dead, all friends slaves. Reason twisted like hemp.

GUBA: From what mad place came you where such happens?

MOTOFUKO: (*Aside*) Name a country where this is not the standard of normalcy. (*To Guba*) Aye, all these I have done. Blinded, I went to worse. Pray you, forgive my sin.

GUBA: What could that be?

MOTOFUKO: (*Uncovering himself*) Murdering a king. (*Stabs him*)

GUBA: Mother of gods! Avenge my death. You kill the wrong man. Yonder—(*Dies*)

(*Guards advance, weapons out.*)

MOTOFUKO: Wrong man, when all men are wrong? Come, dogs, crows, buzzards, tigers. I welcome barks, beaks, claws, and teeth. Make the earth one howl. Damned, damned world where men fight like jackals over the carrion of states! Bare my bones then; they call for rest.

(*Exeunt, fighting. Terrible screams off. Blood flows in from the wings in a river.*)

SOLDIER: (*Aghast*) Horror to report. They flay the ragged skin from him whole!

The Lions are Asleep This Night

"But the hide and fishing stations were hard to run with just slave labor. Not enough criminals could be brought from the White Man's countries to fill all the needs.

"Gold was more and more precious, in the hands of fewer and fewer people in Europe. There was some, true, in the Southern New Lands, but it was high in the great mountain ranges and very hard to dig out. The slaves worked underground till they went blind. There were revolts under those cruel conditions.

"One of the first new nations was set up by slaves who threw off their chains. They called their land Freedom, which was the thing they had most longed for since being dragged from Mother Africa. All the armies of the White Man's trading stations could not overthrow them. The people of Freedom slowly dug gold out of the mountains and became rich and set out to free others, in the Southern New Land and in Africa itself . . .

"Rebellion followed rebellion. Mother Africa rose up. There were too few white men, and the slave armies they sent soon joined their brothers and sisters against the White Man.

"First to go were the impoverished French and Spanish dominions, then the richer Italian ones, and those of the British. Last of all were the colonies of the great German banking families. Then the wrath of Mother Africa turned on those Arabs and Egyptians who had helped the White Man in his enslavement of the black.

"Now they are all gone as powers from our continent and only carry on the kinds of commerce with us which put all the advantages to Africa."

ASHINGO: The ghost! The ghost of the dead king!
RENEBE: What! What madness this? Guards, your places! What mean you, man?
ASHINGO: He came, I swear, his skin all strings, his brain a red cawleyflower, his eyes empty holes!
RENEBE: What portent this? The old astrologer, quick. To find what means to turn out this being like a goat from our crops.
(*Alarums without. Enter Astrologer.*)
ASTROLOGER: Your men just now waked me from a mighty dream. Your majesty was in some high place, looking over the courtyard at all his friends and family. You were dressed in regal armor all of brass and iron. Bonfires of victory burned all

Strange Things in Close-Up

around, and not a word of dissent was heard anywhere in the land. All was peace and calm.

RENEBE: Is this then a portent of continued long reign?

ASTROLOGER: I do not know, sire. It was *my* dream.

His mother was standing behind him, looking over his shoulder.

Robert jerked, trying to close the copybook. His glasses flew off.

"What is that?" She reached forward and pulled the workbook from his hands.

"It is extra work for school," he said. He picked up his glasses.

"No, it is not." She looked over his last page. "It is wasting your paper. Do you think we have money to burn away?"

"No, Mother. Please . . ." He reached for the copybook.

"First you are tardy. Then you stay detention after school. You waste your school notebooks. Now you have *lied* to me."

"I'm sorry. I . . ."

"What is this?"

"It is a play, a historical play."

"What are you going to do with a play?"

Robert lowered his eyes. "I want to take to Mr Fred's Printers and have it published. I want it acted in the Niger Culture Hall. I want it to be sold all over Niger."

His mother walked over to the fireplace, where her irons were cooling on the racks away from the hearth.

"What are you going to *do*!!?" he yelled.

His mother flinched in surprise. She looked down at the notebook, then back at Robert. Her eyes narrowed.

"I was going to get my spectacles."

Robert began to cry.

She came back to him and put her arms around him. She smelled of the marketplace, of steam and cinnamon. He buried his head against her side.

"I will make you proud of me, Mother. I am sorry I used the copybook, but I *had* to write this play."

She pulled away from him. "I ought to beat you within the inch of your life, for ruining a copybook. You are going to have to help me for the rest of the week. You are not to work on this until you have finished every bit of your schoolwork. You

The Lions are Asleep This Night

should know Mr Fred nor nobody is going to publish anything written by a schoolboy."

She handed him the notebook. "Put it away. Then go out on the porch and bring in those piles of mending. I am going to sweat a copybook out of your brow before I am through."

Robert clutched the book to him as if it were his soul.

RENEBE: O rack, ruin, and pain! Falling stars and the winds do shake the foundations of night itself! Where my soldiers, my strength? What use taxes, tribute if they buy not strong men to die for me?
(*Off*): Gone. All Fled.
RENEBE: Hold! Who is there? (*Draws*)
MOTOFENE: (*Entering*) He whose name will freeze your blood's roots.
RENEBE: The son of that dead king!
MOTOFENE: Aye, dead to you and all the world else, but alive to me and as constant as that star about which the groaning axletree of the earth does spin.
(*Alarums and excursions off.*)
Now hear you the screams of your flesh and blood and friendship, such screams as those I have heard awake and fitfully asleep these fourteen years. Now hear them for all time.
RENEBE: Guards! To me!
MOTOFENE: To you? See those stars which shower to earth out your fine window? At each a wife, child, friend does die. You watched my father cut away to bone and blood and gore and called not for the death stroke! For you I have had my Vulcans make you a fine suit. All iron and brass, as befits a king! It you will wear, to look out over the palace yard of your dead, citizens and friends. You will have a good high view, for it is situate on cords of finest woods. (*Enter Motofene's soldiers.*) Seize him gently. (*Disarm*) And now, my former king, outside. Though full of hot stars, the night is cold. Fear not the touch of the brass. Anon you are garmented, my men will warm the suit for you.
(*Exeunt and curtain.*)

Robert passed the moaning white man and made his way down the street, beyond the market. He was going to Mr Fred's Prin-

Strange Things in Close-Up

ters in downtown Onitsha. He followed broad New Market Street, being careful to stay out of the way of the noisy streetcars that steamed on their rails toward the center of town.

He wore his best clothes, though it was Saturday morning. In his hands he carried his play, recopied in ink in yet another notebook. He had learned from the clerk at the market bookstall that the one sure way to find Mr Fred was at his office on Saturday forenoon, when the Onitsha *Weekly Volcano* was being put to bed.

Robert saw two *wayway* birds sitting on the single telegraph wire leading to the relay station downtown. In the old superstitions one *wayway* was a bad omen, two were good, three a surprise.

"Mr Fred is busy," said the woman in the *Weekly Volcano* office. Her desk was surrounded by copies of all the pamphlets printed by Mr Fred's bookstore, past headlines from the *Volcano*, and a big picture of Mr Fred, looking severe in his morning coat, under the giant clock, on whose face was engraved the motto in Egyptian: TIME IS BUSINESS.

The calendar on her desk, with the picture of a Niger author for each month, was open to October 1894. A listing of that author's books published by Mr Fred was appended at the bottom of each page.

"I should like to see Mr Fred about my play," said Robert.

"Your play?"

"Yes. A rousing historical play. It is called *Motofuko's Revenge*."

"Is your play in proper form?"

"Following the best rules of dramaturgy," said Robert.

"Let me see it a moment."

Robert hesitated.

"Is it papertypered?" she asked.

A cold chill ran down Robert's spine.

"All manuscripts must be papertypered, two spaces between lines, with wide margins," she said.

There was a lump in Robert's throat. "But it is in my very finest book-hand," he said.

"I'm sure it is. Mr Fred reads everything himself, is a very busy man, and insists on papertypered manuscripts."

The Lions are Asleep This Night

The last three weeks came crashing down on Robert like a mud-wattle wall.

"Perhaps if I spoke to Mr Fred..."

"It will do you no good if your manuscript isn't papertyped."

"Please. I..."

"Very well. You shall have to wait until after one. Mr Fred has to put the *Volcano* in final form and cannot be disturbed."

It was ten-thirty.

"I'll wait," said Robert.

At noon the lady left, and a young man in a vest sat down in her chair.

Other people came, were waited on by the man or sent into another office to the left. From the other side of the shop door, behind the desk, came the sound of clanking, carts rolling, thumps, and bells. Robert imagined great machines, huge sweating men wrestling with cogs and gears, books stacked to the ceiling.

It got quieter as the morning turned to afternoon. Robert stood, stretched, and walked around the reception area again, reading the newspapers on the walls with their stories five, ten, fifteen years old, some printed before he was born.

Usually they were stories of rebellions, wars, floods, and fears. Robert did not see one about the burst dam that had killed his father, a yellowed clipping of which was in the Coptic Bible at home.

There was a poster on one wall advertising the fishing resort on Lake Sahara South, with pictures of trout and catfish caught by anglers.

At two o'clock the man behind the desk got up and pulled down the windowshade at the office. "You shall have to wait outside for your father," he said. "We're closing for the day."

"Wait for my father?"

"Aren't you Meletule's boy?"

"No. I have come to see Mr Fred about my play. The lady..."

"She told me nothing. I thought you were the printer's devil's boy. You say you want to see Mr Fred about a play?"

"Yes. I..."

"Is it papertypered?" asked the man.

Robert began to cry.

"Mr Fred will see you now," said the young man, coming back in the office and taking his handkerchief back.

"I'm sorry," said Robert.

"Mr Fred only knows you are here about a play," he said. He opened the door to the shop. There were no mighty machines there, only a few small ones in a dark, two story area, several worktables, boxes of type and lead. Everything was dusty and smelled of metal and thick ink.

A short man in his shirtsleeves leaned against a workbench reading a long, thin strip of paper while a boy Robert's age waited. Mr Fred scribbled something on the paper, and the boy took it back into the other room, where several men bent quietly over boxes and tables filled with type.

"Yes," said Mr Fred, looking up.

"I have come here about my play."

"Your play?"

"I have written a play, about King Motofuko. I wish you to publish it."

Mr Fred laughed. "Well, we shall have to see about that. Is it papertypered?"

Robert wanted to cry again.

"No, I am sorry to say, it is not. I didn't know . . ."

"We do not take manuscripts for publication unless . . ."

"It is my very best book-hand, sir. Had I known, I would have tried to get it papertypered."

"Is your name and address on the manuscript?"

"Only my name. I . . ."

Mr Fred took a pencil out from behind his ear. "What is your house number?"

Robert told him his address, and he wrote it down on the copybook.

"Well, Mr—Robert Oinenke. I shall read this, but not before Thursday after next. You are to come back to the shop at ten a.m. on Saturday the nineteenth for the manuscript and our decision on it."

"But . . ."

"What?"

The Lions are Asleep This Night

"I really like the books you publish, Mr Fred, sir. I especially liked *Clio's Whips* by Mr Oskar Oshwenke."

"Always happy to meet a satisfied customer. We published that book five years ago. Tastes have changed. The public seems tired of history books now."

"That is why I am hoping you will like my play," said Robert.

"I will see you in two weeks," said Mr Fred. He tossed the copybook into a pile of manuscripts on the workbench.

"Because of the legacy of the White Man, we have many problems in Africa today. He destroyed much of what he could not take with him. Many areas are without telegraphy; many smaller towns have only primitive direct current power. More needs to be done with health and sanitation, but we are not as badly off as the most primitive of the White Europeans in their war-ravaged countries or in the few scattered enclaves in the plantations and timber forests of the New Lands.

"It is up to you, the youth of Africa of today, to take our message of prosperity and goodwill to these people, who have now been as abused by history as we Africans once were by them. I wish you good luck."

Oskar Oshwenke, Onitsha, Niger, 1889

Robert put off going to the market stall of Mr Fred's bookstore as long as he could. It was publication day.

He saw that the nice young clerk was there. (He had paid him back out of the ten Niger dollar advance Mr Fred had had his mother sign for two weeks before. His mother still could not believe it.)

"Ho, there, Mr Author!" said the clerk. "I have your three free copies for you. Mr Fred wishes you every success."

The clerk was arranging his book and John-John Motulla's *Game Warden Bob and the Mad Ivory Hunter* on the counter with the big starbust saying: Just published!

His book would be on sale throughout the city. He looked at the covers of the copies in his hands:

The TRAGICALL DEATH OF KING
MOTOFUKO
and HOW THEY WERE SORRY
a drama by Robert Oinenke
abetted by

Strange Things in Close-Up

MR FRED OLUNGENE
"The Mighty Man of the Press"
for sale at Mr Fred's High-Class Bookstore
300 Market, and the *Weekly Volcano*
Office, 12 New Market Road
ONITHSA, NIGER
price 10¢ N.

On his way home he came around the corner where a group of boys was taunting the white man. The man was drunk and had just vomited on the foundation post of a store. They were laughing at him.

"Kill you all. Kill you all. No shame," he mumbled, trying to stand.

The words of *Clio's Whips* came to Robert's ears. He walked between the older boys and handed the white man three Niger cents. The white man looked up at him with sick, grey eyes.

"Thank you, young sir," he said, closing his hand tightly.

Robert hurried home to show his mother and the neighbors his books.

Introduction to
Flying Saucer Rock and Roll

*If there was one gripe people had with my previous short story collection (*Howard Who? *Doubleday, 1986) it was that "Flying Saucer Rock and Roll" wasn't in it.*

Well, it wasn't my fault.

When people see a story in a new magazine or anthology, they assume you wrote it last week. Maybe last month. As you'll see by some of the other introductions in this volume, it can take anywhere from six months to nine years from the time you sell a story until it appears.

The easiest way to explain is that "Flying Saucer Rock and Roll" wasn't yet scheduled in Omni *when the Doubleday book was turned in.*

Having said that, I'll take you through some of the Byzantine alleys we call publishing in the SF field. This story was written in October, 1980. At that time I had begun to take friends' advice and send stories to the high-paying markets first. It was bounced by Playboy, Penthouse *and* Omni. *(The* Omni *rejection letter was from Ellen Datlow, at that time assistant fiction editor to Robert Sheckley. It was a nice letter, but it* was *a rejection. This will be important later.)*

Anyway, Terry Carr couldn't buy it for Universe—*"I love it. Take it away," he said—Doubleday, his publisher at the time having a policy against the C, S, F, P and B words, which are sprinkled real liberal-like throughout the story. Marta Randall took it for number 13 of* New Dimensions, *whose editorship she had just taken over from Robert Silverberg, due out from Pocket Books.*

Marta's somewhat prophetic words were, "If this is going to be the last New Dimensions, *I'm going out with the best one ever."*

In April, 1983, two weeks before publication, after review copies and advertising and all that stuff had gone out, Pocket Books cancelled the anthology series.

The official reason was poor sales on # 12. I don't know. Besides this story New Dimensions 13 *contained Connie Willis' "All My Darling Daughters" and Edward Bryant's "Dancing Chickens." Three real strong reasons* not *to publish a book, and besides, if you're pulling a book for sales reasons, you don't send out review copies.*

So while the wrangling on return of rights goes on, "Flying Saucer Rock and Roll" gets a bunch of Nebula recommendations off the review copies.

Then Marta has to announce officially that the book won't be published and that rights are being returned to the authors and please stop recommending stories from the book.

About this time I get a hot letter from Ellen Datlow, who in the meanwhile has become Fiction Editor at Omni *and to whom I've sold a couple of stories.*

"I hear New Dimensions *is dead and authors are getting rights to their stories back. I want to see whatever it is you had there."*

"You've already seen it," I say as I call her, " 'Flying Saucer Rock and Roll'."

Then Ellen did something she had never done before or since. She lied to me. "I did not*," she said.*

"Yes you did."

"I did not. Bob may have rejected it, but I never saw it."

I'm looking at the rejection letter while we're talking.

"Gee, Ellen," I say. "Maybe it was him. Okay, I'll send it along."

She bought it for five times the money I'd gotten from Pocket Books.

About this time somewhere is when I sold the collection to Doubleday. Every other story in there had already come out or was scheduled to appear before the book, but there was no way I could get this one in.

In the meantime, what with George R. R. Martin having such trouble getting assholes in the music publishing business to give permissions to print song lyrics, and Stephen King having to pay $15,000 for those rock lyrics in Christine, *I did a rewrite that turned the words into unrecognizable English phonemes. They work fine when I read them at a convention, but are a*

Flying Saucer Rock and Roll

little tough on readers. You'll have to trust me; that's exactly what they sound like.

The story was published in Omni *in 1985, and was reprinted in both Dozois' and Carr's Bests of the Year. It was both a Nebula and Hugo finalist.*

(In a fit of folly, I had two short stories up against each other—this and "Heirs of the Perisphere"—for the Nebula Award. I thought that if the members of SFWA had all the stories in the world to choose from, and the best they could do was vote for two of mine, well, honor enough. I lost.)

Losing the Hugo was lots easier—they put "Flying Saucer Rock and Roll" up against the first new Fred Pohl story in fifteen years.

Yes, I do know all the words to Billy Lee Riley and the Little Green Men's Sun Records recording of "Flying Saucers Rock and Roll". I hope you enjoy this story. It pays back a long overdue debt to Frankie Lyman and the Teenagers.

Flying Saucer Rock and Roll

They could have been contenders.

Talk about Danny and the Juniors, talk about the Spaniels, the Contours, Sonny Till and the Orioles. They made it to the big time: records, tours, sock hops at $500 a night. Fame and glory.

But you never heard of the Kool-Tones, because they achieved their apotheosis and their apocalypse on the same night, and then they broke up. Some still talk about that night, but so much happened, the Kool-Tones get lost in the shuffle. And who's going to believe a bunch of kids, anyway? The cops didn't and their parents didn't. It was only two years after the President had been shot in Dallas, and people were still scared. This, then, is the Kool-Tones' story:

Leroy was smoking a cigar through a hole he'd cut in a pair of thick, red wax lips. Slim and Zoot were tooting away on Wowee whistles. It was a week after Halloween, and their pockets were still full of trick-or-treat candy they'd muscled off little kids in the projects. Ray, slim and nervous, was hanging back. "We shouldn't be here, you know? I mean, this ain't the Hellbenders' territory, you know? I don't know whose it is, but, like, Vinnie and the guys don't come this far." He looked around.

Zoot, who was white and had the beginnings of a mustache, took the yellow wax-candy kazoo from his mouth. He bit off and chewed up the big C pipe. "I mean, if you're scared, Ray, you can go back home, you know?"

"Nah!" said Leroy. "We need Ray for the middle parts." Leroy was twelve years old and about four feet tall. He was finishing his fourth cigar of the day. He looked like a small Stymie Beard from the old Our Gang comedies.

He still wore the cut-down coat he'd taken with him when he'd escaped from his foster home.

318

Flying Saucer Rock and Roll

He was staying with his sister and her boyfriend. In each of his coat pockets he had a bottle: one Coke and one bourbon.

"We'll be all right," said Cornelius, who was big as a house and almost eighteen. He was shaped like a big ebony golf tee, narrow legs and waist blooming out to an A-bomb mushroom of arms and chest. He was a yard wide at the shoulders. He looked like he was always wearing football pads.

"That's right," said Leroy, taking out the wax lips and wedging the cigar back into the hole in them. "I mean, the kid who found this place didn't say anything about it being somebody's *spot*, man."

"What's that?" asked Ray.

They looked up. A small spot of light moved slowly across the sky. It was barely visible, along with a few stars, in the lights from the city.

"Maybe it's one of them UFOs you're always talking about, Leroy," said Zoot.

"Flying saucer, my left ball," said Cornelius. "That's Telstar. You ought to read the papers."

"Like your mama makes you?" asked Slim.

"Aww . . . ," said Cornelius.

They walked on through the alleys and the dark streets. They all walked like a man.

"This place is Oz," said Leroy.

"Hey!" yelled Ray, and his voice filled the area, echoed back and forth in the darkness, rose in volume, died away.

"Wow."

They were on what had been the loading dock of an old freight and storage company. It must have been closed sometime during the Korean War or maybe in the unimaginable eons before World War II. The building took up most of the block, but the loading area on the back was sunken and surrounded by the stone wall they had climbed. If you stood with your back against the one good loading door, the place was a natural amphitheater.

Leroy chugged some Coke, then poured bourbon into the half-empty bottle. They all took a drink, except Cornelius, whose mother was a Foursquare Baptist and could smell liquor on his breath three blocks away.

Strange Things in Close-Up

Cornelius drank only when he was away from home two or three days.

"Okay, Kool-Tones," said Leroy. "Let's hit some notes."

They stood in front of the door, Leroy to the fore, the others behind him in a semicircle: Cornelius, Ray, Slim, and Zoot.

"One, two, three," said Leroy quietly, his face toward the bright city beyond the surrounding buildings.

He had seen all the movies with Frankie Lyman and the Teenagers in them and knew the moves backwards. He jumped in the air and came down, and Cornelius hit it: "*Bah-doo, bah-doo, bah-doo—uhh.*"

It was a bass from the bottom of the ocean, from the Marianas Trench, a voice from Death Valley on a wet night, so far below sea level you could feel the absence of light in your mind. And then Zoot and Ray came in: "*Oooh-oooh, ooh-oooh,*" with Leroy humming under, and then Slim stepped out and began to lead the tenor part of "Sincerely," by the Crows. And they went through that one perfectly, flawlessly, the dark night and the dock walls throwing their voices out to the whole breathing city.

"Wow," said Ray, when they finished, but Leroy held up his hand, and Zoot leaned forward and took a deep breath and sang: "*Dee-dee-woo-oo, dee-eee-wooo-oo, dee-uhmm-doo-way.*"

And Ray and Slim chanted: "*A-weem-wayyy, a-wee,-wayyy.*"

And then Leroy, who had a falsetto that could take hair off an opossum, hit the high notes from "The Lion Sleeps Tonight," and it was even better than the first song, and not even the Tokens on their number two hit had ever sounded greater.

Then they started clapping their hands, and at every clap the city seemed to jump with expectation, joining in their dance, and they went through a shaky-legged Skyliners-type routine and into: *Hey-ahh-stuh-huh, hey-ahh-stuh-uhh*, of Maurice Williams and the Zodiacs' "Stay," and when Leroy soared his "*Hoh-wahh-yuh?*" over Zoot's singing, they all thought they would die.

And without pause, Ray and Slim started: "*Shoo-be-doop, shoo-doop-de-be-doop, shoo-doopbe-do-be-doop,*" and Cornelius was going. "*Ah-rem-em, ah-rem-em, ah-rem-emm bah.*"

Flying Saucer Rock and Roll

And they went through the Five Satins' "(I Remember) In the Still of the Night."

"Hey, wait," said Ray, as Slim "*woo-uh-wooo-uh-woo-ooo-ah-woo-ah*"-ed to a finish, "I thought I saw a guy out there."

"You're imagining things," said Zoot. But they all stared out into the dark anyway.

There didn't seem to be anything there.

"Hey, look," said Cornelius. "Why don't we try putting the bass part of 'Stormy Weather' with the high part of 'Crying in the Chapel'? I tried it the other night, but I can't–"

"Shit, man!" said Slim. "That ain't the way it is on the records. You gotta do it like on the records."

"Records are going to hell, anyway. I mean, you got Motown and some of that, but the rest of it's like the Beatles and Animals and Rolling Stones and Wayne shitty Fontana and the Mindbenders and . . ."

Leroy took the cigar from his mouth. "Fuck the Beatles," he said. He put the cigar back in his mouth.

"Yeah, you're right, I agree. But even the other music's not the–"

"Aren't you kids up past your bedtime?" asked a loud voice from the darkness.

They jerked erect. For a minute, they hoped it was only the cops.

Matches flared in the darkness, held up close to faces. The faces all had their eyes closed so they wouldn't be blinded and unable to see in case the Kool-Tones made a break for it. Blobs of faces and light floated in the night, five, ten, fifteen, more.

Part of a jacket was illuminated. It was the color reserved for the kings of Tyre.

"Oh shit!" said Slim. "Trouble. Looks like the Purple Monsters."

The Kool-Tones drew into a knot.

The matches went out and they were in a breathing darkness.

"You guys know this turf is reserved for friends of the local protective, athletic, and social club, viz., us?" asked the same voice. Chains clanked in the black night.

"We were just leaving," said Cornelius.

The noisy chains rattled closer.

You could hear knuckles being slapped into fists out there.

Strange Things in Close-Up

Slim hoped someone would hurry up and hit him so he could scream.

"Who are you guys with?" asked the voice, and a flashlight shone in their eyes, blinding them.

"Aww, they're just little kids," said another voice.

"Who you callin' little, turd?" asked Leroy, shouldering his way between Zoot and Cornelius's legs.

A *wooooooo*! went up from the dark, and the chains rattled again.

"For God's sake, shut up, Leroy!" said Ray.

"Who you people think you are, anyway?" asked another, meaner voice out there.

"We're the Kool-Tones," said Leroy. "We can sing it slow, and we can sing it low, and we can sing it loud, and we can make it go!"

"I hope you like that cigar, kid," said the mean voice, "because after we piss on it, you're going to have to eat it."

"Okay, okay, look," said Cornelius. "We didn't know it was your turf. We come from over in the projects and . . ."

"Hey, Man, Hellbenders, Hellbenders!" The chains sounded like tambourines now.

"Naw, naw. We ain't Hellbenders. We ain't nobody but the Kool-Tones. We just heard about this place. We didn't know it was yours," said Cornelius.

"We only let Bobby and the Bombers sing here," said a voice.

"Bobby and the Bombers can't sing their way out of the men's room," said Leroy. Slim clamped Leroy's mouth, burning his hand on the cigar.

"You're gonna regret that," said the mean voice, which stepped into the flashlight beam, "because I'm Bobby, and four more of these guys out here are the Bombers."

"We didn't know you guys were part of the Purple Monsters!" said Zoot.

"There's lots of stuff you don't know," said Bobby. "And when we're through, there's not much you're gonna *remember*."

"I only know the Del Vikings are breaking up," said Zoot. He didn't know why he said it. Anything was better than waiting for the knuckle sandwiches.

Bobby's face changed. "No shit?" Then his face set in hard lines again. "Where'd a punk like you hear something like that?"

322

"My cousin," said Zoot. "He was in the Air Force with two of them. He writes to 'em. They're tight. One of them said the act was breaking up because nobody was listening to their stuff anymore."

"Well, that's rough," said Bobby. "It's tough out there on the road."

"Yeah," said Zoot. "It really is."

Some of the tension was gone, but certain delicate ethical questions remained to be settled.

"I'm Lucius," said a voice. "Warlord of the Purple Monsters." The flashlight came on him. He was huge. He was like Cornelius, only he was big all the way to the ground. His feet looked like blunt I beams sticking out of the bottom of his jeans. His purple satin jacket was a brightly fluorescent blot on the night. "I hate to break up this chitchat—" he glared at Bobby—"but the fact is you people are on Purple Monster territory, and some tribute needs to be exacted."

Ray was digging in his pocket for nickels and dimes.

"Not money. Something that will remind you not to do this again."

"Tell you what," said Leroy. He had worked himself away from Slim. "You think Bobby and the Bombers can sing?"

"Easy!" said Lucius to Bobby, who had started forward with the Bombers. "Yeah, kid. They're the best damn group in the city."

"Well, *I* think we can outsing 'em," said Leroy, and smiled around his dead cigar.

"Oh, jeez," said Zoot. "They got a record, and they've—"

"I *said*, we can outsing Bobby and the Bombers, anytime, any place," said Leroy.

"And what if you can't?" asked Lucius.

"You guys like piss a lot, don't you?" There was a general movement toward the Kool-Tones. Lucius held up his hand. "Well," said Leroy, "how about all the members of the losing group drink a quart apiece?"

Hands of the Kool-Tones reached out to stifle Leroy. He danced away.

"I like that," said Lucius. "I really like that. That all right, Bobby?"

"I'm going to start saving it up now."

Strange Things in Close-Up

"Who's gonna judge?" asked one of the Bombers.

"The same as always," said Leroy. "The public. Invite 'em in."

"Who do we meet with to work this out?" asked Lucius.

"Vinnie of the Hellbenders. He'll work out the terms."

Slim was beginning to see he might not be killed that night. He looked on Leroy with something like worship.

"How we know you guys are gonna show up?" asked Bobby.

"I swear on Sam Cooke's grave," said Leroy.

"Let 'em pass," said Bobby.

They crossed out of the freight yard and headed back for the projects.

"Shit, man!"

"Now you've done it!"

"I'm heading for Florida."

"What the hell, Leroy, are you crazy?"

Leroy was smiling. "We can take them, easy," he said, holding up his hand flat.

He began to sing "Chain Gang." The other Kool-Tones joined in, but their hearts weren't in it. Already there was a bad taste in the back of their throats.

Vinnie was mad.

The black outline of a mudpuppy on his white silk jacket seemed to swell as he hunched his shoulders toward Leroy.

"What the shit you mean, dragging the Hellbenders into this without asking us first? That just ain't done, Leroy."

"Who else could take the Purple Monsters in case they wasn't gentlemen?" asked Leroy.

Vinnie grinned. "You're gonna die before you're fifteen, kid."

"That's my hope."

"Creep. Okay, we'll take care of it."

"One thing," said Leroy. "No instruments. They gotta get us a mike and some amps, and no more than a quarter of the people can be from Monster territory. And it's gotta be at the freight dock."

"That's one thing?" asked Vinnie.

"A few. But that place is great, man. We can't lose there."

Vinnie smiled, and it was a prison-guard smile, a Nazi smile.

"If you lose, kid, after the Monsters get through with you, the Hellbenders are gonna have a little party."

He pointed over his shoulder to where something resembling testicles floated in alcohol in a mason jar on a shelf. "We're putting five empty jars up there tomorrow. That's what happens to people who get the Hellbenders involved without asking and then don't come through when the pressure's on. You know what I mean?"

Leroy smiled. He left smiling. The smile was still frozen to his face as he walked down the street.

This whole thing was getting too grim.

Leroy lay on his cot listening to his sister and her boyfriend porking in the next room.

It was late at night. His mind was still working. Sounds beyond those in the bedroom came to him. Somebody staggered down the project hallway, bumping from one wall to another. Probably old man Jones. Chances are he wouldn't make it to his room all the way at the end of the corridor. His daughter or one of her kids would probably find him asleep in the hall in a pool of barf.

Leroy turned over on the rattly cot, flipped on his seven-transistor radio, and jammed it up to his ear. Faintly came the sounds of another Beatles song.

He thumbed the tuner, and the four creeps blurred into four or five other Englishmen singing some other stupid song about coming to places he would never see.

He went through the stations until he stopped on the third note of the Monotones' "Book of Love." He sang along in his mind.

Then the deejay came on, and everything turned sour again. "Another golden oldie, 'Book of Love,' by the Monotones. Now here's the WBKD pick of the week, the fabulous Beatles with 'I've Just Seen a Face.'" Leroy pushed the stations around the dial, then started back.

Weekdays were shit. On weekends you could hear good old stuff, but mostly the stations all played Top 40, and that was English invasion stuff, or if you were lucky, some Motown. It was Monday night. He gave up and turned to an all-night blues station, where the music usually meant something. But this was like, you know, the sharecropper hour or something, and all they were playing was whiny cotton-choppin' work blues from some damn Alabama singer who had died in 1932, for God's sake.

Disgusted, Leroy turned off the radio.

His sister and her boyfriend had quit for a while, so it was quieter in the place. Leroy lit a cigarette and thought of getting out of here as soon as he could.

I mean, Bobby and the Bombers had a record, a real big-hole forty-five on WhamJam. It wasn't selling worth shit from all Leroy heard, but that didn't matter. It was a record, and it was real, it wasn't just singing under some street lamp. Slim said they'd played it once on WABC, on the *Hit-or-Flop* show, and it was a flop, but people heard it. Rumor was the Bombers had gotten sixty-five dollars and a contract for the session. They'd had a couple of gigs at dances and such, when the regular band took a break. They sure as hell couldn't be making any money, or they wouldn't be singing against the Kool-Tones for free kicks.

But they had a record out, and they were working.

If only the Kool-Tones got work, got a record, went on tour. Leroy was just twelve, but he knew how hard they were working on their music. They'd practise on street corners, on the stoop, just walking, getting the notes down right—the moves, the facial expressions of all the groups they'd seen in movies and on Slim's mother's TV.

There were so many places to be out there. There was a real world with people in it who weren't punching somebody for berries, or stealing the welfare and stuff. Just someplace open, someplace away from everything else.

He flipped on the flashlight beside his cot, pulled it under the covers with him, and opened his favorite book. It was Edward J. Ruppelt's *Report on Unidentified Flying Objects*. His big brother John William, whom he had never seen, sent it to him from his Army post in California as soon as he found Leroy had run away and was living with his sister. John William also sent his sister part of his allowance every month.

Leroy had read the book again and again. He knew it by heart already. He couldn't get a library card under his own name because the state might trace him that way. (They'd already been around asking his sister about him. She lied. But she too had run away from a foster home as soon as she was old enough, so they hadn't believed her and would be back.) So he'd had to boost all his books. Sometimes it took days, and newsstand people got mighty suspicious when you were black and hung around for a long time, waiting for the chance to kipe stuff. Usually they gave you the hairy eyeball until you went away.

He owned twelve books on UFOs now, but the Ruppelt was still his favorite. Once he'd gotten a book by some guy named Truman or something who wrote poetry inspired by the people from Venus. It was a little sad, too, the things people believed sometimes. So Leroy hadn't read any more books by people who claimed they'd been inside the flying saucers or met the Neptunians or such. He read only the ones that gave histories of the sightings and asked questions, like why was the Air Force covering up? Those books never told you what was in the UFOs, and that was good because you could imagine it for yourself.

He wondered if any of the Del Vikings had seen flying saucers when they were in the Air Force with Zoot's cousin. Probably not, or Zoot would have told him about it. Leroy always tried to get the rest of the Kool-Tones interested in UFOs, but they all said they had their own problems, like girls and cigarette money. They'd go with him to see *Invasion of the Saucermen* or *Earth Vs. the Flying Saucers* at the movies, or watch *The Thing* on Slim's mother's TV on the *Creature Feature*, but that was about it.

Leroy's favorite flying-saucer sighting was the Mantell case, in which a P–51 fighter plane, which was called a Mustang, chased a UFO over Kentucky and then crashed after it went off the Air Force radar. Some say Captain Mantell died of asphyxiation because he went to 20,000 feet and didn't have on an oxygen mask, but other books said he saw "something metallic and of tremendous size" and was going after it. Ruppelt thought it was a Skyhook balloon, but he couldn't be sure. Others said it was a real UFO and that Mantell had been shot down with Z-rays.

It had made Leroy's skin crawl when he had first read it.

But his mind went back to the Del Vikings. What had caused them to break up? What was it really like out there on the road?

Was music getting so bad that good groups couldn't make a living at it anymore?

Leroy turned off the flashlight and put the book away. He put out the cigarette, lit a cigar, went to the window, and looked up the airshaft. He leaned way back against the cool window and could barely see one star overhead. Just one star.

He scratched himself and lay back down on the bed.

For the first time, he was afraid about the contest tomorrow night.

We got to be good, he said to himself. *We got to be good*.

In the other room, the bed started squeaking again.

The Hellbenders arrived early to check out the turf. They'd been there ten minutes when the Purple Monsters showed up. There was handshaking all around, talk a little while, then they moved off into two separate groups. A few civilians came by to make sure this was the place they'd heard about.

"Park your cars out of sight, if you got 'em," said Lucius. "We don't want the cops to think anything's going on here."

Vinnie strut-walked over to Lucius.

"This crowd's gonna be bigger than I thought. I can tell."

"People come to see somebody drink some piss. You know, give the public what it wants . . ." Lucius smiled.

"I guess so. I got this weird feelin', though. Like, you know, if your mother tells you she dreamed about her aunt, like right before she died and all?"

"I know what feelin' you mean, but I ain't got it," said Lucius. "Who you got doing the electrics?"

"Guy named Sparks. He was the one lit up Choton Field."

At Choton Field the year before, two gangs wanted to fight under the lights. So they went to a high-school football stadium. Somebody got all the lights and the P.A. on without going into the control booth.

Cops drove by less than fifty feet away, thinking there was a practice scrimmage going on, while down on the field guys were turning one another into bloody strings. Somebody was on the P.A. giving a play-by-play. From the outside, it sounded cool. From the inside, it looked like a pizza with all the topping ripped off it.

"Oh," said Vinnie. "Good man."

He used to work for Con Ed, and he still had his I.D. card. Who was going to mess with Consolidated Edison? He drove an old, grey pickup with a smudge on the side that had once been a power-company emblem. The truck was filled to the brim with cables, wires, boots, wrenches, tape, torches, work lights, and rope.

"Light man's here!" said somebody.

Lucius shook hands with him and told him what they wanted. He nodded.

The crowd was getting larger, groups and clots of people drifting in, though the music wasn't supposed to start for another hour. Word traveled fast.

Sparks attached a transformer and breakers to a huge, thick cable.

Then he got out his climbing spikes and went up a pole like a monkey, the heavy *chunk-chunk* drifting down to the crowd every time he flexed his knees. His tool belt slapped against his sides.

He had one of the guys in the Purple Monsters throw him up the end of the inch-thick electrical cable.

The sun had just gone down, and Sparks was a silhouette against the purpling sky that poked between the buildings.

A few stars were showing in the eastern sky. Lights were on all through the autumn buildings. Thanksgiving was in a few weeks, then Christmas.

The shopping season was already in full swing, and the streets would be bathed in neon, in holiday colors. The city stood up like big, black fingers all around them.

Sparks did something to the breakdown box on the pole.

There was an immense blue scream of light that stopped everybody's heart.

New York City went dark.

"Fucking *wow*!"

A raggedy-assed cheer of wonder ran through the crowd.

There were crashes, and car horns began to honk all over town.

"Uh, Lucius," Sparks yelled down the pole after a few minutes. "Have the guys go steal me about thirty automobile batteries."

The Purple Monsters ran off in twenty different directions.

Strange Things in Close-Up

"Ahhhyyyhhyyh," said Vinnie, spitting a toothpick out of his mouth. "The Monsters get to have all the fun."

It was 5:27p.m. on November 9, 1965. At the Ossining changing station, a guy named Jim was talking to a guy named Jack.

Then the trouble phone rang. Jim checked all his dials before he picked it up.

He listened, then hung up.

"There's an outage all down the line. They're going to switch the two hundred K's over to the Buffalo net and reroute them back through here. Check all the load levels. Everything's out from Schenectady to Jersey City."

When everything looked ready, Jack signaled to Jim. Jim called headquarters, and they watched the needles jump on the dials.

Everything went black.

Almost everything.

Jack hit all the switches for backup relays, and nothing happened.

Almost nothing.

Jim hit the emergency battery work lights. They flickered and went out.

"What the hell?" asked Jack.

He looked out the window.

Something large and bright moved across a nearby reservoir and toward the changing station.

"Holy Mother of Christ!" he said.

Jim and Jack went outside.

The large bright thing moved along the lines toward the station. The power cables bulged toward the bottom of the thing, whipping up and down, making the stanchions sway. The station and the reservoir were bathed in a blue glow as the thing went over. Then it took off quickly toward Manhattan, down the straining lines, leaving them in complete darkness.

Jim and Jack went back into the plant and ate their lunches.

Not even the phone worked anymore.

It was really black by the time Sparks got his gear set up. Everybody in the crowd was talking about the darkness of the city and the sky. You could see stars all over the place, everywhere you looked.

Flying Saucer Rock and Roll

There was very little noise from the city around the loading area.

Somebody had a radio on. There were a few Jersey and Pennsy stations on. One of them went off while they listened.

In the darkness, Sparks worked by the lights of his old truck. What he had in front of him resembled something from an alchemy or magnetism treatise written early in the eighteenth century. Twenty or so car batteries were hooked up in series with jumper cables. He'd tied those in with amps, mikes, transformers, a light board, and lights on the dock area.

"Stand clear!" he yelled. He bent down with the last set of cables and stuck an alligator clamp on a battery post.

There was a screeching blue jag of light and a frying noise. The lights flickered and came on, and the amps whined louder and louder.

The crowd, numbering around five hundred, gave out with prolonged huzzahs and applause.

"Test test test," said Lucius. Everybody held their hands over their ears.

"Turn that fucker down," said Vinnie. Sparks did. Then he waved to the crowd, got into his old truck, turned the lights off, and drove into the night.

"Ladies and gentlemen, the Purple Monsters . . . ," said Lucius, to wild applause, and Vinnie leaned into the mike, "and the Hellbenders," more applause, then back to Lucius, "would like to welcome you to the first annual piss-off—I mean, sing-off—between our own Bobby and the Bombers," cheers, "and the challengers," said Vinnie, "the Kool-Tones!" More applause.

"They'll do two sets, folks," said Lucius, "taking turns. And at the end, the unlucky group, gauged by *your* lack of applause, will win a prize!"

The crowd went wild.

The lights dimmed out. "And now," came Vinnie's voice from the still blackness of the loading dock, "for your listening pleasure. Bobby and the Bombers!"

"*Yayyyyyyyyyy!*"

The lights, virtually the only lights in the city except for those that were being run by emergency generators, came up, and there they were.

Strange Things in Close-Up

Imagine frosted, polished elegance being thrust on the unwilling shoulders of a sixteen-year-old.

They had on blue jackets, matching pants, ruffled shirts, black ties, cuff links, tie tacks, shoes like obsidian mortar trowels. They were all black boys, and from the first note, you knew they were born to sing:

"*Bah bah*," sang Letus the bassman, "*doo-doo duh-du doo-ahh, duh-doo-dee-doot*," sang the two tenors, Lennie and Conk, and then Bobby and Fred began trading verses of the Drifters' "There Goes My Baby," while the tenors wailed and Letus carried the whole with his bass.

Then the lights went down and came up again as Lucius said, "Ladies and gentlemen, the Kool-Tones!"

It was magic of a grubby kind.

The Kool-Tones shuffled on, arms pumping in best Frankie Lyman and the Teenagers fashion, and they ran in place as the hand-clapping got louder and louder, and they leaned into the mikes.

They were dressed in waiters' red-cloth jackets the Hellbenders had stolen from a laundry service for them that morning. They wore narrow black ties, except Leroy, who had on a big, thick, red bow tie he'd copped from his sister's boyfriend.

Then Cornelius leaned over his mike and: "*Doook doook doook doookov*," and Ray and Zoot joined with "*dook dook dook dookov*," into Gene Chandler's "Duke of Earl," with Leroy smiling and doing all of Chandler's hand moves. Slim chugged away the "*iiiiiiiiyiyiyiyiiii's*" in the background in runs that made the crowd's blood run cold, and the lights went down. Then the Bombers were back, and in contrast to the up-tempo ending of "The Duke of Earl" they started with a sweet tenor a cappella line and then: "*woo-radad-da-dat, woo-radad-da-dat*," of Shep and the Limelites' "Daddy's Home."

The Kool-Tones jumped back into the light. This time Cornelius started off with "*Bom-a-pa-bomp, bomp-pa-pa-bomp, dang-a-dang-dang, ding-a-dong-ding*," and into the Marcels' "Blue Moon," not just a hit but a mere monster back in 1961. And they ran through the song, Slim taking the lead, and the crowd began to yell like mad halfway through. And Leroy—smiling, singing, rocking back and forth, doing James Brown tantrum-steps in front of the mike—knew, could feel, that they

Flying Saucer Rock and Roll

had them; that no matter what, they were going to win. And he ended with his whining part and Cornelius went "*Bomp-ba-ba-bomp-ba-bom*," and paused and then, deeper, "*booo mooo.*"

The lights came up and Bobby and the Bombers hit the stage. At first Leroy, sweating, didn't realize what they were doing, because the Bombers, for the first few seconds, made this churning rinky-tink sound with the high voices. The bass, Letus, did this grindy sound with his throat. Then the Bombers did the only thing that could save them, a white boy's song, Bobby launching into Del Shannon's "Runaway," with both feet hitting the stage at once. Leroy thought he could taste the urine already.

The other Kool-Tones were transfixed by what was about to happen.

"They can't do that, man," said Leroy.

"They're gonna cop out."

"That's impossible. Nobody can do it."

But when the Bombers got to the break, this guy Fred stepped out to the mike and went: "*Eee-de-ee-dee-eedle-eee-eee, eee-deee-eedle-deeee, eedle-dee-eedle-dee-dee-dee, eewheetle-eedle-dee-deedle-dee-eeeeee*," in a splitting falsetto, half mechanical, half Martian cattle call—the organ break of "Runaway," done with the human voice.

The crowd was on its feet screaming, and the rest of the song was lost in stamping and cheers. When the Kool-Tones jumped out for the last song of the first set, there were some boos and yells for the Bombers to come back, but then Zoot started talking about his girl putting him down because he couldn't shake 'em down, but how now *he* was back, to let her know . . . They all jumped in the air and came down on the first line of "Do You Love Me?" by the Contours, and they gained some of the crowd back. But they finished a little wimpy, and then the lights went down and an absolutely black night descended. The stars were shining over New York City for the first time since World War II, and Vinnie said, "Ten minutes, folks!" and guys went over to piss against the walls or add to the consolation-prize bottles.

It was like halftime in the locker room with the score Green Bay 146, You 0.

"A cheap trick," said Zoot. "We don't *do* shit like that."

Strange Things in Close-Up

Leroy sighed. "We're gonna have to," he said. He drank from a Coke bottle one of the Purple Monsters had given him. "We're gonna have to do something."

"We're gonna have to drink pee-pee, and then Vinnie's gonna denut us, is what's gonna happen."

"No, he's not," said Cornelius.

"Oh yeah?" asked Zoot. "Then what's that in the bottle in the clubhouse?"

"Pig's balls," said Cornelius. "They got 'em from a slaughterhouse."

"How do you know?"

"I just know," said Cornelius, tiredly. "Now let's just get this over with so we can go vomit all night."

"I don't want to hear any talk like that," said Leroy. "We're gonna go through with this and give it our best, just like we planned, and if that ain't good enough, well, it just ain't good enough."

"No matter what we do, it just ain't good enough."

"Come on, Ray, *man*!"

"I'll do my best, but my heart ain't in it."

They lay against the loading dock. They heard laughter from the place where Bobby and the Bombers rested.

"Shit, it's dark!" said Slim.

"It ain't just us, just the city," said Zoot. "It's the whole goddamn U.S."

"It's just the whole East Coast," said Ray. "I heard on the radio. Part of Canada, too."

"What is it?"

"Nobody knows."

"Hey, Leroy," said Cornelius. "Maybe it's those Martians you're always talking about."

Leroy felt a chill up his spine.

"Nah," said Slim. "It was that guy Sparks. He shorted out the whole East Coast up that pole there."

"Do you really believe that?" asked Zoot.

"I don't know what I believe anymore."

"I believe," said Lucius, coming out of nowhere with an evil grin on his face, "that it's *show time*."

They came to the stage running, and the lights came up, and

Flying Saucer Rock and Roll

Cornelius leaned on his voice and: "*Rabbalabbalabba ging gong, rabbalabbalabba ging gong,*" and the others went "*wooooooooooo*" in the Edsels' "Rama Lama Ding Dong." They finished and the Bombers jumped into the lights and went into: "*Domm dom domm dom doobedoo, dom domm dom dobedoobeedomm, wahwahwahwahhh,*" of the Del Vikings' "Come Go With Me."

The Kool-Tones came back with: "*Ahhhhhhhhaahhwoooo-woooo, ow-ow-ow-ow-owh-woo,*" of "Since I Don't Have You," by the Skyliners, with Slim singing in a clear, straight voice, better than he had ever sung that song before, and everybody else joined in, Leroy's voice fading into Slim's for the falsetto *weeeeoooooow*'s so you couldn't tell where one ended and the other began.

The Bobby and the Bombers were back, with Bobby telling you the first two lines and: "*Detooodwop, detooodwop, detooodwop,*" of the Flamingos' "I Only Have Eyes for You," calm, cool, collected, assured of victory, still running on the impetus of their first set's showstopper.

Then the Kool-Tones came back and Cornelius rared back and asked: "*Ahwunno wunno hooo? Be-do-be-hoooo?*" Pause.

They slammed down into "Book of Love", by the Monotones, but even Cornelius was flagging, sweating now in the cool air, his lungs were husks. He saw one of the Bombers nod to another, smugly, and that made him mad. He came down on the last verse, like there was no one else on the stage with him, and his bass roared so loud it seemed there wasn't a single person in the dark United States who didn't wonder who wrote that book.

And they were off, and Bobby and the Bombers were on now, and a low hum began to fill the air. Somebody checked the amp; it was okay. So the Bombers jumped into the air, and when they came down they were into the Cleftones' "Heart and Soul," and they *sang* that song, and while they were singing, the background humming got louder and louder.

Leroy leaned to the other Kool-Tones and whispered something. They shook their heads. He pointed to the Hellbenders and the Purple Monsters all around them. He asked a question they didn't want to hear. They nodded grudging approval, and then they were on again, for the last time.

Strange Things in Close-Up

"*Dep doooomop dooooomop doomop, doo ooo, ooowah oowah oooway ooowah,*" said Leroy, and they all asked "Why Do Fools Fall in Love?" Leroy sang like he was Frankie Lyman—not just some kid from the projects who wanted to be him—and the Kool-Tones *were* the Teenagers, and they began to pull and heave that song like it was a dead whale. And soon they had it in the water, and then it was swimming a little, then it was moving, and then the sonofabitch started spouting water, and that was the place where Leroy went into the falsetto "*wyyyyyyyyyyyyyyyyyyyyyyyy,*" and instead of chopping it where it should have been, he kept on. The Kool-Tones went *oom wahoomwah* softly behind him, and still he held that note, and the crowd began to applaud, and they began to yell, and Leroy held it longer, and they started stamping and screaming, and he held it until he knew he was going to cough up both his lungs, and he held it after that, and the Kool-Tones were coming up to meet him, and Leroy gave a tantrum-step, and his eyes were bugging, and he felt his lungs tear out by the roots and come unglued, and he held the last syllable, and the crowd wet itself and—

The lights went out and the amp went dead. Part of the crowd had a subliminal glimpse of something large, blue, and cool looming over the freight yard, bathing the top of the building in a soft glow.

In the dead air the voices of the Kool-Tones dropped in pitch as if they were pulled upward at a thousand miles an hour, and then they rose in pitch as if they had somehow come back at that same thousand miles an hour.

The blue thing was a looming blur and then was gone.

The lights came back on. The Kool-Tones stood there blinking: Cornelius, Ray, Slim, and Zoot. The space in front of the center mike was empty.

The crowd had an orgasm.

The Bombers were being violently ill over next to the building.

"God, that was *great*!" said Vinnie. "Just great!"

All four of the Kool-Tones were shaking their heads.

They should be tired, but this looked worse than that, thought Vinnie. They should be ecstatic. They looked like they didn't know they had won.

"Where's Leroy?" asked Cornelius.

"How the hell should I know?" Vinnie said, sounding annoyed.

"I remember him smiling, like," said Zoot.

"And the blue thing. What about it?"

"What blue thing?" asked Lucius.

"I dunno. Something was blue."

"All I saw was the lights go off and that kid ran away," said Lucius.

"Which way?"

"Well, I didn't exactly see him, but he must have run some way. Don't know how he got by us. Probably thought you were going to lose and took it on the lam. I don't see how you'd worry when you can make your voices do that stuff."

"Up," said Zoot, suddenly.

"What?"

"We went up, and we came down. Leroy didn't come down with us."

"Of course not. He was still holding the same note. I thought the little twerp's balls were gonna fly out of his mouth."

"No. We . . ." Slim moved his hands up, around, gave up. "I don't know what happened, do you?"

Ray, Zoot, and Cornelius all looked like they had thirty-two-lane bowling alleys inside their heads and all the pin machines were down.

"Aw, shit," said Vinnie. "You won. Go get some sleep. You guys were really bitchin'."

The Kool-Tones stood there uncertainly for a minute.

"He was, like, smiling, you know?" said Zoot.

"He was always smiling," said Vinnie. "Crazy little kid."

The Kool-Tones left.

The sky overhead was black and spattered with stars. It looked to Vinnie as if it were deep and wide enough to hold anything. He shuddered.

"Hey!" he yelled. "Somebody bring me a beer!"

He caught himself humming. One of the Hellbenders brought him a beer.

Introduction to
He-We-Await

And now the writer dives off the 500-foot platform, not, my friends, into a water tank; no, nor into an ordinary glass of drinking water, but onto this wet cinderblock!

(Girls, you'd better hang on to your boyfriends!)

This story is original to this collection, and appears here, as they say, by permission of the author, me.

And you might as well know the ground rules.

The single culture that has never, ever done anything for me is that of Ancient Egypt. The Tut Exhibit came around and I yawned. BFD. Hieroglyphics leave me cold. Who cares how they built the pyramids? There they are, jocko, take 'em or leave 'em.

About a year ago I was changing my spark plugs in the Barracuda and Pow! Sock! Wham! this story idea came to me, whole.

For those of you who doubt, I'll repeat what every writer has said: Ideas are cheap. What you do with them, how you write the story and what you have to say are the important things.

I sighed. That was no consolation. All I knew was that I was going to have to sit down and research a people and an era I didn't care anything about, all because I'd gotten an idea that couldn't happen anywhere else. And it had to be totally accurate, every detail exactly right, because (in the words of James Cagney in Strawberry Blonde *and of Chad Oliver, Warren Spector and Bud Simons on any given day), "That's just the kind of hairpin I am."*

So I waded in, and this took six months of pure dogged research and writing ten, fifteen, sometimes twenty whole words a day—I hadn't had so much trouble with a story since "The Ugly Chickens" back in 1979.

He-We-Await

I finished the second draft about thirty minutes before I read it at ArmadilloCon last year. The place was packed. There I was, reading from a handwritten draft to a sea of faces. I was playing mental connect-the-dots with the eyeballs of the audience and I didn't know whether I had a story or an afterbirth in my hands.

Eggs-E-Stenchal!

Anyway, here it is. And I found out something else while writing this.

The Ancient Egyptians were pretty neat.

He-We-Await

"In the king-list of Manetho, an Egyptian priest who wrote in Greek in the Third Century B.C., two names are missing.

"They were Pharoahs, father and son. The father, Sekhemet, by legend reigned one hour less than 100 years. Sekhemetmui, his son, a sickly child born to him in the ninety-first year of his rule, lived less than a year after his father's kingship ended.

"I did not say 'after his father died.' No one knows what happened to Sekhemet. Herodotus, who was initiated by the priests into the Mysteries of Osiris, does not mention either father or son in his list, giving credence to some kind of sacerdotal conspiracy.

"A stele, found in an old temple of Sekhmet, had the name of Sekhemet defaced in one of the periods of revision by later kings. The broken and incomplete stele tells of a great project undertaken in his 99th regnal year: 10,000 men set out upriver in 600 boats built for the expedition. Then history is quiet.

"That a century of human life in this time-and-death haunted land are represented only by carvings on a broken rock is a reminder of all that has been lost to us for want of a teller."
–Sir Jorvis Ivane *From the Raj to the Pyramids* Chatto and Pickering, 1888

Always, always were the voices and the cool valley wind.

Ninety-seven times he had made the journey down the River to pray to Hapi, his brother-god, for a good flood. Hapi had been kind eighty-six times and had not denied his prayers for the last nine years in a row, since the birth of his last, his crippled son.

Sekhemet, Beloved of Sekhmet, Mighty-Like-The-Sun and

He-We-Await

Smiter of the Vile and Wretched Foreigner, stood with his retinue on the broad road before his great white house.

Around him was the city he had caused to be built fifty years before, white and yellow in the morning sun. The shadows of the buildings stretched toward the River. Down at the wharf the royal barque was being outfitted for its trip southward up the waters.

Across the Nile were the mastabas of his fathers, and of those before them, cold and grey lumps in the Land of the Dead on the western bank. Here his ancestors slept, their *kas* prayed for, sacrifices offered them, as just in their sleeps as in their lives.

Sekhemet looked back to the balcony of the great house, where his lastborn Sekhemetmui stood watching him. A strange boy, born so twisted and so late, sired in his hundredth year of life, his ninety-first of kingship. Sekhemet did not understand him or his ways.

"The work on the barque awaits your inspection," whispered his chief scribe to him.

Always, always were the voices, more and more voices the older he became, quieter but more insistent.

His ancestors, who had fought up and down the length of the River, had had an easier time of it: uniting the Bee Kingdom and the Reed Kingdom, bringing the Hawk Kingdom under their sway. They had been men and women of action—war pressed on every side, treachery behind every doorway, quick thinking was needed.

Sekhemet had reigned ninety-seven years. All his wars were won while he was still young. Anyone who could offer him treason had long ago been scattered on the desert wind.

The retinue—Sekhemet, his scribes, guards, bearers and slaves—began its walk in the city he had built across from the tombs of his fathers. His own mastaba was being constructed in the shadow of his father's. The workman ferried across the River each morning well after sunup and returned long before dark. No one wanted to be caught on the west bank after nightfall.

So it was that they walked in orderly progress, all eyes of persons they met downcast at sight of them, until they happened by the temple of the protecting god of the city, Sekhmet—she with the hippopotamus-head.

Strange Things in Close-Up

There was a commotion at the temple door—it flew open and the doorkeepers fell back. For, coming out of the courtyard, his garments torn, was the high priest, eyes wild and searching.

He shambled toward them.

"Oh Great House!" he yelled. The guards turned toward him, spears at ready. The priest flung himself to the ground, tasting the dirt, his shaven head smeared with ash from the temple fire. "It is revealed to us—wonderful to relate!—a great thing. A few moments ago, a novice, an unlettered boy from the Tenth Nome - but, it is too marvelous!" The priest looked around him, blinking, seeming to regain his composure. He bowed down.

"Oh Great House! Oh Mighty-Like-The-Sun, forgive me! Sekhemet has given a revelation. We come to you this evening in full pomp. Forgive me!" He backed on his knees to the doorway of the temple, bowing and scraping.

Shaken, his heart pounding like the feet of an army at full run, Sekhemet, Smiter of the Vile and Wretched Foreigner, continued on his way to the royal docks.

After the revelation given by the priests a great flotilla was built. Hundreds of ships were loaded with clothing and tools, provision of garlic, bread, onions and radishes were laid in, jugs of lilly-beer trundled aboard. Work on the mastaba across the water stopped.

The armada was filled with slaves and workmen, artisans, scribes, bureaucrats and soldiers. The ships set out on gold morning following the royal barge up the River.

Somewhere on the long journey south the flotilla put in, for the royal barque carrying Sekhemet and his son Sekhemetmui came alone to Elephant Island where the Pharaoh made his prayers to Hapi and then returned northward.

Nothing was heard of the expedition for a year. The government was run by dispatches sent from somewhere southward of the city on the River.

At the end of the year the royal barge appeared once more at Elephant Island; again Sekhemet and his son supplicated to Hapi for a good flood with its life-giving *kemi*. Those of the island's temple who viewed Sekhemet said he looked younger and more fit than in years, transfigured, glowing with some secret knowledge.

He-We-Await

Then the barque returned northward down the River. It was the last time the old Pharaoh was seen.

Nine months later a small raft came to the dock of the increasingly troubled royal city. Foreigners impinged on the frontiers, there was rebellion in the Thirteenth Nome, the flood had not been as great as in earlier years and famine threatened the Canopic delta.

On the raft was one priest and the son of the old Pharaoh, Sekhemetmui. He was eleven years old and bore on his stunted breast the tablet of succession.

In a few days he was accoutered with the Double Crown of Red Egypt and White Egypt and became Sekhemetmui "The Glory of Sekhmet is Revealed" and Mighty-Like-The-Sun.

He had been a sickly child. Troubles came in waves, inside his body and out. There was fighting in the streets of the capital. He reigned for less than six months, dying one night of terrible sweats while a great battle raged to the east.

He was put into the hastily-finished mastaba across the River which had been started for his father.

Four hundred years after his death his city was a forgotten ruin and many miles down the River the first of the great pyramids rose up into the blue desert sky.

In the empty temple of Sekhmet there was a stele devoted to the old Pharaoh. On it were carved the signs: "I, Sekhemet, shall live to see the sun rise 5000 years from now; my line shall reign unto the last day of mankind."

How it was usually done.:

The body of a dead person would be taken to the embalmer-priests by the grieving family, their heads plastered with mud, their bodies covered with dust.

The priest would demonstrate to them, using a small wooden doll, the three methods of embalming from the cheapest to the most expensive. In the case of a Pharaoh it would always be the latter.

Then the family would leave and go into seventy days of mourning.

One of the embalmer-priests would be chosen by lot. He would take a knife of Ethiopian flint and with it cut into the

Strange Things in Close-Up

left side of the body just below the ribs. The other priests would scream and wail; the chosen priest would drop the knife and run for his life. The others pursued, throwing stones in an effort to kill him, such was their belief about the desecration of a body, and ran him from the House of Death.

Then they would return and dig the brains out of the corpse through the nose with a curved iron hook, procuring most of it in this manner. Then they would pump a solution of strong cedar oil into the brain cavity and plug the nose and throat.

Other priests reached in through the knife-wound and took out the internal organs, placing them in jars with distinctive tops. Into the man-headed jar went the stomach and large intestines. Into the dog-headed they put the small intestines; the jackal-headed vessel got the lungs and heart, and into the hawk-headed went the liver and gall bladder. The jars were sealed with bitumen and capped with plaster.

Into the body cavity they stuffed aromatic spices, gums, oils, resins and flowers, then they sewed the wound closed. They placed the body in a trough of natrum for 69 days, taking it out only to unplug the nose and allow the rest of the brains to run out. They spent the night wrapping the body in linen strips soaked in gum, and placing it in its wooden coffin, which always had eyes painted on it so the soul, or *ka*, of the dead could see.

On the morning of the 70th day the mummy and jars of organs were given back to the family for burial. For Pharoahs this usually meant a resting place in some tomb or mastaba on the Libyan bank of the Nile, the land of the setting sun and of the dead.

None of this happened to Sekhemet.

When a ruler of Egypt wanted sherbet with his meal the next day, word went out to the royal works.

An hour before dawn next morning, several hundred slaves would enter a building divided into hundreds of high-walled roofless cubicles open to the desert air.

The slaves went to the center of the cubicles, from the floor of which rose a pillar 6 feet tall and a few inches in diameter. At its top was a shallow depression, the rim only a fraction of an inch above the bottom of the concavity. Into this tiny bowl the slave sprinkled a drop of water and smoothed it into a film.

Each slave did this in several rooms, and there were hundreds of them.

The temperature of the desert floor never dropped below 34°F. But a few feet off the ground the air, shielded from any wind by the high thick walls, was colder.

Royal attendants, with a thin spoon made of reed and bearing triple-walled bowls, waited outside the rooms a few moments. Entering them and working quickly, turning their heads to avoid breathing in the pillar's direction, they scraped a fingernail of frost from each pillar-top into the bowls.

Going from room to room, each gathered the ice. The many tiny scrapings were placed in one bowl, covered over, closed and packed in datewood sawdust and carried to Pharoah's house.

A few moments before it was to be served it was flavored, one or two small portions to the ruler, his wife, his eldest child and one or two highly-favored guests.

These iceworks, three or four acres in extent, were usually found near the palaces.

Early in the 20th century A.D., an iceworks was discovered far to the south, where no large cities had ever stood. It covered 72 acres and contained 11,000 cubicles each with the wonder-working silent pillars.

THE HOUSE OF THE *KA*: I

... further into the valley. Perhaps my house will not prove to be safe, will be found out, my resting place defiled, my temple defaced. Surely, though, the priests will not let this happen.

Their hands on me like so many clubs. No pain, just sensation, pressure, as if it were happening to someone else. Things I cannot see.

What if the priests are wrong? Is it possible they tell me these things to put me out of the way? They know my son to be weak: if trouble comes he will not be able to hold the Bee Kingdom and the Reed Kingdom together—the nomarchs of the Delta are too shrewd, as they have always been.

What if they have done these things to be rid of my strength? The thought comes to me now—all their talk, the revelation that I go away from the light to wake to a kingdom my line will rule forever . . .

Strange Things in Close-Up

What madness is this I have done? Guards, to me! Let me up, I say! Take your hands from my divinity!

I cannot move. The cold has seeped through me.

What if the priests do not keep their word? I am lost. My *ka* will be dispersed: I am not dead. They have seduced me, deposed me with only words, words of power and glory I could not resist.

Was ever such a fool on the River Nile?

Now there is no more light, no more feeling. All ebbs, all flows away.

Gods. Sekhmet. Protect me. Thoth, find me not wanting on the scales. Let your baboons weigh me true.

The madness of priests . . .

Outside they came and went, some by design, some because they were lost.

At first they spoke the Old Language, or the black tongue of the south, and the barbaric speech from the northeast. Then they used the long foreign sounds unknown in his time, from far across the salt water, Greek, then the rolling Latin.

Then there were desert languages, and those twisted Latin speech patterns of French and Anglo-Norman, the gutturals of German; Italian and Turkish, then French, English, German again, English all against the old desert speech.

They brought their gods with them in waves; Shango, Baal, Yahweh, Zeus, Jupiter, Allah and Mohammed, Dieu, Gott, God and Jesus, Jesu, Gott again, Allah, Allah, Money.

Twice people tried to get in—once by accident. They were crushed by a four-ton block balanced by pebbles, one of six. The second intrusion was by design, but when they saw the powdered skeletons of the first they turned away, fearing one, two, ten more deadfalls ahead.

Once there was a tremor in the earth and the remaining block fell, leaving a clear passage. Once, water fell from a cloud in the sky.

From inside the sounds—voices, earthquakes, rain, deadfall, praises to gods, the sighing of the gentle dusty wind, the slosh and swing of the Nile itself, the groaning of the earth on its axle-tree—were as the long quiet ticks of a slow, sure well-oiled metronome.

He-We-Await

The man ran through the gates of the small town clutching parchment scrolls to him as he stumbled.

Behind him came the drumming of camels' hooves, the clang of their harness bells. The cries of the desert people leaped up behind him.

The running man was old; his head was shaven and his face hairless. He ran by the broken and tumbled building that had once housed the Christian desert fathers, deserted for more than two centuries.

He fell. One of the scrolls broke into powdery slivers under his hand. He cried out and pulled the others to him.

He looked over his shoulder. The camels were closer. Black-garbed riders, swords out, bore down on him. Eyes wild, he ran behind the broken legs of a statue of Dionysus, trying to climb the jumbled stones of a small amphitheater. He saw far out to his left the ribbon of the Nile, beyond the date-palm orchards. He yelled in his anguish.

The riders surrounded him, their camels spitting and stamping. One of them dismounted from his knee-walking animal, swinging up his sword. He held out his hand.

Weeping, the old man turned the scrolls over to him.

He had been at Alexandria when they came out of the Northeast in black flowing waves, putting all who resisted their holy war to sword and fire. He saw them capture the city and tear down the idols. He followed them to the Great Library. He had wept when they began carrying out hundreds of thousands of books and scrolls and took them to burn to heat the public baths—enough parchment and papyrus and leather to keep them steaming for six weeks.

He had come as quickly as he could to this town, the site of the old temple, for these scrolls. He was the only one of the Society of He-We-Await who had made it this far. No one had disturbed their resting place. But he had been seen as he left the ruins and the cry had gone up.

"These scrolls." One of the mounted men leaned forward and spoke in a thick language the old man hardly understood. "If they contradict the *Koran*, they are heathen. If they support it, they are superfluous."

The man on the ground opened one, then another, looked at them, puzzled. He handed them up to the one who had spoken.

"They are in the old, old writing," he said. "They are infidel." He handed them back to the swordsman on the ground.

With no trace of emotion, and some effort, the man jumped up and down on them, grinding them to fine shards which drifted away on the breeze.

"We have no time to light a fire," said the mounted leader, "but that will do. Your conversation will come later. First, the books, then the hearts of men."

They turned their camels and sped back toward the wattle-walled village.

Crying, the old man sank down in the mingled dust of writing and bricks, wailing, gnashing his teeth, rubbing his bald head with hands full of sand.

In the late 19th Century A.D. artifacts of an especially good quality surfaced on the antiquities market.

The Cairo Museum, responsible for all Egyptian archaeological work, investigated.

They found that a graverobbing family from Deir el Bahrani, near the Valley of the Kings, had made a discovery in the cliffs behind Queen Hatsepshut's tomb about a decade before.

The majority of the tombs which had been uncovered in the Valley had proved empty of goods, the coffins missing their contents.

The graverobbers had found, in a shaft dug into the cliff wall above Deir el Bahrani, a forgotten chapter of history.

There was a marker there, hastily carved, a great quantity of goods from many dynasties, and thirty-six mummies.

The marker told the story—in one of the lawless periods before the XXIst Dynasty, the government fell apart, bandits roamed the towns, foreigners attacked from all sides. The priests could no longer guard the tombs in the Valley of the Kings.

Secretly they entered the mausoleums, took out the royal mummies and brought them to the hidden tunnel, with such of the grave goods as they could carry, and secreted them away, hoping their bodies, and the *kas* of the royal lines, would be safe from marauders.

Of the thirty-six mummies, one—Thutmose the IIIrd—had been broken into three pieces. The others were intact, including those of Rameses the Great; Ahmose; Queen Ahmes, the mother

He-We-Await

of Hatsepshut; and Thutmose the Ist and IInd. The rest were eventually identified, except one. That of a very young boy about 12 years of age, in wrappings of a much earlier period than the others. He was entered in the catalogue of the Museum, where the mummies were all taken, as "Unknown Boy (I—IIIrd Dynasty?)."

Dr Tuthmoses looked at the final reports. They were magnetometer scans of the west bank of the Nile, from the Delta, past Aswan to the influx of the Atbara River above the Fifth Cataract, far longer than the extent of the kingdoms of the early dynasties.

All the known tombs were marked; all the new ones found had been checked and proved to be those of later dynasties, of minor officials. The search had gone much further out of the Valley than any burials ever found. Still nothing.

He looked around him at the roomful of books. He was now an old man. There were others devoted to the cause, younger men, but none like him. They were content to sift over the old data again and again, the way it had always been done since the knowledge of the resting place was lost twelve centuries before.

He had devoted fifty years of his life to the quest, through wars, panics, social upheaval and unrest. He had seen his mentor, Professor Ramra, grow old and weak, and embittered, die, with nothing to show for *his* sixty years of diligent search but more paper, more books, more clutter.

Tuthmoses rang the bell for his secretary, young Mr Faidul. He came in, thin and dapper in a three piece suit.

"Faidul," he said. "The time has come to change our methods. Take this down as a record for the Society.

"One: Obtain the best gene splicer possible for a two-day clandestine assignment to be completed on short notice in the near future.

"Two: Send Raimenu and a workaday specialist to Egypt. I want Raimenu to find a woman who wishes to bear a child for a fee of $100,000. Not just any woman. A woman of a family that still worships The Old Way. The specialist is a mitochondrial check—make sure she's from an African First Mother.

"Three: The first two conditions being met, arrange for a

Strange Things in Close-Up

scientific examination of the Deir el Bahrani remains at the Cairo Museum. During this, one of the party is to obtain genetic material from the remains of the 'unknown boy,' who we know to be the son of He-We-Await." (Tuthmoses and Faidul bowed their heads.)

"Four: The genetic material from Sekhemetmui is to be implanted by the splicer into the egg of the mitochondrial First Mother.

"Five: The child of this operation is to be handed over to the Society and placed in my care to be raised as I see fit.

"End of note."

"So it is written," said Faidul.

"So it shall be done," said Dr Tuthmoses.

They called him Bobby. He was raised at first by a succession of nurses in an upstairs room which became his world. He was eventually given everything he wanted—toys, games, insects, fish, mammals.

He had large dark eyes, a small head with a high hairline, a short face, an aquiline nose. One of his arms was bent from birth.

What he read and what he saw was censored by Tuthmoses and his staff—everything was tape-delayed and edited. Other children were brought in for him to play with. He was given tutors and teachers.

He grew up self-centered, untroubled, fairly well-adjusted, with a coolness toward the doctor that seemed to be reciprocated.

They were playing one day; Bobby, the teacher-lady and the kids who were brought in after their school let out.

They had been doing some kind of word games, and Deborah the dark-haired girl got up to get something, then had gone over and started talking to Sally Conroe about something. There had been some quiet talk, and then Deborah did a little dance, humming in a whiny voice:

"Yay-ya-ya-ya-yah yoo yah yoo-yah," and then had sung:
"All the girls in France
"Do the hoochie-hoochie dance
"And the dance–"

He-We-Await

The teacher-lady, at that time a Ms Allen, stopped her with a sharp command.

Bobby found himself staring at Deborah, whom he did not particularly like.

Then Ms Allen got them all doing something else, and soon Bobby forgot about it.

Deborah never came back to the after-school group after that day. Bobby didn't particularly care.

One evening he was going through some books—the ones he had with the big black places on some of the pages—and he was looking in the one on music, way over toward the back.

He turned the page. There was a bright gaudy photograph of a music machine.

He read the caption: *In the 1940s and 1950s, "juke boxes" (like the 1953 Wurlitzer 150 pictured here) brought music to the customers of malt shops, cafes and taverns.*

The machine had disc recordings inside and a turntable he could see. But it was wide and curved, like a box that ended in a smooth round top. It was bright with neon and lights, and the sides had what looked like bubbles of colored water inside.

Bobby stared at the picture and stared at it, as if there was something else there.

He held up his hand slowly toward the photo, moving his fingers closer, staring at the page. His hand curved to grip the picture.

"What do you have there?" asked Dr Tuthmoses, who had come in to check on him.

"A juke box," he said, still looking.

Tuthmoses peered over his shoulder a moment.

"Yes. They used to be very popular."

Bobby's hand was still held over the page.

"What's wrong?" asked the doctor.

"It's—like—"

"Well, now everybody has music at home. They don't have to go where juke boxes used to be. They're anachronisms."

"What are anar—ancho—?"

"Anachronisms. Something that doesn't belong to its time. Something that has outlived its usefulness. One or the other."

"Oh," said Bobby. He put down the book.

Strange Things in Close-Up

Sometimes, late at night, Bobby thought of the word "anachronism." It conjured up for him a vision of a bright orange, yellow and green juke box.

The doctor came to Bobby's room one day when he was 11.

"I've got some tapes we should watch together, Bobby," he said. "You've never seen anything like them. They're about a faraway country, one you've never seen or heard of."

"I don't want to watch the tube," said Bobby. "I'm reading a neat book about American Indians."

"That will have to wait. You should see these."

"I don't want to," said Bobby.

"This is one of the few times you're not going to get your way," said the doctor. He was old and growing irritable. "It's time you saw these."

Then he gave Bobby a mug of hot chocolate.

"I don't want this, either."

"Drink it. I've got mine here. Watch." The old man gulped the thick hot liquid, leaving himself a dark brown mustache.

"Oh, all right," said Bobby, and did likewise.

Then they sat down in front of the television and the doctor put the tape on. It started with flute music. Then there was a cartoon, a black and white Walt Disney, with sounds and a spider inside a bunch of pointed buildings with carvings on the walls.

Bobby watched, not understanding. He found himself yawning. The carvings on the walls, angular people, came alive, strange things were happening on the screen.

Strange things happened inside him, too. He felt lightheaded, like when he had a fever. His stomach was very numb, like the place had been when Dr Khaffiri the dentist had fixed his tooth last year. He felt listless, like when he was tired and sleepy, only he wasn't. He was wide awake and thinking about all kinds of things.

The black and white cartoon ended and another started—a Gandy Goose and Sourpuss one. They were in army uniforms, in the same place with the skinny curved trees and the pointed big buildings, and Gandy went to sleep and was inside one of them, and stranger things began to happen than even in the first

He-We-Await

cartoon. Walls moved, boxes opened and things came out, all wrapped–

Things *came out all wrapped*.

There had been a movie after the cartoon and it was ending. *Things came out all wrapped*.

It had been about the same things, he thought, but it had been like in a dream, like Gandy had, because Bobby wasn't paying attention—he was watching another movie on his half-closed eyelids.

It was like at the hospital only–

Things came out all wrapped.

Only–

Bobby turned toward the doctor who sat very still, watching him, waiting for something.

Bobby's head was tired but he could not stop, not now.

"I . . . I . . ."

"Yes?"

"I want to go there."

"I know. We're ready to leave."

"I really want to go there."

"We'll be on the way before you know it."

"I . . ."

"Rest now. Sleep."

He did. When he woke up he was in an airplane, miles and miles up, and the air above them and the water below was blue and deep as a Vick's Salve jar, or so it seemed, and he went back to sleep, his head resting on Dr Tuthmoses' shoulder.

The launch made its way down the brown flood of the Nile. The sun was bright but the air was moderate above the river. There was no feeling of wind, only coolness.

Bobby sat in a chair, watching the River, taking no notice of the other boats they passed, the fellucahs they met. His hands fidgeted on the arms of the deck chair. He would turn from time to time to watch Dr Tuthmoses. The doctor said nothing; he saw that the wild faraway shine was still in the boy's eyes.

Bobby sat forward. Then he stood. Then he slowly sat back down and slumped in the chair. Tuthmoses, who had his hand up, let it fall again. The launch pilot went back to his fixed stare, whistling a tune to himself.

Strange Things in Close-Up

Another half hour passed in the muddy cool silence.

Bobby shot up so fast Tuthmoses was taken aback.

"Here!" Bobby said. "Put in here!"

Tuthmoses held his hand up, pointed. The pilot turned the wheel and the nose of the craft aimed itself at a large rock outcropping. The old doctor sighed; he had been on an expedition thirty years before which covered this very part of the River and had found nothing. The boat aimed at the western bank, the land of the setting sun and of the dead.

"No, no," said Bobby, jumping up and down. "Not that way. Over there! That way!"

He was pointing toward the eastern bank, the land of the day. And of the living.

THE HOUSE OF THE *KA*: II

The Light! The light! What place is this?

—is this the room where my soul is weighed? Thoth? My brother-gods?

Heavy. My limbs are heavy. My brain is a lump. Why cannot I think? My dreams are troubled. They are swirling colors.

My son. How he hates the traditions. The things that are done in the name of being god. He shall have to marry his half-niece, many years older than he. I should have had a daughter for him to marry, by his mother also. All his older half-brothers died before him. But his birth killed her.

It is too late to sire a queen. I am old. He was so twisted in his limbs. What pain is that in my knee?

I know you tricked me! All of you! These are my last thoughts. You have left me to die; my *ka* to wither away. How did I listen to priests?

What great plan, Sekhmet? To put an old man out of the way?

Where are my eyes? Have they put me in the jars? How do I think? I am going mad mad mad mad mad

My foot itches.

He-We-Await

It took two years and the best people and equipment money could buy and a few times they almost weren't enough.

Bobby was still cared for, but left on his own more and more. He found himself sitting for days, wondering what was happening, what had happened, where he had come in, what his purpose was. He knew he was part of some plan, something to do with the trip he barely remembered.

Dark places in the books disappeared, he could have anything he wanted. Books on Egypt were brought to him when he asked. The television now jibed with the *TV Guide*. He watched the news—depressing stuff on wars, plagues, fires, human misery, suffering, death, live and in color.

Sometimes he thought the old way, the days before the trip, were better.

Nothing told him *anything* he really wanted to know.

Dr Tuthmoses, old and subject to palsy, came to him for the first time in months.

"Tomorrow, Bobby," he said. "Tomorrow we will take you up there with us. There will be a ritual. You will need to be there. We will bring you clothes for it. You get to carry things needed in the ceremony. You're an important part of it. I hope you'll like that."

"I'm going to get to see him?"

Tuthmoses' eyes widened.

"Yes."

"Doctor?"

"Yes?"

"That time, before we went on the trip. When you showed me the cartoons and the movie. You also put something in my chocolate, didn't you?"

"Yes, I did, Bobby. It was to help you remember."

"Would you give it to me again?"

"Why?"

"If I'm going to be part of this, I want it to *mean* something. I want to understand."

"Don't you have everything you want?"

"I don't have a place," said Bobby. "I don't understand any of this. I've read the books. They're just words, words about

Strange Things in Close-Up

people a long time ago. They were interesting, but they've been gone a long time. What do they have to do with *me*?"

Tuthmoses studied him for a few seconds. "Perhaps it's for the best." He got up shakily and walked to the bookcase jammed with titles by Wallis Budge, Rawlinson, Atkinson, Carter. He picked one up, turned pages. "I'll have the drink brought to you tonight. After you finish it, read this chapter." He held the book out to Bobby, held open with his long thumb to a chapter on ritual. "Then you'll understand."

"I want to," said Bobby.

Tuthmoses opened the door. He turned back. "In a year or so you might be able to leave here, go anywhere, do anything you wish. By then it won't matter what you know or whom you tell. But until then, you have to stay."

"I guess I don't understand."

Tuthmoses' shoulders dropped. "I wish I had been a better guardian, a father to you," said the doctor. "It was not to be. Perhaps, later on if I live, and events do not deter, He-willing, we can learn to be friends. I would like to try."

Bobby stared at him.

"Well, that's the way I feel," said the doctor. "Rest now. Tomorrow is the greatest day."

"Of *my* life?"

"Of all lives," said Tuthmoses. He left.

He was brought into the great long room with the large curtain at the end.

Dr Tuthmoses, Faidul and the others were dressed in loose grey robes. Their heads and beards were fresh-shaved.

On the walls were murals, hieroglyphs, evocations to the gods. At one end of the room stood the hippo-headed statue of the god Sekhmet, its thick arms raised in benediction. In front of it was a throne of ivory, facing the curtain.

The room was brightly lit though it was early in the morning. When the door opened and Bobby was ushered in, his dark eyes were blinking. He was dressed in a short kilt, he had bare arms, chest and legs. A white headdress spilled down onto his shoulders.

In his crossed arms were a hook and a flail.

He-We-Await

Tuthmoses had told him what the ceremony was; the book and drink the night before told him what it meant.

In the early days, once a year, the chief priest would chase the Pharoah with a flail around a courseway. As long as the Pharoah could run, his youth and vigor were renewed by the ceremony.

In later years when the kingdoms were united this was changed. A young man was chosen to run the course before the priest, and his vigor would transfer by magic to the ruler. This was the ceremony of *heb-sed*.

Bobby was the chosen runner.

The course was outlined by barechested men, standing four feet in from the walls of the room, holding in their hands bundles of wheat.

Before the throne on a low table were symbols of life and death—four empty canopic jars, their effigy-tops unstoppered, an empty set of scales, an obsidian embalmer's knife, the figure of a baboon.

Another door opened and all in the room, except Bobby and the men holding the wheat along the course, dropped to the ground.

There was the sound of small steps, shuffling feet. Bobby watched the four men bring the shrunken figure in between them.

He was old, old and bent. They had dressed him in another simple kilt. His skin was pitted and wrinkled, stained in patches of light and dark from chemicals.

He doddered forward, eyes looking neither right nor left. His head had been shaven; there were corrugations in his skull like a greenhouse roof. His legs were twisted. One arm was immobile.

They placed him on the throne, then the attendants fell to their faces.

Dr Tuthmoses stepped forward, bowed.

On the old man's head he placed first the red crown of the Bee Kingdom, then the white crown of the Reed Kingdom. The old man's eyes focused for the first time at the touch of the crown's cloth.

He looked slowly around him.

"*Heb-sed?*" he croaked.

Strange Things in Close-Up

"Yes, *heb-sed*," answered Tuthmoses.

The ancient man leaned back in the throne a little, the edge of his mouth fluttered as if he were trying to smile.

Tuthmoses waved—a priest stepped forward, came to Bobby, took the flail from the hand of his bad arm. Music began to play through hidden speakers, music like in the first of Bobby's dreams while watching cartoons two years before.

Bobby stepped past the men with the wheat and began to run. The priest's naked feet slapped on the Armstrong tile floor behind him, and the first of the knots on the flail hit him, drawing blood from his shoulder.

He jerked. Faster and faster he ran, brushing by the standing men, and at every third step the flail kissed him with its hot tongue and he yelled.

Some of the wheat covered the floor by the second circuit. On the third Bobby saw spots of blood on the tiles ahead.

They passed the starting point—Bobby kept running. The expected stroke did not come. He looked back over his shoulder. The priest had stopped at the marker, arm still raised. He motioned the boy back and handed him the flail.

Bobby's shoulders twitched as the priest guided him next to Tuthmoses. He was sweating and his chest heaved.

Bobby looked at the old man on the throne—was it only the nearness or did he look less ancient, more human? The music rose in volume, drums, flutes, strings. The old man's eyes grew bright.

"Oh Great House!" said Tuthmoses in the Old Language. "We wait to do your bidding. Behold," he said, waving his arm, "the sun rises 5000 years later!"

The room lights went out.

The curtain pulled back. Dawn flooded the room twenty-two stories up over Central Park. Great towers rose up on all sides, their windows filled with lights. The ocean was a flat smoky line beyond, and the slim cuticle of the sun's red edge stood up.

The old man stared in wonder.

"I have lived to see it," he said. Then he looked at Bobby. His lip trembled.

"Boy," he said. "Here," he lifted his twisted blotched arms toward him. "My flail, my scepter."

Tuthmoses motioned him forward, indicating that Bobby hand them over.

He-We-Await

Bobby stepped up on the dais, watching the shaking in the old man's hands as they closed on the sacred objects, pulling them to his breast.

Bobby stepped backwards, picked up the obsidian knife from the table and jammed it under the ribs of the old man and twisted it.

He made no sound but slid up and over his own knees and spilled forward off the throne onto the floor, the scepter breaking on the chair's arm.

"You were the worst father anyone *ever* had!" yelled Bobby.

There was a gasp of breath all around the room, then the sound of someone working the slide on an automatic pistol. The doctors made a rush toward the bloody old man.

"Stop!" said Bobby, turning toward them, knife in his hand.

They froze. Faidul was aiming a pistol at Bobby's head. Tuthmoses stared at him, eyes wide, breath coming shallowly.

"He has seen the sun rise 5000 years from his time," said Bobby. He dropped the Ethiopian knife back onto the table, knocking over the baboon figurine. "*Now*, his line is ready to reign until the last day of mankind."

He walked to the throne, the barrel of Faidul's pistol following him.

"Only this time," said Bobby, "I'll do it *right*."

He sat down.

Beginning with Tuthmoses, and one by one, they bowed down before him, prostrating themselves to the floor tiles. Last to go was Faidul, whose hand began to tremble when Bobby gave him a withering stare.

"What is your first wish, Oh Great House?" asked Tuthmoses from the floor.

"See that my late father is given seventy days' mourning, that his tomb is made ready, that his *ka* be provided for through all eternity."

"Yes, He-We-Await," said Tuthmoses, beginning to tear at his robe and gnash his teeth.

Bobby watched the orb of the sun widen and stand up from the horizon, grow brighter, too bright to stare at.

"Get busy!" he said, turning his head away.

So began the last days of mankind.

The Left-Handed Muse

by Lewis Shiner

It was the second ArmadilloCon ever, October of 1980, held in two rooms of the Quality Inn in South Austin. Gardner Dozois was guest of honor. On Saturday, Ugly Shirt Day[1], Gardner read a story he'd just written with Jack Dann and Michael Swanwick called "Touring."[2]

"Touring" is a little ditty about how Buddy Holly (and the Big Bopper and Richie Valens) arrive in Moorhead, Minnesota and find they're sharing the bill with Elvis Presley and a foulmouthed Texas girl named Janis. Well, suffice to say that the socks were knocked off every foot in the room. And Howard Waldrop stood shaking in his newly bare feet.

Because next day, Sunday, he was to read "the rock and roll story."

Of course it wasn't written yet. But the actual reduction of one of Howard's stories to words on paper is only the last, almost insignificant stage in its genesis.

The story begins with a name. Not a title, necessarily, just the label by which Howard knows it. For example, "the Hemingway story," which would, in time, be known as "Fair Game." Or "the Egyptian story" which became "He-We-Await." Or "the Mound-Builder novel" which became Them Bones.

There is no warning. Suddenly the name appears in conversation. You're talking about Shakespeare and Howard says, "sure, it's just like the Africa story." You, of course, have never heard of the Africa story. Howard stares at you as if you're

---

[1] In all honesty, mine was uglier than Howard's. But then I'd been saving it since 1970 with something like this in mind. And it was the only shirt I had that ugly. Which cannot be said of Howard's.

[2] It was in *Penthouse* in April of '81, reprinted in *The Year's Best Horror Stories X* from DAW (edited by Karl Edward Wagner). As Howard would say, "Check it out."

The Left-Handed Muse

mad. "The Africa story," he says patiently. "You know." Then a year, maybe two, later, after you've been hearing on and off about the Africa story long enough that you think you know what's going on, you're talking about the convention next week. You ask Howard what he's planning to do for his reading. "The Africa story[3]," he says confidently.

"Oh," you say. "You're ready to write it."

It is common knowledge that if you need a story from Howard, you pray for a convention. Conventions (and the occasional Turkey City Workshop) are the impetus that fuels the final stage of the process, the words-on-paper bit.

At the 1985 NASFC in Austin, Howard sat in the hallway and finished the longhand draft of "Night of the Cooters" with literally seconds to spare. "Man Mountain Gentian" was written on a pink Snoopy pad while on a Greyhound from Austin to Dallas. It was the only paper they had in the bus station. Waiting in growing panic for the Jetboy story[4] Howard had yet to finish (i.e. begin transcribing), George R. R. Martin began secret negotiations to get Howard to a local convention, where the con committee was to insist he read.

Sometimes it takes years. "Man Mountain Gentian" (a.k.a. the Sumo story) had become such a familiar item to most fans that when artist Jim Odbert painted a tribute to Howard, a fake F&SF cover devoted to Howard's work, he included a scene from the story. One wonders how many people knew that the story was not only unpublished at the time, but that Howard had not yet set pen to Snoopy pad on its behalf.

Is a picture emerging here? Do you begin to see these stories as Howard sees them? As independent entities, perhaps already written, typed, and published in an alternate world? Waiting only for Howard to see them clearly enough to copy them down?

Lately as much effort has been spent downplaying the separate functions of the brain's hemispheres as was ever spent touting them. But. In some cases split-brain theory provides valuable—even inarguable—insight.

---

[3] Published, of course, as "The Lions Are Asleep This Night" and included in this volume.

[4] "Thirty Minutes Over Broadway!" from Martin's *Wild Cards* (Bantam, 1987).

Strange Things in Close-Up

Briefly, the left brain (which controls the right half of the body) is analytical, mathematical, given to dissection. The right brain is primitive, intuitive, holistic.

The left-brained writer makes outlines, flow charts, lists of characters and the contents of their pockets. This writer begins work at the first scent of an idea and sculpts it gradually into a story through repeated, painstaking drafts.

Howard? Once Howard is ready, that is, once one of the stories is ready for him, Howard stays up all night, writing longhand on whatever paper he can scrounge. He reads it at the convention the next day, types it up during the next week (with virtually no changes) and away it goes.

And if Howard does have to revise (as he did "Heirs of the Perisphere"—and, I might add, improved it greatly), you don't want to be around to hear about it. The entire story must be deconstructed and rebuilt from scratch in Howard's head, for even the slightest change. He must, in effect, seek out another parallel world where the change had already been made.

So here's Howard, it's Saturday night, one of his best friends in the world has just read one of the best stories he's ever written, worse yet, a rock and roll story, and Howard is under the gun.

So, what does he do? Come up with a new story? In less than 24 hours? Don't kid yourself. Cancel the reading? No way. He goes home and writes exactly the story he would have written all along. The story whispered to him across the corpus callosum from the dark recesses of his right brain. Whisked from holistic image to marks on paper without conscious intervention.[5]

The rest is of course history. The mad applause and, in some cases (I won't mention my name here) actual tears shed when Howard, terrified, shaking, voice cracking, finally read "Flying Saucer Rock and Roll" that Sunday morning.

Nor will I dwell on the aftermath—the sale to New Dimen-

---

[5] I can prove this. Howard cannot punctuate. Which is to say, his right brain cannot punctuate. His left brain knows the rules, but he is unable to execute them while in the process of writing. QED, the right brain is firmly in the driver's seat.

sions 13[6], *perhaps one of the great anthologies of all time, never published due to the bungling of Pocket Books. The eventual sale to Omni, the nominations for both the Hugo and the Nebula, and so forth. All that matters is that it was written—transcribed, whatever—and it is here, with six other priceless, irreplaceable Waldrop stories.*

Treasure them.

LEWIS SHINER
Austin, TX

---

[6] Everyone knows this story. Howard always preferred to sell his best stuff to *Shayol*, but he had to give this one to Marta Randall for *New Dimensions*. Had to because he'd pulled "The Ugly Chickens" from Marta so he could sell it to *Universe* for less money. But then everyone knows of Howard's lifelong compulsion to get the least money for his work, and I won't go into it here.

A Selection of Legend Titles

☐ Eon	Greg Bear	£3.50
☐ Forge of God	Greg Bear	£3.99
☐ Falcons of Narabedla	Marion Zimmer Bradley	£2.50
☐ The Influence	Ramsey Campbell	£3.50
☐ Wyrms	Orson Scott Card	£3.50
☐ Speaker for the Dead	Orson Scott Card	£2.95
☐ Seventh Son	Orson Scott Card	£3.50
☐ Wolf in Shadow	David Gemmell	£3.50
☐ Last Sword of Power	David Gemmell	£3.50
☐ This is the Way the World Ends	James Morrow	£4.99
☐ Unquenchable Fire	Rachel Pollack	£3.99
☐ Golden Sunlands	Christopher Rowley	£3.50
☐ The Misplaced Legion	Harry Turtledove	£2.99
☐ An Emperor for the Legion	Harry Turtledove	£2.99

Prices and other details are liable to change

ARROW BOOKS, BOOKSERVICE BY POST, PO BOX 29, DOUGLAS, ISLE OF MAN, BRITISH ISLES

NAME..

ADDRESS..

....

....

Please enclose a cheque or postal order made out to Arrow Books Ltd. for the amount due and allow the following for postage and packing.

U.K. CUSTOMERS: Please allow 22p per book to a maximum of £3.00.

B.F.P.O. & EIRE: Please allow 22p per book to a maximum of £3.00.

OVERSEAS CUSTOMERS: Please allow 22p per book.

Whilst every effort is made to keep prices low it is sometimes necessary to increase cover prices at short notice. Arrow Books reserve the right to show new retail prices on covers which may differ from those previously advertised in the text or elsewhere.

Bestselling SF/Horror

☐ Forge of God	Greg Bear	£3.99
☐ Eon	Greg Bear	£3.50
☐ The Hungry Moon	Ramsey Campbell	£3.50
☐ The Influence	Ramsey Campbell	£3.50
☐ Seventh Son	Orson Scott Card	£3.50
☐ Bones of the Moon	Jonathan Carroll	£2.50
☐ Nighthunter: The Hexing & The Labyrinth	Robert Faulcon	£3.50
☐ Pin	Andrew Neiderman	£1.50
☐ The Island	Guy N. Smith	£2.50
☐ Malleus Maleficarum	Montague Summers	£4.50

Prices and other details are liable to change

ARROW BOOKS, BOOKSERVICE BY POST, PO BOX 29, DOUGLAS, ISLE OF MAN, BRITISH ISLES

NAME..

ADDRESS..

....

....

Please enclose a cheque or postal order made out to Arrow Books Ltd. for the amount due and allow the following for postage and packing.

U.K. CUSTOMERS: Please allow 22p per book to a maximum of £3.00.

B.F.P.O. & EIRE: Please allow 22p per book to a maximum of £3.00.

OVERSEAS CUSTOMERS: Please allow 22p per book.

Whilst every effort is made to keep prices low it is sometimes necessary to increase cover prices at short notice. Arrow Books reserve the right to show new retail prices on covers which may differ from those previously advertised in the text or elsewhere.

A Selection of Arrow Books

☐ No Enemy But Time	Evelyn Anthony	£2.95
☐ The Lilac Bus	Maeve Binchy	£2.99
☐ Rates of Exchange	Malcolm Bradbury	£3.50
☐ Prime Time	Joan Collins	£3.50
☐ Rosemary Conley's Complete Hip and Thigh Diet	Rosemary Conley	£2.99
☐ Staying Off the Beaten Track	Elizabeth Gundrey	£6.99
☐ Duncton Wood	William Horwood	£4.50
☐ Duncton Quest	William Horwood	£4.50
☐ A World Apart	Marie Joseph	£3.50
☐ Erin's Child	Sheelagh Kelly	£3.99
☐ Colours Aloft	Alexander Kent	£2.99
☐ Gondar	Nicholas Luard	£4.50
☐ The Ladies of Missalonghi	Colleen McCullough	£2.50
☐ The Veiled One	Ruth Rendell	£3.50
☐ Sarum	Edward Rutherfurd	£4.99
☐ Communion	Whitley Strieber	£3.99

Prices and other details are liable to change

ARROW BOOKS, BOOKSERVICE BY POST, PO BOX 29, DOUGLAS, ISLE OF MAN, BRITISH ISLES

NAME..

ADDRESS...

....

....

Please enclose a cheque or postal order made out to Arrow Books Ltd. for the amount due and allow the following for postage and packing.

U.K. CUSTOMERS: Please allow 22p per book to a maximum of £3.00.

B.F.P.O. & EIRE: Please allow 22p per book to a maximum of £3.00.

OVERSEAS CUSTOMERS: Please allow 22p per book.

Whilst every effort is made to keep prices low it is sometimes necessary to increase cover prices at short notice. Arrow Books reserve the right to show new retail prices on covers which may differ from those previously advertised in the text or elsewhere.

Bestselling Fiction

☐ No Enemy But Time	Evelyn Anthony	£2.95
☐ The Lilac Bus	Maeve Binchy	£2.99
☐ Prime Time	Joan Collins	£3.50
☐ A World Apart	Marie Joseph	£3.50
☐ Erin's Child	Sheelagh Kelly	£3.99
☐ Colours Aloft	Alexander Kent	£2.99
☐ Gondar	Nicholas Luard	£4.50
☐ The Ladies of Missalonghi	Colleen McCullough	£2.50
☐ Lily Golightly	Pamela Oldfield	£3.50
☐ Talking to Strange Men	Ruth Rendell	£2.99
☐ The Veiled One	Ruth Rendell	£3.50
☐ Sarum	Edward Rutherfurd	£4.99
☐ The Heart of the Country	Fay Weldon	£2.50

Prices and other details are liable to change

ARROW BOOKS, BOOKSERVICE BY POST, PO BOX 29, DOUGLAS, ISLE OF MAN, BRITISH ISLES

NAME..

ADDRESS...

....

....

Please enclose a cheque or postal order made out to Arrow Books Ltd. for the amount due and allow the following for postage and packing.

U.K. CUSTOMERS: Please allow 22p per book to a maximum of £3.00.

B.F.P.O. & EIRE: Please allow 22p per book to a maximum of £3.00.

OVERSEAS CUSTOMERS: Please allow 22p per book.

Whilst every effort is made to keep prices low it is sometimes necessary to increase cover prices at short notice. Arrow Books reserve the right to show new retail prices on covers which may differ from those previously advertised in the text or elsewhere.

Bestselling Thriller/Suspense

☐ Skydancer	Geoffrey Archer	£3.50
☐ Hooligan	Colin Dunne	£2.99
☐ See Charlie Run	Brian Freemantle	£2.99
☐ Hell is Always Today	Jack Higgins	£2.50
☐ The Proteus Operation	James P Hogan	£3.50
☐ Winter Palace	Dennis Jones	£3.50
☐ Dragonfire	Andrew Kaplan	£2.99
☐ The Hour of the Lily	John Kruse	£3.50
☐ Fletch, Too	Geoffrey McDonald	£2.50
☐ Brought in Dead	Harry Patterson	£2.50
☐ The Albatross Run	Douglas Scott	£2.99

Prices and other details are liable to change

ARROW BOOKS, BOOKSERVICE BY POST, PO BOX 29, DOUGLAS, ISLE OF MAN, BRITISH ISLES

NAME..

ADDRESS...

....

....

Please enclose a cheque or postal order made out to Arrow Books Ltd. for the amount due and allow the following for postage and packing.

U.K. CUSTOMERS: Please allow 22p per book to a maximum of £3.00.

B.F.P.O. & EIRE: Please allow 22p per book to a maximum of £3.00.

OVERSEAS CUSTOMERS: Please allow 22p per book.

Whilst every effort is made to keep prices low it is sometimes necessary to increase cover prices at short notice. Arrow Books reserve the right to show new retail prices on covers which may differ from those previously advertised in the text or elsewhere.

Bestselling General Fiction

☐ No Enemy But Time	Evelyn Anthony	£2.95
☐ Skydancer	Geoffrey Archer	£3.50
☐ The Sisters	Pat Booth	£3.50
☐ Captives of Time	Malcolm Bosse	£2.99
☐ Saudi	Laurie Devine	£2.95
☐ Duncton Wood	William Horwood	£4.50
☐ Aztec	Gary Jennings	£3.95
☐ A World Apart	Marie Joseph	£3.50
☐ The Ladies of Missalonghi	Colleen McCullough	£2.50
☐ Lily Golightly	Pamela Oldfield	£3.50
☐ Sarum	Edward Rutherfurd	£4.99
☐ Communion	Whitley Strieber	£3.99

Prices and other details are liable to change

ARROW BOOKS, BOOKSERVICE BY POST, PO BOX 29, DOUGLAS, ISLE OF MAN, BRITISH ISLES

NAME..

ADDRESS...

....

....

Please enclose a cheque or postal order made out to Arrow Books Ltd. for the amount due and allow the following for postage and packing.

U.K. CUSTOMERS: Please allow 22p per book to a maximum of £3.00.

B.F.P.O. & EIRE: Please allow 22p per book to a maximum of £3.00.

OVERSEAS CUSTOMERS: Please allow 22p per book.

Whilst every effort is made to keep prices low it is sometimes necessary to increase cover prices at short notice. Arrow Books reserve the right to show new retail prices on covers which may differ from those previously advertised in the text or elsewhere.

Bestselling Non-Fiction

☐ Complete Hip and Thigh Diet	Rosemary Conley	£2.99
☐ Staying off the Beaten Track	Elizabeth Gundrey	£6.99
☐ Raw Energy: Recipes	Leslie Kenton	£3.99
☐ The PM System	Dr J A Muir Gray	£5.99
☐ Women Who Love Too Much	Robin Norwood	£3.50
☐ Letters From Women Who Love Too Much	Robin Norwood	£3.50
☐ Fat is a Feminist Issue	Susie Orbach	£2.99
☐ Callanetics	Callan Pinckney	£6.99
☐ Elvis and Me	Priscilla Presley	£3.50
☐ Love, Medicine and Miracles	Bernie Siegel	£3.50
☐ Communion	Whitley Strieber	£3.50
☐ Trump: The Art of the Deal	Donald Trump	£3.99

Prices and other details are liable to change

ARROW BOOKS, BOOKSERVICE BY POST, PO BOX 29, DOUGLAS, ISLE OF MAN, BRITISH ISLES

NAME..

ADDRESS..

....

....

Please enclose a cheque or postal order made out to Arrow Books Ltd. for the amount due and allow the following for postage and packing.

U.K. CUSTOMERS: Please allow 22p per book to a maximum of £3.00.

B.F.P.O. & EIRE: Please allow 22p per book to a maximum of £3.00.

OVERSEAS CUSTOMERS: Please allow 22p per book.

Whilst every effort is made to keep prices low it is sometimes necessary to increase cover prices at short notice. Arrow Books reserve the right to show new retail prices on covers which may differ from those previously advertised in the text or elsewhere.